TEMPLE

"Paulie Bindel is a stunning fictional creation: wise beyond his years, witty, sensitive and perceptive, and with a point of view as fresh as that of Holden Caulfield. . . . The dialogue is simply brilliant." —*Publishers Weekly*

"*Temʃ le* has all the standard ingredients—crackling humor, deep sadness, plenty of *shtick*. . . . What's new . . . is the experience of the sixties. . . . Greenfield writes brilliant dialogue and has a light, deft touch with character. For all its funny surface . . . *Temʃ le* is about something called soul." —*Newsweek*

"*Portnoy's Comʃ laint* is the prototype; Bruce Jay Friedman's *A Mother's Kisses* and Mordecai Richler's *St. Urban's Horseman* bear a strong family resemblance. So does Robert Greenfield's *Temʃ le,* but the author's energy is so abundant that the entire genre seems revitalized. . . . Greenfield manages that most difficult recipe: a blend of acrimony, humor, regret, and hope. . . . Memorable." —*Time*

"Not since Ken Kesey and Tom Wolfe has a writer come along who can take you for a ride from the first page and make you wonder what hit you when you turned the last."
—*The Telegram* (Worcester, Mass.)

TEMPLE

Robert Greenfield

A LAUREL BOOK
Published by
Dell Publishing Co., Inc.
1 Dag Hammarskjold Plaza
New York, New York 10017

Laurel ® TM 674623, Dell Publishing Co., Inc.

ISBN: 0-440-38488-5

Reprinted by arrangement with Summit Books, a Simon & Schuster Division of Gulf & Western Corporation.

Printed in the United States of America

First Laurel printing—September 1984

FOR SANFORD MENDEL,
WITHOUT A DOUBT

"In this our life there are no beginnings but only departures entitled beginnings . . ."
DELMORE SCHWARTZ, "The World Is a Wedding"

Prologue:
ANOTHER
YEAR

EARLIER, LONG BEFORE the sun had come up, he had methodically shaved himself for the new year. Dipping the old Gillette into the bowl of the sink, he had drawn it carefully across the tender skin of his face, all the while peering into the dim bathroom mirror as though at any moment he fully expected someone to come up behind him, clamp a heavy hand on his shoulder, and say, "This is *verboten*. This you cannot do."

After he had finished, large clumps of snowy white lather had still remained scattered across his face. East and west, one stood at the tip of each cheekbone. The largest of them was located farther south, just below his mouth at the bulb of his chin. Precipitously, it hung there like an iceberg that would never move no matter how hard the wind began to blow.

Each snowy mound hid a tiny cut from which blood had slowly seeped. Gradually, the lather turned bright red. Using bits of wadded-up toilet paper moistened with water from the tap, he did what he could to halt the flow of blood by affixing the paper to his face. Soon enough, each wad also became red. Then they dried, clinging so persistently to his skin that he was forced to peel them off with a gentle, probing finger, taking care not to break the small, crescent shaped scabs that were only just beginning to form on his face. Only then had he dressed himself and set off for *shul*, arriving long before any of the others.

That a man who had lived so long simply could not learn to do well what he had to do each and every morning, Shabbos and certain holy days excluded, was a continuing mystery to him, a problem apparently without solution. Perhaps some day soon, the scientists would come up with a miraculous new razor blade that would never wear out or ever cut, scratch, or nick human skin. It would give him great pleasure to be alive to use this blade.

Now he stood on a narrow footbridge looking out at the surrounding bay on a bright blue brilliant September afternoon, the very first one of a brand new year. The fishing boats had just begun coming in, bringing back men who fished in groups for pleasure. All that they had caught would soon be sold off on the docks to those willing to clean and scale the fish by hand.

Today, the bay seemed to him like a great and silent bowl, God's very own *schissel*, alive with color reflected back from the clear blue sky. Within the blue of his eyes, the bay and all that it encompassed could be seen in miniature, reality captured in a fluid lens. A momentary blink, an adjustment in the setting of the lens, and the blue was tinted by a sudden, milk white cloudiness, the hue of confusion and failing memory. Looking in every direction at once, he struggled to remember.

Around him stood all the others who had also walked slowly down the avenue to the bay to perform *Tashlikh* at the water's edge. As the rabbi droned on and on in his hoarse, grating voice, reciting the ancient prayer on the rickety bridge, the members of the congregation began reaching impatiently into their pockets for the tiny bits of bread they had put there earlier in the day to symbolize the sins of the previous year that they were no longer willing to carry around with them. In a moment, the crumbs would be thrown into the water down below.

He himself could remember a time when this ritual had been far more real. The good Jews of the *shtetl* where he had been born had made a point of never leaving their little houses without a chunk of rich, dark cornbread wrapped in a handkerchief shoved deeply into their pockets. If ever they found themselves far from home when hunger struck, they would not be forced to eat *trafe* food. Now, there were lunchboxes and kosher restaurants, thermos bottles, aluminum foil, and refrigerators, all the great innovations of which the modern world was so proud. Now a man could be a good Jew without ever having to carry his lunch around in his pocket. Yet he still regularly cut himself each morning when he shaved.

He was still trying to remember. An experience that had been digested so thoroughly by his consciousness that it now formed an essential part of his nature, the literal core of his very being, from which he drew his strength.

A piece of bread had figured prominently in the experience, a tattered crust that at the time had seemed more precious than life itself. There had been a basin as well, an ordinary *schissel* like the one his daughter-in-law now kept under the bed for him at home so that he would not have to walk down the hall to the

10

bathroom in the dead of night to empty a bladder that seemed always to be full.

Taking one hand off the cool metal railing before him, he shaded his eyes against the blinding sun and blinked once more. Despite the brilliant play of light across the surface of the water, or perhaps because of it, he could not see the entire bay all at once. Today, the great bowl was broken into a hundred gleaming secants. It was as though some dark body had eclipsed the pupil of his eye, blacking out everything save for a single shining sliver of light shaped like the crescent of a quarter moon. The crescent gleamed before him without ever changing shape or size, challenging him to recall what had once been as familiar to him as his very own heartbeat.

Reaching slowly into the side pocket of his old brown suit, he brought forth the handful of crumbs that his daughter-in-law had put there for just this purpose. Leaning forward, he scattered them towards the rippling water down below. Above his head, dappled gray and white gulls turned in lonely circles, cawing and crying like hungry children. The fishing boats were in. Soon the birds would eat. At his back, the breeze suddenly stiffened, reminding him that yet another winter was on the way.

It was now time for him to walk back home and rest so that he could go to *shul* once again before the sun set. Another year had just begun. Perhaps he would soon remember what he could not now recall for the life of him. If not, then at least, *denken Gott*, he was still able to walk without anyone's help all the way down the avenue to the bay for *Tashlikh*, if only to realize once he got there that he no longer even knew why he had wanted to come so badly in the first place.

11

I
THE
CHARITY
WARD

CHAPTER ONE

IT ALL REALLY starts as I come up the front steps after work on Thursday. What is there about a Thursday that always annoys me? For one thing, it is almost the end of the week, but not quite. Already, I feel paranoid. I can hear a man's voice in the apartment and it does not belong to me. I push through the open door into the living room. Some guy I have never seen before sits with his feet up on the coffee table. He is wearing boots, which somehow makes it worse. As he leafs through my copy of *Cowboy Kate* by Sam Haskins, he is calling out to Lesley in the kitchen. Soon, the book and everything else in the apartment will belong to him.

It is a scene right out of Yiddish theater, where my father used to take his father in better times. An overly made-up blonde who has already buried two husbands and is eagerly searching for a third turns on her side on a chaise lounge by the pool. The pool is a canvas flat smeared with paint, so you have to use your imagination. The blonde looks everywhere for a likely prospect. Then she spies the little man across the way. Although he is not so likely, she rattled her diamonds at him. *Tell me, doll-link*, she asks. *Who you?*

The little man grins. He doffs his famous hat. The audience roars in appreciation, already knowing what is to come. He tugs at a curl. *Der kennst mir?* he inquires, talking to them and not her. You know me? *Der vaist vee ich bin?* he demands. You know who I am? Then the little man waits. The laugh builds beyond all proportions simply because of who he is. Then he delivers *the* line, the one that made him famous. *Doos bin ich*, he proclaims for all the world to hear. This is me. *Menashe!*

Doos bin ich, Paulie. That is what I should tell them all. The ones who are already sitting in my living room as I come up the stairs after work. The ones whose names get mumbled when they are introduced so that I know right away that they are dealers on

15

their way back from Mexico, with a brand-new shipment hidden under the floorboards of the VW bus parked outside. The musicians, who are perpetually down on their luck, like the guy who came up the front steps only last week, clutching a battered electric guitar case to his chest as though it was all he had left in the entire world.

By way of introduction, before I could get a word in edgewise, he launched immediately into a story of the fabled night he jammed with B.B. at the Ark and every last record scout in the place ignored the King of the Blues from Indianola, Mississippi, to ask, "Who the *hell* is that white kid with the long blond hair?" In the morning, before I could get out of bed, he was already gone. After having borrowed twenty bucks from Lesley in the hall, money we cannot afford to part with that I know we will never see again.

Before they go, they all manage to ask the very same question of me. *Who are you?* When they think that I will not notice, they stare sideways at me, trying to gauge how long I will last in this apartment where so many others have lived. What can I tell them, when I myself do not know? *Who are you?* they all want to know. Who are you and what are you doing here with her?

Today, I have no answers left. The false smile that crinkles up the corners of my eyes with aching insincerity as I try my best to be nice to them simply will not come. I turn my back on the stranger in the living room. I rush down the stairs into the street. I start to run. Running is perfect. It is the only move I have. Whenever I come into any room, the very first thing I do is check out all the fire exits so that I will know which way to go when the time comes for me to bolt.

As I run, all of Cambridge streams by. Its very earnest student reality has been smeared on to large canvas flats that seem to whirl past me like gaily painted horses on some great old merry-go-round. I feel as though I am standing still as it all revolves around me. Outside Cahaly's and Tommy's Lunch, the young mothers with one baby in the stroller and another already on the way are shopping for an extra quart of milk. I can tell that they are all sick to death of eating ground round for dinner three nights a week while they wait for their graduate student husbands to stop being so damn brilliant and full of promise and start making a decent living. But I have no time to help them.

By the Lampoon Building, I dodge past four guys in morning coats. They are waving empty champagne glasses in the air while chanting the name of Harvard's current president over and over, as though it is some kind of very expensive mantra. Preppie penguins, with perfect wheat blond hair that falls in neatly pleated strands just to the edge of their starched white collars. They laugh and stumble down the steps. One gives me the finger as I pass, just for good measure.

• I angle towards the river. The faint, briny smell of lobster comes floating off the water. Today, the Charles is dull and still. Nothing moves on the river except for a racing shell manned by a full crew in sweats. Intently, they stroke for Eliot Bridge. A V-for-victory shaped power ripple flows out behind them. Soon, they will circle back to dock at some musty old boathouse. They will lift countless beers in celebration with their arms draped across one another's shoulders. They all know just what they are doing here. They belong.

Music comes blasting from a window in one of the dorms along the Drive. A stereo has been turned all the way up. The room in which it stands has become a little loudspeaker. It reverberates with sound, a single cell vibrating faster than all those surrounding it. A party is in progress. Yet one more to which I have not been invited.

Wherever I look, the extremely weird Chinese pre-engineering students are out in force. They sit on benches in their short sleeve oxford shirts with button down collars. The white plastic penholders in their front pockets are stuffed with automatic lead pencils and cheap Bic pens. Textbooks lie open on their laps. A slide rule is balanced between the thumb and first finger of one hand. They are all hard at work advancing the frontiers of their impossibly cloistered fields. Madly, they scribble columns of figures, covering the pages of their notebooks with a slanting, spidery scrawl.

These are the boys who really scare me in Cambridge. On the very first day of the term, they march confidently into class and demand to be given the final exam. Naturally, they pass it with flying colors, adding yet another ace to their already awesome transcripts. Then they move on to something they can *really* sink their teeth into, the final equation that leads directly to the ultimate doomsday weapon, the one that will make the H-bomb look like a windup toy.

Probably when you get to know them, they are the nicest guys in the world, eager to please, grateful to be here on scholarship, tremendous at Ping-Pong, yet really humble, willing to give you

17

the shirt off their back if you ask for it. After all, *someone* has to do the dirty work of making the world safe for democracy. So why not them? Even if it does mean sitting hunched over all day long on benches by the river, never once looking up until after the sun has set and it is already night.

Leaving them all behind, I cross the river and go running through an open gate into the stadium itself. Big stone portals rise up over my head, one following the other in endless succession. Every last seat in the house is empty. Today, the stadium belongs entirely to me.

The playing field is so green that it looks as though they cover it with dollar bills each night. The grass glows green and ghostly in the fading light of late afternoon. The chalk lines beneath my feet are thick and luxurious. I nearly stumble over them as I go from the fifty to the thirty, then down the far sideline. Untouched, I cross into the end zone. Under the goalpost I go, scoring the winning touchdown to absolutely no applause.

Then I am out of the stadium and in a phone booth. My hand trembles as I dial the number. My shirt is soaked with sweat. My hair is damp. My chest heaves so badly that I literally cannot draw breath. All I want now is to go back to the apartment. Only I cannot. *He* might still be there. No matter who *he* happens to actually be, I know already that he is everything I can never become, no matter how hard I try.

"Is he *still* there?" I ask after she picks up the receiver. *Doos bin ich*, Paulie. The last in a long line of small, anxious men. See my hat? My famous grin?

"Who?"

"Your ex-boyfriend . . ."

Because of me, they are all her ex-boyfriends now. Because of me, Lesley has made The Supreme Sacrifice, giving them up like some junkie who has sworn off heroin or an alcoholic who has taken the pledge. I hate her for doing this just as I would hate her for not doing it, knowing that it is only temporary, subject to change at a moment's notice should market conditions suddenly improve.

"I'm sorry, Paulie," she laughs, making it into a joke. "You'll *have* to be more specific . . ."

"The guy in the living room . . ."

"*Rob?* Paulie, will you please stop *trying* to be so crazy? Rob is a friend of Anita's . . ." Because she is whispering, I know for certain that *he* is still there, watching and listening. "Returning something she borrowed from me and inviting both of us to dinner tomorrow night. Where *are* you?'' she pleads. Now, she is upset. I can hear tears forming in her voice. Rob is getting her entire range in a single phone call. He must be special. "Just come home, will you?'' she begs. "We can have . . . big fun.''

Big Fun. That is what we have together all right, Lesley and I. Every night, with a single cranberry scented candle burning down by the side of the old brass bed she rescued from some junkyard, in the little room at the very back of the boxy, three-decker house in which she has lived for years, we have big fun. Fucking Lesley is all there is. We cannot talk about anything without arguing. We disagree on every subject. Shadows cast by her former lovers block out the sun for me except when we are in bed together. Then she is happy and I am happy and it all makes sense.

For Lesley knows only what is hip, and not what is real. The greasy chitlin' and ham hock soul of people like Rufus Thomas, Shorty Long, and Koko Taylor offends her. She prefers the J. Geils Band, currently playing nightly at The Charity Ward. Not that there is anything wrong with the J. Geils Band. For white boys. Only they know where they got it all from and so do I.

Not Lesley. She was raised not to know, in a big white clapboard house on Staten Island, not far from the zoo where the snakes are regularly fed live white mice. For the past thirty years, the house itself has belonged to Dr. Alfred Gold and his hysterical wife, Gloria. In her time, Gloria has swallowed more than one of Lesley's suitors whole. Live and wriggling, they struggle to free themselves from her powerful jaws. To no avail. They are gone before they know it.

Degrees from Columbia University line the walls of Dr. Alfred's ground floor office. "P and S" is what he calls his alma mater. Lesley has informed me that this stands for "Physicians and Surgeons." Dr. Alfred is neither. On Saturday, after he has read *The New York Times* at the breakfast table, which he has had delivered, of course, no driving down to the ferry terminal to grab a grimy, ink-stained copy of the *News* off a stand for him, Dr. Alfred spends his time filing down molars. He *has* to work six days a week. Whatever he makes, Gloria spends.

In the background, WQXR is turned up loud. Gaily, Dr. Alfred waves his probe around in time to the sound of the Texaco-sponsored broadcast from the Metropolitan Opera House. In his office not far from the zoo where live mice are regularly fed to hungry snakes, Dr. Alfred is Toscanini himself, with baton, in white dental smock and richly polished cordovan loafers.

Meanwhile, Gloria is somewhere across the waters, shopping in Bloomingdale's. Lovingly, she selects new pairs of tights and hand knitted leg warmers for her baby girl, whom she raised to become a dancer. As a family, the Golds worship culture, breeding, and refinement. Me they hate with a passion. And for good reason. I am none of those things, in spades.

In Cambridge these days, every girl I know claims to be a dancer. Only Lesley is the real thing. Lesley Gold, with hair the same, spun in ringlets that cling tightly to her face. Lesley has the sculpted cheekbones of a high fashion model and great, searching blue eyes. She is thin, really thin, yet always worried about her weight.

The play of the long muscles in her flat stomach and powerful thighs is always plainly visible as she strides purposefully down the hallway without any clothes on after her evening bath. Her hipbones actually curve out, throwing dark blue shadows across her groin whenever she pauses for a moment with the light behind her. Lesley always stands with her legs bowed out. Even in the street, she walks with the swift, pigeon toed gait that marks her unmistakably as one who dances, seriously.

Lesley bruises easily. She is always black and blue in the strangest places from doing floor work in class. Whenever she is not working part-time for the welfare department, she is taking classes. She knows she is now too old ever to dance professionally. Yet she cannot give it up. Black and blue and pink with dusting powder, she stands each night by the bed, holding onto the brass frame for support as she does stretching exercises so she will be able to lie down without throwing herself around the mattress all night long. She is one very nervous sleeper.

Lesley has a dancer's body but she is not a dancer. Pale and demanding, her body at times seems geometrically absurd, as though it was put together the wrong way around. "Think you're pretty?" I sometimes ask her. "*Know* I am," she always responds. I cannot argue the point. Lesley is beautiful. She is also hard to satisfy. At first the sex between us was awful. Now, it is great. Sex helps Lesley relax. Myself, I am more nervous than I have ever been.

Although Lesley can be kind and giving, sooner or later she always has to touch the thing that hurts the most. She cannot help herself. Putting her fingers on the newest bruise she has only just

20

brought home from class, she will probe and push and squeeze at it until she screams. As a child, she often edged the very best glass in the house towards the edge of the dining room table when no one was watching, just to hear the sound of good crystal as it shattered.

To Lesley, every warning is an invitation. If there was a sign hanging on her life, it would read, DANGER— HEARTBREAK DEAD AHEAD. Shaky ground is all she walks on. Take her to the seashore and she will head immediately for the far end of the pier where the boards are rotten clear through and you can look right down and see the ocean lapping around the crusty pilings. Sometimes I think she wants to put the whole world into her mouth, just to see how it tastes.

Lesley and I met at a party. I had already given up on graduate school and she was looking for a "meaningful job." We spent two weekends together, then I moved right in. Sometimes, I can be impetuous. Now we both live not far from the great New England Confectionery Company building. If ever I wrote home and told my parents that I was but a stone's throw from the factory where they actually stamp out those pastel tinted, slightly medicinal tasting wafers and then press them tightly into rolls, they would both say, "*Necco?* You're living by where they make those Necco wafers? Like we used to buy you on the avenue when you were a kid? You could never get enough of them, even then. Fine. Good! *Wonderful!* Do they sell them any cheaper up there?"

I do not write my parents. The phone is easier, although more expensive. Whenever I call, I reverse the charges. Lesley cannot stand to listen as I talk to them. She leaves the room whenever I dial their respective numbers. I have never yet taken her home. It would be too complicated. Lesley Gold is the original girl who you take to a night club and the whole band knows her name. She has been around. More times than I can number. Yet now we are a pair. We have caught one another's disease.

Soon I will be limbering up by the bed at night before I go to sleep. Although we are sick to death of one another, neither of us is willing to find the cure. I think they call it love.

CHAPTER TWO

BY THE TIME I get back to the apartment, Rob is gone. Lesley and I kiss and make up. Then we do other things. We do everything we can think of. Then Lesley invents a few all on her own. Back home, Rosh Hashanah has come and gone. Soon, it will be Yom Kippur. I cannot help but think of my grandfather. He is a small man, not unlike Menashe Skulnik in appearance, only not so funny. He does have a tremendous sense of humor, though. The fact that he is still alive is a constant source of amusement to him.

Against my better judgment, I call my mother. I wish her a Happy New Year. She asks when I am coming home. Soon, I tell her. She says my grandfather is doing fine, all things considered. Fine, I say, knowing enough to hang up while I am still ahead, even if the rates are cheaper after six.

The next morning, I wake up two seconds before the automatic alarm clock radio automatically switches itself on. My head is killing me. My heart pounds out a series of jungle rhythms in wild four-four time. The syncopation is rotten. Air rasps noisily through my tortured sinuses, the sound that of a rusty file being drawn slowly across a dull blade. The local ragweed pollen index has hit a new all-time high. I am about to have an attack.

Any second now, my mother will come through the bedroom door with an old-fashioned vaporizer in her hands, her face half-hidden in a whirling cloud of Vicks Vapo Rub scented steam. Reaching under the bed for the white porcelain basin I have filled during the night with phlegm thicker than the yolks of a dozen eggs, she will replace it with one that is brand new and spanking clean. Then she will remove the tin wastepaper basket embossed with a map of the world that stands by the wall, carting away another load of clotted tissues that resemble sorry, broken carnations without stems. All my life, I have watched myself slowly disappear into three-ply Kleenex tissues. Soon, there will be nothing left of me but tissues.

Only today my mother is back home and I am all alone in the apartment. Hours ago, Lesley got up to ride the MTA to work. Where she slept during the night, the bed is now cold. I reach out with my hand to feel the sheet. A damp stain shaped like the subcontinent of India marks the site of our lovemaking. During the night, it has stiffened and dried. Now, it is crusty to the touch, like a piece of toast burned so badly that it cannot be saved.

I reach for my little white plastic inhaler. A single pump, a sharp intake of breath, and the sour-tasting spray is on the back of my throat. Up, up, and away. Another day begins. Reaching out with both my hands for the sides of the mattress, I lean my head against the cold brass bed frame, bracing myself for the rush.

When it comes, I go right with it, arching my body into the torrent of words spilling from the radio beside my head. "*Wawk* with me and *tawk* with me, Bosstown," Cole T. Walker shouts, having already worked himself up into a fine evangelical frenzy that somehow seems completely appropriate despite the hour. "Put yore hands on the radio and yore feet on the floor and come *alahv!*" he howls. " 'Cause this mornin', chillun, the Reverend Doctor Cole ain't puttin' out *no* jahv!"

For as long as I can remember, I have depended on such disembodied voices to get me through both the night and day. From out of the ether, the voices would come floating magically into my bedroom when I was a teen-ager, taking me away. I have a short but complete list of those that I consider to be truly immortal. Jerry Blavat, the Geeter with the Heater, the Big Boss with The Hot Sauce, out of Philadelphia on a station that could sometimes be heard when atmospheric conditions were perfect. Ralph Cooper, Coopy-Doo For You, who rhymed everything that he said from midnight to dawn on a ten watt station that could best be heard at the entrance to the Forty-Second Street IRT station. Jocko Henderson, the captain of Jocko's Rocket Ship, maniacally chanting "Eee-tittly *okk!*/ You know this is the *Jock!*/ And I'm back on the scene/ With the r-r-record ma-*cheen!*" Jay Lawrence, the Jaybird, from Cleveland, who of a winter's night at three A.M. liked to play handball in the studio with his newsman, the two of them alternately doing play-by-play. B. Mitchell Reed, Your Leader, BMR, who dominated New York for a single year from seven to eleven at night before fading into the sunset and heading west, confidentially revealing during his very last hour on the air that his first name was actually Burton.

In Bosstown, Cole T. Walker is now the unchallenged king of the airwaves, the merry young soul of morning radio. A white boy with both soul and gumption, he has ratings that allow him to do, say, and play whatever he likes. Without question, Cole is the hippest thing happening in the city, for those who know.

Rolling over onto my side, I shove open the curtain and look out the window at the day. Our backyard, like every other one on the block, is filled with old trash, broken glass, and rusted bedsprings. Rusted bedsprings grow everywhere in our neighborhood, sprouting from the earth as though carefully planted there by hand. Across the alleyway, wet wash hangs in slanting diagonals on the back porches of all the other boxy triple-decker houses. Somehow, the hazy golden sheen of yet another perfect colonial morning in New England makes it all look fresh and new.

Currently, we are enjoying our single week of Indian summer in Boston. It will be followed immediately by crisp, red apple autumn. Then endless, dead cold, slushy gray winter will take over. The local bars will fill with those eager to watch and discuss endless televised replays of great breakaway Bruin goals and heroic Celtic comebacks. Forcing myself out of bed, I go down the hallway. The cracked linoleum beneath my feet is unbelievably cold, the first sure sign that winter will soon come.

Halfway through a commercial for a chain of stereo stores that sell second-rate equipment at first-rate prices, Cole stumbles badly over a word. He tries desperately to recover, then completely cracks up instead. Forgetting the ad entirely, he decides instead to throw in a free plug for his favorite local group. The J. Geils Band will be back at The Charity Ward tonight, he says. Cole notes that he himself might well drop by during the first set. Those who are interested will find him at the bar, accepting free drinks from whoever feels like buying. As always, he is completely open to any and all offers of payola. Maybe, Cole says, if you ask them nicely, the boys will even get around to playing this one tonight.

There is a moment of silence. Then, a hairy-throated voice shouts, "Uno, dos . . . one, two, three . . . *cuatro*." Another momentary pause. Then Sam the Sham and all his Pharaohs blast into "Wooly Bully." It is all I can do to keep from dropping my

24

toothbrush into the sink. "Hallie told Mallie," Sam screams. "A lotta things she saw. Two big horns. And a wooly dog. Woo-lee bul-lee. Woo-lee bul-lee. Woo-lee bul-lee."

Right in back of Sam, the Pharaohs struggle for traction. Their rear wheels skid madly across the icy slick rhythm track. *"Drive, Drive!"* Sam orders in the background. I drive, leaning over to spit foam into the sink without ever missing a beat. Although I do not dance, I do have rhythm. Although my voice is lousy, I know the words to all the songs.

"Let's not be el seven," Sam implores. Although I have no idea what he is talking about, I agree wholeheartedly. "Come and learn this dance," he urges. If only I could, Sam, I most surely would. The song is definitely a bit of classic wax. A dusty musty. An ingot from the golden grooveyard of Bosstown's all-time greatest hits. Who else but Cole would have the absolute bad taste to play it at this time of day?

I am sorry that Lesley is not around to hear him do it. Cole is an old friend. Or so Lesley says, insisting that she knew him way back when, before I appeared on the scene. Now that Cole is famous, their friendship has lapsed. Which is just the way it is with Lesley and other people. She gives and they take. Had I the time and energy, I could spend my days fighting duels to avenge her honor. As things now stand, all I can do is passionately hate those who have treated her badly. Of course, it is entirely possible that someday I too may be counted among them.

Today, Lesley is somewhere across the river in fabulous Bosstown itself, dispensing government checks to the needy. Although it is not our welfare she is looking out for, perhaps she does provide some of the local underprivileged with relief. The day that one of those angry petitioners for Federal aid gets a good look up Lesley's skirt and discovers that she did in fact go to work again without wearing any underwear, it will be all over for her. She will never make it home alive. Still, we do need the money that they pay her. For funny things, like rent and food.

I go back into the bedroom. Slowly, I slide open the door of what is supposed to be *our* closet. Lesley's clothes hang all the way from the door to the far wall in mad disarray, incontestable proof that Gloria definitely knows a bargain when she sees one. My things are jammed into a six inch space in the near corner. No matter how hard I try, I cannot ignore the metaphor. This is how I am living in Cambridge. Shoved into the first six inches of a closet, with not one really expensive wooden hanger to call my own.

I hate Lesley's clothes. I hate the warm, sweet smell of her body that comes off them even when she is not around. If I had a knife, I would run it through the entire closet, shredding every last little jumper and pleated skirt into tattered shreds. But I have no knife. They do not let me play with sharpened implements any more.

Reaching into the closet with both hands, I manage to wrestle a fairly clean shirt into plain view. By the time I put it on, the shirt is already so creased that it looks as though I have worn it to work each day for a solid week. One thing I know for sure. My mother would never have let me leave the house looking like this.

Sitting down on the bed, I start putting on my hiking boots. They have expensive red-and-gray braided laces and inch thick Vibram soles. Each shoe has to weigh at least a pound. The manufacturer guarantees them to be effective in temperatures of down to ten below. Why I am wearing footwear designed for attempts on the north face of Everest to work in a bookstore, I have no idea. Nearly everyone I know in Cambridge dresses this way, as though at any moment the current will be shut off forever more and we will all have to begin living off the land in those orange nylon mountaineering tents that are perpetually on sale in Central Square. Lesley hates the entire look. Contemptuously, she calls it "collegiate rustic."

Bent over nearly double, I am pulling on the laces when I see the pill. A small red dome, it sits sparkling brightly in its very own shaft of dusty morning sunlight. I lean over some more and peer beneath the bed. On all sides, the pill is surrounded by turned-out jazz shoes and worn ballet slippers that Lesley no longer dances in but likes to keep within easy reach, just in case. I lean all the way over, nearly putting my forehead to the floor.

In front of the battered old blue suitcase without a handle that I keep under the bed, just in case, I see the pill's identical twin. Scooping both pills up into my hand, I get to my feet and hobble over to the window to examine what I have found in the full light of day. Carefully, I turn both pills over in my palm. Neither one bears the markings of any of the well-known manufacturers of pharmaceuticals whose products are preferred for recreational use on the street. Where they actually came from, I have no idea.

26

The only drugs I ever use are epinephrine and ephedrine, strictly the real thing, for hard-core sufferers only.

Since no one but Lesley and I ever come into this room, I immediately start getting nervous. It is something I am really good at. The sensation begins down in my stomach and spreads quickly through my chest. Tiny flutterings that feel like the beating of a butterfly's wings work their way up to my Adam's apple. Without realizing what I am doing, I clear my throat three times in a row, doing my very best to swallow without gagging.

I look over at the little clock on the radio by the bed. Already I am late for work. Sliding the pills into the wrinkled front pocket of my shirt for safekeeping, I edge around the bed. I take my jacket from its hook by the door and go out into the hallway. Then I turn and head back into the room for my little white plastic inhaler. Without my inhaler, I am not fully dressed.

My chest has now really started to tighten up on me. My sinuses throb. I have the kind of headache usually associated with wolfing down an entire cup of Italian ices in a single swallow on a blazing hot summer's day. The little vein above my right eye pulses like mad, a sure sign that before the day is over I may yet have to live through an authentic, full blown attack.

My throat is what really bothers me. No matter how many times I try to clear it, I can still feel something down there, tickling away like mad just out of reach. Any minute now, the terrible eczema I suffered from as a child will once again burst into flower across the skin on my cheeks and forehead.

I remember something that Lesley's best friend, Anita, once told me about the emotionally disturbed souls that she sometimes counsels for a living. *Some people never have a nice day.* Without doubt, I am one of them. As soon as I have the time, I am going to make that statement my family motto. Emblazoned on a tiny crest that Lesley will sew under protest onto the front pocket flap of my thick, woolly red-and-black lumber jacket, it will look tremendous. Collegiate rustic, all the way.

CHAPTER THREE

WHAT I HAVE never told either of my parents is that the block on which Lesley and I live is right in the middle of a completely black neighborhood. They just would not understand. The neighborhood is a little village. We have our very own corner bar where people often start talking as soon as they come through the big front door. We have a barbecue hut made of white stucco that is run by the members of an obscure cult who wish to be allowed to migrate back to Africa at government expense. We have the little store without a name and, of course, the schoolyard.

Geographically, the schoolyard stands right at the very heart of our little village. Each morning, I cut across it to get to work. The concrete beneath my feet is visible only in a few scattered places. Cardboard boxes crushed flatter than apple pancakes lie beneath a layer of broken glass ground into granules that sparkle like sugar in the sun.

Although we are but five minutes from the great university that dominates all of Cambridge, we might as well be living on another planet. Or, as an old black man cheerfully told me one night as we both waited patiently in line for our chicken and ribs, "Round here, boy, Harvard don't mean *shit*." It is a sentiment with which I am in complete agreement.

Most mornings, I cannot even tell whether the little store without a name is open until I rattle the rusted knob on its old front door. Its windows are coated with grime. Inside, the only light comes from a single bulb hanging from a wire that dangles over a filthy glass counter containing Ring-Dings, Yodels, and Yoo-Hoos that date from prehistoric times. On the back shelves, the same cans of food stand in the exact same order day after day. The store itself is more like a museum than a market.

When I push open the door, a tiny brass bell above my head tolls, announcing my arrival. The little black man who runs the store looks up from his paper. He sits in the exact same place

28

each day, perched on a high stool by the ancient cash register. He wears a dark green shawl-collar sweater that President Lincoln would have looked good in, baggy blue train conductor's pants that A. Philip Randolph may well have owned once, and thick soled shoes without any laces.

His face is small and smooth, a chunk of hard, dark wood that someone has painstakingly carved into a set of impassive features and then carefully oiled. Both his face and clean shaven skull are a single color, a dark, warm chocolate that has only just come bubbling from the stove.

The little man has only a single expression, one that I recognize immediately without knowing why it seems so familiar to me. No surprises, the look says. No sudden changes. Nothing to worry about, or fear. Just the same old same old, day in and day out. Each morning, I know that he will be there, sitting quietly on his stool in a store where it is always twilight. The little man is marking time in the murky gloom until a wrecker's ball takes down the building and both he and the store without a name are no more.

Stooping over the ragged pile of newspapers by the door, I bypass those that have already been handled by other people, selecting an unblemished copy from underneath. I carry the paper to the counter and put it down, reaching into my pocket for a dollar bill so that the little man will know that I am a serious customer, here to do cash business.

"Morning," I say, trying to be friendly. "How you doing today?"

The little man grunts. Like my grandfather, he is doing as well as can be expected, all things considered. Slowly he slides off the stool. He eases himself around the counter to the register so he can ring up the sale. "Can I get some chips?" I ask, pointing to the ten cent bags of potato chips, both regular and barbecue, that he keeps clipped to heavy metal rungs by the register.

"*Wun?*" he asks, so softly that I have to strain to hear what he is saying.

"Just one," I say. I never, ever buy two. Still, he asks me the same question every day, as though it is only a matter of time until I break down under the pressure and double my order.

"Reg-u-lah?" he inquires. "Oah bobb-e-keww?"

"Bobbekew," I say, trying to make it easy for him to understand me.

29

Pulling a bag off the nearest rung, he drops it onto the counter. "Tin sint," he says.

"Ten and fifteen," I say, showing him the newspaper. He reaches for my dollar with one hand, pulling open his money drawer with the other. I stand patiently, waiting for my change. It comes slowly, first two quarters, then a dime, then a nickel, then incredibly, ten pennies, counted out one by one.

"Thanks," I say, putting it all into my pocket. "You have a good day now." I smile to let him know that I am only telling him this for his own good. He dips his head in answer. Then he moves out from behind the counter, easing himself back up to his stool.

"See you tomorrow," I call out over my shoulder as I go through the door. The tiny brass bell above my head tinkles goodbye. By the time I am out on the street again, he is already back where he was when I first came in, waiting for his next customer to appear.

I am starting to get to him all right. I can tell. Pretty soon, we will be having regular conversations with one another. See what the Sox did last night? How about that Yaz? Is he something, or what? And them Mets? Are they making a stretch drive, or not? Yeah, it's a miracle all right. No lie.

Having someone to talk to in the neighborhood will give me the feeling that I really belong. I mean, although I am not black, I *can* quote Curtis Mayfield, chapter and verse. Just like Curtis, I got my pride and a move on the side. So I *got* to keep on pushing.

Rolling up my newspaper, I stick it under my arm as I set off for the Square. As I munch the barbecue chips that are my breakfast, it suddenly occurs to me why I like the little man in the store without a name so much. It is so very simple that I cannot imagine why I have not thought of it before. The way he sits without talking, the clothes he wears, and that look on his face. He reminds me of my father.

30

CHAPTER FOUR

THEN THERE IS E.C. E.C. manages the bookstore where I work. If all the Totally Sincere Guys Who Really Know the Score in Cambridge ever hold an election, my money is definitely on E.C. He will win in a landslide, going away. E.C. has Dem Authentic, Living on the Road Is Getting Me Down, François Villon Blues. Funky, man. You know? With a stockbroker father living in Litchfield, Connecticut, who makes more in a single week than my old man takes home in an entire year.

E.C. is thin. He never eats, at least not where anyone can see him do it. E.C. is rangy. He always looks as though he has only just come off a dusty palomino that he has ridden hard and then left to graze by the MTA station in the middle of the Square. E.C. rolls his own, of course, sprinkling Bull Durham tobacco salted with an herb he calls "deerfoot," but that I know to be reefer from a little leather pouch that he can actually draw shut with just one hand and his teeth.

E.C. always seems to be peering myopically at something just out of everyone else's sight. Maybe he really is a visionary. His hair is long and blond. On the old guitar that E.C. claims he bought for eight bucks in a pawnshop in Okemah, Oklahoma, he plays those hard driving, white boy blues. He is perpetually going down the road, feeling sad.

E.C. is currently in his sixth year of some obscure and very experimental four year program at Harvard that somehow combines musical theory, statistics, and existential philosophy into a single major. In my opinion, E.C. is making the program up as he goes along. What really impresses me is that he was admitted to it without ever having graduated from any of the private schools to which he was sent after his mother died. E.C. likes to hint darkly that she committed suicide but I cannot be sure. He could be lying.

E.C. does have his finger on the pulse of Cambridge. He was

the very first person in the entire world to ever order a "pint of mild" at The Plough and Stars. Then he showed them how to make the nearest thing to it by mixing light beer and dark, half and half. Now, no one would think of drinking anything else there. Some people claim that E.C. was paid to start hanging out at The Charity Ward at night, making it *the* place to go long before Geils ever began playing there.

For all I know, the story may be true. Little rages are always running through Cambridge. Like ripples spreading out behind a racing shell on the Charles in late afternoon, they peter out only when they reach the bank. The same no doubt is true for E.C. In his heart of hearts, I know that E.C. loves money. Otherwise, why would he continually proclaim his dislike for it in such ringing tones?

Two years ago, when E.C. and Lesley were seeing one another semi-regularly, he borrowed two hundred and twenty-eight dollars from her. So far, she has not seen a penny of it back. E.C. is also not paying her any interest on the money. Even E.C.'s father would have to call that smart business.

What amazes me is that people do not find it strange that a full bore, forty-five-caliber outlaw like E.C. manages a bookstore. Not just any bookstore either, but the one that dominates the Square, no matter which way you come through it. Years ago, the store was a hotbed of good vibes and tradition. The eccentric old character who ran the place did not care at all about making a profit. He would just let everyone browse for as long as they liked. He made a policy of actually lending books to students who could not afford to buy them. He kept the store open all night long during Finals Week so people could study there. Now they show Bogart films non-stop at the Brattle instead. Which tells you a lot about what has happened to Cambridge in the ensuing years.

Back then, I am told, the walls of the store were covered with autographed pictures of all the famous judges, politicians, plastic surgeons, and tenured professors who never would have made it out of Harvard in the first place if not for the old guy's generosity. Many of these people actually attended his funeral. Then they went back home and a conglomerate of young and groovy million-aires from Aspen bought the store lock, stock, and barrel.

First, they renamed it. Then they tore out the front window and replaced it with a big red double door that came off a barn somewhere up in Vermont. The door is fitted out with a tiny stained glass window on which an old fashioned quill pen floats magically above a volume of Boswell's *Life of Johnson*. The title faces the wrong way round so that everyone coming into the store who can read will know immediately that they are entering a class establishment. Above the door hangs a huge ship's timber on which a single word has been burnt in curving script: TOMES. Which is the name of the store now. So help me God.

People love it. Seven days a week, from nine in the morning until well past midnight, Tomes, the literary supermarket, does land office business, selling books that no one really reads. In Tomes, all the walls are covered with thick, weathered slabs of graying wood. Spider ferns and wood geraniums that are perpetually in bloom stand everywhere. Even during the very darkest days of winter, in Tomes it seems as though spring is just around the corner.

In Tomes, browsing is specifically discouraged. Once or twice a year, E.C. gathers together all the brand new salespeople. Personally, he demonstrates how to hang out right on top of someone who is looking at a book. Either they buy it or they leave. Although I have seen distinguished looking men stand their ground, with one aging professor actually going so far as to make a little speech defending his right to read for free as a Cambridge tradition of long standing, it does not happen very often. Try reading with someone breathing right into your face and see how you like it.

Naturally, the little storeroom at the very back of the store has never been modernized. No plants grow within its walls. The walls themselves are made of damp plaster that comes up under your nails when you scrape your fingers along the surface. The fetid smell of the dank hole that is the employees' toilet drifts into the room, winter and summer alike.

As I come into the storeroom today, I do my best not to breathe too deeply, as always. I hang my lumber jacket on its usual hook. Then I transfer my little white plastic inhaler to my shirt pocket, just in case. I am now ready to work. So far, I am having one authentically great morning. Although I am half an hour late, I have not yet seen E.C. I know that my luck cannot last.

Taking up my regular position at the buy-back window, I unlock the little cash drawer to which I have been entrusted with a key of my very own. Out on the floor, I would not last a week. I do not have the personality for it. Back here, however, I am free to wheel and deal as I see fit, buying textbooks that people no longer need or want. Actually, I like the bargaining. The corrosive give-and-take that occurs when money is on the line makes my blood run faster.

Not that there is ever any more in my pay envelope at the end of a week when I have made some particularly brilliant deals. My salary is always the same, tied directly to the current Federal minimum wage. It is still better than having to act like a cop in the aisles.

"Paulie," E.C. says, coming up behind me so quietly that I do not even realize that he is there until he speaks. No wonder browsers flee when he approaches. E.C. has the technique down to an exact science. He even wears shoes that do not squeak. "You," he notes, "are late."

I nod my head in agreement. Although I hate the fact that E.C. calls me by the same name that people like Lesley and my parents use when they talk to me, there is nothing I can do about it. For months after he took over as day manager, E.C. referred to me as Bindle, rhyming it with "spindle." For some reason known only to him, he simply could not accept the fact that my last name should be pronounced Bin-*del*. So now we have settled on Paulie. It is a compromise that neither one of us likes but then I do not even know what E.C. stands for. I have never asked.

"E.C.," I say casually. "How about paying Lesley back that two hundred and twenty-eight dollars?"

I say this to E.C. every morning, whether or not I am on time. It is my way of letting him know what I think of outlaws who borrow money from ladies with no intention of ever paying them back.

"You know," E.C. says, shaking his head slowly in that sorrowful southwestern way I am certain he has practiced many times in front of a mirror. "Maybe you *should* start working nights with Norris. He's more your speed anyway, isn't he? Being a fellow member of an oppressed minority and all . . ."

"Maybe I should," I say, knowing that there is no way I ever will. "Then you can just start slipping around my back to see Lesley whenever you feel like it."

This gets to him. He laughs so I will think that it does not but I know better. Under that hard, existential shell, E.C. has feelings. A few of them anyway. Really casually, he says, "Hey. Don't be el seven, man." *El seven.* Is E.C. hip, or what? He actually introduced Lesley to Cole T. Walker. E.C. and Cole are still good friends, even now. Half the music that Cole plays on the radio E.C. probably turned him on to in the first place. The man is just an all around cultural force.

"El seven," I call out after E.C. as he starts to move away. "El seven," I say again, having no idea at all what the expression means. "You don't have to worry about me where that's concerned, E.C. No way. El seven is . . . something I'll never be."

Of course, E.C. is well aware that I do not even know what el seven means. That is why he said it to me in the first place. To be mysterious. Still, he finds it upsetting to deal with me. I am so thoroughly hostile.

Before going back into his little office, E.C. takes momentary refuge in the corner of the store where all the science fiction is stacked, drawing strength from the books that he prefers over all others. Never trust anyone who reads too much science fiction. That is my motto. Or at least one of them.

I am about an hour and a half into my day and already looking up at the clock every ten minutes or so to see whether it is time yet for me to go to lunch when the first ringer comes in. He is a really young kid, maybe seventeen or so, definitely a freshman at Northeastern or some place like it. The scholarship they gave him is not enough. I can see right off that he needs a little extra money on the side to make it through the year.

His hair is slicked back and he has pimples on his chin. Although it is only September and still plenty warm outside, he wears a thick woolen muffler draped casually around his neck. Probably he read somewhere that this is how you dress when you go to college.

In his hands, he holds the gigantic art history book that every school in the area now uses for their required course in the field. Brand new, it sells for thirty-five bucks. Everyone is always looking to get one second-hand but since the demand is so constant, even used copies bring anywhere from twenty-six to twenty-eight dollars. Just before I left the store yesterday afternoon, I saw a whole shipment of them that had just come in from the Colorado warehouse. If they last a week, I will be surprised.

Yet now I am being offered one that looks brand new. I decide to take the kid over a couple of jumps. "Art History One, huh?" I ask, turning the book over in my hands.

"Yeah," he says nervously. "Gut course. All the way."

"Duccio, Michelangelo, Botticelli. . . ."

35

"Great painters, man."

"Cassini," I say, thinking of the brothers Oleg and Igor. "Hon. Vincent Impellitteri . . ."

"One of the best," the kid confirms, nervously clearing his throat. "If you like that style."

This is great news. Every single day of my childhood, I had to walk into school past a brass plaque that read, "This building constructed by the City of New York, Hon. Vincent Impellitteri, Mayor." The kid standing before me knows as much about Art History One as I do concerning E.C.'s current sex life. Which is nothing. The kid never took the course.

"Give you sixteen bucks for it," I offer.

"Great," he says too quickly. "I'll take it."

I turn the book over in my hands. "Nope," I say. "Back cover's nicked. I can only go fourteen."

"Fine by me. I just want to get rid of it. . . ."

I count the money out of the cash drawer and hand it to the kid. At fourteen bucks, the book is a steal. In fact, the book itself is stolen. On the inside back flap, I see the little red paper dot that identifies all stock originating from our Colorado warehouse. Whoever works the front register is supposed to peel off the dot before ringing up a sale. I am buying back one of our own books that we have never even sold. Neat.

The kid takes his money and leaves. He probably has a lot more stops to make before he is through for the day. No doubt, he gets a flat fee for every book that he unloads. The guy who is running the scam is the one making the real profit. For months now, my friend Norris Rice, who also happens to be the night manager of the store, has been dropping little hints to me that something weird is going on in Tomes.

Books do not balance. Shipments disappear before they can be stacked. It is nothing very big, Norris says, just something I should keep my eye on so that I do not get blamed for the problems. Although I have never been a very great fan of Sherlock Holmes, I do not need to do very much detecting to know who is behind all of this. Only E.C. has a key to the stock room. Selling us back our very own books, while taking a percentage of the store's commission when the book is sold again, is the ultimate E.C. touch. I have to hand it to the boy. He does have *chutzpah*.

Myself, however, I just do not feel like being part of his lousy scheme. I consider my choices. I can place a long distance call to the main office in Colorado, collect, of course. If they accept it, I can explain to the groovy young millionaires that while they are up on the slopes praying for snow, they are being robbed blind in Cambridge by their most trusted employee. No doubt, this will win me a raise and a battlefield promotion. Maybe they will even give me E.C.'s job.

Only, I do not want it. The Colorado millionaires are the ones who destroyed the store in the first place, turning it into a greenhouse for functional illiterates who like to look at books filled with pretty pictures. I am caught on the horns of an authentic moral dilemma. The criminals are stealing from one another and I am supposed to decide which ones are truly guilty. It is definitely time to consult the Talmud.

E.C., I am sure, thinks he is striking a blow for the common man. He is Robin Hood, Jesse James, and Pretty Boy Floyd all wrapped up in one. To me, he is just another skinny hippie from a rich family who is ripping off the system and calling it politics. No doubt, the money that he makes gets funneled directly to his dealer friends to finance their runs to Mexico for reefer and bootleg pills. E.C. doubles his take by investing in a tax-free business. Yet he still has not paid Lesley back what he owes her. One thing I know for sure. E.C. will be a millionaire long before I am.

I lock up my cash drawer in disgust. Although it is still early, I have had it. My morning is over. It is now officially time for lunch, no matter what the clock says. As I go out through the big front door into the street, E.C. comes after me. This is his first big mistake. Walking over to the bike rack, he unlocks the shiny ten-speed he rides to work each day. Then he wheels it towards me, cool as can be. "Catching a breath of fresh air, Paulie?" he inquires. "Little oxygen break?"

"Actually," I tell him, "I'm going to lunch."

"*I'm* going to lunch," he notes. "You must be confused."

It is high noon in the Square all right. The sun is straight up over our heads. Our shadows run from our feet across the sidewalk. Then they drip slowly into the black and oily gutter. Two Zen cowboys with big irons on our hips, we turn slowly to face one another. It has been a long time coming. Once this showdown is over, one of us will *have* to leave town. Cambridge is just not big enough for the both of us.

"They teach you how to steal at Harvard, E.C.?" I ask. "Or you just picked it up all on your own?"

"Harvard's a myth, Paulie," he sniffs, neatly sidestepping my question. "You shouldn't be so hung up on it. Just because you never went there . . ."

"Tell that to the Chinese pre-engineering students," I say, doing my best to be just as cryptic as him. "*Before* they blow up the world. Or are they a myth, too?"

"You're talking shit now, man. You know that?"

"Am I, E.C. ?" I say. "How about paying Lesley back that money you owe her?"

This is the point right here. I do not really give a damn about what E.C. is doing in the store. It is Lesley that I care about. For me, this has become an absolute point of honor. I demand satisfaction. And today, it looks as though I am finally going to get it.

"How about kissing my ass?" E.C. suggests.

"How about trying to make me, *scumbag?*" I shout, taking a threatening step in his direction. In about two seconds, I will have him off that bike. Then I will wrap it around his skinny neck like a woolen muffler.

But E.C. is too quick for me. The original advocate of non-violence, especially when the violence is directed at him, he loops one leg over the frame of his bike, puts both feet on the pedals, and boosts himself up onto the seat. Wheeling the bike in a tight circle, he crouches low over the handlebars like a racer. He starts to move away from me. "You know, Paulie," he says in a calm, conversational tone, as though we are only discussing the weather. "Sometimes I wonder about your ethics."

"*Ethics?*" I scream as I run after him, my voice cracking so that it suddenly becomes a high pitched girlish falsetto. E.C. picks up speed, his thin legs pumping like crazy as the wheels spin faster in whirling circles. "Ethics?" I demand, still screaming. "Motherfucker, you don't know the meaning of the word."

People walking through the Square stop dead in their tracks to stare at me. And why not? For them all, this is just another piece of street theater, with no admission charge. E.C. does not even bother turning around. He is too cool. Instead, like the perfect preppie he once was, he sticks his arm straight out from the elbow as though to signal for a turn. Then he gives me the finger, holding it proudly aloft for everyone to see, like a candle against the night.

No one in the crowd can mistake the gesture. Soon this too will become part of the ever increasing E.C. legend. Behind me,

38

people start laughing. I cannot blame them. It is definitely funny all right. I am just sorry that I was not around to watch it all myself.

As E.C. pedals away through traffic, I stand there on the sidewalk feeling like a complete idiot. Once again, I have tried to fight someone else's battle. I have tilted against the windmill and come out second best. Although I have both might and right on my side, I have been denied the satisfaction due me. E.C. has won again. It is what he is good at. The bastard.

CHAPTER FIVE

FOOD HELPS. MY mother told me this many times over when I was a child. Naturally, I did not listen. Now that I am on my own, I recognize how truly great a nugget of folk wisdom this actually happens to be. *Food helps.* Those of us who rarely get our way in this world can always sit down at a back table in Bartley's, the Burger Cottage with soul, order a melted cheese sandwich on rye bread with french fries on the side, and then hide behind the sports section of the *Boston Globe* until it arrives.

With every bite, I start feeling better. As I eat, I am being serenaded by the seductive south of the border sizzle of burgers cooking on the griddle in the front window. Arranged in a neat double line, they slide to and fro in tiny pools of their very own grease, doing a red hot, meaty little samba. Castanets begin clicking madly in the background. Soon, Carmen Miranda herself will appear at the front door wearing a hat made of bananas, coconut shells, and odd bits of costume jewelry purchased at discount in Filene's basement. Bartley's will be magically transformed into the old Copacabana.

In back of me, thick lipped china cups bob soapily in a big double sink, surfacing and sinking only to resurface once again. They clang softly against one another like buoys out at sea signaling the approach of an on-coming storm. The mantle of fog along the Newfoundland banks grows thicker. Spencer Tracy appears through a hatch on the lower deck with a corncob pipe in his mouth to haul in the hand lines. On his head, he wears the Vita Herring hat. Bartley's becomes a commercial fishing trawler plying the open sea.

Instead, Norris Rice strolls through the door looking as though he has only just rolled out of someone else's bed. Norris can barely keep his eyes open. The two longest fingers of his bony right hand are busily curling ringlets in the bushy black beard that shrouds his face. Any day now, Norris' beard is just going to rear up and devour his entire head. At the moment, it climbs slowly up one side of his jawbone, explodes into a huge black shrub atop his skull, then descends peacefully once again along his other cheek to his chin. Right at the very top, a narrow patch of mottled, cocoa-brown scalp is visible, a tiny clearing hacked by hand in the heart of the darkest jungle known to man.

Surrounded by all that hair, Norris' little teak-colored face seems at first to be almost insignificant. Women, however, like it just fine. Norris' big waffle-iron eyes are almost octagonal in shape. Whenever he is attracted to someone new, mumbling under his breath, "Look out now fellas, 'cause mah nose is *open!*", his eyes gleam like a traffic signal shifting from red to green. Women respond automatically, pressing the accelerator all the way to the floor so they can catch up with him before he is gone. I have seen it happen more times than I can number.

In Cambridge, the jury is still out on Norris Rice, trying to decide whether anyone is home there or if it has all become just a riff for him. In some ways, I guess that Norris is kind of a burnt-out case. A six foot seven inch former high school All American with a deadly, looping jump shot and a very real B-plus average, Norris was recruited to bring some respectability to Harvard's basketball program. Somewhere along the line, though, he just lost interest.

Norris is now a permanent fixture in the Square, a local legend who stands on the corner each Saturday in a see-through shirt and a pair of bold, double-knit slacks, softly talking trash to all the sweet young coeds who are out shopping. On Sundays, he plays three-on-three half court for horse caps of mescaline in the little schoolyard by my house, the winners getting so wasted that by the time they finally lose, it has all just become a laughing matter.

Many of those recruited along with Norris to bring various other basketball programs in the area back to respectability have fallen on harder times. They shoot up over sinks filled with blood as Isaac Hayes gets down on the long version of "By the Time I Get to Phoenix." In his own way, Norris is a success. He works as the night manager in Tomes and he has me for a friend. What more could any man ask?

"Norris," I call out anxiously, waving my hand at him. "Over here, buddy."

As though his body is made of separate, collapsible sections, Norris sinks slowly into the chair across from me. "Try and keep it down to a low roar today, huh, Paulie," he suggests. "Feel like ah got carpet tacks in mah brain."

"Carpet tacks in the brain," I parrot. "Could be the name of a hot new band. An album title. A fad, even."

"Could be ah only got up, too. They got any orange juice left?"

"Not for members of your race, no. Sorry, Norris. But *someone* had to tell you."

Norris looks at me sideways, grinning. *"Tico!"* he shouts, waving at the madman who has worked behind the counter in here for longer than anyone can remember. "How's mah breakfast comin'?"

"Already came," Tico shouts back, revealing a matching pair of solid gold teeth in the front of his mouth. "Then it went. Now she gone for good." Tico waves a large carving knife in Norris' direction to back his statement up.

Norris smiles with only his teeth, as though Tico has just said the funniest thing he has heard this year. Under his breath, he mumbles, "This is one sick mother, Paulie. Any time he's ever holdin' *any* kinda knife on you, y'all jes' keep smilin' at him."

"You in good mood today, hah, Norris?" Tico calls out. "How come? You get suction all night long, hah?"

Two really sweet looking girls who have been lingering over lunch at the counter suddenly decide it is time they paid their check and got back to the Medieval Studies department at Radcliffe. Tico stares hungrily as their tweed skirts twitch in time on the way out. Then he laughs like Richard Widmark. "Hokay," he says. "But only for you, Norris."

Grabbing four eggs that he balances perfectly between his fingers, Tico breaks them with one hand against the lip of a large bowl. He throws in salt, water, and pepper. With a fork, he begins scrambling them rapidly, restaurant style. Pouring the yellow mixture onto the griddle so that it forms a thick, brim-

41

ming puddle, he rims it with four strips of raw bacon. Effortlessly
he splits an English muffin in two with the point of his knife. I
suddenly understand the wisdom of Norris' advice. With a knife
in his hands, Tico is definitely one funny guy.

Popping both halves of the muffin into a large toaster, Tico
slides a large china plate on to the counter. Then he starts
whistling something that to me sounds suspiciously like "Wooly
Bully." I am impressed. Cole T. Walker's standing with the
working people in Cambridge has never been higher. The man
crosses over into every market.

"So, son?" Norris says, his long spidery fingers slowly drawing an unfiltered Camel from the pack he is never without. "How
y'all been? Makin' it and takin' it?"

"Not so good, Norris," I say. "Me and E.C. gave each other
some more shit this morning."

"I ast for the news, baby, not the weather."

"I been thinking that maybe I should quit."

Norris shrugs. In his time at the store, he has seen them come
and go. Which is why he works nights. After six P.M., he gets to
do just as he likes. No one ever jumps on his case or tells him a
thing. For weeks he has been after me to come and work with
him. Only I cannot do it. I am afraid to leave Lesley alone in the
apartment at night. It would be like giving a pyromaniac a full
book of matches and a can of kerosene. And I would be the one
reduced to ashes by the ensuing blaze.

"A man's got to do . . . what a man's got to do," Norris says
slowly, tapping his unlit cigarette against the tabletop for emphasis.
"That's what ah always say. Dig?"

"Possibly," I say. Even to me, Norris looks particularly wasted
today. His arms are broomstick thin, his little face gaunt. He will
never again be the awesome physical specimen that he once was,
but then, these days he is into an entirely different game. I mean,
being able to get any woman you want is no small feat. It is a
kind of power that has nothing at all to do with money, as least
as far as Norris is concerned.

"Norris," I say, leaning in towards him, "what's your secret,
man?"

"What is?"

"You know. With women . . ."

"Ain' no secret, Paulie," he says, grinning. "Just treat all the
women like little girls and all the little girls like women. Young

42

ones like bein' rushed. Doan ask me why. Old ones want you to take it slow. It's in the blood."

"Right," I say, as though he has finally opened my eyes on the subject. I mean, there *has* to be more to it than this. "Got you."

Then I sit all the way back in my chair and laugh out loud. Norris Rice, the living legend. Making his way in the white man's world and doing just fine, thank you. At least, most of the time. When things get tough for him, I am not the one who hears about it. No one does.

"How's Lesley holdin' up?" he asks suddenly.

"Fine," I say, suddenly nervous because he has brought her name up in the conversation. Although I have never thought about it before, it now occurs to me that it is entirely possible that the two of them actually spent a night or two together way back when. I do not want to think about it. Not at the moment. "Good as expected," I add.

"Now she," Norris says significantly, "is different. She's *people*, you know?"

Sure I do. And people just cannot help themselves. Left to their own devices, they will almost always fall into bed with one another. It is one of the basic laws of nature. Still, what came before came before. I cannot run from it. Of course, I cannot live with it either. Unfortunately, there is also no one in the entire world that I can talk to about it, Norris included.

Reaching into my shirt pocket, I take out the two little pills I have been carrying around with me ever since I left the house. I roll them on to the table in front of Norris like a pair of miniature red dice that will come up snake eyes no matter how many times I try to make my point.

"Hello, fellas," Norris says happily, bending over to address the pills directly. "How y'all been keepin'?"

"You know what these are, Norris?"

Before he can answer me, Tico appears carrying the plate on which Norris' massive breakfast has been arranged. Only Norris gets this kind of service in here. Coolly, he closes one large hand over the pills, grinning at me so I will know enough to keep my big mouth shut. Tico puts the plate on the table. He winks broadly as though he *knows* that we are discussing something illegal. Then he moves away.

Picking up his fork, Norris digs a huge, triangular wedge from the quivering mound of perfectly scrambled eggs steaming before

43

him. He shoves the wedge into his mouth, ignoring a tiny bit of yolk that falls on to his beard. Then he goes to work on the muffin. He smears strawberry jam from a tiny packet all over its cratered, pockmarked surface. Taking a huge, jagged bite out of it, he sighs, a man totally at peace with himself and the world.

Chewing contentedly, he says, "Now, where'd y'all say you got hold of these?"

"Uh . . . a friend gave 'em to me?"

"If that's your best story, cool. Y'all wanna know what they are, or should ah make one up too?"

"Just tell me, Norris."

"MDA," he says, his jaws bulging with food. "Distant cousin to the Peace Pill and/or the Love Drug, which y'all may or may not remember was *the* hip trip last spring. These babies came in right after."

"You're sure?"

"Hell, yeah," he says, his little face wrinkling up with righteous indignation. "July Fourth weekend, we held ourselves a little tourney-ment over in the schoolyard by your crib. House rules. Everyone who played kicked in one of these, winner take all. Did guys get high? *Hey!* People *still* talkin' on that day. We had everybody down. E.C., Cole T. Walker . . . everybody. Can't say as I remember you bein' there though."

"I wasn't," I say, remembering the pitched battles Lesley and I fought about what we were going to do that weekend. "I went camping with Lesley on the Cape," I tell Norris, failing to mention that while we were there, we got bitten over every square inch of our bodies by vicious, blood sucking mosquitoes. For three days, we argued non-stop inside a tent too small for either of us to stand up in. Big fun, all the way.

"How was that?" Norris asks, not the least bit interested. "Bunch of white people squattin' around in the dirt, discussin' 'What is oxygen?' "

"Something like that," I admit.

"Tell you one thing," Norris says. "Fast as these little suckers came into Cambridgeburg is how fast they got gone again. So somebody been sittin' on these babies for a *long* time. 'Cause at the moment, there is just none around. None."

Norris looks up over my head at the clock on the wall. "What time you got to be back in the store, Paulie?" he asks.

"Now?"

"*Right* now," he says, nodding his head. "Even as you sit here jivin' with the master, you already late."

I turn and look up at the clock. As always, Norris is dead right. I get to my feet. Grabbing my check, I scoop both pills off the table in the very same motion. "Y'all gonna be at Anita's house tonight?" Norris asks, going back to work on his eggs.

"Shit," I say. "I didn't even know you were invited."

"Hell, yeah," Norris grins. "They askin' me to *all* the best parties these days. Just like white folks."

"Don't you have to work?"

Norris shrugs. Work has never before interfered with his social life. So why should he start making exceptions now? "Y'all doan see me at Anita's," he says, "ah'll fall by The Charity Ward later on. Round about midnight, like Miles once said. You'll see mah smilin' face."

I nod. Then I look down into my hand. One of the little pills is starting to crumble around the edges from the sweat in my palm. Putting both of them back into my shirt pocket, I wave goodbye to Norris. Then I head towards the register to pay my check.

Pushing open the big plateglass front door of Bartley's, the Burger Cottage with soul, I move back into the swirling confusion of the Square. All the while, I am busily clearing my throat as though I have swallowed something that I can neither get all the way down or ever bring back up. It is just another one of the maddening little habits I have developed of late. Annoying, certainly, but not necessarily fatal.

CHAPTER SIX

ANITA SAFTIR IS what my mother would call an "eccentric girl." She lives in a building that matches her personality to perfection. I cannot ever see the place without wanting to break down immediately into tears. Struggling writers have starved to death in the garrets beneath that gabled roof. Unrecognized artists have gone blind squinting at their masterpieces in those gloomy one room studios. The place just reeks of tuberculosis. Any day now, I fully expect to see Proust himself come stumbling down the hallway, manuscript in hand. There is nowhere else in Cambridge that Anita could live.

After I knock loudly on her front door for the third time, Anita finally opens it to let me in. She wears the same loose green-and-purple silk rag of a robe in which she almost always receives her guests. Her fingernails are painted forest green. Her toenails are purple. An unlit cigarette dangles from one corner of her wide, fleshy mouth. In her right hand, she holds a safety razor.

"Anita," I say dutifully, handing over a bottle of cheap wine wrapped in a brown paper bag that I can only hope she will not open until after I am in the apartment. "I made sure not to come late. I know it's a real fetish with you."

"God," she says. "That sounds dirty." Accepting the wine without even looking at it, Anita giggles. Her robe falls open. As always, she is naked underneath. I do my best not to look. Anita is Lesley's best friend. Although she is slightly overweight these days, she too is a dancer. To Anita, everything always sounds dirty. Anita thinks the little hallway leading to her bedroom is the most coveted bit of real estate in all of Cambridge. For all I know, she may be right.

"Shaving?" I ask, pointing to the razor.

"Just my legs," she says. I wonder if she thought I meant her face. "Come in," she says, stepping back to admit me. "No one else is here yet but . . . come in."

Before I step over the threshold, I say, "Anita, you *did* put away the cats, right?"

Anita nods. Her face is sad. A look of utter tragedy fills her soft brown eyes. "The poor babies," she whimpers. "I had to lock them all in the bathroom."

"Better them than me," I note. Then I move past her into the living room. Tiny bits of kitty litter crunch loudly beneath the rippled soles of my hiking boots. The heavy claustrophobic odor of cat spray, cat fur, and cat urine hangs over the entire apartment. In here, it always smells as though a very large wheel of Camembert cheese is slowly going bad beneath the sofa. Puffballs of cat hair as big around as desert tumbleweeds dot the faded Persian rug.

Slowly, I slink into the sprung cushions of Anita's Salvation Army sofa. I am Jonah in the belly of a cat, God's very own messenger swallowed whole by an ordinary household pet. Should

46

just one of those puffballs become airborne, lodging itself in my trachea, they will have to call an ambulance. I will be dead on arrival at Peter Bent Brigham, the hospital with soul.

For safety's sake, I reach into the front pocket of my shirt for my little white plastic inhaler. A quick blast of spray onto the back of my throat and I breathe a little easier. Not deeper, but easier. "Why don't you just go ahead and make a fire, Paulie?" Anita calls out as she retreats down the hall. "I haven't had one in months."

"Kind of warm for a fire, isn't it?" I ask.

"So?" Anita demands. "We'll open all the windows."

How can I argue? Anita's logic is always infallible. Like Lesley, she is accustomed to getting her own way. Anita's parents are so rich that Lesley invariably refers to them as "The Rothschilds." Yet Anita lives right at the poverty level. It is not something I can understand.

Systematically, I begin crumpling up old copies of the violently radical underground newspapers that Anita reads religiously, searching for news of old comrades who have fallen in battle and are now part of the middle class. Wadding the newspapers into large balls that crinkle noisily in my hands, I line them up on a blackened metal grate covered with a thick layer of cold gray ash. I then take six pieces of kindling from the basket on the hearth. I break each one in half across my knee, just to hear the sharp, crackling sound reverberate through the silent apartment.

Making a little pyramid with the wood, I reach for a long starter match and crouch back down. The ritual of making a fire never fails to give me pleasure. No doubt, this is because I grew up with steam heat that issued forth from paint caked radiators on which Number Ten pineapple juice cans half filled with water had to be placed at night in order to ensure that my nasal passages would not completely seal up before morning.

For no good reason, it suddenly occurs to me that the flue may well be closed. Although I am no expert in such matters, Anita herself has told me that it has been months since anyone made a fire in here. It would be just like her to tell me to start one and then have to run to the phone to call the nearest hook and ladder company to put it out again.

Boldly sticking my head right into the fireplace, I look straight up, expecting to see a rectangular shaped patch of darkened sky at the very top. I see only blackness. The flue, I decide, is definitely shut. Reaching out for the soot covered black metal

47

handle on the back wall, I give it a rough jerk, turning it one hundred and eighty degrees around. Somewhere above my head, a metal plate slides into place. At the very same time, someone knocks on the front door.

"Anita?" I call out. "People."

"Be a big sweetheart, won't you, Paulie, and let them in?" she calls back. "I've got Gillette Foamy halfway up to my crotch. . . ."

This image stays with me as I go to the door. In the bathroom down the hall, surrounded by mewling cats, Anita Saftir stands completely naked. One tiny turned out pink little foot is perched delicately on the very edge of the bowl. Slowly, she leans forward with razor in hand. Odalisque in her bath, taking special care not to leave a trace of stubble anywhere. I open the front door. To my amazement, Lesley stands in the hallway next to a guy who looks vaguely familiar.

Of course, I am expecting her. Over the phone earlier today, she told me she would come to Anita's apartment straight from work in order to save time. Certainly, I recognize her. It is only that whenever I see her outside of our little bedroom, I am surprised. It is as though she does not really exist anywhere but there, and inside my head.

I stare at the guy next to her. He is a real Maccabee, an authentic Jewish warrior with a full head of curly black hair, a strong hooked nose, and a set of truly great teeth. He wears boots. The boots I like. His hair I hate. The nose as well. I hate his mouth and all the brilliant, phony insights that will soon be coming from it. There are hundreds of guys who look just like him in Cambridge. I hate them all.

On the absolute coldest day of the year, I see them striding confidently through the Square wearing only a torn T-shirt, faded wheat jeans, and a sleeveless vest. Their biceps wink at the freezing winter. They need no coats or bulky hand-knit sweaters. They have their love to keep them warm. When the sun comes out in the spring and everyone else is in shorts, they wear perfect, cream-colored raincoats hung all over with loops and buckles. Always, they look as though they have only just come from another wildly successful audition at the Green Street Playhouse.

They all share a single dream. Some day, with a faithful woman by their side and a good dog for company, they will move to the Berkshires. There, they will open the perfect little art movie house, serving bowls of homemade popcorn with real butter and mugs of steaming, cold-pressed apple cider to those culture-starved locals who have not yet seen *Jules et Jim* at least fifteen times.

Stepping forward, Lesley plants a wet kiss on the side of my face. I hardly notice. I am too busy trying to place this guy. "Paulie," she says, "this is Rob Rosen."

"I know you?" I ask, putting out my hand. Rob Rosen takes it, squeezing down as hard as he can. I squeeze right back. The two of us go right on smiling. In a moment we will both reach for spiked clubs and begin bashing each other's brains out. The one still standing when it is over will get to drag Lesley and Anita by the hair to the bedroom down the hall.

"Don't think so," Rob says.

"You met Rob yesterday, Paulie," Lesley points out, giggling in spite of herself. "Only for a second, though. Then you went for your regular little Thursday run? Through the stadium and back again?"

"Oh, right," I say. "Right. Anything to stay in shape, you know?"

"Rob's a therapist," Lesley adds. "Sometimes Anita and I refer people to him."

"You Anita's boyfriend?" I ask, eager to get everything clear in front.

"Paulie," Lesley says, rolling her eyes in disapproval like someone's maiden aunt at a dinner party.

"She refers people to me," Rob says, smiling in a reassuring manner. "And we are good friends . . ."

Just then, Anita appears. She has put on a dress and pinned up her hair. She now looks exactly like the kind of girl you would take to the Saturday night dance at the country club if only you could ever get up enough nerve to first talk to her at the pool.

"Sorry I'm late, 'Neeta," Rob says, smiling to beat the band. "I had some trouble getting away. *Jenny*," he says, as if that explains it all. Turning towards me, he adds, "My wife. We don't live together any more but she has custody of our daughter."

I am impressed. Rob definitely has lived. He has a wife, a daughter, and who knows what else. To me, the entire concept of marriage is completely terrifying. Just after we first began living together, Lesley and I were walking hand in hand through the Square one day. I realized that we could easily be married to one another. Immediately I felt so weak that I had to sit right down in the street until the strength came back into my legs. Not Rob, though. He is a *man* all right, in every sense of the word. "I've brought some *very* nice wine," Rob announces suddenly. That it has to be better than the stuff I bought, I do not doubt. "Would you like to open it?" he asks, thrusting the bottle in my direction. Its expensive French label is aimed directly at my heart.

"Thanks," I say, showing him the long wooden starter match I am still holding in my hand. "But I've got fire detail tonight."

"Lovely," he croons, rubbing his hands together. "Nothing finer than a toasty blaze."

Suddenly, making a fire seems like the single dumbest thing a person can be doing. Why, I do not know. Without speaking, I turn and head back into the living room. With the steel reinforced tip of my boot, I drop kick one of the wadded balls of newspaper towards the back of the fireplace. I am now officially sulking. It is one of the few things that I am really good at. First, I pout. Then I get a headache.

Lesley follows me into the room. I turn to look at her. She is more tired than she has ever been before. The strain of living with me is definitely wearing her down. The hollows beneath her eyes are smudged inky black. Her pale skin is almost translucent. She is so thin that I can almost see the light shine right through her bones. "Paulie," she says softly, unable even to look me in the face. "Why are you starting already? We haven't even sat down to dinner yet."

"Who's starting?"

"Why can't you be *nice* to people for a change? Would it kill you to try?"

"I don't know. What if I try and it kills *me*?"

Lesley stares at me. Silently, she is begging me to stop now, before it really begins. But I cannot do this. The tom-toms have started pounding loudly in my brain. Messages are traveling at the speed of light along the jungle telegraph of my central nervous system. A bonfire burns brightly inside my head. "Why do we have to eat *here*?" I demand. "Why can't we just go home?"

"Paulie, I only just came through the door. . . ."

"Let's see if it swings the other way, okay?"

"Paulie," she hisses. "Lower your voice. They're only in the other room. They'll hear you."

"So? Let them hear."

"What the *hell* is the matter with you tonight?"

"Nothing."

"You had a fight with E.C. at work today, didn't you? I can tell. I know something must have happened because you're taking it out on me."

As always, Lesley is right. I would like to explain my basic problem to her. Only I cannot do this without asking for another blue book so that I can expand my answer to include some badly needed historical perspective.

Back in the neighborhood where I grew up, I often found myself sitting at the very back of the avenue bus when the big Catholic school by the post office let out for the day. The girls would stream aboard in number, white thighs flashing from beneath their gray green uniform skirts. Invariably, the worst looking of them would plop herself right down next to me and announce in a hard, nasal voice, "I had to go to confession today. With Father Paul. He's *so* dreamy. I told him what Vinnie made me do last night."

Gasps of horror and admiration all around. Little palpitations in those gray green, Irish Catholic hearts. "I mean . . . I *had* to." Hand jobs on the hood of a parked car, Father Paul. I had to. Vinnie *made* me. He's *so* dreamy that if I didn't, he would be taking Carol Ann to the dance on Friday night. And everyone knows what she does. *Everything.* Carol Ann is a *total* pig. So what else could I do?

Somehow, in Cambridge, I have become that girl. My reputation is constantly being dragged through the mud. All I can do is sit at the very back of the bus, complain about it, and go to confession, again and again. *Doos bin ich*, Paulie.

"How come you never told me about Norris?" I demanded.

"Oh, shit," Lesley groans, stamping her foot on the rug so that a fine layer of dust rises a good six inches into the air before falling back down again. "Is that what all this is about? I don't believe it. I do not believe it. It was *years* ago. Actually, at the time, everyone was doing it. I mean, it was like a sorority initiation or something."

"How sick is that?"

"This is better?"

It is a fair question all right. Before I can answer it, Anita leads Rob into the room. She holds four expensive looking wine glasses in her hand. In her apartment we usually drink out of empty shrimp cocktail jars. So tonight must be special. "Little appetite stimulant?" Rob asks smugly. "Already got one rolled."

51

"Goody," Anita says, putting down the glasses. "Whoever wants to smoke right now . . . raise your hand."

Lesley puts her hand right up in the air. She must have some of whatever is going around. Getting high only adds to her confusion, making everything more dramatic and less so, all at the very same time. "All right," Anita says approvingly. Then she looks directly at Rob.

Rob reaches slowly into his jacket as though he is going to draw on me from a shoulder holster. Instead, he produces a tightly rolled, pencil thin joint. Norris would have laughed himself sick over it, saying, "Throw it back till it gets big enough to smoke, brother." Not Rob. "I feel I should warn you," he announces with a completely straight face. "This is *very po*-tent stuff."

In a second, Rob will begin telling us the thrilling story of where the dope was actually grown and how it was smuggled into the country. Even though I do not use the stuff myself, it does not bother me to see other people do so. As long as I am spared the details of its origins and effects.

Lighting up, Rob takes a single cautious, therapeutic toke. Then he passes it on to Lesley. She takes three monstrous hits, holding the smoke down deep in her lungs until her eyes cross. Giggling, she sinks slowly into a rocking chair by the fireplace. As Norris always says, if you are going to get high, you might as well get *high*.

"Not smoking?" Rob inquires, his eyebrows fluttering up towards his forehead.

"Never do," I tell him. "It's a physical thing with me."

"Asthma?" he asks.

"Among other things. How'd you know?"

"The cats," he says. "They are conspicuous in their absence tonight. What else affects you like that?"

"Depends. What else have you got?"

"You know," he offers, "there is a whole school of thought that holds allergies and asthma to be psychophysical. Trauma-related. If you'd like, I could arrange for you to come to the clinic where I work. Actually you'd be doing me a favor. Right now the field is wide open. I'd *love* to approach it from the counseling end. No charge to you, of course. . . ."

"Of course," I say. "You got a card? I always like a card."

"Certainly."

Reaching into the same pocket from which he took the joint,

Rob hands me a small white card that I immediately put away without ever intending to take out again. "Lesley?" I say. "Can I talk to you for a second? In the bedroom?"

"Now?" she asks. Her eyes are totally glazed. There is a smoky plate-glass window between her and the rest of the world.

"*Now*," I say.

Together, we go down the hallway to Anita's bedroom. The walls are painted purple. The bedspread is green. God only knows the last time the sheets beneath it were changed. The only light comes from a lamp by the bed with a red bulb in it. Lesley and I stand inside a large microwave oven, waiting for someone to turn on the heat. Then we will both bubble over and start turning brown around the edges.

"What the *hell* is this, Lesley?" I hiss.

"This reefer?" she asks, really out of it. "I don't know. Mexican, I think . . ."

"This clown. This idiot, Rob. You set this up, right? You and your lunatic best friend, Anita. You talked to this guy about me, right? You told him how fucked up I am. . . ."

Without pausing for breath, I say, "You think I need therapy? You think I'm flipping out? Go check my medical records. When I was eight weeks old, I had eczema so bad they had to take me to the hospital. What was my psychological problem back then? Too small a crib?"

"Paulie," she pleads. "Calm down. You'll get an attack. . . ."

"I get an attack *every* time I come here," I shout. "Maybe if Anita really cleaned this place up instead of sticking her nose into my business, I wouldn't. I don't need any help. Not from someone like that. Understand?"

Having rounded the final curve, I am now headed rapidly for the straightaway that leads directly to my throwing things and beating my hands black and blue against the wall. Words are flying out of my mouth so fast that I cannot possibly keep track of them. I am actually spitting as I talk, which is something both my father and I do whenever we get really angry.

Lesley stands there taking it. Her face is wrinkled with concern. Suddenly, she looks really old to me. She has aged fifty years since we came into this room. I see all this, yet I still cannot do anything to slow myself down. Adrenaline kicks around my bloodstream. I shift into a higher gear. I am out of control.

"Just admit it, for Christ's sake," I yell. "You talked to him about me, right? Told him *all* kinds of shit, right? *Right?*" The

53

last word I scream directly into her face, just to make certain that she will really hear it.

"I only did it for your own good, baby," she sniffs, a single tear forming in the corner of her right eye. "To help."

All my life, people have been doing things for my own good. So far, none of them has helped. "Worry about me the *right* way," I scream. Of course, I myself have no idea what this is. No one knows. But then I am long past making sense. All I want to do now is grab the lamp that stands by Anita's bed and smash it into a thousand pieces. Then I will rub the hot, sharp splinters into my hands until all the burning hot redness comes dripping out of me onto Anita's disgusting sheets.

"Paulie, *please*," Lesley begs. "Let's go back inside. They'll come in here otherwise."

This is what she really fears. Desperately, I try to think of something that I can say to her that will really hurt. I need some feedback to keep the argument going. All on my own, I am running rapidly out of gas. I feel tired and weak, far too exhausted to continue on by myself. Lesley sees this. She jumps in with a suggestion.

"Right after dinner," she says, "we'll go home. I promise. We'll have big fun. We won't even go to The Charity Ward tonight. Only we can't leave now. Anita cooked."

"After dinner?" I repeat, wanting desperately to believe her. "You promise?"

She nods. Just that quickly, it ends. All the sudden, swirling craziness that flooded through my brain disappears. Automatically, I reach for her hand. Amazingly, she lets me take it. This is what Lesley loves best about our relationship, the rollercoaster up and down. The anger and the yelling and then what comes afterwards. The making up. The big fun. It is the only way she can be certain that she is still alive. By stubbornly staying with me. It is at moments like this that I know I am going insane.

Lacing our fingers together, we walk back into the living room like high school sweethearts. The star halfback and the captain of the cheerleaders have patched up their little quarrel. Now, they will walk down life's rosy path, forever holding hands. In the living room, Anita crouches by a low lacquered table, setting out little plates all in a row. Rob sits by her side with his legs crossed in the lotus position. He piles mounds of soft white rice into bowls. Atop the rice go what look to me like tiny sections of old gray inner tube.

"You know," Anita says kindly, "people sometimes go into that bedroom and are *never* heard from again." She giggles. "Mainly it's the red light, I think. Start the fire, Paulie. Then we'll eat."

Grateful to have something to do with my hands, I go over to the fireplace and strike a long wooden starter match against the stone hearth. I touch the match to a ball of wadded up newspaper and step back. A single tongue of bright orange flame begins licking its way upwards. The paper crumples backwards before it, returning to the void from which it came. As the paper disappears, the kindling begins to crackle and burn.

"Anita?" I say, moving away from the fire. "What's the funny looking stuff on top of the rice?"

"Nee-gree," she says.

"Great. What's that?"

"*Nigiri sushi,*" Anita says, clarifying the issue not at all as far as I am concerned.

"A great delicacy," Rob notes. "Renowned for its effect on sexual potency."

"Paulie," Lesley explains, "it's raw fish."

I stand there with my mouth open, trying to think of something to say. Fish is the only thing I absolutely cannot eat in any form whatsoever without breaking out immediately into two distinct and very violent skin rashes. On my arms, strawberry colored blisters as big around as quarters form. On my face, tiny white pustules crop up from under my skin. This is how I react to fish that has been *cooked*. Eaten raw, there is no saying what the stuff will do to me. Peter Bent Brigham, here I come.

Before I can inform Anita about any of this, a large cloud of stinging smoke rolls out of the fireplace right into my face. Without thinking, I breathe in. The smoke goes deep into my lungs. My throat is now paved with broken glass. Actual tears run down my cheeks. I begin coughing and hacking like a man in the final throes. Death by tuberculosis, here I come.

A second cloud of smoke, far larger than the first, comes billowing into the room. Yanking open the window behind me, I stick my head outside. I begin breathing deeply through my mouth, as I was taught to do as a child whenever I woke up in the middle of the night already in the midst of a major attack.

Instantly, Rob Rosen springs into action. Wrapping one of Anita's Japanese cloth napkins around his arm, he vanishes into the smoky haze that now obscures the fireplace. Heroically, Rob reaches right into the very heart of the fire. There is a loud, twisting sound. Somewhere above our heads, a metal plate slides open. Miraculously, the smoke immediately begins retreating back into the fireplace, just as it is meant to do. Once again, man has conquered fire.

Looking as though he has only just rescued a family of six from a burning tenement building while having his picture taken for the front page of the *Daily News* all at the very same time, Rob sinks onto the couch. He is exhausted. His face is blackened with smoke. "Someone . . . closed . . . the flue," he manages to gasp between choking breaths. "*Dumb* fucking thing to do," he notes.

Who else but you know who? *Doos bin ich,* Paulie. The one who closed the flue instead of opening it. The one who cannot eat fish in any form without breaking out into several rashes. The one who can only sit down to dinner if an entire herd of entirely innocent kitty cats have been unfairly imprisoned in the bathroom. Cruelty to animals is added to the long list of charges against me. I am guilty on every last count. A jonah of the first degree, I must be thrown overboard at sea during any storm so that all the others will be spared. There is no use in denying it any longer. I simply do not belong out in public anymore. My condition is far too serious.

Moving faster than I have since I made my brilliant touchdown run in the empty stadium, I head for the door. I am nearly there when the steel-reinforced tip of my hiking boot catches the very edge of the low table by the couch. In extreme slow motion, the table tips over just far enough to dump every last tiny plate onto the floor. Mounds of soft white rice and little slabs of raw gray fish combine with the furry fuzzballs of cat hair on the rug to form a sorry looking sooty mixture that no one will ever eat.

The evening is now complete. I want to apologize but I do not know where to start. Instead, I yank open the door. I keep going until I am out in the hall. Taking the steps two at a time, I bound and rebound from one landing to another, going down. The wooden banister scorches my palm as I hang on desperately for balance.

Finally, I hit the street. My chest feels as though I have just run a sub four minute mile. My nose and throat are on fire. Panting, I try to catch my breath. At any moment, I know that a window high above my head will fly open and someone will call out in darkness for me to come back up. I will be forgiven completely for what I have done.

Only no window opens. No head peers forth in darkness to call my name. Instead, I stand by myself in the street watching the fish-eyed headlights of cars moving slowly towards the Square. I am drenched with perspiration, yet cold all over. My hands tremble. My joints ache. I am tired, yet I cannot go home. I have no home to go to.

Haltingly, I begin to run down the street. My legs are stiff. My arms flap wildly. I need a drink and the sound of music blasting in my ears. Misery such as mine must have company.

CHAPTER SEVEN

TONIGHT THE CHARITY WARD is rocking. Going round and round. Reeling and a-rocking. What a crazy sound. And it will never stop rocking. Till the pain goes down. At the bar, guys sit elbow to elbow, banging their beer glasses in time to the music. Before them, little pools of what they have already spilled but will never miss shimmer brightly in the light. The tables are jammed with damp, sweaty couples already in the grip of overheated passion. Fellow patients all, I salute them.

On the little stage by the door, Peter Wolf, the chief resident, leaps into the air. He vaults into the house for a beer. Draining it in a single gulp, he fights his way back to the band. It is safer up there. He grabs Magic Dick by the neck to say hello. Into the mike, Wolf howls, "Time to get *cray*-zee, bay-bee!" Behind him, J. Geils himself stumbles in place, guitar in hand, lanky hair falling into his eyes. Geils nods to the drummer. They kick into "Rockin' Robin." Everyone sweats.

Peter Wolf sings a verse. Then he turns it loose, letting Magic Dick burn down the building with his harp. The solo nearly chokes him. After he empties his harmonica of every last note, he flings it contemptuously into the house. J. Ceils and the bass player stalk one another across the stage, fighting a musical battle to the death. The building rises miraculously from its ashes as the drummer goes sixteen bars all on his own.

Everyone lights up fresh cigarettes. Peter Wolf coughs, desperately trying to clear his throat just as I have been doing all day long. Then he clams right on stage. People cheer. I fight my way to the bar for a drink. Someone grabs me by the shirt. "Give him one of these, one of these, one of these, and one of these," Norris shouts to the bartender, pointing to the glasses lined up before him.

The bartender nods obediently and moves away. Norris Rice has spoken. Here, as everywhere else in Cambridge, his word is law. "What you doin' here all on your own, son?" Norris demands. "You get parole?" I nod without speaking. What can I say? "Then how come you look like you dyin' slow and feelin' poorly about it, boy?"

"Ah, Norris," I say, feeling it well up inside of me so that suddenly all I want to do is cry. "I'm fucking up. All over the place."

"You due," he says. "Hell, you *overdue*. Relax and meet my friend here. What'd you say your name was, honey?" he asks the girl beside him.

She brushes a strand of white blond hair out of her eyes. "Honey," she says.

"Right," Norris laughs. "Right the first time. Paulie, whyn't you and Honey here go dance some? Shake a leg and loosen yourself up?"

"No thanks, Norris."

Honey makes a face. "Pardon me for living," she says in a nasal, working class accent. Here is a girl who has started more than one serious bar fight in her time.

"It's just not what I'm good at," I tell her. Not that she even listens. As soon as the bartender sets down a rock glass filled with brown whiskey meant for me, she sweeps it away. Squeezing it in her hand like an old friend she has not seen in far too long, she puts the drink away in a single swallow. Honey is definitely feeling no pain. It is a condition to which I aspire with all my heart.

"Let me get you another, son," Norris says, motioning to the bartender for a refill. "Now, since the music is right and the feeling is tight, guess ah might. Ready?" He looks at Honey. She nods without having heard the question. What does it really matter? Norris slides off his stool. He takes Honey's hand and begins leading her towards the tiny dance floor in front of the stage.

Over his shoulder, he calls back to me, "Y'all hold the fort for us now, Paulie. Guard them seats with your life. Either that or give me half of what you sell 'em for. . . ." Cackling loudly, he disappears into the crowd.

I nod. Holding the fort is what I am good at. Dropped behind enemy lines on a secret mission, I will steadfastly withstand every form of torture known to man without ever disclosing any information that might help my captors. Death before dishonor, every time.

I boost myself up onto the stool that Honey has only just vacated. It is still warm with the imprint of her tight, blue-jeaned ass, now swinging in dangerous circles on the dance floor. The bartender sets a brand new drink in front of me. Just as Honey did, I drain it in a single gulp. The fire spreads down into my stomach. Then it moves up towards my head. The relief I crave is on the way. "Again," I order. Miraculously, the bartender obeys. A second shot follows the first down my throat. I only cough a little. Then I demand another.

"This seat taken?" someone asks from in back of me.

"That's right," I say, without even bothering to turn around. "By a large and militant Negro person who very possibly may be armed."

"I'll take my chances."

E.C. stands behind me. He is the one person I absolutely have no desire to see tonight, so naturally he is here. Where else would he be, as Peter Wolf dances like a rag puppet at the very edge of the stage. E.C. boosts himself up onto the stool next to me. Fondly, he drapes his arm over my shoulder. Right away, I know that he is drunk. In E.C., friendliness of any kind is distinctly unnatural behavior. "Listen, E.C.," I say. "I don't want to hear word one about what went on today. . . ."

"Forget it," he says. "I have."

Magically, two more glasses appear on the bar. E.C. picks one up and screws it into my palm like an electrician putting a brand new bulb into an old socket. "For a smart guy, Paulie," he says, leaning in close so that I can smell the whiskey on his breath, "you can be a real asshole sometimes, you know?"

"Thanks, E.C. I'll drink to that."

We clink glasses and drink. The effect of too much alcohol on the human personality can never be underestimated. Tonight,

E.C. seems almost human. "It's Norris, you know," he says. "Always has been. Right from the start."

"What is?"

"It's Norris who's stealing books out of the storeroom. Then he sends in those kids to sell them back to us. I been on to him for weeks," E.C. notes, with more than a trace of pride in his voice. He belches softly for emphasis. "Damned if I know what to do about it, though. . . ."

"E.C.," I say, looking him right in the face, "you are so full of shit that it's coming out of your earholes."

"I'll drink to that," he says. Again we clink glasses. We drink. "You ask him," he says. "See if he denies it."

I am about to pursue the matter further with E.C. when the band suddenly crashes into silence behind me. The song they are playing falls over, dead. There is much applause, some screaming, and a few loud grunts of approval. E.C. himself lets fly with a wild rebel yell that comes straight from the heart of Dixie by way of Litchfield, Connecticut.

On stage, Peter Wolf sashays coolly to the microphone. *"Hey!"* he shouts. "Applause is nice but it won't buy rice. We need *money!"* The drummer hits a rim shot to punctuate this demand. "Nickels, dimes, quarters, E Bonds, whatever. Now, we gonna take our break! Be back in a shake! But don't stop sippin', it gets the honey drippin'. And, bay-bee, I do want to be your King Bee." Bang, bang, bang. Three more rim shots. Show business, I love it. "Remember what Confusion say—the drunker *you* get, the better *we* sound. Later!"

Peter Wolf knows no fear. Hopping off the stage as though he is in his very own living room, he begins making his way through the crowd. Naturally, he heads straight towards E.C. People at the bar begin looking at the two of us with newfound respect in their eyes. Who knows? Maybe I *am* somebody.

"Hey!" Peter Wolf shouts to the bartender. "Attila the Hun! Three double ryes. The cheapest you got. No, make it Seven and Sevens. Four of 'em. . . ."

If only Lesley could see me now. I am actually cheek to jowl with the great Peter Wolf himself. Her idol. "E.C.," Peter Wolf says, ignoring me completely. "You seen Cole?"

"Try the john," E.C. says. "He could be giving back everything he drank up on your tab."

"Cole T. Walker is *here?"* I say in amazement. *My* idol.

"None other, brother," Peter Wolf notes. "Cole T. Walker.

The Pear-shaped Talker. Only don't beat your meat in the street about it. Just jump back, Jack. . . ."

"Peter Wolf," E.C. says, making introductions even as he neatly slides a drink off the Wolf's tray into his hand. "Paulie Bindel . . ."

"Pleased and diseased," Peter Wolf says, looking bored.

"Mr. Wolf," I say. "I wonder . . . can I ask you a question?"

"Shoot. Time and answers is all I got, youngblood."

"What becomes of the broken hearted?"

"Come again? If you can . . ."

"You know, who had love that's now departed? I know I've got to find. Some kind of peace of mind . . ."

"I'll be searchin' everywhere," Peter Wolf says, picking up on it. "Just to find someone to care . . ."

"I'll be looking every day," I say as E.C. stares at us both in wonder. "I know I'm gonna find a way. Now, name it and claim it."

Peter Wolf grins. " 'What Becomes of the Broken Hearted?' " he says, naming the song whose lyrics we have been reciting together.

"By?"

"Jimmy Ruffin, brother of the great David, lead singer of the temptin' Temptations."

"Label?" I demand.

"Motown. No, hold on. *Soul*. Followed by?"

" 'Gonna Give Her All The Love I Got.' "

"Right the first time. Go again."

"I will build you a castle with the tower so high," I say, "it reaches the moon . . ."

"I'll capture melodies from birdies that sing and compose you a tune," he counters.

"Chorus coming now," I note. "Every day, we will play. On the Milky Way. And if that don't do . . ."

"Then I'll try something new," Peter Wolf says, singing the lyric the way it should be sung. "Smokey gold. Give me a pound on it."

Wolf lays his hand out, palm up. I slap five with him. E.C. cannot believe what he is seeing. I am getting over with Cambridge's number one star. "Mr. Wolf," I say, taking a drink off his tray for myself, "for a white boy, you *do* have soul."

Peter Wolf nods. He understands. And why not? He is half crazy himself. The only difference between us is that he is making money from it. "Anytime at all you wanna come back-stage and rap," he says, "feel free. Just ask for the Wolf. I'll pull you through." Then he looks down at his tray. "Shit," he mutters. "Them drinks just ee-vap-o-rated on me. Got to find Cole before he passes out. He's holdin' our piece of what they took in at the door. Later, gator, gotta go."

I down the shot. What a moment. It is just too bad that Lesley was not here to see it happen. But it did occur. The night itself is young. There is no telling what may transpire before it ends. "E.C.," I say grandly, "I am going to the john. Why don't you hold the fort for me here while I'm gone. Anyone wants to buy these seats, make sure you get top dollar and I'll take half. . . ."

E.C. has never been treated like this. He wants to shut me up with a smart remark but the words will not come. "Oh, and E.C.," I tell him, "do me one more favor, huh? Pay Lesley that two hundred and twenty-eight dollars you owe her."

Before E.C. can throw his drink in my face, I walk away. Score one for the good guys. I am definitely on a hot streak. Not even the deadly stink in the john bothers me tonight. I am out on my own and feeling fine. By-passing the line by the urinals, I go into a stall. I can hear the guy next to me giving up both his lunch and supper, loudly. Then the toilet flushes and the stall door slams.

From outside, I hear someone say, "Cole? You all right, man?"

"Five pounds thinner without my dinner," he says, that unmistakable radio voice smoother than a silk glove even in here. "But always ready for another round. Who's buyin'?"

I shake myself off as quickly as I can. Carefully, I do up my zipper. I cannot bother to flush. I *have* to see what Cole looks like. Only by the time I get outside, he is already gone. The two of us just are not meant to meet face to face. Still, I did get to stand beside him for a while. I cannot wait to tell Lesley all about it.

When I get back to the bar, everyone I know is gone. Either they are outside getting high or the best set of the night is already over. Coming in through the front door, however, bigger than life and twice as ugly, is none other than Rob Rosen. Lesley stands next to him on tiptoe, scanning the room for a familiar face. Her skin is pale. Her eyes gleam brightly. To me, she has never looked more beautiful. Anita trails behind, obviously confused.

I have to get out of here before they find me. But there is just one door, and, at the moment, Rob Rosen happens to be standing in it. As they begin heading my way, I slide off the stool and head for the exit through which Peter Wolf disappeared backstage. My path is blocked by a black man not quite as tall as Norris but much bigger around. A tiny gold star gleams threateningly from his right ear. He does not look friendly. "I've got to see the Wolf," I tell him.

"You an' the rest of the world," he notes. "China, too."

"He *knows* me."

"Come back tomorrow mornin'. Seven A.M. We ain' here, start without us. . . ."

Rapidly, I gauge my chances of slipping around him and then screaming for Wolf at the very top of my lungs as this guy begins slamming me repeatedly against a solid brick wall. Then Peter Wolf comes strolling by. He has one arm looped casually over the shoulder of a girl who looks like Honey's twin sister.

"Wolf!" I cry out. "It's me, man. Tell this guy I'm cool . . ."

Peter Wolf nods. The behemoth by the door steps back, granting me access to the inner sanctum. For this one small act of grace, I will be eternally grateful. What I will now say to Wolf himself, I have no idea.

"Didn't exactly expect to see you again *this* soon," Peter Wolf says. "What's the haps?"

"It's just . . . uh . . ." I am running away from my life and need a place to hide. Surely, I can tell him this. Wolf has already seen and heard it all. Once I do, though, I will lose all the precious points I have only just scored with him. Still, I *have* to tell him something.

"Hey, man," Wolf says. "You can talk to me. I'm just the same back here as I was out there. Humble."

Blurting out the very first thing that comes into my head, I say, "I have to ask you . . . I mean, I figure that you, of all people, would know. Wolf . . . what does 'el seven' mean?"

Peter Wolf's little face lights up with joy. For years he has been waiting for someone to ask him this very question. I could not have come to a better source. My reputation with him will remain intact. "Plain as the nose on your face," he grins. "Take an *L*, put it up to a 7, and what you got?"

"I don't know, Wolf. Tell me. . . ."

As befits a star of his magnitude, Peter Wolf's patience in such

63

matters is infinite. "Look," he says, forming an *L* with the thumb and first finger of his right hand. Holding the *L* up for me to see, he fits it neatly to the rough, upside down 7 he makes with the thumb and first finger of his left hand. All the while, Honey's twin sister looks on in stupefaction. "Now," he says, "name it and claim it."

"A box?" I say tentatively.

"A *square!*" he shouts triumphantly. "Dig? *Don't be el seven.* Don't you be no square. Come and learn this dance." Turning in a circle where he stands, he executes three intricate little dance steps. Then he comes up singing, "Woo-lee bul-lee." "Woo-lee bul-lee," he chants happily, leading his white blonde friend down the hall. "Woo-lee bul-lee."

With Wolf out of the way, I head immediately for the fire exit in front of me. Pushing open the door, I find myself outside the building in a narrow brick alley that leads directly to the street. I start breathing regularly once again. I will be no square. This I swear is true. In fact, just as soon as I am safely back within the familiar confines of Lesley's little bedroom, I will do everything in my power to actually learn this dance. Woo-lee bul-lee.

CHAPTER EIGHT

IN THE LITTLE bedroom where my day began, I lie sideways in the fetal position with my knees drawn up to my chest. A single cranberry scented candle burns down in a ceramic holder by the radio. Above my head, spidery, webbed shadows creep slowly across the ceiling. My throat is red and raw. Someone has spray painted my lungs with wet cement. No matter how hard I try, I cannot block out the memory of how Rob and Lesley looked standing together in the doorway of The Charity Ward. Already, they are a couple. I can see them clinging damply to one another even now, clothed only in a fine film of perspiration. I am driving myself crazy.

Forcing myself out of bed, I go down the hall to the phone. I will call The Charity Ward. Asking for Lesley by name, I will demand to speak to her. If they have already left, I will obtain Rob Rosen's home number from information. I will keep on dialing until someone answers. The sound of the ringing phone will destroy his rhythm. I will render him impotent from afar.

As I stand there with the receiver in my hand, I glance over at the chipped blue wall before me. On it, in pencil, Lesley has scrawled all the numbers that she calls regularly. The numbers are small and cramped. They slant backwards, like flowers drooping after a heavy rain. It is the handwriting of a girl who is still in junior high school, worrying only about what she will be doing on Friday night. I put the receiver down again. It is all I can do to keep from bursting out into tears.

Returning to the bedroom, I throw myself across the bed. I reach for my little white plastic inhaler. I pump a massive dose of spray onto the back of my throat. My heart tightens like a boxer's fist. Behind my forehead, a beautiful red white and blue striped balloon starts to rise slowly towards the stars. I go right with it, letting the spray take me higher.

The balloon disappears. Now, I am sailing on a black freighter through tropical waters to some quiet island. There, on a cream-colored beach, I will sit beneath a palm tree watching the scalloped waves roll in from the horizon. I will sit there forever more. Not exactly dead but at peace. On a permanent vacation from life and all its various problems. No clock radios will suddenly click on to announce the coming of a brand new day. No one will make any demands on me that I cannot satisfy.

Then I hear someone unlock the downstairs door. Lesley has come home. She has chosen me over Rob, at least for the time being. Tiny footsteps come trailing through the kitchen and then down the hall. The bedroom door swings open. Lesley stands there looking at me with pity in her eyes. "Boy," she says, shaking her head in wonder, "are you crazy."

I nod. There is no sense in arguing the point. We both know that it is true. "What did you do after I left?" I ask slyly, testing her to see if she will tell me the truth.

"Nothing much. Rob insisted that we go to The Charity Ward but we didn't know a soul. . . ."

"He brought you home?"

"No, I walked. Of course he brought me home. But it just wasn't the same without you, Paulie. No exploding smoke bombs, no riots. Nothing."

Lesley takes off her jacket. She drapes it over a chair. Then she starts unbuttoning her blouse. She walks around the bed with it half open. Then she pulls it over her head and throws it on the floor. Having worn it once, the blouse is already dirty laundry as far as Lesley is concerned, to be treated accordingly. It is the way she was raised by Gloria and Dr. Alfred.

"Rob must think I'm insane," I say, still probing for details.

"He *was* impressed, I will say that. He'd probably pay you to come see him now."

Turning sideways, she reaches behind herself to unsnap her skirt. Her breasts come up and out, stretching the sheer, pebbled fabric of her bra to the limit. For a thin girl, Lesley has tremendous breasts. The bra quickly follows her blouse to the floor. She stands before me, completely naked.

Her body is made of pure white marble seamed with tiny blue veins that pulse right beneath the skin. This is all that we have left now. It is the single thing that keeps us together. In the flickering light of a single cranberry scented candle, Lesley addresses the room at large, as though I am no longer even in it. "All in all," she says, "just another pleasant little Friday night at Anita's. It may be *months* before we're asked back."

Then she climbs up on to the foot of the bed. She poses there for a moment. Then she giggles and tumbles forward, pinning me to the mattress. Lesley's calves are thick with muscle. Her thighs are corded and powerful. Her hands are everywhere at once. She grins in my face, daring me to respond. I slide out from underneath and push her on her back. She lies there without speaking, perfectly willing to wait now that she knows it is going to happen for certain. Big Fun.

I start to get undressed. With the tip of a finger, Lesley traces lazy circles across her breasts, amusing herself until I am ready. One minute I am struggling with my belt. The next I am inside her. The scalding wetness shocks me but only for a moment. Lesley's hips urge me on. Her rhythm is insistent, demanding. The urgent slap of flesh on flesh is the only sound until she begins humming softly to herself. I recognize the melody immediately. Sam the Sham and all his Pharaohs doing "Wooly Bully."

In my mind, I am working on a wall. I am placing new stones on top of the old ones. Getting them to fit perfectly without using any mortar demands all of my concentration. A stone at a time, the wall begins to rise above our heads, enclosing both of us in a rocky little fortress. Then I realize that Lesley is trying to tell me something. I strain to listen. "I . . . forgot . . . my . . . diaphragm," she moans.

While this bit of news is certainly interesting, there is not all that much I can do with the information at the moment. Keeping the rhythm going seems far more important. We are both plugged into a transformer that is discharging powerful jolts of high voltage current. Motion is all that counts, going round and round until our bodies fuse and there is nothing left of either of us but twisted, smoking metal.

The wall I am working on develops severe structural problems. The rocks themselves begin to burst, exploding like Molotov cocktails. A large crack appears above my head and begins to widen. Then the entire wall starts to give way. It folds over on top of itself as wc plunge towards the ground and certain death. I signal to Lesley with my hands.

All of Lesley's years of strenuous training in jazz, tap, and classical ballet do not desert her. Somehow, she manages to fling herself backwards without falling off the bed. She turns a near impossible half-gainer. She resurrects an older and simpler form of contraception. Moving in tandem, we keep on going.

The transformer powering us both kicks over into the red zone. A circuit-breaking rush of current flows up my spine into my brain. My head flies back. My mouth comes open. I lose all feeling in my hands. My toes curl over. I brace myself for what comes next.

One moment I am in bed with Lesley in Cambridge and the next I am soaring through a pure blue sky in brilliant sunshine, headed for the open ocean and that quiet island. Birds cry to one another beside my head. Then the sky itself shatters. Tiny bits of blue firmament reflect the brilliant sunshine back into my eyes. I am blinded by the glare. I go deaf and dumb. I scream and shout and pray. Then I laugh uncontrollably. It is over. I open my eyes, eager to see where my journey has brought me.

Lesley sits against the bed's old brass frame. She wipes her mouth with a tissue. Then she rapidly discards the tissue into a wastebasket by the door. My contribution to the evening can now be hauled off to the local dump for burning. Soon, there will be nothing left of me but crumpled Kleenex three-plys.

"God," I say, letting out my breath. My voice sounds shaky even to me. "What *was* that?"

67

"Just a thing I do," she says casually. "Admit it. You *do* feel better, right?"

I feel fine. In fact, I am nearly unconscious. Instead of speaking, I reach for a pillow. I come up with my crumpled shirt in my hand. Rearing back, I toss it towards the closet. In the cranberry scented candlelight, the shirt turns a perfect circle in the air. The two little red pills fall from the front pocket to the floor. I look down. Then I pick them up in my hand.

They are cool and smooth to the touch, two bits of ancient, polished stone. The pure blue sky reassembles above my head. Then it vanishes. Angry black storm clouds now dot the horizon. The birds who flew beside me come back to roost by a garbage can in the gutter. Shitting and cawing, they will cluck out their miserable little lives in the filthy street. Nothing has changed. I am still trapped. Everything is just as it was before. What seemed so simple is complicated once again. I can either let the whole thing pass or begin the inquisition. And there is no way I can let it pass.

"Lesley," I say, "can you look at these?"

I roll over onto my side. Not that it will make much of a difference. If she is going to lie to me, she can do it just as well right to my face. Opening my hand, I show her the pills. "Oh, *those*," she says brightly. "I wondered where they were. . . ."

"They're yours?"

"Sure."

"Where did you get them?"

"Paulie," she says, lightly flicking at my arm with the tip of a finger, "are you playing District Attorney with me?"

"It's a simple question, Lesley. Where did you get them?"

She leans out of bed, taking down the robe that hangs from the door of her closet. Right away, I know that this is going to be even worse than I thought. Lesley is getting dressed for it. A formal argument.

"A friend gave them to me," she says, slipping one arm into the robe.

"Anyone I know?"

"Not really, no." I can see that she is annoyed. "Is this twenty questions?" she asks. "Will it be my turn soon?"

"*Who*, Lesley? Just tell me who . . ."

"Someone I haven't seen in a very long time that I ran into unexpectedly."

"Try a name."

68

Lesley shoots me a look of pure, unadulterated fury. Then she laughs. "Cole," she says. "Cole T. Walker. Boy, has he gotten fat. Success has gone right to his stomach. I told him that, too."

"Where did you see him?"

"In the Square."

"You saw him in the Square, told him how fat he had gotten, and he gave you the last two of these little red pills in existence?"

"Who says they're the last two?"

"Norris."

"*God,* Paulie. Did you give this story to the *Crimson,* too? Maybe the wire services will pick up on it. They'll send a TV crew. Then I can watch myself on the evening news. . . ."

Just like Dr. Alfred Gold on a Saturday afternoon, I stand poised with the high-speed drill in my hand. My radio is tuned to WQXR. The sounds of opera seep into the room. I lean in close. The diamond tip begins whirring in buzzing circles. Any minute now, I will break through hard enamel to the soft green decay hidden inside.

"Did you have lunch with him?" I ask.

"You bet," she says. "With what he's making now, he can afford to buy an old friend a meal."

"Lunch and what else?"

"What do you mean 'What else?' "

The small white gold flame that has been burning along the braided fuse of our conversation finally reaches the cache of dynamite hidden in my brain. The dynamite explodes. Large boulders, some big around as Cole T. Walker himself, fly straight up into the air. Mighty oaks go sprawling. Entire sections of the landscape are disrupted. I throw back the covers and get out of bed. The least I can do is hear this standing up.

I slide open the door of the closet, looking for my robe. All I see are Lesley's clothes. Little pleated skirts, corduroy jumpers, and pastel blouses with Peter Pan collars that Gloria purchased on sale in Bloomingdale's on Saturday afternoon. On the stage of the Metropolitan Opera House, Joan Sutherland hits an unusually piercing note. It travels by radio wave to Dr. Alfred's ground-floor office. Dr. Alfred's hand slips. The drill goes right through a nerve, coming to rest in solid bone. His career ends with a scream, not a whimper.

Madly, I begin tearing blouses off their hangers. I fling them to the floor, one after the other. "What *else?*" I shout.

69

"Paulie, *stop!* Go crazy in the other closet, where I keep my jeans. Those are my good clothes."

"You aren't going to need any good clothes, Lesley," I scream, as the blood rushes in my head. "You're never leaving this room again. Not until you tell me . . . *what else?*"

In a calm and quiet voice, as though she is describing something someone else did, she says, "We went back to look at this house he's living in near the Common. He's going to buy it, I think."

"*And?*"

"I did him."

There it is at last. The simple statement I have been working so very hard to extract from her mouth, bloody roots and all. A complete confession, admissible in any court of the land. The prosecution now rests, Your Honor.

A sudden gush of sour tasting vomit gets as far as the back of my throat before I manage to choke it down again. I am crazy all right. I have to be, trying to live with someone who cannot be trusted to walk through the Square in the middle of the day without winding up in someone else's bed.

I feel dizzy. I am sick all over and nauseous, yet strangely calm. I still need more information. "You *slept* with him?" I ask.

"Don't be ridiculous."

"You didn't?"

A small glimmer of hope flickers before me. It is no bigger than the reflection of the candle flame in the bedroom window, yet it is still there. "It was in the afternoon," she says, instantly snuffing out the flame. "Who had time to sleep?"

"Then . . . what happened?" I stutter, not knowing exactly how to pose the question.

"I just *did* him, silly. Like at the end with you. Only he was standing up." She giggles. Obviously, the memory amuses her. "He couldn't believe it either," she says, taking note of the look on my face.

"*Why?*" I ask, searching for a reason, an excuse, anything.

Lesley stares at me as though I have finally asked the single dumbest question of all time. Then she shrugs, "I don't know, baby," she says. "There didn't seem to be any reason not to."

I wonder if Dr. Alfred and Gloria are still up. I want to call and congratulate them on the way they raised their only daughter. Guilt is an emotion Lesley has never experienced. She is freer

70

than I will ever be. "Besides," she says, "it's not as though I went out looking for someone new or anything. I knew Cole long before I ever met you. . . ."

There it is, all right. Cole T. Walker just got in line before me. The little bakery ticket with his number on it was still good so Lesley stamped it for him one more time, out of friendship. I am not even angry now. I am not hurt and I am not upset. I am finally, perfectly dead. A chilling paralysis has taken control of my entire body, numbing me from head to toe. It is not personal with Lesley. It never has been. We are just from two entirely different neighborhoods. No bus line runs between them, either. I bend down and reach under the bed for my old blue suitcase without a handle.

"Don't do that, Paulie," Lesley says nervously. "Not even as a joke. You know how much I hate it when you do that."

Methodically, if there is a method in total madness, I begin pulling my shirts from the closet and throwing them into the suitcase on the bed. A mound of wrinkled clothing rises before me. I do not belong here. I never have. I do not even speak the same language as these people. No matter how hard I try, I will never be able to learn it. I am el seven, born and raised. Back home, the old man has a battered couch that opens up into a bed in the living room of his apartment. He and my mother can fight for the privilege of having me as a house guest.

"You'll never get it any better anywhere else," Lesley says, trying to make it all into a joke. I am not laughing. Turning away from her, I go out into the hallway to the chest of drawers where I keep my socks. When I come back in, she is getting out of bed. "Where are you going, Paulie?" she demands.

"Home," I say bitterly. "But don't bother getting up for me. Rob Rosen might want to drop by after I'm gone."

"Cute," she says. "Really cute."

I grab for my suitcase. It trembles at the very edge of the mattress like a drunk in the Combat Zone about to go head first off a curb. Then it tumbles from the bed to the floor. Clothes spill out everywhere. Lesley giggles in spite of herself. It is funny all right. Even I can see that.

Picking the suitcase up by its hinges, I throw it as hard as I can into the far corner of the room. It crashes into a chair, turns over, then slides onto the little table where Lesley keeps all her little glass animals and expensive bottles of French perfume. For some reason, the sound of breaking glass sets me off again.

"Fuck all this," I shout. "Fuck you and Cambridge and the bookstore and all your friends. I'll *send* for my stuff."

Grabbing my little white plastic inhaler off the table by the bed, I shove it into the front pocket of my red-and-black checked lumber jacket. I head for the door. The two little red pills lie before me on the rumpled sheet, twin spots of blood straight from the heart, hers and mine. Picking them up, I throw them at Lesley. Anything to hurt her the way she has hurt me.

"These are yours," I scream. "You keep them. For when you and Cole walk by the river on Sundays."

I storm out through the hallway into the kitchen. I take the front steps two at a time, stumbling over my own feet so that I have to reach out for the wall to keep from falling down. Running is the only move I have. No one has ever been half as good at it as I am, either. The minute I come into any building, the very first thing I do is memorize all the escape routes, taking careful note of all available emergency exits, just in case I have to leave at a moment's notice.

I am at the very bottom of the stairs and about to go out into the street when I realize that I still have the key to the apartment in my pocket. I take it off my key ring and place it carefully on the bottom step. Lesley will find it there on her way out to work tomorrow morning. I know that I will not be needing it any more.

No matter what time of night I get to his apartment, my father will be more than glad to let me in. It is a service he is only too happy to provide. Although neither he nor my mother expects me, they will not be all that surprised to see me back again either. They have both been waiting for my return since the day I left.

Having only so recently put it all behind me for good, I am heading right back into it again. I am going to join my people. The dead, the aged, the sick, the dying, and yours truly, Paulie Bindel. Back together again, for the very first time.

SHABBAT SHUVAH

CHAPTER NINE

EVEN FROM WHERE Esther was standing, one hand resting comfortably on the knob of the door that was still open in back of her, the smell of raw ammonia in the beauty parlor was so strong that it nearly took her breath away. At the far end of the shop, behind flocked red-and-gold drawstring curtains, Marlene, the new girl, was carefully pouring industrial strength hair dye from a large gray plastic gallon jug into a row of small white bottles bearing the "Contessa" label. A facsimile of Toni Assante's handwritten signature adorned the label of each and every bottle, boldly proclaiming the lie that Toni herself had personally formulated the product within to her own exacting standards.

How Marlene could actually work right on top of that stuff without a mask, her thick black shag cut Italian hair falling into her eyes while an unlit cigarette dangled casually from her lips no less, Esther simply could not imagine. Maybe they taught them secret breathing techniques in beauty college these days. That, and how to wear their blue jeans tighter than a second skin. Every time Marlene leaned forward, the crack of her ass opened up like the earth giving way after a heavy rain.

Uf mir gezugt, Esther thought. I should only be so lucky. With a figure like Marlene's, it didn't matter *what* your hair looked like. You could be bald and still never spend a Saturday night at home alone. Shutting the door softly behind her, Esther moved slowly into the shop. Almost always, she felt at home here, as though all the Saturday mornings she had spent in the shop had somehow made it her own.

Hanging up her coat on the same tarnished brass hook she always used, Esther reached for one of the cups that stood upside down on the little table by the appointment desk. The cups were reserved solely for Toni's regulars, the women who had kept her in business for years in this same location on the avenue.

Esther filled her cup halfway to the top with coffee from the

75

oversized aluminum percolator on which the little red light was never allowed to go out. Using a wooden stirrer for a spoon, she added non-dairy creamer and saccharin. Before she even lifted the cup to her mouth, Esther knew already just how it was going to taste. Thin and bitter, like bile. Despite what they said on television, there simply was no substitute for real cream and sugar. Not if you could afford the calories.

Although it was not yet nine o'clock, Esther was already having a terrible morning. On the one and only day of the week she ever got to sleep late, Morty had called at the ungodly hour of seven-thirty to let her know that Paulie was in, and staying with him. Esther knew just how much pleasure it gave Morty to be able to deliver such messages. In her most refined tone of voice, she had asked politely to be allowed to speak to her son.

"You wanna talk to him?" Morty had whined in that annoying tone she had come to hate so much over the years. "How can you talk to someone, Esther, when they're still asleep?"

Fighting the urge to scream, she had quietly asked Morty to have Paulie call her when he got up or just come by the house any time after eleven. Until then, as Morty well knew, she would be busy. Unable to get back to sleep, Esther had begun her day lying in bed, tormented by questions to which she had no answers.

After making herself crazy for a solid hour, she had gotten dressed and walked down the avenue to Toni's shop, knowing that although she would be early for her appointment, she could at least find someone to talk to there. That something had gone seriously wrong in Boston, she was certain. Why else would her son come home in the middle of the night without giving anyone advance notice?

Of course, she had been dead set against his moving up there in the first place. Not that it had done any good. Once Paulie made a decision, you could talk until you were blue in the face and he would not change his mind. Her greatest fear had been that if she said too much against this girl that he had found, this dentist's daughter from Staten Island whom she herself had never met, he might just marry her out of spite. Her son could be just like that sometimes. With every passing year, Paulie was becoming more and more like his father.

Still, whatever made him happy would make her happy. Esther had told her son this little lie for so many years that she now wholeheartedly believed it herself. All she asked from him was a little consideration. A little consideration and some of the respect

76

that was due her. Coming home without telling her was bad enough. Staying with Morty in his awful three room apartment on the avenue made it only that much worse, adding insult to injury.

At the back of the shop, Marlene straightened up and stripped off the thin rubber gloves she had been wearing to work with the dye. Quickly, she rinsed her hands under the tap. Then she wiped them dry on a towel. Running her still damp fingers through the chopped ends of her ruffled hair to give it yet more body, Marlene pushed through the flocked drawstring curtains into the beauty parlor itself.

Esther could not help but stare at the girl's fingernails. Every last one of them had to be at least two inches long, painted a garish shade of red that she herself would have called "Chinese orange." How Marlene kept her nails so perfectly, Esther had no idea. Her own were almost always chipped or split. Week after week, Toni begged her to have them done here professionally once and for all, free of charge of course.

Esther always refused. She was a working woman. For years now, she had supported herself all on her own. Her nails testified eloquently to this fact. It gave Esther far more pleasure to just cut them short with a cuticle scissors herself and forget about them than to walk around like some female vampire on the prowl.

Realizing that she was no longer alone in the shop, Marlene stared at Esther with an expression of dumb surprise on her face. Without actually speaking, she formed the word "Hi" in very small letters on her lips. Then she went directly to the appointment desk and opened up the book. With her other hand, she switched on the radio. Esther smiled in spite of herself. Another one who could not live without noise always going in the background. Her son was the exact same way. The television generation, never happy unless something electrical was plugged in and humming loudly.

"You got an appointment?" Marlene asked nasally, tracing the outline of her bee-stung lips with the tip of a Chinese orange finger.

Esther stared at her in amazement. The girl had seen her in here at least a dozen times. More than once, Toni had introduced Esther to Marlene as ". . . my very best customer, and my oldest friend. You always make sure and take *very* good care of Esther, Marlene. She's *special*." Yet now Marlene was asking if she had an appointment. It was unbelievable.

"If not, it's okay," Marlene said quickly. "I can do you now. *Before*."

"Only Toni does me, dear," Esther noted icily.

"She's away this weekend. . . ."

"I know," Esther sniffed. "Paradise Island."

"You want Enid, she just ran out for danish."

"I can wait."

"You want something to go with your coffee?" Marlene asked, trying to be nice. "I could always run out and grab her. She only went down the block. To Shucker's."

"Very sweet of you to offer, dear. But no, thanks. I *never* eat danish."

"I know what you mean," Marlene said conversationally, as though the two of them had been friends for years. "Nothing worse for you than white sugar. 'A moment on the lips, forever on the hips,' I always say. Myself, I had to cut out sweets. Entirely."

Esther stared at the girl in amazement. Marlene wasn't rude. She was just a little stupid, and very young. Suddenly, Esther felt very protective toward her, as though she were her very own daughter. "Even this gum," Marlene said, popping a freshly unwrapped stick into her mouth. "Sugarless."

"With your figure, dear," Esther noted. "You could afford to chew the regular kind. Me . . ." She laughed, letting the rest of the sentence trail away, as though to say, I know how fat I must look to you.

"Oh, *please*," Marlene said sincerely. "You've got a *beautiful* face. I wish I had your skin. Honestly."

For a moment, neither woman spoke. Marlene's large myopic eyes swept rapidly around the shop, searching for something to say that would prolong the conversation. Staring at Esther's coat with a look of unconcealed envy, she said, "What a *lovely* color. Is it new?"

"Lane Bryant," Esther confirmed, naming the store where she had bought the coat only a week ago, on sale. "Whenever I want something nice, I go there or to Roaman's."

From the look on the girl's face, Esther could tell that she never heard of either store. Marlene was thin. She could just grab some *shmatta* off the rack on the Highway or Eighty-sixth Street and on her it would look tremendous. When you were Esther's size, you had to search in over-priced stores for hours in order to just find something that would actually fit. Never mind what was

78

in fashion. Fashion was for women who weighed less than a hundred and fifteen pounds.

For Esther, shopping had always been an ordeal. Having to look and look for clothing until her eyes fell out and her head began to spin made her physically ill. When finally she allowed herself to buy something, it was usually expensive and made to last. She had no other choice.

Before Esther could ask Marlene whether anyone had yet heard from Toni, the door to the shop swung open and Enid came in. Shorter than either Esther or Marlene, Enid was attractive in a sweet and simple way. In her hand she held a white paper bag. Esther took one look at the bag and knew immediately that it contained more calories than she would permit herself to eat all weekend long.

"*Ee*-nid," Esther said, stepping back with her hand in the air like some policeman halting traffic at a busy intersection. "Don't even *try* and tempt me. I'm being good."

"So be good, Esther," Enid said, smiling. "See where it gets you. Me, I'm going to eat."

Setting the bag down on the appointment desk, Enid took out a plain danish covered with glazed white sugar. She bit down on it as though she had been waiting for hours to do just this. Chewing enthusiastically, she said, "I know where I'm going when I die. Why should I make it any easier for them to carry the coffin?"

"Enid," Marlene said quickly. "Bite your tongue." Turning to Esther, she said, "Do you believe how she talks?"

"God forbid," Esther answered. Then she added, "On my worst enemy I wouldn't wish it." She said this to take the sting out of Enid's remark, which she understood in a way that she could never explain to Marlene.

Without being asked, Enid reached around behind the appointment desk and brought forth a brightly colored picture postcard that she handed to Esther. "From Toni," she explained. Esther skimmed the message on the back. Toni was having the time of her life. The weather was perfect, the beach fabulous. Toni was so dark from the sun that they had tried to stop her from going into the casino one night, mistaking her for a native.

"And Dom?" Esther asked, looking directly at Enid.

"She doesn't say," Enid said. "But as long as he's down there gambling with *her* money, I'm sure he's happy."

Esther nodded in agreement. Dom was a smooth talking hustler who sometimes did hair for Toni when the shop got so

79

crowded you literally could not get your foot inside the front door. Esther had never liked him. For Toni, she liked him even less. A man that good looking could never love anyone but himself. Although they had never discussed it with one another, Esther knew that Enid felt the exact same way.

Enid herself had her hands full. Her husband worked only when he was in the mood. Most days, he was out at the track, perfecting his system. Enid had to spend her Saturdays in the shop to make certain that their three kids would have enough to eat whenever the system crapped out, which was just about all the time. More than once, Enid had confided that she wished she had the guts to do to her husband what Esther had done to Morty. Just throw the bastard out into the street and go it alone. With three hungry mouths to feed, Enid was still hanging on, hoping things would get better.

Marlene moved to the second chair. Methodically, she began snapping her gum as she set out her combs and brushes on the narrow counter by the mirror that ran the length of the shop. "How come nobody likes Dom but me?" she asked innocently.

"Because," Enid said, "to you, he's always nice. Gee, I can't imagine why." Enid then made a face that left no doubt as to the reason. Esther laughed out loud. Turning towards Esther, Enid said, "So, sweetheart? What brings you in with the chickens today?"

"My son," Esther said simply, delighted to have a chance to talk about it. "He came home from Boston late last night. I wanted to get out early for him."

"Lucky you," Enid clucked, congratulating her. "What is he in for?"

"The High Holy Days," Esther said quickly, making the answer up right on the spot. "He came to spend Yom Kippur with his grandfather in shul."

"Nice," Enid said succinctly. "In this day and age, that's nice to hear. So how does he look, Esther? Still a stringbean?"

"He looks beautiful," Esther said, although it had been months since she herself had seen him. "You wouldn't recognize him." If and when Paulie finally decided to let her know that he was home, she hoped that she would.

"Have him come by," Enid said slyly, winking. "We'd *love* to see him, wouldn't we, Marlene?"

Marlene shrugged and snapped her gum. "Thanks," she said. "But I got a boyfriend."

"Is that what you call him?" Enid asked sarcastically. "Mr. Clothes Horse?"

Marlene was about to come to her boyfriend's defense when Esther cut her off. "He's too busy," she said. "Whenever he comes home, he runs around like crazy. I'm lucky if *I* get to see him."

"Isn't that the way it is?" Enid said. "First they take up all your time. Then they don't want any of it. There's no happy medium."

"He's staying by Morty," Esther blurted out suddenly, unable to keep the bad news to herself a moment longer. "Morty himself called to tell me. At seven-thirty this morning."

"He just couldn't wait, could he?" Enid said softly, understanding immediately. Esther nodded in response, fearing that if she spoke, her voice would crack.

"Soon," Enid said. "It's coming. For all of us. Every dog has his day. No, Esther? You yourself told me this."

"Me?" Esther laughed. "*I* told you this?" She shook her head. "Couldn't be. Doesn't sound a bit like me, does it?"

Enid and Esther looked at one another and laughed. Then Enid picked up the glazed danish from the appointment table. Slowly she brought it to her mouth. "Why am I eating?" she said out loud, addressing the question directly to the danish. "I need this like another hole in my head."

Putting the danish back down, she reached for Esther's hand. "Come, sweetheart," she said, leading Esther towards the big double sink in back. "I'll give you a nice wash. It'll make both of us feel better."

By ten-thirty, the little shop was so crowded that Esther could barely hear herself think, much less actually tell how she was feeling. Although both Dom and Toni were away, a record number of women were seated in the cracked red leatherette armchairs by the front door, impatiently waiting their turn. Many held rolled-up movie magazines in their laps. Some wore green smocks. Nervously they crossed and uncrossed their legs, kicking them straight out from the knee to mark each passing minute. To Esther, the women looked like weathered veterans of some long-defunct Broadway chorus line, still in shape and ready to dance, should the opportunity suddenly present itself.

Each and every one of them smoked intently, crushing out one cigarette after the other into standing chrome ashtrays that had to be emptied constantly as the morning wore on. Less than half an hour ago, the smoke collecting in the shop had gotten so thick that Enid had sent Marlene to the hardware store down the avenue for a rubber wedge to keep the front door open so some of the fumes would filter into the street.

For a solid hour, a delivery boy who could not have been more than thirteen years old, but who everyone agreed was absolutely adorable nonetheless, had been making regular trips from the luncheonette on the corner. With him he brought the highly recommended diet plate, cold tuna (whole can), with lettuce, cottage cheese, and tomatoes. Although it was still fairly early in the day to be eating lunch, the women waiting just inside the front door of the shop were bored. As soon as the first plate of food had come into the beauty parlor, they had all suddenly gotten hungry and begun to order.

Esther, who never ate any lunch at all on Saturday, sat regally in the first chair, congratulating herself on having been smart enough to come in early today. For although the shop was already a mob scene, in an hour it would be even worse, filled with so much noise, *shreying*, and *gareider* that nothing could have lured her inside the door.

Leaning all the way back in the chair with her eyes closed, Esther relaxed completely as Enid's powerful fingers stroked and pulled at her hair, which was now clean again for the first time in a week. Although Enid was talking away no more than six inches from her ear, Esther could not hear a word she was saying. In back of the shop, the dryers were going full blast. The deep rolling roar of their airplane engines obliterated all other sounds.

The women sitting beneath the dryers with large plastic bubble caps snapped over their foreheads, waiting patiently for Enid or Marlene to come back and pronounce them "done," were also talking. Often two women in adjoining seats would look at each other, shout sentences that neither could hear, then nod their heads in vigorous agreement.

As far as Esther could tell, Marlene had not yet sat down at all this morning. The pale green smock she wore over her clothing was stained with water and dye. The makeup on her face was streaked with sweat, revealing patches of skin that were red and scaly. Marlene was now a completely different person than the cool, self-assured vision who had greeted Esther earlier in the day. The transformation was so astonishingly complete that Esther felt slightly ashamed of the way she had treated the girl. After all, Marlene was only trying to make a living in here.

At the front of the shop, a discussion had swirled in an apparently endless circle for the past five minutes as to whether or not it was true that Chasidic wives only got to sleep with their husbands three times a month, and then through a hole in the sheet, neither husband nor wife ever seeing the other without clothes, which, as one woman had pointed out, was the way God had made them.

"My marriage, exactly," Ruthie Bender cracked. A woman whose naturally dark brown hair had been streaked silver by Toni Assante and then cut into the thatched, artichoke style that was rapidly gaining popularity in the neighborhood, Ruthie had a voice that cut through the din with ease. "Only in my sheets," she added, "there's *lots* of holes."

"Tell us, Esther," Enid asked after the laughter had subsided. "You work in shul. This is true?"

"True," Esther said, letting Enid's capable fingers do their work. "It's true. When they have their period, they're unclean. Then they go to the *mikvah* to bathe. Then they make another baby. Contraception they don't believe in."

"My marriage, exactly," Ruthie Bender said again, putting a king-sized Kent into an ashtray so that its lipstick rimmed filter stuck out just over the edge. "Maybe Sol's Chasidic. I know he's got something wrong with him."

"Say what you will about them," Esther noted. "And I want you to know that to them, my father-in-law is no better than a *goy*—they do take good care of their children. They treat them like kings."

"Oh," Enid said, her left eyebrow rising to punctuate the remark. "And we don't?"

"It's not the same," Esther said. "Theirs don't laugh at them."

"That *is* different," Enid conceded.

Something she had long been keeping within herself welled up suddenly from Esther's heart. "They *all* laugh at us," she said bitterly. "We talk too loud. We love too much. I swear to God, Enid, we make them all feel good they're not us."

To Esther, it seemed that everyone in the shop had suddenly stopped talking in order to listen to her. Even the roar of the dryers in back had quieted. Whatever came out of her mouth now, everyone would hear.

"You know what I always say, Enid?" Esther asked. Enid put down her comb and stepped back from the chair.

"What, Esther? Tell me."

"A fire *uf zey*."

Grinning broadly, Esther shifted her weight in the chair. Then she repeated the remark in English, so that all the girls would understand. "A fire on them," she said. "Let them burn."

All around the narrow, crowded beauty parlor, women shook their heads in agreement. One or two put down the magazines they were holding to reach for fresh cigarettes. Ruthie Bender jangled the thick gold charm bracelet dangling from her thin, speckled wrist and called out, "You tell 'em, Esther. From your mouth to God's ear. What *do* they know?" Under the dryers in back, women turned to one another and repeated the phrase so as not to forget it before they got back home. A fire *uf zey*. Let them burn. All of them. After all, what *did* they know?

Half an hour later, her hair perfect, Esther left the shop in a mad flurry of shouted goodbyes and see-you-next-weeks. She made extra sure to be especially nice to Marlene so the girl would never again mistake her for just another customer. Without being able to put her finger on it, Esther felt as though she had accomplished something important this morning. She had said what was in her heart.

Although it was probably a sin even to think this way, somehow Esther felt as though she had said it not in Toni Assante's little beauty parlor on the avenue but in temple, where her father-in-law prayed so faithfully each Shabbos and God himself was said to hear every word.

CHAPTER TEN

JUST FROM LOOKING at what she was about to give her father-in-law for his Shabbos lunch, Esther could feel her stomach begin to turn. Overnight, the spicy brown gravy of the rich goulash she had made him for dinner on Friday night had hardened into a murky, evil looking solid. Bits of pebbled chicken skin, glistening with oil and cold to the touch, lay trapped beneath the surface like the wreckage from a collision out at sea. The splintered ends of several large bones stuck straight up through the thick layer of caked yellow fat coating the bowl.

As far as Esther was concerned, there was something truly awful about food both before and after it was cooked, first a horrible rawness, and then a dead finality, that defeated appetite. Yet a person had to eat to live. Only when something had been prepared by someone else and then set before her on a plate, preferably one made of the finest china, did Esther feel hungry, eating more than probably was good for her.

The rest of the time it was all she could do to pick tentatively at her food like a nervous little bird pecking for seeds scattered on the ground. Unlike most of the people she knew, Esther did not live to eat. Still, she was as big as a house and getting bigger. It was her special curse. She alone had to pay twice for pleasure she had never known in the first place.

Since it was Shabbos, she could not even warm the goulash up on the stove. Orthodox law prohibited her from making a fire. Had she remembered, she could have set the bowl out this morning before going to the beauty parlor. Only back then, her mind had been on other things. Feeling slightly guilty while knowing that she had really done nothing wrong, Esther sat herself down at the far end of the dining room table. Glancing up at the electric clock on the wall, she realized that her father-in-law was already late. In itself that was not unusual.

Still, she could not help but worry that today would be the day when he would miss a curb somewhere, step sideways into the gutter, and fall awkwardly onto the hard asphalt. Shattering a hip, he would lie there helplessly like a dog in the street until someone found him. It was a nightmare that might soon become real.

Stubbornly, Esther fought the urge to rush to the phone to call the shul in order to find out if he had already left. In shul today no one would answer the phone except for Solomon, the colored janitor. More likely than not, Solomon would be too asleep to tell her anything that she did not already know. All she could do was wait.

To make the time pass more quickly, Esther automatically began counting the faded yellow roses on the wallpaper Morty had put up in the dining room nearly twenty years ago. Although she had hated the pattern from the first day it had gone up, it still soothed her nerves to try and calculate precisely how many butter-colored flowers were stretching their heavy heads along the rungs of a painted trellis towards a sun no one had ever seen.

Giving up the count before she was halfway through, Esther got nervously to her feet and walked to her bedroom at the front of the house. From her closet she withdrew the gift she had rescued for her father-in-law from one of the Care packages that constantly came through her office in the shul. A pair of old-fashioned black leather shoes that were almost new. The smooth, uncracked leather from which they had been made still smelled faintly of polish. The shoes themselves were tiny, as though fashioned for a child to wear. It was for this reason that she had brought them home. The old man's feet, like his hands, were small and fine boned. She was certain that the shoes would be a perfect fit.

Returning to the dining room with the shoes in her hand, Esther sat herself down once more at the table. More times than she could remember, she had sat here waiting for her son to come home for dinner. Sooner or later, she would always give in to the urge to call him. Stalking angrily to the front window, she would throw it open and shout his name out into the street. This practice Esther now recognized as being distinctly lower class.

It was lower class to scream from the window to your children in the street below. It was lower class to squeeze fruit in the market on the avenue while *hondling* like crazy with the store-keeper over price. It was lower class to dress yourself to the teeth for every last social function in temple so as to dazzle all the other women present with the sheer, aggregate cost of your outfit.

Still, Esther could not bring herself to get rid of the large gold rings set with semiprecious stones that she wore on the fingers of both her hands. To look down at her hands while she worked and see something of value there gave her pleasure. Whether or not this too was lower class, sometimes a person just had to do what they felt was right.

Deciding that she would not go to the front window to watch for her father-in-law in the street, Esther lit her first cigarette of the day instead. That it was only her first was in itself a minor miracle. The girls in Toni's smoked like chimneys. Of course, to smoke at all on Shabbos was forbidden, the simple act of striking a match on a day meant for complete rest and devotion prohibited by one of the many laws of Torah.

To Esther, it made no sense. On Shabbos you could not

smoke. Yet on Rosh Hashanah, the Jewish New Year, she had watched the men of the temple rush out on to the front steps during every break in services to eagerly light up cigarettes. That was permitted. Only today it was a sin.

Dragging deeply on her cigarette, Esther took the smoke all the way down into her lungs before letting it back out through her nose. For the minor sins of smoking on Shabbos and wearing gold rings set with semiprecious stones, God would have to forgive her. All things considered, she was doing the best she could.

The sound of a key being put into the downstairs door made Esther sigh out loud with relief. Thank God. The old man was finally home. Getting quickly to her feet, she stubbed out her cigarette in the small round cut-glass ashtray on the dining room table. Like a young girl ashamed to be caught in the act by her parents, she fanned what was left of the smoke above her head towards the open kitchen window. Her father-in-law himself smoked, seven cigarettes a day, but none on Shabbos. There was no need for him to walk into a house that reeked of tobacco today. He had spent the entire morning praying.

Esther listened as he slowly made his way up the front stairs. Each one creaked in noisy protest beneath his feet. Never a very big man, over the years her father-in-law had grown even smaller and lighter. Still, the steps were very old. The wood from which they had been made was now cracked and starting to rot. Like so many other things in this house, they were badly in need of repair. There was no denying that for such tasks, a man's touch was required.

Finally, the door came open. Hesitantly, her father-in-law stepped over the threshold. For a moment, he looked confused, as though not entirely certain that he had come to the right place or of the welcome that he might receive here. Esther quickly surveyed him from head to toe, checking for breaks, bruises, or minor injuries.

Because it was Shabbos, he had not shaved himself before going to shul this morning. Stubby white hairs, each one short, stout, and abrupt, poked their stubborn heads through the fine mesh of the skin along his jaw. His face had a slightly simian cast to it that usually went unnoticed because of his eyes, which were blue and very clear.

Only his hands betrayed how really old he was. From the wrists down, the skin was thinner than water spotted parchment.

Beneath the parchment, the blood vessels were knotted and purple. Each of his fingernails was like a tiny slab of thick, clear amber, so hard that Esther could trim them only with a pair of garden shears.

Bones that had been broken more than once over the years had knitted poorly, twisting once flexible joints into impossible positions. As a result, he now stood before her with his head bent slightly forward. Still, he walked everywhere without a cane. His hearing was good. When the occasion demanded it, he could write out his name in a strong, cursive European hand. Almost always, he knew precisely where he was and what he was doing. In many ways, he was in better shape than she was. Despite his age, his body had not yet betrayed him.

Having found a telltale trail of tiny drops leading from his bedroom to the bathroom down the hall one morning, lately Esther had begun putting a *schissel* under his bed at night. It was the very same cracked porcelain bowl into which her son had coughed and spat as a boy during his terrible attacks of asthma. But this situation was nothing to be alarmed about. Even as a younger man, her father-in-law had told her, he had never been able to wait in line in any toilet. When he had to go, he had to go.

"*Gudten Shabbos,*" he said, fumbling for the key that dangled in swinging circles from the old-fashioned pleated gold chain hanging from the belt loop of his pants. The suit he was wearing today was the exact same color of the cold goulash he would eat for lunch. Like nearly everything else he wore, the suit had come to Esther through the shul. Although she had given it out to be altered more than once, it still fitted him like a hand-me-down. Nevertheless, she knew it to be his favorite.

"Shabbos," she answered, watching the key stubbornly elude his grasp for another moment before he finally seized hold of it. Quickly he tucked it away into his pocket. "*Du hust gudt gedovendt?* she asked.

The old man considered the question for a moment. Had he prayed well this morning? He shrugged. The answer was beyond his knowing. Slowly, he began moving towards the little tea trolley on wheels in the far corner of the dining room. With care, he laid to rest the small blue velveteen bag on which the word *tallis* was embroidered in golden letters. Neatly folded inside the bag were his prayer shawl and the long white robe Esther herself

88

had specially laundered for him by hand a week ago so he could wear it in shul during the High Holy Days.

"Who made the *Kiddush* today?" she asked him. "Weiss?"

"Stryker," he said, turning his back toward her as he moved into the kitchen to rinse his hands before eating. "Pickled herring, rye bread, *ziessen* cake. *Zer gudt.*"

"Schnapps?" she asked.

"A *bissel bromfen*," he allowed over the sound of running water. "*Nisht gefalich.*"

"Paper cups?"

The old man nodded. Then he went over to the rack from which the dish towels were hanging. Selecting the one used only for meat meals, he wiped his hands on it. "Nat couldn't afford to put a whole bottle on the table?" Esther asked scornfully. "Yesterday afternoon Sol sent half a case to the shul for him to use."

The old man said nothing. What Nat Weiss did with Sol Stryker's whiskey was no concern of his. Coming back into the dining room, he moved around the entire table before finally taking his usual seat at the other end. Unconsciously, Esther reached for her cigarette, forgetting that it was already dead in the ashtray. Sol Stryker was far too important a man ever to actually make *Kiddush* himself. He simply donated the goods and then let his brother-in-law, Nat Weiss, do the work for him. Knowing Nat Weiss the way she did, Esther was certain that most of that whiskey had already found its way into his big house on the other side of the avenue, never to be seen in shul again.

Little went on in Ahavath Mizrach that Esther did not find out about sooner or later. For the past five years, she had worked as the shul's recording secretary, spending five days a week behind an old, scarred wooden desk in a drafty little office at the back of the building. As recording secretary, Esther sent out mailings. She billed those who had made pledges to the shul that they had not yet honored. She made certain that the big ballroom downstairs was never booked for two events on the same evening, something that had happened with astonishing regularity before she had taken the job.

The work itself was definitely beneath her abilities, the money she was paid to do it hardly worth mentioning at all. She had taken the position simply to get out of the house during the day. To go looking for a real job in the city now, at her age, was not possible. The idea of riding the train back and forth to work each day during the rush hour terrified her.

Besides, there were definite advantages to the job. As recording secretary, Esther got to attend all the numerous business and financial meetings held in temple almost every night of the week. At these meetings, she often talked on a first-name basis with truly influential people like Sol and Sylvia Stryker. Esther could not help feeling that it was to her advantage to know such people well. Especially now that her son was home again.

Esther was about to show her father-in-law the present she had for him when she saw that he was sitting with his eyes closed, silently reciting the *Kiddush* to himself once more. She padded quietly into the kitchen. The bowl of cold goulash standing by the sink looked no better to her now than it had before. Using just the very tips of her fingers, she slowly eased three pieces of chicken from the cold, clinging jelly the gravy had become. Her father-in-law loved the parts that other people never ate, the wings, the neck, and the ass, rich with greasy fat.

After she had walked back into the dining room and set the plate down before him, he exhaled loudly through his nose. Then he said, "*Kalte* chicken. *Gudt.*"

Knowing that he would have said the exact same thing no matter what she had given him to eat, Esther went back to her end of the table and sat down once again. Between the two of them, the chairs that had once been occupied by her husband and her son stood empty. She and her father-in-law still sat this way at every meal, as though at any moment the chairs might suddenly be filled again.

With his right hand, her father-in-law reached for the little red plastic basket before him, taking out a piece of bread. He ate bread with every meal—morning, noon and night—with chicken both hot and cold, as well as every kind of fish, liver, veal, eggs, sour cream, pot cheese, and even *latkes*, the starchy potato pancakes that all by themselves would lay for hours in your stomach like a stone. To him, bread was more than just food. As long as there was bread on the table, all was well. Life went on.

Despite the way he ate, so far as Esther could tell, he never gained an ounce. She could not say the same for herself. Every last diet that had ever been the rage in the neighborhood, Esther had tried, to no avail. Even after a solid week of starving herself at every meal, she would step up onto the little Detecto scale in the bathroom only to watch the needle swing inexorably towards the higher numbers.

Willpower was not the problem. She had enough willpower for two people. It was something else entirely. Lately, whenever anyone bothered to ask how her current diet was going, Esther just told them, "Oh, I don't diet any more, dear. With me, it's *glandular*." For all she knew, this could well be the truth. She had no desire at all to go to some overpriced specialist to find out for sure. What if there *was* something seriously wrong with her? A massive tumor that would not stop growing until it had taken over her entire body? It would not help to know. She had a condition. There was nothing more to be said about it.

As a fat woman without a husband who was rapidly growing older, Esther was well aware of just how awfully cruel people really could be. She had always sympathized wholeheartedly with other oppressed minorities—blacks, homosexuals, Puerto Ricans, and everyone without enough money in the bank to buy happiness in this world. Somehow, she could not help feeling that she personally had gotten just what she deserved. God had chosen to punish her. For what reason, she was not sure.

The only real pleasure Esther got from food these days was by watching her father-in-law eat. At the moment, he was going at it with both hands, shoveling chicken into his mouth with his fingers while sopping up the cold gravy with a torn piece of seeded rye bread. Unlike her son, the old man had always been an eater.

Esther reached into her pack for a fresh cigarette. Rolling it around between her fingers, she stared at her father-in-law, trying to decide whether this was the time to tell him the news. She could wait no longer. "Paulie's home," she announced suddenly, just like that.

The old man looked up in surprise, his mouth filled with food. Still chewing, he asked, *"Vo ist der den?"*

"By Morty," Esther said, unable to believe how painful it was for her just to have to say this out loud.

It was well past noon. By now Paulie had to be up. The least he could have done was to call. But he had not called, he had not come over, nothing. There could be no excuse for such behavior. None.

"Ach," the old man said, nodding. "By Morty. *Gudt*."

Then he put his head back down and went right on eating. To him it made no difference whether Paulie was in this house or

91

Morty's apartment. Both were home. As long as his grandson was safe and sound, nothing else mattered. *"Ven kommt er du den?"* he asked, more out of simple curiosity than anything else.

"Ich vaiss nisht," Esther said, which was the truth. He had been invited. He certainly was expected. When he might actually arrive was another story altogether.

"I'll give a call over there," she said, watching as the old man began wiping what was left of his bread in careful concentric circles around his plate. "If he comes now . . . he can catch you before you go back to shul."

The old man shook his head vigorously from side to side. Then he waved his hand in the air to make certain that Esther had not misunderstood his first gesture. *"Ven er kommt,"* he said, *"er kommt."* When he comes, he comes. From long experience, Esther knew that this would be the old man's final word on the subject.

Once her father-in-law finished his meal, Esther realized that she would have the entire day to herself. She would be free to do whatever she pleased. Suddenly the afternoon seemed to stretch away before her like some vast, barren wilderness through which there was no path. By all rights her son should have been here by now.

Letting go with a noisy belch to signify that he was nearly done, the old man swallowed. He smacked his lips, then reached for a paper napkin. Carefully, he wiped his mouth with it. Then he blew his nose into the flimsy paper and crumpled it into a ball. Looking around slowly, as though he was seeing this room for the very first time, he smiled. *"Er hat geheissen hant es Shabbat Shuvah,"* he said.

Although Esther worked each day under a large Hebrew calendar on which every last minor feast and half holiday was outlined in red, she herself had forgotten that today was *Shabbat Shuvah*, the Sabbath of penitence and return, falling between Rosh Hashanah and Yom Kippur during the holiest ten days of the year. She knew that Paulie would have no idea at all that today was special. She made a mental note to tell her son about it as soon as he came over so that he would not disappoint the old man with his ignorance.

"Uf Yom Kippur," the old man said, *"ich gae duchenen."*

Esther nodded, wondering what this had to do with anything. On Yom Kippur, her father-in-law would ascend the red-carpeted steps of the pulpit with the other *kohanim* of Ahavath Mizrach and chant the special blessing over the congregation. The ritual itself was ancient. Since women were not permitted to participate in it, Esther really did not know very much more about it except that she could never listen to the old man say the blessings without starting to cry.

"*Paulie kennt mir helfen,*" her father-in-law said now.

How could Paulie help him? For a moment, Esther was certain that the old man had gotten confused, mistaking Paulie for his very own son. Long before she had met Morty, he too had participated in this ceremony. That particular Morty was a man she had never known, her ex-husband having rarely gone to shul while they were married and then only to say *Yizkor* in memory of his mother on Yom Kippur. Paulie, she was certain, had never once taken part in the ritual of *duchening*.

Before she could question her father-in-law about it, he was up and out of his chair and on his way into the living room. There, Esther knew, he would sit by the front window for precisely an hour, staring into the street. Then he would return to temple. "I have something for you," she called out after him.

"What?" he asked, turning around.

"Shoes," she said, bringing them up from the floor so he could look them over carefully with his cobbler's hands.

The old man took a single step back into the dining room. When he saw the shoes, the expression on his face changed entirely.

"*Ken nisht,*" he said hurriedly, backing away from the shoes as though they were contaminated.

"Why not? They're like new. . . ."

"*Shvartze shich?*" he said, shaking his head. "*Ken nisht. Danke* but . . . *nein.*"

Then he turned and walked away. Esther sighed. Perhaps he did not want them because he was not permitted to wear leather shoes of any color to shul on Yom Kippur. Or perhaps there was some other religious reason for his refusal. It was all so complicated. Esther herself knew that she did not even understand a tenth of it.

Just like that, the meal was over. Sitting by herself in the empty dining room once again, with the shoes that her father-in-law had rejected still in her hand, Esther could not help noticing how badly the roses on the wallpaper had faded over the years. They were now an entirely different shade of yellow than they had once been. To do the room over she knew would be hard, messy work. First, the old wallpaper would have to be pulled off in long, curling strips. After much scraping, the wall itself would have to be smeared all over with dripping paste before new paper could be put up. It was the kind of job Morty had loved, as though grateful for any opportunity to spend hours in the house without having to talk to her.

It occurred to Esther that perhaps Paulie could find someone who would do the work for her. Perhaps he might even want to do it himself. To pursue the project all on her own seemed impossible. It was just too depressing to consider. Realizing that she had not eaten a thing today, hungry, yet at the same time unwilling to put food into her mouth, Esther rolled the unlit cigarette between her fingers. Then she slowly got to her feet to collect her father-in-law's empty plate.

Today, she weighed more than she ever had before. She was so big around that she could barely stand up without having to hold onto the back of a chair. In a kind of awful waking dream, she saw herself as one of those monstrous helium-filled balloons that floated down Broadway each year during the Macy's Thanksgiving Day parade.

Although to all the spectators on the sidewalk it seemed as though she was being kept aloft by the wind, Esther had only to look down to see that in fact she was being carefully steered along the parade route by a complex series of fine guy wires. Each and every wire was being held by a man, all of them with thick black beards and black skullcaps on their heads, their hairy black forearms sticking out of cheap white nylon short-sleeve shirts.

She had a condition all right. There was no saying she didn't. Had she only known of another beauty parlor in the neighborhood where they wouldn't have recognized her the minute she came through the door, Esther would have gotten dressed and gone there right this minute to have her hair done all over again. Anything to get out of this silent, empty house filled with ghosts and fading yellow wallpaper, to be part of something other than her own bitter and unending loneliness, if only for a little while.

CHAPTER ELEVEN

SIMPLY, THE FEELING was too frustrating for words. One moment it was right there, close enough to touch, and the next it was completely gone, out of sight and out of mind, as though he had never known anything about it in the first place. But of course he had. Why else would it be bothering him so constantly now? Such were the rewards of growing old in a country where age itself did not automatically command respect, perhaps with good reason.

Annoyed with himself for not being able to focus sharply on what had once been so clear to him, and a bit ashamed to have to admit this fact to himself, Mendel Bindel, the *shamus* of Ahavath Mizrach, slowly rounded the corner on his way back to shul. As always, he was not so much looking where he was going as steering a course by his very own special set of local landmarks.

To his right stood the splintered wooden telephone pole with the chipped silver metal 9 on it. The configuration of the number itself was similar to one he seemed to remember from another time. At the moment, though, he could not be certain where he had seen it first. To his left ran the long chain-link fence behind which King, the fierce *menshenfresser* of a German shepherd lay crouched and waiting in the shadow of a large flowering bush. Thick ribbons of white saliva dripped from the fleshy folds of the dog's black mouth. Its large yellow eyes gleamed brightly in the shade.

The old man knew that at a moment's notice, without any kind of provocation whatsoever, the dog might suddenly hurl itself headlong against the fence, barking like crazy while baring its savage teeth. One day soon, King was going to spring *over* the fence onto public property. Mendel Bindel would be ready for him. Seizing a metal garbage can cover or a broken broomstick from the gutter, or just by using the point of his shoe to deliver a swift kick to the animal's balls, he would make certain that King would never again leave his little yard without thinking twice about it beforehand. In America, as everywhere else, even an old man had the right to defend himself.

What continually surprised him about this country to which he had come with the best years of his life already behind him was not how different it was from all that he had known but how similar. As he walked to and from the temple each day, always following the exact same route, his eyes picked out only those details that reminded him of the past.

Moving towards the gutter, a narrow asphalt speedway along which cars raced madly in an endless contest to beat the light on the avenue up ahead, the old man made sure to look both ways before crossing. Taking care to stay within the two thick yellow lines the city had been kind enough to paint in order to guide him on his way, he crossed slowly to the other curb.

Having reached the safety of another sidewalk, he resumed his steady pace once more. Shoving one hand deeply into the side pocket of his old brown pants, he began searching with his fingers for something. All the while he was thinking of those nearly new, lamp-blacked shoes with high tops that laced up the front.

His daughter-in-law had just presented him with those shoes. Although they *had* been black, they did not have high tops. He was thinking of another pair. Still, it was *verboten* for him to wear them. Why, he could not say. As he considered the problem, the lines in his forehead doubled in number. The small muscles surrounding his mouth puckered in sympathetic harmony. For some reason it seemed very important that he work all of this out *now* so that he could explain it to his grandson before Yom Kippur came and went. Precisely why he needed to do this was another mystery altogether.

Suddenly his fingers found what they had been looking for. Several of the crumbs he had carried with him to *Tashlikh* at the bay had lodged themselves in the lining of his pants pocket. Although they were now as hard as stone, their presence was oddly reassuring, one more link to what had come before. There seemed to be so many pieces to this puzzle confronting him that he could not fit them all together without losing his mind.

Looking up, he saw the great stone steps of the temple before him. He no longer had any time left to think about the past. Reaching out with his hand to the smooth metal banister for support, he took the steps one at a time, not pausing for breath

96

until he was standing in front of the shul's oversized oak doors. Automatically, he touched the fingers of his right hand to the small *mezzuzah* mounted on the doorpost. He put his fingers to his lips, then back to the *mezzuzah* once again. Only then did he permit himself to pull open the door and go inside.

Before him the temple seemed to stretch away forever, endless rows of gray wooden benches running in orderly fashion towards the Ark. There, behind the beautifully beaded, pure white curtains that were used only during the High Holy Days, the sacred Torahs themselves were kept. The Eternal Light, a single red bulb that always burned, swung suspended high above from a gilded chain.

As always, the room itself was silent, the only sound being the regular rasp of air rushing out his nostrils and then back in again through his mouth. This silence was always here to greet him like an old friend when he arrived before the sun was up each morning for the first service of the day. It remained behind to bid him goodbye when he left again after *Ma'ariv* each evening. In this silence, for him there was meaning.

Moving down the center aisle, he began slowly gathering up the *Siddurim* that the congregation had left scattered along the benches when they had bolted for home this morning after the singing of *Adon Olam* had been completed. Despite the rebbe's constant pleas from the pulpit, people were always in such a great hurry to get home once Shabbos services were over that they neglected to put the books back where they belonged. It was his job to do this for them.

Once, his grandson had worked alongside him, stacking the books into piles far heavier than he himself could lift and then carrying them to the big walk-in closet at the very back of the shul. Now that he did the work alone, the job took longer. Still, he did not mind. At the moment, the temple belonged entirely to him, as it never could when there were others present.

Filling his arms with books, he turned and began walking back the way he had come. As always, he made very sure not to take any more *Siddurim* than he could safely carry. If one fell to the ground, he would have to pick it up immediately and press its binding to his lips, a sign that no disrespect had been intended to the name of the Lord, which was written on nearly every page of every volume.

Nudging open the closet door with his knee, he went inside. The sheer weight of the books he was carrying made his arms

97

ache. He longed to switch on the light bulb hanging from a string above his head but this was not permitted. Only Solomon could do it for him. From long experience, he knew that Solomon was down in the kitchen taking a nap. Solomon worked as hard as any man. There was no need to disturb him when he was resting. So he worked on in darkness.

Placing the books on the shelf where they were kept, he stepped back, rubbing away the fire that was burning in the muscles of his forearms. Sighing with relief, he looked around. As *shamus* of Ahavath Mizrach, it was his responsibility to maintain the closet in perfect order. A single glance told him that this was work enough for a committee of men, with Nat Weiss always breathing down their necks to make certain that the job was done correctly.

The closet was hopelessly crowded with cardboard boxes. Some were empty and had always been so, yet no one ever threw them out. Others were filled with extra prayer shawls made of shiny acetate and flimsy nylon for those who came to shul without one of their own. On every wall of the closet large, glossy calendars hung at crooked angles. All had been supplied free of charge by eager salesmen from the Lower East Side who were anxious to make certain that the name of their firm would be familiar to the Finance Committee when the time came for the temple to make a new block purchase of prayer books or shawls.

Ezrin Brothers of Hester Street. Mankiewicz and Morer, Ludlow Street. Cohen and Cohen, corner of Second and Delancey. Caterers to the trade, each firm proudly proclaiming itself in large black letters to be absolutely the oldest and most reliable supplier of strictly Orthodox goods in America. Although the old man had never once visited any of their fine establishments, and had no say at all as to which firm the shul might actually buy from, he had spent so much time looking at the calendars that he considered them all to be his friends.

Where the shelves of the closet ran out into darkness, the old man knew that a single bottle of good whiskey, Seagram's V.O. or Canadian Club, could be found. Always a single bottle and never more. Although the bottle was meant to be used only for the *Kiddush*, important officers of the shul, Nat Weiss foremost among them, often took their friends in here for a quick shot, knocking the stuff straight back from a tiny pleated paper cup.

Neither eating nor drinking was permitted in shul itself. But the closet was not shul. Once its doors had been shut, shul was left behind. Among the glossy calendars and empty cardboard boxes, men were exempt from the many laws governing how they were meant to act in the presence of the holy Torahs. Or so Nat Weiss had informed the rabbi, and the rabbi had not disagreed.

Of all those who used the closet, only Mendel Bindel, the *shamus*, knew precisely where everything in it could be found. He alone could descend into its crowded depths in the midst of any service and return with the requested prayer book, *tallis*, or yarmulka in hand. Grinning like a triumphant explorer just back from the darkest regions of central Africa, he would hand the item over, grunt with satisfaction, and say, "*Na. Nem es.*" Here. Take. I have found what you needed, once again.

His other duties as *shamus* of the shul were equally simple. He was required to be present for all services, *Shaharith* in the morning, *Minchah* before sunset, and *Ma'ariv* just after, seven days a week, week in and week out, winter and summer alike. For this he was paid nothing. It would never have occurred to him to ask for money. Instead, he paid himself in other ways, taking home the occasional bottle of whiskey he was certain that no one would miss, selling wine and matzohs from Israel at Passover for a small profit. Most of his income, which he used primarily to keep himself supplied with cigarettes and razor blades, came from saying *Kaddish* for other people.

This practice was nearly as old as the religion itself. Orthodox law decreed that for a year after the death of a mother or father, a son had to pray for the deliverance of their souls each day, both morning and evening. But not everyone had the time, patience, or desire to do this. Still, Orthodox law prescribed. So, for a certain sum of money, the old man could be hired to perform the task instead.

Currently he was saying *Kaddish* for three different people, whose Hebrew names he had laboriously written out on a tiny piece of paper which he would withdraw from the side pocket of his jacket before beginning the prayer each day in order to remind himself for whom he was praying. Once the year of required mourning was over, the paper would be nearly transparent, the ink smudged from the sweat of his hand. Only then would he throw it away, knowing that the name of the deceased would take its rightful place on a bronze plate bolted to one of the great tablets mounted on the temple's back wall.

Next to each name was a tiny bulb which Solomon would light on the anniversary of the death. On Yom Kippur, all the lights would blaze forth, the wall taking on a life of its own, a life composed of many deaths and whatever it was that came afterwards. For a while after becoming *shamus*, the old man had wondered about the people for whom he was being paid to pray. Most he had never known in life. Now they were dead. What kind of people had they been? Good people? *Frum?* Of the book? Or backsliders, who only in death had their names sounded before the holy Torahs?

Now, he no longer bothered to think of such things. Instead, he took his fee and said the *Kaddish* without worrying about the lives of the dear departed for whom he was praying. They were dead, and the prayer needed to be said. The words themselves had the power to touch his heart so that he always felt as though he was praying for his very own parents, dead these many years. There was no need for him to do anything but repeat the words, exactly as they had been written.

Still, it made him far happier to be able to teach some young man to say the prayer for himself, for his own mother or father. As far as he was concerned, this was the proper way to remember the dead. Over the years, many of the men he had instructed in the *Kaddish* had begun returning to the shul on the High Holy Days, filling the cheap seats at the very back of the temple so as to be near him when they prayed.

On *Kol Nidre* night they would all be here, filling this great room with their nervous energy. His grandson would be present as well. As the old man moved from the closet back out into the shul, he could see their faces before him. Good boys every one, with good hearts, all of whom always had a handshake and a smile ready when they saw him coming. Soon he would see them all again, on the evening that began the Day of Atonement and the solemn twenty-four-hour fast that followed.

It was of that evening that he was thinking as he gathered together another armful of *Siddurim*. Straightening up again, he saw that he was no longer alone in shul. At the very front of the temple, where only the rich men sat during the High Holy Days, the rabbi himself was standing over his special cabinet, pushing aside one book after the other while mumbling softly to himself.

The old man cleared his throat to let the rabbi know that there was someone behind him. When the rabbi turned to look at him, the old man inclined his head in a gesture of respect he had been taught nearly seven decades earlier, as a schoolboy in short

100

pants. Then he lifted his head once more and stared at the larger man standing before him.

The dark stubble coating the fleshy edges of the rabbi's jaw was positive proof that he had not touched a razor to his face since before the sun had set on Friday. Concerning the rebbe's piety, there had never been any question. Something else about him, a certain lack of *menshlichkeit*, bothered many in the congregation. Simply, Reb Simeon Hakveldt was not the man that his predecessor, Saul Abrams, had been. Rabbi Hakveldt's dark, glowering countenance worked against him, putting people off. *Shvartze Simeon*, someone had once called him. Dark Simeon. The name had stuck, although the old man himself never used it.

Greeting the *shamus* with a formal nod, the rabbi looked at the *Siddurim* in the old man's arms, then at all the books still scattered on the empty benches surrounding both of them on every side. Then he sighed. "*Der bucher*, eh, Mendel?" he said, addressing the old man by his first name, as was his habit. "So many to be put away. Every Shabbos."

The old man shrugged. Putting away the books was not a job he minded. "And all so old as well," the rabbi went on, reaching out to pick one up. "Who knows?" he said, talking more to himself than to the *shamus* now. "Maybe that is why they never remember to put them back themselves."

Holding the *Siddur* at arm's length, the rabbi surveyed it critically, looking down at it over the curving incline of his nose. The prayer book in his hand was cracked and torn, its cover just beginning to fray around the edges. In contrast, the oversized volume containing the sections of the Torah to be read from the pulpit that he had only just taken from his cabinet was brand-new. Its pebbled cover was in mint condition, the gold letters embossed along the spine shining as brightly as the sun.

The rabbi looked from one book to the other. Then he shook his head and made a little clucking noise with his tongue, as though words alone could never express what he was feeling. "A first-class shul," he said, the phrase having only just occurred to him, "must have first-class *bucher*."

"*Denken Gott*," the old man replied quickly, thinking of other shuls he had known in other places, "we have *bucher* at all, Rebbe."

"But we need *neier bucher*, Mendel," the rabbi insisted, stressing the Yiddish word for "new." "*Der kennst der demannen* how I fought for *neier Mahzorim*?" he asked. The old man nodded. He remembered the rabbi's battle for new High Holiday prayer books very well. "In *Enn*-glish *andt* Hebrew. No more running for page numbers during *Musaf*, eh?"

The rabbi smiled suddenly, his large horse teeth blazing forth from the middle of his olive drab face. The old man shook his head, recalling how things had been when Saul Abrams was still the rebbe of Ahavath Mizrach. Back then, the shul had been far too poor to afford a single edition of the High Holy Day prayer book for the entire congregation. Instead, on both Rosh Hashanah and Yom Kippur, people would pray from their own books.

Treasured relics carried by hand from every corner of Europe, the books had for the most part been ancient, older even than their owners, with soot-black covers soiled beyond recognition and torn bindings covered with tape. These were books that had traveled, each and every one with a history of its own. More often than not, some of their thick yellow pages would tumble to the floor of the temple during the most critical part of the *Musaf* service. Having been used in a hundred different shuls, the books followed no set pattern. Instead, the prayers that they contained were scattered through them in every conceivable kind of order.

On Yom Kippur especially, when the shul was crowded with people who rarely if ever came to temple on any other day, a steady stream of congregants would make their way toward the corner where the old man sat, seeking help. Up at the Torah, the reader would be racing through some prayer in a rumbling monotone, trying to make up for lost time. Without help, no one who did not know the entire service by heart could determine precisely where in his own prayer book he was meant to be.

Handling each book gently, like a newborn infant unexpectedly thrust into his hands at a circumcision, the old man would flick quickly through the pages with the tip of his forefinger. Finding the proper place, he would hand the book back to its owner, saying "*Na*. In *der mittel*. Read. . . ."

To go over and ask Mendel Bindel for help during Rosh Hashanah and Yom Kippur became in Ahavath Mizrach a kind of unofficial custom. Unlike Saul Abrams, however, Rabbi Simeon Hakveldt did not approve of the practice. In his opinion, the constant moving about, the shuffling, and the talking had distracted from the sanctity of the service itself.

Making an eloquent plea to the Finance Committee during one of their regular Wednesday night meetings, Rabbi Hakveldt had persuaded the leaders of the temple to invest five thousand dollars in a set of brand new *Mahzorim*, a single edition, with page numbers and English translation throughout. Sol Stryker had donated most of the money all by himself. It was now his name that was embossed on the front of every book even though the books themselves were only used twice a year, on Rosh Hashanah and Yom Kippur.

Although the old man understood the reason for the change, he still missed the old books. The rough feel of their thick, textured pages on his fingers and the dry dead smell of age that had come off their tattered covers had been both entirely familiar and very comforting to him. It was the world those books had come from that he missed. Once the books were gone, the world itself would exist solely in his memory, which lately had been none too good at all.

He himself still stubbornly continued to pray from the same weathered black *Mahzor* he had always used. He had no need of page numbers or English translation to follow along with the service. To him, English was but another of the many languages of exile.

The rabbi stared at the small old man standing before him. Then, as though he was about to address the entire congregation on a matter of great importance, he spread out both his hands, palms facing the floor. "*Siddurim* to match our *Mahzorim*, eh, Mendel?" he said. "A new set, *complete*."

The old man did not answer. Fearing that perhaps he had not been understood, the rabbi added, "Only for that, we need money." The old man stood before him, still not speaking. "*Gelt*," the rabbi clarified. "*Gelt macht der velt*, eh, Mendel?"

Money makes the world. It was a saying that the old man had heard throughout his life without ever really believing it to be more than half true. And if you did not have money, what then? You lived anyway. The rabbi, however, seemed delighted with his own cleverness. He laughed out loud, his upper teeth protruding over his thick lower lip.

Nodding as though to indicate that he would have liked to stand here and talk with the rabbi all day long but that he had more pressing work to do at the moment, the old man began to move away. Then he stopped, looked up at the rabbi, and said, "*Uf yom Kippur, Rebbe. Ich gae duchenen.*"

It was now the rabbi's turn not to answer. Why the old man had chosen this precise moment to bring up the matter of the priestly blessing, he had no idea. One could never be too careful when dealing with these aged but clever operators from the other side. No matter how confused they seemed at times, nothing escaped their notice for long. Always, they knew how to stick the needle in just where it hurt the most.

Unlike his worthy predecessor, Saul Abrams, who along with all his other many talents had actually been born a *kohen*, a priest, Rabbi Simeon Hakveldt was a *yisraelite*. On Yom Kippur, when the *kohanim* ascended to the pulpit to pronounce the priestly blessing just as it had been performed back when the Temple still stood in Jerusalem, Simeon Hakveldt would have to step down to join those waiting below.

In this of course, there was no shame. A man could be born a *yisraelite* and still become a great rebbe. Only with Simeon Hakveldt it had always been a sore point, as though his admittedly humble origins had been scrutinized and found to be lacking in quality. While some young boy born a *kohen* could *duchen* as soon as he was bar mitzvahed, he, the rabbi of this great temple, never could.

In order to show what kind of man he truly was, Rabbi Simeon Hakveldt refused to give in to what he was feeling at the moment. Instead, he smiled kindly and said, "*Gudt,* Mendel. *Gudt.* That *der kennst* still *duchenen,* at *deinen* age"—the rabbi shook his head from side to side to indicate that this at the very least was a kind of miracle—"*denken Gott.*"

The old man looked up at the rabbi with an odd expression on his face. Then he said, "*Ver muzzst denken Gott . . .*" He let the rest of the sentence trail away, as if to suggest that there could be no one else responsible.

Feeling as though he had already been bested in this little encounter without knowing how or why it had happened, the rabbi cleared his throat. Then he smiled and nodded his head, a gesture he hoped would serve as goodbye. He had no more time to waste here. Only a few days remained before he would give his Yom Kippur sermon, after which the most important appeal of the year would be made. With the entire community gathered together first to listen and then to respond by pledging both their spiritual and financial support, he would once again be on trial. All eyes would be upon him. Everyone would listen closely to what he had to say. Before the day was over, he would be judged, both by God and by those who paid his salary.

On that one day of the year more than any other, the rabbi rightfully felt that the power was in his hands. The power to bring people back, if only for a little while, to the faith that they always seemed to slowly lose once again over the course of the year no matter how many social, cultural, and religious events the synagogue sponsored to keep them interested. Breaking with tradition, he had decided to begin composing his Yom Kippur sermon today. But only in his mind, of course, for he was forbidden to take a pencil in hand and commit anything to paper on Shabbos.

It was for this reason that he had made a special trip back to shul for the oversized volume containing the *Maftir Yonah*, the Book of Jonah, which would be read aloud during the afternoon service on Yom Kippur. The story itself was of course well known to him. God had commanded Jonah to go to Nineveh to warn the people that they were about to be destroyed for their wickedness. Jonah had refused, going off to sea to escape the Lord. A great storm had washed him overboard, where he had been swallowed up into the belly of a whale. Begging the Lord for forgiveness, Jonah had been delivered from the great fish. Then he had gone to warn the city, which had immediately turned away from wickedness and thus was spared.

It was precisely at this point in the story that the rabbi always lost the central thread of the tale. Seeing what the Lord had done, Jonah had gotten angry and demanded to die. He had gone off to sit alone on the east side of Nineveh. The Lord God had made a gourd grow up over Jonah's head to shade him. This had pleased Jonah. At dawn, God had made a worm to destroy the gourd. A hot east wind had come up, the sun had beaten down on Jonah's head, and he had fainted. Again, Jonah had angrily demanded to die.

It was then that the Lord had said unto him, "You would spare the gourd, though you spent no work upon it. . . . Should I not then spare the great city of Nineveh with more than a hundred and twenty thousand beings, who did not know their right hand from their left, and much cattle?"

Who did not know their right hand from their left. What a phrase. To the rabbi, it was as completely inexplicable as the precise symbolism of the gourd or the source of Jonah's apparently unquenchable anger, not to mention the three days and nights Jonah himself had spent inside the belly of a whale.

Simeon Hakveldt was no great Biblical scholar, who had only to study a text once to extract every last drop of meaning from every word. He had known this ever since he had been a young boy in *cheder*. And yet, it was in the Book of Jonah that he hoped to find some central theme on which to base his Yom Kippur sermon. The theme of charity, certainly. The charity shown by the Lord toward both Jonah and Nineveh.

"On Rosh Hashanah, their destiny is inscribed, and on Yom Kippur, it is sealed." So Rabbi Amnon had written in the *unesanah tokef*, the great devotional prayer that would be read aloud by the entire congregation on the Day of Atonement. "How many shall pass away and how many shall be brought into existence, who shall live and who shall die; who shall come to a timely end and who to an untimely end . . . who shall be at peace and who shall be molested; who shall become poor and who shall become rich; who shall be lowered and who shall be raised. But repentance, prayer, and charity cancel the stern decree."

It was that feeling exactly that the rabbi wished to evoke with his words on Yom Kippur. But the words themselves were so hard to find. It was at moments like this that Rabbi Simeon Hakveldt was certain that it had all been said before, and by finer minds. Still, Ahavath Mizrach was *his* shul. On Yom Kippur people would fill this great room to capacity to hear him speak. He alone was expected to make them feel, to ache, and then to give with generosity so that the shul would prosper in the coming year. That terrifying weight was upon him once again.

Truly, the Hebrew calendar was like a great stone wheel rolling ever onward as man stood helplessly in its path, watching it slowly come closer. Once again the year had come full circle. Once again it would soon be Yom Kippur. Once again he would have to find something both new and vital to say to the congregation.

But repentance, prayer, and charity cancel the stern decree. The phrase echoed in the rabbi's mind. Repentance. Coming to God with an open heart. Prayer. *With* devotion, not as one unloading a burden and then moving on, as Rambam, the great Moses Maimonides, had written. Charity. *Tzedakah.* The very essence of the religion. To give without specifying who was to receive.

The absolute highest form of charity, the rabbi knew, was a partnership, the strong taking in the weak. The partnership of temple and congregant, striving together to raise enough money for a new set of *Siddurim.* There it was all right. A beginning for his sermon, the one he had come to shul to find.

Glancing around, the rabbi realized that he was now alone in

106

the temple. Having already quietly completed his work, the old man had gone home. Striding out through the door to which he had his very own special key, the rabbi was surprised to see that it was still only early afternoon. The sun was shining brightly, the air so soft and warm that it felt more like a day in May than mid-September.

With any luck at all, the weather on Yom Kippur would be just as fine. There was no telling how many more people would come to temple in sunshine than if the skies suddenly opened, streaks of jagged lightning tore across the ragged clouds, and the streets were soaked with stinging rain. Let the weather be as it is today, Rabbi Simeon Hakveldt thought, and I will do my part once more.

Although he himself would never have described it in such terms, the rabbi had just concluded another one of his little bargains with the Lord. At home he knew that his midday meal was probably already waiting for him on the dining-room table. A great stomach-churning pang of hunger coursed through his entire body. Suddenly famished, he began hurrying down the street towards his house.

As he went, the rabbi could not help feeling that no matter how much he rushed, he was already late and would always be so, all the various forms of charity available to him notwithstanding.

CHAPTER TWELVE

THE HOUSE IN which Simeon Hakveldt had lived rent free ever since becoming spiritual leader of Ahavath Mizrach was two stories high and made of brick. It stood on a corner within easy walking distance of the synagogue and was owned by the eminent Sol Stryker himself through a company named Rosalie Properties, Inc., Rosalie being the name of the Strykers' eldest daughter. At the time of incorporation, Rosalie Stryker had been both single and extremely eligible, a condition that her father made certain was altered soon afterward, through marriage to an accountant.

Rosalie Properties, Inc., was itself the child of Stryker Togs, the business that Sol Stryker's father, Eli, had founded during the Depression to manufacture children's clothing. Although nearly every one of Eli Stryker's fellow cutters in the garment center had warned him that to try and sell shirts and pants for infants when most of their parents did not even have enough money for food was madness, the firm had been an immediate success. Over the years, it had grown steadily, becoming larger and more prosperous than anyone could have predicted.

Most of his profits from the business Eli Stryker had invested in real estate, buying up a large number of two-story houses made of brick in neighborhoods scattered throughout the borough. Every last house stood on a corner. It was Eli Stryker's belief that only a prosperous man could afford to own property where two streets met to form an intersection.

For nearly twenty years, as the local real estate market stagnated and both city taxes and the cost of maintaining these houses in good repair mounted, Sol Stryker tried desperately to sell off his father's holdings at a profit. Unable to do so, he finally donated the largest of the houses to Ahavath Mizrach for use by its rabbi. This simple act of charity, prorated over a period of years, provided Rosalie Properties, Inc., with enough of a cushion to weather a series of small recessions. Then the boom in urban real estate began. Eli Stryker's many houses, all of them two stories high, made of brick, and standing on corners, increased in value to nearly seven times their original cost, thereby validating what the elder Stryker had often told his son. Own *things*, not paper. *Never* make a show.

This last piece of advice Sol Stryker had taken thoroughly to heart, keeping his family in the neighborhood long after he could have easily afforded to move them to one of the richer suburbs out on Long Island. As the very backbone of the Ahavath Mizrach community, the Stryker family attended shul regularly. They endowed various temple projects with both their blessings and large sums of money. Once a year they came to dine with the rabbi, his wife, and their two children in the rent-free two-story brick house on the corner.

In Simeon Hakveldt's considered opinion, Sol Stryker was the very model of a good Jew, courteous, polite, cultured, and wealthy, a perfect gentleman in every sense of the word. About

Sol's brother-in-law, Nat Weiss, the rabbi could not say the same. Having failed to rise any higher in the family firm than second vice-president in charge of regional marketing, Nat Weiss had made the temple his very own special concern.

It was Nat Weiss and not Sol Stryker who three times had been President of the synagogue. It was Nat Weiss who patrolled the center aisle of the shul each Shabbos like a lion that had just been released from its cage, handing out *aliyahs* to friends as though they were his own personal property so that they could have the honor of reciting the blessings over the Torah. It was Nat Weiss who kibitzed and suggested and planned, making the rabbi's life more difficult than anyone knew.

Thankfully, it was Sol Stryker who came with his wife, Sylvia, to dine once a year with the rabbi, and not Nat Weiss. Even in a rent-free house, a man had the right to choose his dinner companions. Or so the rabbi believed. Unfailingly, the night on which the Strykers finally sat themselves down at his table, upon which Leah had set out only the finest crystal, the best plates, and the special silver, was a wondrous occasion, the room itself expanding with hearty laughter and brilliant conversation.

Never was that evening very far from the rabbi's mind. Even as he came into his house today, placing his wide-brimmed black felt hat on the table by the door, then feeling automatically with his fingers to make certain that the small black yarmulka he always wore was still in place at the very top of his head, the rabbi was thinking that the time had come once again for Leah to send the Strykers one of her beautifully handwritten invitations. After *Sukkoth* and before *Chanukkah*, the Strykers would honor both him and this house with their presence.

Peering through the open doorway into the dining room, the rabbi noted with satisfaction that both of his children, Rachel and Daniel, were still seated at the table, waiting for him to come home before they finished their midday meal. Catching sight of him, Daniel waved happily and smiled. Rachel stared myopically at her father through her thick glasses. Then she went right on eating. The rabbi sighed. Going into the small downstairs bathroom to wash his hands, he carefully said the blessing first in a soft, gurgling undertone before turning on the water.

He himself had heard many tales, nearly all of them apocryphal, about the rabbi's beautiful daughter and her fate. His daughter was not beautiful. Rather, she was plain, in an extravagant manner, one of those creatures designed by God for use rather than esthetic pleasure. Rachel was ruddy, sturdy, and rotund. Perhaps she would make some man a good wife in time. But even that was not certain.

In nearly every way the girl was unlike her younger brother. It was as though they had come from two separate wombs. Smooth and shiny, quick and clever, Daniel moved through life like an eel. The boy shimmered brightly in the rabbi's eyes as though he was always damp from the sea. The awesome difference between him and his sister was positive proof of the inexplicable nature of God's handiwork.

By the time the rabbi went back into the dining room, his daughter was already gone. This in itself did not displease him. He had no great desire to argue with Rachel before eating today. Daniel had taken advantage of his sister's absence to squirm from his seat onto the table itself. With both hands he was grabbing for the elaborate silver candelabra which had completely fascinated him for the past few days. "Daniel," the rabbi said gently, lifting his son off the table and putting him back on the floor, "the table is for eating, not crawling." Daniel looked up at his father with a puzzled grin on his face. Smiling, the rabbi said, "Upstairs, Daniela. *Gae.*"

Still grinning, his son bolted from the room. Upstairs, Daniel could occupy himself in any way he pleased except by turning on the television and sitting before it staring mindlessly at the screen. This the rabbi had expressly forbidden either of his children ever to do in the house on Shabbos.

Seating himself in his usual chair at the head of the table, the rabbi began drumming his thick fingers against the starched white tablecloth. He stared across the room at the ornate mahogany breakfront that Leah had brought to their marriage from her parents' once fine home in Williamsburg. Every last plate and goblet within the breakfront was shining brightly to welcome Shabbos, the queen of the week, to their house. Although the sight pleased him, the rabbi still felt annoyed. He had been home now for a good ten minutes, yet his wife had not presented herself. Instead, he was sitting here all alone like some stranger waiting for a bus in the Port Authority. Above the loud sound of his stomach rumbling, he could hear his wife humming contentedly to herself over the kitchen sink.

"*Leah!*" he called out, his voice ringing through the silent house. "*Du hust der* window *uffen?*"

Leah's first response was to laugh. "Why, Simeon?" she

110

called back in that mocking, derisive tone he had come to know so well over the years. "You're worried about people passing by?"

"On *Shabbat Shuvah*," he said sharply, "the rebbitsen shouldn't be singing out a window. *Mi' tornisht*." It was forbidden.

"And why not?" Leah demanded, pushing open the kitchen door with her elbow. In one hand she held a bowl of cold borsht, in the other, a plate of the special pickled herring the rabbi loved so much. A day-old loaf of yellow *challah* was balanced precariously between her arms, resting against her ample chest. Expertly, as though she had been a waitress in some former life, Leah slid her armload of plates onto the table without spilling a thing.

"Only this morning in shul," she said, "Sylvia Stryker herself told me I had a voice good enough for the Broadway stage."

The idea was so absurd that for a moment the rabbi made no reply. It was just like Sylvia Stryker to plant such an idea in his wife's always restless and fertile imagination. Was it any wonder that he had been having so much trouble lately with Rachel? The girl came by her rebellious attitude naturally, having learned it as a child at her mother's knee. Much in the same way that he had looked over the worn *Siddur* in shul, the rabbi critically surveyed his wife as though he was seeing her for the very first time.

Although they had now been married for nearly twenty years, the rabbi having prudently waited until he was almost thirty to take a wife, he still had not gotten used to her appearance. Not that Leah wasn't an attractive woman. In many ways she was now even more beautiful than when he had first met her during his term of service as rebbe of Shaare Zion in Williamsburg. It was only that for a rabbi's wife, Leah was too voluptuous. Even her name suggested a kind of ripeness that he himself had always found to be both unnecessary and a bit embarrassing.

Leah was slim in the waist, yet full breasted. She wore her long black hair pulled harshly away from her face into a narrow braid that hung down her back like the line on a carpenter's plumb bob. Her large brown eyes were penetrating, her nose straight, her hands, wrist, and throat unadorned with jewelry other than the plain gold wedding band that had once belonged to his mother. Only Leah's mouth, which was too wide, and her breasts, which had somehow weathered the onslaught of two hungry, nursing children to retain their proud outline, seemed out of place to the rabbi.

By all rights he should have married a Miriam, with thin, pale arms, a tight, *f crimpda* little mouth, and the knob ends of her bones always butting up against the plain cloth of her dull, sensible dresses. A nervous hummingbird of a woman that the entire congregation could have first pitied and then embraced as a true daughter of Israel. As it was, Leah had few friends among the Sisterhood, most of whom found her "aloof" and "hard to work with." Those were the exact words that Nat Weiss's wife, Ceil, had once used to describe Leah to the rabbi at a wedding reception where both the wine and music had flowed. He had never permitted himself to forget them, knowing that his future at the shul depended in large part on the opinions of such people.

Since then, Leah had added insult to injury by openly demonstrating her preference for the company of Ceil Weiss's sister-in-law, Sylvia Stryker, above that of all the other women in temple. Leah acted as though it was only natural for the rabbi's wife to move in such rarefied social circles. This both pleased and angered the rabbi at the same time.

It was of Sol Stryker's wife that Leah now began to speak, saying, "Simeon, you'll never guess what else Sylvia told me this morning." The rabbi held up his hand to cut short whatever gossip she was about to repeat. It was no business of his. Besides, talebearing was a sin. Leah ignored him completely, prattling on. "Nat was parading up and down in front of the women's section like a little rooster. You know the way he gets? With his chest all puffed up and his head held like so?"

Leah leaned her head to one side. Adopting a haughty expression, she transformed her features into an exact replica of Nat Weiss's face. The rabbi could not help laughing. There was no denying that Leah was an excellent mimic. Whenever Nat Weiss was the subject of her impersonations, he was forced to admit that he did enjoy watching her perform. "Looking all of us up and down as he walked, like so. . . ." Leah's eyes darted first this way, then that. "I *had* to laugh, Simeon. Not that he saw me," she added quickly. "Sylvia understood, immediately. 'Leah,' she said to me, 'isn't it hard to be a woman and keep a straight face when Nat is around? Believe me, dear, I know.' "

Unconsciously, Leah slipped naturally into a perfect imitation of the way Sylvia Stryker always stared sideways at a person when she talked to them, as if everyone in the entire world had been born to live beneath her feet. " 'He hasn't looked at me once in twenty years without completely undressing me with his eyes,' " Leah went on, quoting Sylvia. " 'When Sol and I still used to visit Nat and Ceil at home, I'd turn to Sol as soon as we got into the car and ask, 'Am I still naked, Sol? Because your brother-in-law didn't leave me with a single stitch on at the table. . . .' "

In spite of himself, the rabbi laughed out loud, far more amused by the story than he thought he was going to be when he first heard his wife use the word "undressed." His mother had never talked this way in front of her family. Now women spoke boldly not only to one another but to men as well. There was no denying the changes that were sweeping across America, the land of plenty. The land of plenty *tsouris*.

In nearly all of his feelings about the nation in which he had been born, Simeon Hakveldt was extreme. When he loved America, primarily for its tradition of religious tolerance and respect for civil liberties as expressed in the Bill of Rights, he did so with great zeal, expressing far more emotion than those who actually controlled the destiny of the land.

When he hated America, for its rapacious appetites, foolish blunders, and total lack of order, discipline, and direction, he did so with a ferocity that was medieval in nature, dating back to those *shtetl* rabbis who had railed and thundered in private against the civil authorities while speaking only of religion from the pulpits of their tiny shuls. In nearly every way Simeon Hakveldt was a first-generation American, not really at home here in the land of his birth, yet comfortable nowhere else but in this neighborhood where a rough mixture of English, Yiddish, and Hebrew was still understood perfectly by almost everyone with whom he came into contact.

So far, Rabbi Simeon Hakveldt had not been fortunate enough to visit the Promised Land, where he might enjoy the great *mitzvah* of praying before the last standing wall of the Temple. If Ahavath Mizrach's Board of Directors ever saw their way clear to send him, he surely would go. Until then, he was more than content to live in and criticize the United States of America, the land where no one with two nickels to rub together had ever gone hungry because of their religion.

"*Genug*, Leah," he said, in order to put a halt to her little show. "*Ich vil eppes essen.*"

Busily, Leah began setting out the food before him. The rabbi carefully studied her face as she did this. With a Miriam for a wife, he might well have spent the rest of his life in fourth-class *shlepper* shuls like Shaare Zion. Instead, he was now at Ahavath

113

Mizrach, a jewel of a temple, living rent free in this luxurious house while earning a bountiful salary of nearly twenty thousand dollars a year, not to mention the fees he collected on the side for officiating at weddings and funerals. All in all, he was doing well. It put virtually no strain on his finances for him to pay the rent each month on the spacious, three-room apartment in which his mother now lived in Brighton.

The life he shared with Leah pleased the rabbi. If only men would not always look twice at his wife when they first met her and then look once again at him, as though entirely reappraising their original opinion of him, he would have been completely happy. Years ago Nat Weiss had told him, "Without a beauty for a wife, Rebbe, who knows? We might well have hired someone else for the position, qualified though you were." The words had always stayed with him.

Putting all such thoughts from his mind, the rabbi lowered his nose to the bowl of carmine-colored borsht. He breathed in the rich smell that came from the beets themselves. Then he loudly smacked his lips. *"Zehrr geshmak,"* he said, drawing out the phrase. "Leah," he asked. "You'll also sit and eat?"

"I ate already, Simeon," she said. "With the children."

The rabbi nodded. To eat a meal all by himself, in peace, was a special pleasure in this house. He could put the time to good use by thinking some more about his Yom Kippur sermon. Reaching out for the slice of bread with which he began every meal, he carefully fingered the egg-rich *challah.*

"Challah?" the rabbi said scornfully, his face registering disapproval. *"Vo ist der frische* rye bread then?"

Only yesterday, well before sunset, he himself had brought home the small round rye with seeds, unsliced, twenty-seven cents for everyone else but given to him free of charge each Friday afternoon by the baker on the avenue who came regularly to shul each Shabbos. He had also stopped off in the market for the special pickled herring that he preferred above all others. Unfortunately, ham was also sold in that market, sometimes over the very same counter as the fish. But what else could he do? The taste of their herring was unbelievable. No other kind even came close.

"Der frische rye," Leah said levelly, looking right through him with those clear and penetrating eyes, "is *en der* kitchen. *Der villt es?"*

"Voo den?" the rabbi asked in a singsong manner, as if there could be no question about it.

Because it was Shabbos, Leah offered no argument. Instead, she turned around and went back into the kitchen to bring him what he had asked for. The rabbi heard the soft rustle of waxed paper as the bread was taken from its bag. Then he smelled its familiar thick and yeasty aroma, spiced with the tang of tiny, sour caraway seeds.

Even as a boy, Simeon Hakveldt had been mad about bread. On his way home from *yeshiva* each day, he had made it his business to cut through the rough cobblestone alley underneath the Williamsburg Bridge just so he could pass by the neighborhood's biggest bakery. Stopping before the patched screen door that led to the bakery's ovens, he would stand with his eyes closed as the traffic rumbled overhead, breathing in the incredibly rich and tantalizing aroma of hot, fresh bread.

Never once had he been able to just reach into his pocket for a pair of nickels, walk confidently through that door, toss both coins on the counter, and then plunge his hands wrist deep into the great wire rim baskets in which the rolls were dumped still steaming from the oven, one mound of seeded and one of seedless, searching and searching until he found the absolute hottest, freshest ones.

The rolls he had taken home to his mother had come instead from the big wooden bin out back. That bread was one day old, and stale. Harder than stone, it had already been handled and rejected by others. But it was free. To bring it home was a *mitzvah*. So his mother had told him, and so he had believed.

Still going strong at eighty, Rebeccah Hakveldt was even now a remarkable woman, living proof that he came from noble stock. In her, he constantly saw his own son. Daniel was a raw and precious diamond that could be sculpted into a million brilliant facets so long as the hand holding the blade was steady. Steadier than his father's hand, Simeon Hakveldt knew his own to be.

What he had made of himself would be nothing compared to what Daniel could achieve if he put his mind to it. With all the important people he had come to know as spiritual leader of Ahavath Mizrach, Sol Stryker foremost among them, there was no door that would be closed to Daniel, no goal that he could not reach.

Rachel was something else again. For months now, they had been at war with one another. Leah insisted that it was merely a

115

stage, one that all adolescents went through on their painful way to becoming adults. If so, it was a stage that he himself had never known. A good son, he had honored both his mother and father through all the years of his life, as the Torah commanded a man to do. All that he was today the rabbi owed to his mother. It was a debt he could never repay. His only hope was that somehow he could pass on what she had given to him to his children, provided that they were willing to accept it from him.

The rabbi looked up from his plate as Leah slid the rye bread he had brought home only yesterday onto the table. Reaching for it eagerly, he twisted a great hunk off the end with his fingers. Then he stuffed it hungrily into his mouth so that even before he began to eat, he was already choking on it a bit.

"Chew a *little*, Simeon," Leah pleaded, in the same tone of voice she used with the children whenever they did something wrong. "If only for me." Then she laughed, as she almost always did when he ate this way.

How could he even begin to explain to her how much he loved the taste of fresh bread? No meal could begin without it. He had never gotten enough as a boy growing up in Williamsburg. Now, even as a man, it still sometimes seemed to him that he would never get his fill, no matter how much of it he ate in his fine two-story brick house on the corner, within easy walking distance of the shul that unquestionably was his very own.

CHAPTER THIRTEEN

ALREADY IT WAS growing dark, the light failing so rapidly that the rabbi could no longer make out the fierce expression on the faces of the twin lions of Judah that pranced proudly across the top panel of the stained glass window above his head. Only a moment ago he had been able to see them both as plain as day. Now, they were gone, absorbed by the soft twilight of autumn in the city. Another Shabbos, and a great one as well, the Sabbath of repentance and return, was nearly over. Another week had disappeared down the drain of time, never to come again. Already it had been forgotten by nearly everyone.

The rabbi sighed. Leaning his shoulder against the wall, he surveyed the great room before him. As always, he was not at all pleased by what he saw. Traditionally, in Ahavath Mizrach, *Minchah* and then *Ma'ariv* on Shabbos were the most poorly attended services of the entire week, the *minyan* of ten adult males required before worship could begin in any Orthodox shul always in doubt.

Tonight they had made their quota, but only barely. Simeon Hakveldt himself had been forced to cross the street in order to enlist the services of a young boy who had just been bar mitzvahed. Since the boy lived so close to the shul, he had been unable to refuse the rabbi's heartfelt request that he come and make it possible for them to pray. What the boy might say when he was asked to come again next Shabbos was another problem altogether.

Most of those who had dragged themselves from their homes to return to synagogue after spending the entire morning there in prayer had done so only because they were charged with the solemn responsibility of saying *Kaddish* for a recently deceased parent. Although they grudgingly remained in shul for the entire service, the rabbi knew that this was only because that particular prayer happened to come at the very end.

Despite the fact that the *Kaddish* had only just begun, most of those standing scattered in ones and twos throughout the temple were already hopelessly lost, stumbling in total confusion over words they should have known by heart. Their voices were weak and pitiful, with none of the power and majesty that the rabbi associated with truly effective prayer. Not that Simeon Hakveldt blamed any of them for this. It was the *shamus* who had led them astray.

Standing all the way at the back of the shul with one hand on the edge of the bench before him for support, Mendel Bindel was off and running. From memory, without glancing down at any book, he was barreling through the prayer as though trying to set a new land speed record for the *Kaddish*. Words tumbled from the old man's mouth like boulders being swept down a mountainside by a roaring avalanche. As he neared the end, he seemed only to gather momentum, his rhythm growing even faster.

As the others *fumphered* and stuttered, trying desperately to keep pace, the *shamus* slammed through the last line. Loudly he belched "Or-*mayn*." He wiped his lips with the side of his hand,

117

as though he had only just polished off a particularly refreshing glass of beer. Then he sat back down, his business for the day concluded.

The rabbi shook his head in silent disapproval. Simply, this would never do. Was this Ahavath Mizrach or the Belmont racetrack? In order for any prayer to ascend properly to God's ears, it had to be said slowly, each and every word pronounced just as it had been written, sounded with both reverence and respect. This was the way in which the rabbi himself always prayed, in order to set an example for the others. To race madly through the *Kaddish* as the *shamus* had just done simply was not proper.

Rabbi Simeon Hakveldt realized that he had overlooked this sorry state of affairs for far too long. The time had come for him to explain to the *shamus* in his most kindly tone of voice that here in America, there was time. No soldiers waited outside the front doors of the temple to massacre the congregants as they walked back home at night, thank God. The old man did not have to rush.

As soon as *Ma'ariv* was over, Rabbi Simeon Hakveldt walked slowly all the way to the very back of the shul to speak to the old man. Mendel Bindel stood in front of the door, talking to Solomon, the *shvartze* janitor. What the two of them had to discuss the rabbi could not imagine. The results of the Belmont *Kaddish* perhaps, with the names of those who had finished in the money to be posted on the temple's back wall in the morning.

Patiently, Simeon Hakveldt waited for their conversation to end. As though the old man already knew what was on the rabbi's mind, he quickly went out through the door into the night before the rabbi could intercept him. So be it, Simeon Hakveldt thought to himself. What he had to say to the *shamus* could wait until tomorrow. Turning around, he walked back the way he had come.

It was now Solomon's duty to lock all of the temple's doors, an absolute necessity in these days of increased lawlessness against shuls even in the richest suburbs out on Long Island. If he hurried, the rabbi realized that he might be able to get home in time to put his son, Daniel, to bed. This would be a rare pleasure indeed. Making his way through the side door, he went out into the street.

Simeon Hakveldt was both shocked and dismayed to see a long line of men standing before him on the sidewalk. Many held little bags in their hands, as though awaiting transportation to some distant work camp. For *Minchah* and *Ma'ariv*, he himself had been forced to go looking for a *minyan*. Yet to use the little annex behind the shul now that Shabbos was over, men were more than willing to stand in line. Like so many other facets of life in Ahavath Mizrach, this too was Nat Weiss's doing.

Nat himself had personally spearheaded the fund-raising drive to convert the unused annex into a modern gymnasium complete with steam bath, lockers, and a shiny four wall handball court. Nat had claimed that a gym would serve to bring the younger men of the community back to the temple and the Finance Committee had believed him. So far, it had brought them only to the gym.

Had it not been for the annual one hundred dollar surcharge that these men paid in addition to their regular temple membership dues, the rabbi would have long since appealed to the Finance Committee to shut the annex down. Ahavath Mizrach was a synagogue, a house of God, and not a health spa. Sadly, the shul needed every last cent of revenue that Nat Weiss's driven mind could generate. For reasons the rabbi had never been able to understand, at the end of every year the shul always finished in the red.

It occurred to the rabbi that he should say something to these men. A few well-chosen words might serve to stir their consciences, bringing them back *inside* the shul, where they were needed and where they rightfully belonged. Looking over the line carefully, the rabbi realized to his horror that he did not even know most of these men. Whether they would actually listen to what he had to say, he could not tell.

Clearly the situation demanded more than a few casual words spoken in the street at twilight. He would have to take the matter up with Sol himself when the Strykers came to dine at his house. Right now it seemed far more important that he get home and put his son to bed. Nodding perfunctorily in the general direction of the line, the rabbi began walking quickly away.

From the very front of the line, Morty Bindel turned to watch the rabbi go. Pursing his thin lips, he reached with his finger behind the lenses of his old fashioned metal-frame glasses to flick an imaginary speck of dirt from his eye. Even if the rabbi *had* nodded to him, Morty was damned if he would say hello to the bastard. He had far better things to do with his time.

Although it was still early autumn, Morty was already wearing

119

the outfit that would take him through the winter. His soft battered felt hat was pulled low over his eyes. Beneath his orange nylon ski parka lined with kapok, he had on a yellow, Perry Como–style cardigan on which a printed pattern ran in an elongated loop around the neck and then down along the buttonholes in front. Made of some brand-new miracle fiber, the sweater was guaranteed never to shred, pill, unravel, or wear out.

Although the sweater did sometimes cause sudden bursts of static electricity to leap from the tips of his fingers, Morty would wear it day in and day out from now until June. Purchased during a midsummer clearance sale at the discount outlet down at the far end of the avenue some three years ago, with but a single hole in the sleeve, the garment had been an unforgettable bargain at four dollars and fifty cents. Whenever Morty put the sweater on, the memory of what he had paid for it made him warm all over.

Checking to make certain that the rabbi was definitely out of earshot, Morty turned to Mo Tannenbaum. "Also a rabbi, huh, Mo?" he said softly, not really expecting an answer. "Nat Weiss's ass he kisses like it was sugar candy. My father he doesn't have a good word for, *ever*. Lives in a better house than you or me without paying rent, buys herring where they sell ham . . . only in America, huh, Mo?"

Mo Tannenbaum grunted. It made no difference at all to him what kind of man the rabbi truly was. In less than eighteen months, Mo would be retiring from his clerk's job at the post office on half pension. Then he would move to Florida and take up residence in one of those massive condos outside Hollywood Beach. Mo was a lucky stiff all right. His wife, Bea, had worked for years in a knitting store on the avenue, saving every penny so that Mo could afford to retire early. Morty Bindel's wife had handed him divorce papers only two months after Paulie had been bar mitzvahed. Morty Bindel would still be selling postcards behind the counter in Avenue Station when he was seventy.

Morty himself had actually been to Florida once, with Paulie and Esther, in the month of August, years ago. The trip had been a disaster that he had never forgotten. Esther had blamed him for everything. The strange food. The hard motel beds. The swarming bugs. The killing heat that had come off the narrow black tar roads in endless shimmering waves.

Wherever they had looked, ancient washing machines from Sears and Roebuck were standing on the front porches of rotting wooden shacks. The *shvartzes* who lived in those shacks had swayed silently back and forth in cracked bamboo rocking chairs. Most of all, Esther had complained about the poverty. So much poverty, and right by the road as well. It was depressing.

But then she had not sat up for nights on end beforehand, carefully planning their route with maps spread out all over the living room floor. That was the part that Morty had enjoyed the most. To him there was something truly wonderful about a map. Like the Talmud itself, a map could tell you everything you needed to know while being completely unintelligible all at the very same time.

Fayetteville. Sumter. Myrtle Beach. Okeechobee. The place names themselves had captured Morty's imagination, making him feel, even as he sat in his very own living room, that he would be the very first white man ever to journey through the region. The very first Jew from the neighborhood to do so, he might well have been. For what Morty had not bothered to ask anyone was why those with money went to Miami Beach only in the winter. In August Morty Bindel got his two weeks of annual vacation. So it was in August that they had gone.

Although Esther had made him miserable, the trip had been without incident until the ancient car that he still drove to this day had blown a tire on a deserted stretch of two-lane road in the middle of nowhere. Wrestling with the wheel, Morty had somehow managed to bring the car to a sliding stop on the gravel by the side of the road, saving all their lives. Even as he got out of the car to change the flat, Esther was already letting him have it with both barrels, going on and on about how Triple-A hadn't been good enough for him. No, Morty Bindel alone had to map out his *own* route to Miami Beach, using the straight ruler and compass that he had bought for his son to take to school.

Without answering her, Morty had managed to get the punctured tire off the wheel, brutally cutting both of his hands in the process on the metal rim that burned like a fire from the sun. All the while, the old car had swayed dangerously above his head so that he could only pray that the rusty jack would hold. Red-faced from exertion, feeling as though he might yet faint from the heat, Morty had opened the trunk to find their only spare just as flat.

Leaving Esther behind to guard the car and all of their precious belongings, he and his son had set off, rolling the tire with their hands along the very edge of the road in the pitiless heat. High noon in the deep South. The blazing sun beating down oppressively on his head. A million mosquitoes whining in his ears.

Beside him, his young son had walked in silence, somehow trusting that his father would get them both out of this godforsaken place in one piece.

"See that?" he had asked the boy, pointing to a scummy little pond of water without a name on which thick green crud had dried like the icing on a cake no one would ever eat. "This is *real* country, Paulie. No-man's-land. Not like Prospect Park."

The boy had nodded and smiled without speaking. Without having to ask, Morty had known that the kid was dying of thirst but unwilling to say so. Poor Paulie. As a child, he had suffered horribly from every last allergy known to medical science. Yet he had never complained. When it came to pain, the kid was just like his grandfather. A regular soldier.

After walking for what had seemed like miles, they had come to a tiny wooden shack half hidden in a patch of skinny, crooked pines. A single battered red gas pump had stood in front of a faded red-and-white Coca-Cola sign ventilated with what had looked like bullet holes. To himself, Morty had thought, "If the guy who owns this place depends on the tourist trade for a living, he starved to death years ago." He had not said a word to his son, not wanting to scare the boy any more than Esther already had by ranting and raving about the night riders and Ku Klux Klan *meshuggeners* she claimed were lying in wait for them behind every bush.

Rolling the tire into the cool darkness of the shack, Morty had looked up to see pure blue sky overhead. The roof itself was so full of holes that he had wondered whether someone had dropped a bomb on the place. Everywhere, blocking his path no matter which way he turned, there were swaybacked tables groaning under the weight of worn jacks, stripped wrenches, nuts, bolts, and bits of greasy metal so twisted that they no longer even had names.

At the very back of the shack, an aging *shvartze* with steel gray hair stood in a pair of faded blue coveralls. Morty had been tempted to tell the guy, "Mister. Nobody told you? Lincoln *freed* the slaves." Instead he had kept his mouth shut, silently offering him the shredded tire instead. Here he was, stranded in the middle of the wilderness, in desperate need of help. The *shvartze* could charge him an arm and a leg and he would have to pay. What else could he do? Call the local Better Business Bureau to complain?

Without speaking, the *shvartze* had run the tips of his broad fingers over the worn tread like a blind man reading Braille. His hands were smooth and very fine, like a doctor's. Even though it had to be over a hundred degrees inside the shack, the *shvartze* was not even sweating. He had long since learned how to live with such heat. Slowly the *shvartze* had licked his lips, his tongue very pink against his dark and pebbled skin.

"*Mmm*," he had said, finally lapsing into speech. "Fifty-fahv Plymouth, ain't it? Raht front wheel?" Morty had nodded, not knowing what to say. The man was right on every count.

For seventy-five cents, the *shvartze* had patched the tire on the spot, silently handing Paulie a grape soda, some strange brand that Morty himself had never seen before. He had let the kid drink it right down without saying a word. If Paulie had gotten sick from it, he would have made up some kind of story to tell Esther. Anything to avoid offending the squat little man on whom his life depended.

Even after all these years, Morty still had not forgotten the incident. Last night, when his son had come home unexpectedly from Cambridge, ringing his doorbell only hours before he himself had to get up to go to work, Morty had sat Paulie down in the living room to *shmooze* for a while. Nothing serious, just how are you and what are you doing. Running out of things to say, Morty had leaned back in his chair and asked, "Remember that *shvartze* in Carolina, Paulie? Never even *asked* what kind of car the tire had come off. Took one look at it and *knew*. Probably never been any further in his whole life from that shack than to the outhouse across the road. But . . . *tires*." A roll of the eyes. A wave of the hand. "Forget it. He could tell you everything. A *mayven*."

Paulie had not answered him. The look on his face had said it all. The kid just did not like it when he talked about *shvartzes*. Morty himself knew that he was not prejudiced. In Avenue Station, he worked side by side with men of every race, creed, and religion. Most of them were not worth the time it took to talk to them. Still, he treated them all just the way they treated him, regardless of their color. Paulie, however, was a little crazy on the subject. Rather than continue the conversation, Morty had gone back to bed instead, reading until the alarm clock went off, telling him that it was once again time for him to get dressed for work.

Turning to Mo Tannenbaum now, Morty kicked the front tire of the car that they were both leaning against. "Mo," he said, "I

123

ever tell you about the *shvartze* who fixed my tire for me that time down in Carolina?"

"You told me, Morty," Mo replied in a tired voice. "More than once."

"Right," Morty said quickly. "Then you don't need to hear about it again."

"How's the TV, Morty?" Mo asked, using a toothpick to remove from between his teeth what was left of the fine dinner that Bea had made him. Morty himself had eaten alone tonight, out of a can.

"Hah?" Morty asked, distracted for the moment by someone walking on the other side of the street who in profile looked faintly like his son.

"The TV you bought after comparison-shopping everyone on the avenue into the ground, Morty. The one they were *begging* you to buy."

"Fine," Morty said enthusiastically. "Wonderful. Works like a charm. Excellent make. A Zenith," he added, just in case Mo had forgotten the brand that Morty had finally decided was superior to all the rest.

"You changed the channel yet, Morty?" Mo asked with a knowing grin, throwing the toothpick into the street.

"Laugh, Mo," Morty said, as his friend proceeded to do just that. "But for your information, that happens to be the proper way to break in a set. You leave it on only one channel."

"For six weeks, Morty?"

"Even longer if you have to. It softens the tube," Morty told him. "You get twenty percent longer life *and* better brightness. The resolution, of course, is unbelievable."

"What channel?" Mo interrupted.

"I beg your pardon?"

"What channel did you leave it on for six weeks, Morty?"

"Nine," Morty said. "What else? *Million Dollar Movie* and all the sports. Who needs to watch anything else? They even got their own news people. *Tremendous* local coverage. If you ask me, the best."

"If you ask me, Morty," Mo said. "Your *head* is getting a little soft, not the picture tube."

Morty was about to answer Mo when a sudden shaft of light fell across his friend's face. Morty looked in the direction from which the light had come. The annex door was now wide open. Solomon, the *shvartze* janitor, stood in front of the door with a confused expression on his face, a pencil in one hand and a clipboard in the other.

"So who are you going to be tonight, Morty," Mo asked, picking up his bag, "when Solomon asks for your name?"

"Nat Weiss," Morty said bitterly, picking up his own bag with one hand while grabbing for Mo's arm with the other so that the two of them would not be separated in the crush of men pressing towards the annex door. "And if that don't work, I'll tell him I'm your guest for the night. You think he'll argue? The way he takes care of my father?"

Morty Bindel himself did not play handball. Instead, he came to the annex each Saturday night to take some steam, believing it to be good for his lungs. All his life, he had been troubled by sudden shortnesses of breath that would come upon him without warning, forcing him to sit right down no matter where he happened to be at the moment. It was nothing serious. That he knew for certain. Lately, he had become convinced that he was slowly being poisoned by all the shit floating around in the city's air. Bus fumes, the smell of garbage waiting to be picked up, and the stink from sewers that were blocked up on the avenue all worked their way into his body during the week. The only way he could get it back out of his system again was to sit with his head slumped forward in the *shvitz*, breathing in hot steam through his mouth.

Nat Weiss did the exact same thing each Saturday night. The only difference was that Nat had the power and the connections to get the shul to build him a place in which to do it. In Morty's opinion, Nat was an unlearned man. He had never read history, as Morty did each night to put himself to sleep. Despite this, Morty Bindel was expected to pay an extra one hundred dollars a year for the privilege of sitting next to Nat in the steam room.

So far, Morty had not paid them one red cent. Why should he? He did not play handball. He only came to the annex once a week, taking up but a single place on one of the wooden benches in the steam room. With all that his father and ex-wife had done for the shul, the least they could do was let him in for free. If they really wanted his hard-earned money so badly, let them bill him for it. Esther herself would address the envelope, if she still remembered where he lived.

After Morty had taken off his clothes in the locker room, shoving them into his little bag for safekeeping because he had not been issued a locker of his own, he pushed open the double thick steam room door. The little room was gloomy with humid heat, safe, warm, and wet. After a good long *shvitz*, he would feel like a new man again, ready and able to put up with another week of nonsense in the post office.

"Close the door, willya?" someone shouted at him in a harsh voice from atop the bench to his left. "You're lettin' out all the best steam."

Morty looked around, waiting for his eyes to adjust so that he could identify who had shouted at him. "You paying for it by the pound?" he asked softly. Already he could feel the scalding hot vapors going up his nose and into his throat, burning out the poisons.

"Jesus H. Christ, Morty," someone else complained. "Take your time about it, why don't you?"

"Jesus is not here tonight," Morty replied with great dignity, as the door slammed shut behind him. "Unless that was him out on the handball court and I missed him."

No one said a thing. Morty slowly began making his way up the benches past the pale, sweating bodies toward his favorite seat in the far corner. Where the wall and the ceiling came together, there was a spot that was a natural heat trap. Here the steam was most intense, collecting in billowing clouds. Sitting down, Morty looked up over his head. A small puddle of super-heated water hung from the ceiling as though it had no intention of ever falling to the floor below.

Sighing with pleasure, Morty stuck out his right leg straight in front of him. Leaning over, he slowly began kneading the big, knotted muscle in his thigh with both of his hands. The sweat was really starting to pour off him now, running in little rivers down his face, then cascading in a steady waterfall from his chin to his chest. It had been just this hot that day in Carolina when he and Paulie had walked for miles to get that tire fixed. On old bones, such heat felt good.

Morty looked across the room at Mo, who was sitting with his eyes closed and his fat, pleated stomach hanging down between his knees, slowly breathing in steam through his mouth. Following Mo's lead, Morty put both of his forefingers to his nostrils, pinching them tightly shut. Then he tilted his head forward, holding in the air until he thought he would faint. When he could stand it no longer, he inhaled deeply through his mouth. The steam hit him in a whirling rush all the way down in his lungs. Immediately he began coughing and spitting. With interest, he

126

watched it all run out through the cracks in the boards between his feet.

When he looked back up again, Morty saw that Marvin was sitting no more than two feet away from him. To Meshuggener Marvin, he did not have to say hello. How Marvin actually managed to drag himself here at night, Morty could not imagine. The poor kid was a case all right. He belonged in an institution, not out on the street. But all the institutions were full. So Marvin walked around like a normal person, driving everyone else crazy.

No one at Ahavath Mizrach knew who Marvin's parents were or if he even had any. No one knew where he lived or how he lived. One Shabbos he had just appeared at services. No one had turned him away so he had just kept right on coming. Now he was a regular.

On Yom Kippur, Morty knew, Marvin would be at the very back of the shul, *clupping* himself madly in the chest as he bobbed up and down in his filthy white sneakers. For an idiot Marvin was very religious. More than anything else, Morty pitied the kid. Marvin had just never had a chance in this world. He had been born damaged.

"Marvin," Mo called out, starting up with him to pass the time. "You're sweating? How come?"

"*Hot*," Marvin said, his oversized head swaying from side to side on his spindly neck. One of Marvin's eyes did not quite match the other. No matter how he looked at you, he still seemed to be staring at a point somewhere above your head.

"By you it's hot?" Mo said, stringing him along. "Not so hot by me. . . ."

"*Sweating*," Marvin said, wiping the perspiration off the dead white, pimpled skin around his nose with the tips of his crooked fingers. Even from where he was sitting, Morty could smell Marvin. The stink coming off his body was awful, a dank, rotten odor like the stench from a mound of fish left for too long in the sun. "Like a pig," Marvin added, trying to be helpful.

"*Mo*," Morty cautioned, trying to stop what he knew was coming. "Leave him alone, huh?"

"It's all right, Morty," Marvin said, giving Morty that sickly grin that never failed to make chills run up and down his spine. Marvin thought he was just like everyone else. Normal. "I like Mo. I like to talk with him."

"Not a pig," Mo said, ignoring Morty's plea. "In shul, you can't sweat like a pig.

127

"And why not, Mo?" Marvin asked.

"It's not kosher."

A few of the men sitting on the benches laughed. They had heard it all before, yet to them it was still funny. You never knew what might come out of Marvin's mouth. "Is that so?" Marvin asked, astonished. "You know something, Mo? You're right. I'm sweating like a . . . *fish.*" Marvin looked around. Then he laughed out loud at his own little joke.

"A small salted fish," someone called out from across the steam room.

"Seriously, Marvin, tell me," Mo demanded, "what do you eat? I mean, at home. . . ."

"An egg," Marvin said simply.

"That's it?" Mo said in disbelief. "Just an egg?"

"An egg," Marvin repeated.

"From an egg you got a gut like that, Marvin?" Mo laughed. "I don't believe it."

"I got," Marvin said, obviously delighted to be the center of attention.

"Maybe he's pregnant," someone called out.

Marvin stared down at his bulging white stomach in alarm. He poked at his flesh. Very earnestly, he leaned over with one hand cupped behind his ear, as though listening for a heartbeat. Laughter rang through the steam room.

"You're fine, Marvin," Morty reassured him. "Just fine. Don't worry about it. You sonsabitches," he said, addressing the steam room at large, "ought to know better than to put things into his head."

"Why not?" someone demanded. "It's empty, ain't it?"

"Excuse us," someone else said. "We got Doctor Spock with us here tonight. The expert on child care. . . ."

"So how's *your* kid doing, Morty?" Mo asked softly. "Still looking for work?"

Just then, the door to the steam room swung open. Morty waited for the usual chorus of abusive comments to begin. Instead, there was only silence. Framed in the doorway stood Nat Weiss, president of Ahavath Mizrach. A short, stocky man, Nat somehow always seemed bigger than he really was. A large six-pointed Star of David made of platinum lay nestled in the tangled white hair on his thick barrel chest, dangling from a chain of fine white gold. Next to the thick gold wedding band on the third finger of Nat's left hand, a gigantic diamond ring, the stone cut into the shape of a teardrop, covered his entire pinky. Unlike the other men. Nat had not bothered to cover himself with a towel. Instead, he stood in the doorway naked, his big, thick purple *shvantz* hanging in plain sight for everyone to admire. The man was definitely an animal. An animal with money.

"*Nat,*" Mo Tannenbaum called out eagerly, scooting over on the bench. "Room for you right here."

Magnanimously, Nat waved his hand in the air, settling down instead next to Marvin. "Moish," Nat said, looking up at Mo Tannenbaum, "remember that pocket tape recorder I told you I was going to buy for my daughter Steffi? The one with the *voice?* Sings like an angel."

"I remember, Nat. You told me," Mo said, leaning forward.

"You can't believe how small they make those things these days. I could have brought it in here with me and you wouldn't see it. . . ."

"And where would you hide it, Nat?" Morty called out. "Under your equipment?"

Nat Weiss jerked his head around, searching for the man who had said this to him. Unable to pick Morty out in the steamy gloom, he went right on talking. "She wants it to record herself singing along with some of her albums. So I got her one. . . ."

"Jap?" Mo Tannenbaum asked innocently, just to keep the conversation going.

"What *Jap?*" Nat demanded in an outraged tone of voice. "I don't buy Jap, Moish. *Ever.* I got a guy on Fourteenth Street gets me everything I need *American.* TV, tape player, radio, you name it. So guess what I paid for the recorder. . . ."

"Sixty bucks?" Mo Tannenbaum ventured, unwilling to offend Nat any more than he already had.

"*With* cue and review," Nat said proudly. "Built-in condenser mike picks up sound from across the room. Works on current *or* batteries."

"You paid sixty bucks, right, Nat?" someone called out.

"Got a little needle that shows you when the batteries are weak," Nat continued. "Carrying case and three sixty-minute cassettes thrown in free of charge. Guess how much?"

"Sixty bucks, Nat," Morty said suddenly, his voice booming through the little steam room. "They're market priced. You get the same discount no matter where you buy."

Nat looked up into the far corner. "Morty," he said, his face lighting up with pleasure, "I shoulda known it was you up there

129

in the peanut gallery. Still ridin' free yet makin' more noise than anyone, huh?'' Clearing his throat, Nat announced, "Seventy-two fifty. *Without* tax.''

Mo Tannenbaum whistled softly in appreciation. "Very next day—" Nat said, wiping a thick finger across his forehead so that a single drop of water rolled to the very tip of his manicured fingernail. For a moment, it hung there, glistening like a diamond-shaped tear. Then Nat flicked it contemptuously to the ground. ''—Saw it in Gimbel's for ten bucks more.

"You shoulda given me a call, Nat," Morty said softly. "I could have gotten you top of the line. Panasonic. A guy in the station sells them on the side."

"What kinda stuff, Morty?" Nat demanded. "Damaged goods? Fell off the back of some truck in Jersey?"

"All I know is what they cost," Morty said simply. "Sixty bucks. No more, no less."

"*Sixty*, huh?" Nat said, considering the figure as though he had only just heard it for the very first time. "And who did you say makes them?"

"Panasonic," Morty repeated.

"Right. That's what I thought you said." Nat smiled. "They put out a pretty good product for a couple years, Morty. Then there was a buy-out. Now, they're *Jap*."

Morty Bindel's face collapsed. "You got it all wrong, Nat," he protested. "You're thinking Sony. Panasonic is . . ."

Before Morty could complete the sentence, Nat Weiss was on his feet. "Moish," he said looking right at Mo Tannenbaum. "Little *schnapps* before you head home? Just a quickie? I got a bottle in my office."

Honored at having been selected for this great privilege, Mo Tannenbaum scrambled quickly to his feet. All across the steam room, men began standing, groaning as they wrapped towels around themselves. Saturday night was suddenly over, the long haul towards next weekend having already begun.

Within seconds, only Morty and Meshuggener Marvin were still sitting where they had been, Marvin with his eyes shut and his head back, apparently asleep. As Nat Weiss moved towards the door, Morty suddenly got to his feet. Desperately, he lunged for Nat Weiss's arm. "*Nat,*" Morty called out, "my kid is home. I tell you that?"

"The one that lives out of town?" Nat asked, stopping in the middle of the steam room.

"That's the one," Morty replied.

"What brings him back?"

"He came to sit with my father in shul on Yom Kippur," Morty said, making it up as he went along.

Nat Weiss nodded in approval. "Your father," he said, as though it was his own family he was now discussing, "is a *prince*. Few more like him and this shul wouldn't have any problems. He *always* pays his own way."

Morty grinned, beaming with pride. "My kid is just like him, Nat. They're two of a kind. I want you to meet him. He only just got home. Did I tell you that?"

"You told me, Morty," Nat said, his voice suddenly very cold. "What do you want me to do about it? Organize a parade down the avenue for the both of you? Do everyone a big favor and pay the surcharge, huh, Morty? Otherwise, I can't let you in here no more. It just isn't fair to the others." Then Nat swept out of the steam room, leaving the door wide open so that all those trailing in his wake could follow.

Feeling suddenly very tired, Morty leaned his forehead against the hot, damp wall by his side. Closing his eyes, he breathed in deeply through his mouth. They were all alike. Nat, the rabbi, Sol Stryker, and the rest of the big shots who ran the temple. The power was in their hands and they were squeezing it so tightly that an ordinary man never stood a chance.

From somewhere down below, Morty heard someone stirring. Then a damp hand touched his knee. Opening his eyes, Morty saw Meshuggener Marvin standing before him with just a moth-eaten towel clinging to his bulging, soft white belly. Marvin looked for all the world like a little kid who had lost his way back home from school.

"Morty," Marvin said, his voice very small in the deserted steam room. "You're sweating? How come?" Then he grinned, sending chills up and down Morty's spine.

YOM
KIPPUR

CHAPTER FOURTEEN

GATHERED BEFORE ME tonight in a single room are all the faces. Craggy ones made of ancient stone, sharply hewn by wind and time, with bent noses and fixed, rigid grins. Weatherbeaten ones tanned the color of old, dry oak, framed by shaggy white sideburns that cling like moss to sculpted cheekbones. Surely I must have seen such faces on the narrow, cobbled streets of Cambridge. But I never noticed. I was too busy running away from myself while worrying about the extremely weird Chinese pre-engineering students by the river. I have actually forgotten what *we* look like, in a group.

The faces smile, gold teeth flashing. The arms move forward, hands offered for the shaking. Blue gabardine suits say hello to natty houndstooth jackets. Tightly buttoned vests with expensive silk ties knotted into a double Windsor, a healthy and happy New Year *and* an easy fast. Under the big crystal chandeliers, the yarmulkas revolve in celestial orbits. They are beaded and blue, plain white, smooth velvet black, and hot, shocking pink.

I can hardly believe that there are still so many faces left. In the neighborhood, on *Kol Nidre* night, they have all turned out once more to proclaim that the Lord is One. In some places, the religion may be dying. Back here, it is not yet dead. The old ways live on.

Sweet perfume drifts into my nose from the women's section. The smell is tinged with the high, piercing odor of camphor. Only hours ago, all the finely knitted woolen suits were still hanging in the bedroom closet, keeping the mothballs company. As were the shawls, the stoles, and the hats with feathers on them that tilt upward at a rakish angle. Now, they are all assembled here.

Soon, the cantor will approach the Ark. Softly, he will beg God to forgive the congregation for all the vows they may make to Him in the coming year and then fail to carry out. I wish him all the luck in the world.

A crowd of latecomers rushing through the doors carries me forward into the shul itself. Despite the heat in the room, I feel cold all over. Automatically, I look towards the far corner where my grandfather always sits on a chair that he drags in by himself from the Talmud Torah next door. Although I have been home for days, I have not yet seen him. Why, I do not know. Other things just seemed to keep getting in the way.

His chair is there but he is not around. Then the door to the closet behind the chair opens. Out he comes. The *shamus* of Ahavath Mizrach. No two ways about it. The original is still the greatest.

Tonight, my grandfather looks even smaller and lighter than I remember him. By March, the month that comes in like a lion and goes out the very same way in the city, any sudden gust of rain-soaked wind will be more than enough to carry him away. Like some human kite, he will be borne off into the sky.

Over his long white linen robe, my grandfather wears his old heavy wool *tallis*. It is the one that he will be buried in, as Orthodox custom decrees. Once the *tallis* was white. Now it is yellow. A cracked painter's yellow that is the precise color of tired cheese. Draped across his thin shoulders, it falls in long cylindrical folds down his back like a pair of wings that he will soon unfurl. Whenever he raises his arms, the thick black bars of color that run across the shawl first flutter and then converge.

With his thumb and forefinger, he twirls the tiny white hairs that sprout in his nostrils. A steady stream of people come up to greet him, shaking his hand and wishing him an easy fast. His clear blue eyes sparkle against his pale white skin. His face shines like the sun. My grandfather looks good. This shul is where he really lives. Tonight, he is completely at home.

I edge past the people who will spend the entire night shifting from foot to foot against the back wall. Already, I am nervous. I cannot be certain that my grandfather will even know me. Not that his memory is bad, or anything. It is just that whenever he puts on that long white linen robe and that old heavy wool *tallis*, he becomes someone else entirely. Mendel Bindel, *kohen*. I should have made it my business to see him earlier in the week.

"*Gudt Yomtov*," I say, putting my hand out to him like all the others have done.

"*Gudten Yomtov*," he answers, adding, "*andt a gudten yure.*"

Then he blinks his eyes and starts to smile. He knows who I am all right. To him, it makes perfect sense that I am here tonight. Where else would I be?

"*Du hust gegessen?*" he asks. As always, with him business comes first.

"I ate, yeah. With Mom at home. After you left for shul."

"*Andt* Morty?"

I shake my head. Without the old man at the head of the table, staring vacantly into space as my mother piled food in front of him, the meal was just not the same. After letting her really load up his plate, he would always look down at the food and then at her and ask, "Esther? You're sure you made enough? I mean, you're positive? The whole Russian Army *is* coming to sit down with us tonight, no? If not, I can always take the leftovers to shul with me tomorrow for lunch."

When it came to Yom Kippur, he could really be a scream, the old man. Something about the day would just set him off early. Sooner or later, he would always say something that got to my mother. An actual, screaming fight would break out over the dinner plates. Shouts and curses and tears on *Kol Nidre* night, my mother getting so completely rattled that she would forget to bring in some dish that she had spent half the day slaving over in the kitchen.

Tonight, though, it was dead quiet in the house. Just the wallpaper, my mother, and me. The two of us sat at the table trying to think of something to say to each other. It was then I knew for sure how definitely great it felt to be back home again.

"Morty's in the apartment," I say, watching my grandfather's face to see how he will take the news.

"*Er kommt du fir Kol Nidre?*" my grandfather asks.

"I don't think so," I say, knowing that at the moment the old man is sitting in the living room in his skivvies, trying to decide whether or not to turn on the television. "But he is coming tomorrow for *Yizkor*. Also, he said I should wish you *Gudt Yomtov*."

He did not say exactly that. But then my grandfather does not have to know. The old man has been strangely silent about Yom Kippur this year. For all I know, he is boycotting the entire event. Whether he is even going to fast, I cannot say. Most years, he limps along until about four in the afternoon. Over and over, he tells everyone how it is absolutely killing him not to eat. Then he goes up to the apartment and puts on a pot of coffee.

The smell drives everyone who lives in his building and is fasting completely crazy. The way he figures it, as soon as the sun goes down behind the bank on the other side of the avenue and he cannot see it any more, the day is over. The old man has what you might call his very own private version of the Hebrew religion. I think he makes it up as he goes along.

How someone as completely Orthodox as my grandfather could have raised a son like Morty, I will never understand. Maybe the feeling just skips a generation. *"Du bist here,"* he says. *"S'genug."* Then he takes my arm just above the elbow and turns me in a circle. He begins introducing me to the men who always sit near him on the High Holy Days. I shake hands with Murray Friedberg and then Sidney Meyers. I first met both of them years and years ago. But they do not remember. They are too aggravated.

"The calendar board outside says, *'Kol Nidre,* six forty-five, sharp,' " Murray notes bitterly, twisting his head around so that he can talk to my grandfather and look at the clock on the back wall all at the very same time. "Already it's five past seven. This is 'sharp' by them?"

"Murray, please," Sidney Meyers counsels. "Keep your trousers on. They start this late, there's no way they can make an appeal tonight. Am I right, Mendel?"

As always, my grandfather is the final authority on all such matters. Before he can speak, Murray snorts loudly through his nose. "This rebbe should miss an opportunity to *shnorr* money?" he asks. "On a night like this? Go *on.* Never happen."

"They'll call names?" Sidney asks, obviously terrified by the prospect. "Or cards?"

"Carten," my grandfather says, stating a fact. Reaching into his worn, blackened *Mahzor,* he pulls out a card that my mother probably ran off on the addressograph machine in her office. I take the blue-and-white card from his hand. Across the top runs a row of tiny tabs. Each tab has a dollar amount printed on it, ranging from eighteen, or *chai,* to fifteen hundred, for big givers only. Since no Orthodox Jew is permitted to write or to even tear paper on Yom Kippur, some fund-raising genius has devised this foolproof method. Merely by folding down a tab, people can give, even on the holiest day of the year.

I turn the card over. On the back, there is a psalm that David Ben-Gurion, former prime minister of Israel, is said to have read at the dedication of the monument in the national martyr's forest in the Promised Land. Below the psalm, in parentheses, it says, "This is to be treated like a prayer and not discarded."

Even if I do not fold down a tab and make a donation, I cannot throw the card away. Instead, I have to walk around with it stuck inside my pocket all night long as the guilt mushrooms like a malignant tumor inside my heart because I have not given, I have not contributed, I have not done my part to make *Eretz Yisroel* strong for the coming year.

"They'll still call names," Murray Friedberg says. Obviously, a man who has seen it all before. He *knows*. "Mark my words. Sol Stryker and Nat Weiss's gifts, they'll announce more than once, as a *spur*."

Sidney Meyers looks as though he is about to faint. No doubt, he has no intention of giving all that he can afford. Now, everyone will know. They will announce his measly little donation in front of the entire congregation, in the presence of the holy Torahs no less, and his name will be immediately stricken from the Book of Life. Unless, of course, he somehow manages to come up with an extra twenty-five or so at the very last moment. Religion was invented to comfort people in just such situations.

Swallowing hard, Sidney says, "Still, we'll be out by nine. No. Mendel?"

"And ten is no good by you, Sidney?" my grandfather asks quietly, smiling.

"*Ten?*" Murray says, his big frying pan of a jaw dropping open in utter astonishment. "At Beth-El, where my brother-in-law has a seat, they're out by *nine* every year. Like clockwork."

"Murray," my grandfather says gently, as though he is talking to a child, "Beth-El is Reform."

"So?" Murray demands, unable to let the matter rest. "It's not the same God?" Without waiting for an answer, he keeps right on going. "We finish later. The seats here are twice the price. They make an appeal tonight *and* tomorrow and . . . the bottom line is . . . who knows if it even does any good?"

My grandfather clears his throat. It is a small, dry sound, like a baby's rattle rolling around in a crib but with much more authority. "Murray," he says. "It does good. Believe me. It does."

Then he looks towards the back doors. A broad smile creases his face, "*Gib a kuk*," he says, poking me in the ribs with a finger. "Here *kommt* Marvin."

139

Making his way slowly along the back wall, headed directly for our corner, is Meshuggener Marvin. The old man has told me all about him. Still, he looks even worse than I expected. From some garbage can on the avenue, Marvin has rescued a worn and shiny gray rayon suit. The cuffs and collar on his white shirt are frayed. Around his neck, he wears the kind of string tie they sell in five-and-dime stores for less than a dollar brand new. This one is definitely used.

Marvin carries a big white plastic shopping bag in his hand. Stopping right in the middle of the crowd that is jammed up against the back wall, he takes off the small silver yarmulka he is wearing, replacing it with one made of plain white nylon from his bag. "Light . . . *weight*," he explains to no one in particular. Right away I start to get nervous. If this were a movie theater, they would have already thrown Marvin out. On *Kol Nidre* night, however, the doors of the shul are open to everyone. It is a tradition of long standing.

"*Yomtov*," Marvin says, grabbing my hand without having the faintest idea of who I am. Solemnly, he moves on, shaking hands with my grandfather. Then he leans over to work the row in front.

"Wonderful," Murray says, grudgingly giving him his hand. "Now that you're here, Marvin, we can start."

"*Yomtov*," Marvin says again. His needle is stuck on automatic repeat. He reaches for Murray's hand once more, just to make sure.

"You already got me tonight, Marvin," Murray tells him, clasping his hands together before him. "Relax."

Stepping back, Marvin reaches into his big white plastic shopping bag. He pulls out a *Mahzor*. Shoving the book right into my face, he flicks madly through the pages until he gets to the *Kol Nidre* service. Pointing to the prayer that the cantor will soon recite, with a fingernail so black it looks as though he dipped it into coal oil, he says, "*Spain.*" I nod my head. In Spain, Jews forced by the Inquisition to convert to Catholicism used *Kol Nidre* to renounce their vows. "It started there," Marvin says, breathing directly into my face to make certain that I get the point.

"Marvin," my grandfather says quietly, "*kim aher*. Stand by me."

Amazingly, Marvin obeys. Moving behind my grandfather, he leans against the closet door. Holding his prayer book up to his chin, he begins reading to himself from it. His lips move rapidly. No sound comes from his mouth. Balling his right hand into a fist, he thumps it lightly against his heart. This gesture is meant to be used only when reading from the section of the *Amidah* that enumerates the sins a person has committed during the year.

Marvin sways back and forth. His eyes are closed. His head bobs like a cork floating on a windblown lake. The skin on his face is crusted with strawberry-colored plaque. To me, Marvin smells like an old coat that has never been dry cleaned. With the back of his hand, he begins striking himself repeatedly in the forehead, the chest, and the side of his face. Marvin has definitely had one hell of a year. The sins for which he is atoning tonight are too numerous to count without pencil and paper.

Murray Friedberg stares at him for a second. Then he looks at me. Putting his forefinger to the side of his face just below the temple, he twists it in tight circles. As far as he is concerned, Marvin is completely nuts.

"Marvin," my grandfather says, *"shlug zer nisht kopf en vant."* Do not beat your head against the wall. It is definitely sound advice, for all of us. But Marvin is not listening. *"Langsam,"* my grandfather says. Slowly, *"Langsam,"* he repeats. "You got the whole night and all day tomorrow to *doven*, Marvin," he says gently. *"S'genug."*

Marvin closes his *Mahzor*. His entire body goes limp. Then he begins to smile. He plays with the fringes of his cheap white nylon *tallis*. "Is he . . . uh, all right?" I ask my grandfather in a whisper.

"Who? Marvin?"

I nod. "S'a good boy, Marvin," he says. *"A bissel meshuggeh* but . . . a good boy. At heart."

Where my grandfather developed this kind of patience, I cannot say for sure. Of course, I have a pretty fair idea. As a kid, I would often quiz him about what it was like in the camps. Never once has he told me anything about it. "And if I told you," he would say, "then you would know? Better you should worry about other things. *Denken Gott*, you won't have to live through what I did." But what if I do? I need to know how he made it. More than anything, my grandfather is a survivor.

"Uh-*huh*," Murray Friedberg thunders, his voice so loud that it gets everyone's attention. "Now comes *el presidente*, Nathan Weiss. His brother-in-law, Sol, must need a tissue to blow his nose."

141

I watch as Nat Weiss picks his way through the crowd. He is smiling and nodding without ever really looking anyone in the face. I should introduce him to E.C. The two of them would get along just fine. I can tell.

Nat Weiss's face is all bone, as though some invading army has stripped it of all flesh. Beneath skin as thin as tissue paper, tiny blood vessels lie coiled like twisting ropes strung between the two violent peaks of his cheekbones. His *tallis* shimmers white gold in the light. The collar is trimmed with thick brocade. When he reaches up to adjust the broad, flat yarmulka perched on his perfect silver gray hair, the large diamond on his pinky catches the light, breaking it up into colors.

Just by looking at the man, I can tell that he is only slumming. His seat is all the way up front, close to the rabbi and the cantor and the holy Torahs and, for all I know, God as well. There is not a single thing about Nat Weiss that I like and I am doing my best to be charitable tonight.

Marvin has no such worries. Sticking out his hand, he shouts "*Yomtov*" really loud right in Nat Weiss's face. Brushing Marvin aside, Nat just keeps on coming. Finally, he reaches my grandfather. He grunts. "Mendel," he says, "what's with the air conditioning?"

My grandfather shrugs. The big Fedders unit in the stained glass window above his head is banging away like crazy. The entire wall throbs with the vibration. "What's with it, Nat?" he asks.

"Solomon. He turned it on when I told him to after *Minchah?* Or just ten minutes ago?"

My grandfather shrugs once more. He knows the answer all right. Only he is not about to give it to Nat Weiss. Not ever. Experts have worked him over and come away with nothing. Against him, Nat Weiss does not stand a chance. "*Der villt Alaska, Nat?*" my grandfather asks. "*By mir, ess kalt.*"

"I want my brother-in-law Sol, who donated five tousaint dollars to the shul for a Fedders, not a Carrier system, that throws ten tousaint BTU's a minute after it's been on for half an hour, to feel at least a little chill on his bones when he comes to hear *Kol Nidre.* Is this asking too much?"

"Tell him to take off his jacket, Nat," Murray Friedberg suggests. "He'll feel a chill."

"Give it a couple minutes," my grandfather says. "*S'ganz kalt veren.*"

"*Kol Nidre* starts, we shut it off," Nat says. All the fleshy cords in his neck are throbbing. He is one nervous fellow all right. "Rabbi's orders. So the *chazzan* doesn't have to shout. . . ."

"Must be quiet for *Kol Nidre*," Marvin notes. Then he puts his finger to his lips. He leans right on top of Nat Weiss and goes "*Shhhh!*" so loudly that for a second I expect Weiss to keel over from the spray alone.

"*Teppeta*," Nat mutters instead. "Mendel," he says, turning to my grandfather. "*Du hust* a second? *Kim mit mir.*"

Nat Weiss backs my grandfather into the corner by the closet. He whispers into his ear like he is telling him the biggest secret of all time. I catch Solomon's name being mentioned a couple of times but nothing else. Then Nat Weiss turns around and heads back the way he came. Unfortunately, I happen to be standing in his way. He has to deal with me. Looking me up and down, he says, "Morty's kid, huh?"

"That's it," I tell him.

"The one that lives out of town?"

"Two for two."

"Figures," he sniffs. Then he walks away. No "Good *Yomtov*," no "Nice to see you here in shul tonight," no nothing. Just the knife, slipped in deftly between the ribs where it will do the most damage without being seen. It is the way they deal with you in the neighborhood once they can no longer actually grab you by the hair on your way home from school and shove your head into a parked car again and again, just to see what kind of sound it will make. It is not personal, either. They just do not like anyone leaving, and then coming back. It makes them paranoid. Maybe you do not love them.

"What's *his* problem?" I ask my grandfather as Nat Weiss disappears back into the crowd.

"Nat?" he says. "*S'gefalich*, no?"

Before I can pursue this line of questioning any further, Solomon appears. Solomon I actually happen to like. He has been around the shul since some time before the dawn of creation, doing all the little things that Orthodox Jews are not permitted to do on Shabbos and the High Holy Days. Solomon actually attended my very own bar mitzvah. He wore what I would swear on my life is the exact same suit he has on tonight.

Aside from his hair, which is grayer than I remember and fluffed out into a wild-looking Afro topped off with one of those pointy black rayon yarmulkas that they hand out to mourners at funerals, Solomon still looks the same. "Nat Weiss *crazy* tonight, Mendel," he complains to my grandfather. Then Solomon sees me. "Hey, *Paulie!*" he cries, sticking out his hand for me to shake. "When'd you get in? Been a *long* time, huh?"

Reaching for his hand, I give him the soul shake, thumb to thumb. Solomon expects the ordinary palm-to-palm model. Our fingers intertwine. Both of us laugh. "Nice to see you, Solomon," I say. "Really nice."

Solomon is not listening. Instead, he is turning from side to side, pointing his chest first towards one corner of the shul and then the other. For some reason, I alone notice the bulge under his coat just below the heart. I mean, I know that things are bad. But this is ridiculous. "Solomon," I say. "What are you doing, man?"

"Practicing," he says.

"Solomon," I say, leaning in close so I can whisper. "You packing a *gun?*"

Solomon laughs and shakes his head. "Aw, Paulie," he says, "you know me better than that. It's that Nat. Like I said. He gone *crazy* tonight. I swear. . . ."

Suddenly, the air conditioner above my head coughs and dies. The noise level in shul actually drops a couple of decibels. All the people caught talking to their friends across the rows immediately get embarrassed. They cover up by loudly shushing everyone who is still making noise. Half an hour late, with people still streaming in through the doors *Kol Nidre* is about to begin.

I look towards the front of the shul. The entire pulpit has been draped in white to mark the sanctity of this great day. Before the Ark, the rabbi sits in a high backed chair. Nat Weiss is to his immediate right. Hesitantly, as though he fears that at any moment Nat Weiss may order him to sit back down, the *chazzan* approaches the pulpit. He too is dressed in white.

Stepping up beside me, my grandfather grabs hold of my arm. For one so old, his grip is surprisingly strong. "Sol Stryker," he whispers. *"Der zahst im?"*

Getting up on tiptoe, I strain to see over the heads of those in front of me. Several well dressed men are hurrying down the center aisle to their seats. Any one of them could be the great Sol Stryker. "Which one?" I ask.

Instead of answering, my grandfather shoves a *Mahzor* into my hands. Opening it for me, he flicks through the pages until he reaches one headed, "Evening Service for Yom Kippur."

144

"Biyashevoah shel ma'aloah," he announces, pointing to the three lines in the middle of the page. I stare down at the Hebrew for a moment. Then I shift my eyes to the facing page, on which the English translation is written. It says, "By the authority of the heavenly court/And by the authority of the earthly court/With the consent of the Omnipresent One/And with the consent of this congregation/We declare it lawful to pray with sinners."

A little note at the bottom of the page informs me that this passage was inserted into the *Kol Nidre* service some seven hundred years ago by Rabbi Meir of Rothenburg. I have to give the old reb credit. Even back in the thirteenth century, long before there was color television, soul music, Greyhound buses, or cheese you could squeeze from an aerosol can directly into your mouth, he understood my basic problem.

In Ahavath Mizrach, Yom Kippur is officially about to begin. If I am to make it through the day to come without totally losing what little is left of my mind, I need to at least know why I am here. And there it is right before me, in black and white.

CHAPTER FIFTEEN

I WAKE UP feeling hollow clear through. All night long, I have dreamed of workmen. Day laborers who toil for the hourly wage and then fight for overtime in order to feed their families. The workmen have sandblasted my insides. There is nothing left in there now but wood shavings and bare, smooth walls. My heart thumps loudly in my chest, echoing and rebounding off exposed beams and the raw, unpainted rafters of my rib cage. All because I went to bed hungry, as some people do every night of their lives.

Across the living room, the old man sits hunched over the dinette table. He is hard at work on his precious plate blocks. Beside him, the radio plays. He wears khaki skivvies and his old-fashioned steel frame glasses. Although he never says so, something good must have happened to him in the Army. Twenty-five years after they handed him his discharge, he still dresses as though he expects reveille to blow at any moment.

The plate blocks on which he works are his legacy to me, my single inheritance. All my life, he has told me just how much they will be worth some day. The radio is a gift that he bought for himself. It is one of the few luxury items in the apartment aside from the brand new color television set which he absolutely refuses to let me touch. Only he knows how to change channels without damaging the tuner. Or so he says.

Every morning, the old man sits fiddling with his radio, pulling in stations from as far away as Hartford, Connecticut, and Babylon, Long Island. Should the Russians, the Chinese, the Turks, or the Mongols ever invade our fair land, he will be able to follow their progress along the East Coast, conquest by conquest.

The old chipped white china mug filled with coffee that usually sits by his elbow is nowhere to be seen today. So maybe he is fasting after all. I know better than to ask. Instead, I sit up slowly. I feel more than a little dizzy. Because the cratered mattress inside the couch slants backwards, I have spent the entire night with my head lower than my feet. According to my mother, it is never good to have too much blood in your brain. It makes things that already seem vague only that much more confused. Then again, perhaps sleeping this way helps my condition. Since I have been home, I have not used my inhaler once.

"You up?" the old man asks without turning around.

I grunt in answer. He nods, satisfied with my response. Then he goes right on working. I take advantage of the opportunity to study him for a moment. I cannot remember my father ever looking any other way than he does right now. No doubt, this God-given ability to forget the past keeps all of us from blowing out our brains. Still, there is no denying that lately my father's mainspring seems to be running down. Some days, his clock ticks so slowly that I can barely hear the sound.

Once upon a time, Morty definitely must have shown a flash of real promise. Why else would my mother have married him? Where that lightning has gone I cannot say. The everyday routine of the old man's life has worn him smooth. Now there are no rough edges left. Morty knows only the same and the same again and then once more the same, day in and day out. Nothing new ever happens to him. Nothing ever will.

Still, he lives. He puts himself to bed each night by reading

146

from one of his books on European military history. The next morning, from out of the blue, he will say to me, "Frederick of Prussia, Paulie. *Brilliant* man!" Then he goes into the bathroom to brush his teeth. With him to Avenue Station each day he takes his own bar of fine Swiss soap, hard-milled and made of goat's milk. Throughout the day, he leaves his little cage and goes to the bathroom to wash his hands, fearing that the germs he picks up from dealing with the public will do him in.

At night, he peels off the Supp-Hose socks he wears because of the varicose veins in his legs. He reaches for the tube of Ben-Gay so he can rub some on his aching back. Going to the refrigerator, he eats ice cream straight out of the carton, never from a bowl. He reads himself to sleep and then it all starts over again in the morning when he gets up to carefully iron by hand the uniform pants that he wears to work. Frederick of Prussia could not have led my father's life for more than a single week.

Although he grew up over here, I think in his heart the old man feels himself to be entirely European. He has never become accustomed to life in this rough and brawling land. My grandfather has done a far better job of adjusting to America, but then he has his religion to pull him through. All the old man ever does is work.

Knowing that he would never talk to me of such matters, I once asked my mother what Morty had been like when she first met him. "Your father, dear," she said, "had *such* wonderful manners. He was so polite. Almost formal. He courted me. I, of course, was charmed. All the other boys couldn't wait to get inside my sweater. But not your father. He was a perfect gentleman."

So he still is, in a way. A perfect, divorced gentleman who sells stamps in the post office on the avenue and is a member in good standing of the Jewish War Veterans. Although Morty hardly ever goes to temple, at least he does not work on Yom Kippur. For such small favors, I suppose I should be grateful.

Getting out of bed, I pull on my pants. In less than a minute, I am completely dressed and ready to go back to shul. On Yom Kippur, all the ordinary day-to-day business of life is edited out. I am not allowed to eat breakfast. I am not allowed to wash my hands or brush my teeth. Instead, I can put the time to good use by contemplating how truly miserably I have acted during the previous year as well as all the ways in which I can improve, provided that my name is actually included in the Book of Life for the year to come.

"You going back?" the old man asks, finally looking up from his stamps.

"I thought I might," I say. "Pop's there all alone. I thought he might want some company. . . ."

"Why not?" he says, throwing it right back to me again. Talking to the old man is like playing tic-tac-toe against a machine. Every *X* automatically makes an *O* appear on the board, even though no one else is actually playing.

"*Yizkor* is at eleven," I tell him.

"So?"

"I thought you might want to know."

For as long as I can remember, the old man has always made it to shul on Yom Kippur to say *Kaddish* for his mother. At Ahavath Mizrach, as in all other Orthodox temples, they say *Yizkor* four times a year. Today's service is the one that really counts. It is like Midnight Mass on Christmas Eve for renegade Catholics. People who never, ever go to temple at any other time show up in such numbers that my grandfather has to go to the Talmud Torah next door to conduct assembly line sessions in one of the classrooms. He ushers one group in, leads them in the mourner's *Kaddish* and *el molay rachamim*, then shows them the way back out so the next group can have their chance.

There is nothing more terrifying in the entire world than *Yizkor* on Yom Kippur. Since both my parents are, thank God, still alive, I have never actually seen it. The moaning and sobbing that begins when the names of those who died during the previous year are called out from the pulpit is enough to make me want to get as far away from shul as I can while that part of the service is in progress. All my life, I have always known that the day will come when I will have to stay behind. Then, and only then, I will truly be an adult. Today, I can still take myself for a little walk. I am exempt, a child both at heart and in the eyes of the shul.

"I'm going," I tell him.

"See you," he grunts, reaching towards his radio to turn up the news.

Closing the door to the apartment behind me, I go out into the hall. The entire building smells of potato pancakes and stuffed cabbage. Not that anyone is cooking today. They would not dare.

148

The smells have just gradually eaten their way into the woodwork. They are part of the general ambience.

The building itself is starting to fall down. Someone has smeared dumb graffiti over all the staircases. The walls are chipped. Wherever I look, paint is peeling off in big, gray green strips. No one even knows who the landlord is anymore, the old man says. So go find someone to complain to about it.

Outside, it is definitely autumn in the city. That great smoky odor of burning leaves come floating into my nose from somewhere far away. It is the time of year when everyone gets to start over from scratch again with a completely clean slate next to their name. Soon enough, though, it will be winter. The sun will shrink, becoming no more than a ten watt bulb in the dead gray sky. The streets will be covered ankle deep with applesauce slush. Holding their coats tightly closed before them, people will walk on the avenue against the wind with their heads down. Not that I will be around to see them do this. I am getting out. Exactly where I am heading this time, I have no idea. Cambridge, however, is definitely not on the list. I have already been there once.

Crossing the street that marks the border of the Italian section of the avenue where the old man and but a few of his fellow *lantzmen* live because the rents are cheaper, I head towards the Jewish side. The pork stores and salumerias disappear, giving way to huge discount marts where everything is always on sale so long as you pay cash and do not bother asking for a receipt. Today, every last store is locked up tight, so as not to offend any of the regular customers.

I leave the avenue and head towards shul. Here, the streets are lined with squat little red brick houses that sit glaring at one another across the narrow black gutter. In front of every house is the tiny patch of rough concrete that passes for a patio in the neighborhood. Some are rimmed with flowers, pale yellow lilies and dead pink roses that droop lifelessly behind the sharp metal spires of chain-link fences. Everywhere, there is dog shit in the street.

I am almost halfway across the schoolyard where once I lined up each day to march into class past the brass plaque with Hon. Vincent Impellitteri's name on it when I realize that two kids are actually playing ball on the first court. On a day when even the wildest, toughest Italian kids in the neighborhood keep a *very*

149

low profile, this is madness of the first order. A major sin, punishable by instant death.

What makes it even worse is that both of them are Jewish. They have to be, decked out in three-piece suits, white shirts, ties, and brightly polished black shoes. One of them is really big. Although his friend, a short, runty kid with a razor-sharp face obviously has all the moves, the giant is the one with a future. His height will be his ticket out of the neighborhood. Maybe I should give him Norris' phone number up in Cambridge.

Out of habit, I look towards the very top of the school building. There, high upon the bricks for as long as I can remember, the words "Fox and Grapes" were written in thick white paint. Just who was crazy enough to write them there, six stories up with nothing but hard concrete below and no ledges anywhere to stand on while doing the work, I never knew.

Not that it matters. For me, the words themselves were enough. As a kid, I had to see them each day on my way home from school to make certain that the sun would rise again in the morning. Only now they are gone. There is nothing up there but neat red brick and pale cement. It figures. In the neighborhood, no matter how high up on the bricks you make your mark, someone always comes along after you to rub it out again.

Only the buildings themselves remain, made of stone so hard they can only be defaced, never really altered or destroyed. Once I knew nearly everyone on these streets, as well as their parents, brothers, sisters, and grandparents. Now I am a stranger. Although the two kids playing ball on the first court in suits do not know it, they will not last either. Soon enough, someone new will take their place, even if their names actually do happen to be Fox and Grapes.

I hurry down the last few blocks towards the temple. After going up the front steps, I put the fingers of my right hand to the *mezzuzah* on the door post. Then I kiss them as a sign of respect. Why miss touching any of the bases today? Inside the shul, the great excitement of *Kol Nidre* night has been replaced by the quiet reality of Yom Kippur itself, the long haul marathon of prayer that will continue until after the sun is gone for the day. My grandfather will not set foot outside this building until it is dark once more.

Before empty benches that look like the sun bleached, skeletal remains of some great whale beached on the shore, the hard core regulars of the shul stand. These are men who know no other

150

way. Wrapped in prayer shawls with yarmulkas on their heads, they face east, silently reciting the *Amidah*. Some pause occasionally to wipe their mouths with pocket handkerchiefs. Others twist the fringes of their mustaches as they pray. Some sway rhythmically from side to side. One man suddenly clears his throat. The noise is like that of heavy furniture being scraped against a wooden floor.

Others do not pray at all. Instead, they stand in place, blinking their eyes. The *Mahzor* is open before them. They are waiting for a wave of sound to carry them forward, towards the Ark and the holy Torahs.

I am about to go and join my grandfather. Then I decide it would be wise if I first used the downstairs bathroom. Passing by the tiny office where my mother works five days a week, I head towards the men's room. Solomon stands on the landing. He is holding open the door that leads outside, talking to someone I cannot see. "*Nat?*" he says. "That water fountain got to *stay* turned off, no matter what?"

"*Off!*" Nat Weiss calls back, his voice loud and unmistakable, even on Yom Kippur. "Someone wants water, let them go to a candy store. A public park. This is an Orthodox shul. On Yom Kippur, you can't even get a drink of water here. Noth-*ing*."

"This for a girl, Nat," Solomon explains.

"Applies to girls as well as boys," Nat Weiss answers. "Women as well as men. Solomon," he complains, "can't you see that I'm busy out here?"

"Nat," Solomon says, "this for a *little* girl. Maybe five years old."

Nat Weiss finally makes an appearance. He is wearing a different suit than the one he had on last night. On his feet are a pair of those dark blue canvas weave shoes that the old gin rummy players who sit around the cabanas in Miami Beach prefer. "So turn it on," he barks. "You got to come to me on every little thing, Solomon? Only once she gets her drink, right off again. We're not running no refreshment stand for kids here today."

Solomon heads towards the water fountain upstairs, shooting me a tired look as he goes. I stare at Nat Weiss. To me, he looks exactly like a lizard. I can see him sitting on a hot, flat rock in the middle of the desert, basking in the blazing midday sun. Flick. Out comes his long, white spotted tongue. Flick. Another fly dead and gone. Flick. Flick. Flick. He never misses a one.

Looking up at me, he says, "You heard the awful news?" Before I can answer, he says, "They killed fifty *yeeden* in *Eretz Yisroel* this morning. The assassins. Women and children. On Yom Kippur, no less."

"Who did?" I ask, stunned.

"Who?" he repeats. "The guerrilla murderers. Who else?"

"Who told you this?" I ask.

"Who?" he repeats. "Your very own father. He ran right over as soon as he heard it on his radio. On the short-wave band, from Europe."

"*My* father?" I say dumbly. The last time I saw the old man he was still in his underwear at the dinette table. "Where is he then?"

"Outside. He refuses to come in until *Yizkor* starts. Typical Morty *mishegass* but this, this news . . ." Nat shakes his head, unable to summon the words to express what he is feeling.

"Murray Friedberg," Nat sings out. "You heard?"

"What, Nat?" Murray asks, stopping by for a moment on his way to the john.

"They invaded a settlement in the Negev with bombs and guns and slaughtered people as they slept in their beds."

"My God!" Murray cries out. "How many, Nat? How many dead?"

"How *many?*" Nat shouts, drowning me out before I can supply the number. "Does it matter? They can't count the bodies, they're stacked so high. Those *vilda chaia*. Death isn't good enough for them. They should be hung by their heels on the Dizengoff in Tel Aviv. They should smear their *batesem* with honey and tie them to anthills in the desert. That they should die like they kill us . . ."

"Listen," I say, trying to make some sense out of what I am hearing. "Are those *confirmed* reports?"

"So what are they?" Nat demands. "Lies? You need confirmation? Go talk to your father. Did they not even bomb near the wall in June? What do they care for what is right or holy?"

There is no way in the world that Nat Weiss is going to listen to me. My grandfather is only the *shamus* of the shul, an employee of the temple who is paid nothing for his work. My mother sends out mailings in the office upstairs. My father is a clerk in the post office on the avenue. We are not pillars of the community who kick in with big gifts whenever the shul is in need. My opinion does not mean a thing to Nat. Because if any

152

of us are so smart, if we know anything at all, then how come we are not rich? Until I can answer that question, Nat Weiss will never hear me out, no matter what I say to him.

"On our most sacred day, no less," Nat shouts, slamming the flat of his hand against the wall so hard that I know it has to hurt. Not that he is bothered by the pain. Nat is flying on an authentic rush of pure adrenaline. "Do we attack them in their mosques?" he demands. "Do we kill their caliphs and sultans, who are the worst anti*semitts* of all, and want only to see us driven into the sea?"

I myself do not have an answer ready in time. Nat turns away from both Murray and me, grabbing for Sidney Meyers. Sidney is coming down the steps with nothing more on his mind than making it into the men's room in time.

"What's all the *gareider*, Nat?" Sidney asks good-naturedly. "You're catering a little brunch down here for your friends?"

Just then the rabbi appears, accompanied by Judah Benjamin, the cantor. Sidney goes red in the face. "*Gudt Yomtov, Rebbe,*" he croaks in a hoarse whisper.

The rabbi nods at Sidney. Then he turns towards Nat. Immediately, Nat begins his story all over again from the top. When he finishes, there is silence. Then Judah Benjamin, who I have always liked, says, "So how did you find all this out, Weiss? You got a transistor in your *tallis?*"

"Someone told me," Nat says, knowing better than to supply them with my father's name while I am standing here. "They heard it on the news. Short wave. What does it matter? I *heard*. That's all."

The rabbi considers the issue. He seems a thoughtful man. Not necessarily brilliant but thoughtful. Stroking his cheeks with his long, curving fingers, he shakes his head sorrowfully from side to side. His left thumbnail must be at least two inches long. Whether this is in accordance with some obscure law of Torah, I have no idea. His face is black with stubble. The sharp points of his cheekbones are prominent beneath his tired eyes.

"*Shrecklich,*" he says, pronouncing official judgment on the event. "Just *shrecklich*."

"Words alone are not enough, Rebbe," Nat insists. "We must *respond*."

The rabbi considers the challenge for a moment. Then he says, "What can we do but pray?"

It seems a fairly reasonable answer. But then I am not Nat

Weiss. The fires do not burn as brightly within me as they do inside him. Nat is a man possessed. Fiercely, he takes the rabbi by the arm. Then he leads him into the men's room, so that they can talk in private.

I look from Judah Benjamin to Sidney Meyers to Murray Friedberg and then back again. None of them knows any more about this than I do. They have all come downstairs to perform a simple bodily function only to learn that Armageddon is once again just around the corner in the Middle East.

Just outside the shul, waiting for *Yizkor* to begin, stands my father. He is the only one who has actually heard the report. He alone knows what they really said. I do not go to him. Upstairs, with a *Mahzor* in his hand, oblivious to everything save the simple fact that this does happen to be the absolute holiest day of the year, is my grandfather. I go to join him instead. The rabbi is right. What else *is* there to do but pray?

CHAPTER SIXTEEN

UPSTAIRS, THEY HAVE already begun slowly making their way through the first Torah reading of the day up at the pulpit. Before I can say a word to him, my grandfather hands me a *Mahzor*. He orders me to go stand in the corner and make up for lost time. I am to begin at the *Kedushah* ("Holy, holy, holy is the Lord of hosts: The whole earth is full of his glory"), not to return until I have gotten through *Ovenu Malchenu* ("Our Father, Our King"), the prayer that ends the section of the *Amidah* I missed while wasting my time downstairs with the power brokers of the temple.

The *Amidah* itself is said repeatedly on Yom Kippur. It was said last night during *Kol Nidre* and it will be said again today, during *Musaf*. They will say it once more after the Book of Jonah has been read aloud from the pulpit and then for the last time during *Ne'ilah*, the concluding service of the day. The way in which it is said is also repetitive. Each person first reads it silently by himself. Then he listens as it is read aloud in somewhat longer form, with many of the passages being chanted in unison by both the man at the Torah and the congregation at large.

At the very heart of the *Kedushah* is the *Shema*, the single line that proclaims, "Hear, O Israel, the Lord is Our God, the Lord is One." Supposedly, no matter how close to death you happen to be, whether you are being tortured to renounce your faith in some medieval dungeon or about to go head first off the top of some tall building, as perhaps the guy who painted "Fox and Grapes" on the wall did, all you have to do is recite the *Shema* and you will be taken back into the fold. Some people, I am positive, not even the *Shema* will help. After all, it is only six words long.

The *Shema* itself is part of a larger prayer containing two hundred and forty-eight words. In ancient times, this was the exact number of parts the human body was thought to contain. On Yom Kippur, the *Shema* is said twice. It is preceded by two blessings and followed by one in the morning. It is preceded by two and followed by two in the afternoon, thereby fulfilling the Biblical prescription, "Seven times a day I praise thee."

For those who know how to look, the entire *Mahzor* is filled with hidden meaning. Secret passageways open suddenly onto great vaults filled with gleaming treasure. The book is an intricate road map to a higher world.

Each word of the *Mahzor* is a little building block. Although the power of the word is mighty, when the word becomes the line, the line the passage, the passage the prayer, and the prayer one of the five separate services that make up the day's worship on Yom Kippur, the final effect is far too much for any one man to grasp.

The words of the prayer that I now stand reading to myself proclaim that we are the children of the Lord, His servants, community, vineyard, and flock. But we have acted brazenly, viciously, and fraudulently. We have acted willfully, scornfully, and obstinately. Perniciously, disdainfully, and erratically. More times than we can number, we have turned away and transgressed.

Today we are seeking atonement for the sin we have committed forcibly and willingly, and by acting callously. For the sin we have committed unintentionally and by idle talk. For the sin of offensive speech and oppressing a fellow man. The sin of evil thought, lewd association, and insincere confession. The sin of foolish talk and evil impulse. We are asking:

Forgive us all sins, O God of forgiveness, and grant us atonement.

For the sin of wanton glances, haughty airs, and scornful defiance. Sordid selfishness and levity of mind. Talebearing and swearing falsely. Groundless hatred, breach of trust, and a confused heart.

Forgive us all sins, O God of forgiveness, and grant us atonement.

For sins requiring a burnt offering. For sins requiring corporal punishment, forty lashes, or premature death. For sins for which the earthly courts would have imposed four kinds of death penalty: stoning, burning, beheading, or strangling.

Forgive us all sins, O God of forgiveness, and grant us atonement.

For the breach of positive commands and the breach of negative commands. For sins known to us that we have already acknowledged, and those not known to us that are indeed well known to Thee.

Forgive us all sins, O God of forgiveness, and grant us atonement.

The list is long and never ending. Each sin is to be enumerated with the loosely balled fist *clupped* lightly against the heart. Only even as I stand in temple, reciting the prayer, my mind begins to wander. I keep thinking of the night I first went to the Apollo Theater on a Hundred and Twenty-fifth Street in Harlem. On stage, a hapless victim was dragged before a high bench to be tried for his crimes. Left all by himself in a white hot spotlight, he stood there, quaking.

Without warning, the band pounded into "Here come da judge, Here come da judge." The curtains flew open. A skinny old black man in flowing robes and a huge yellow fright wig shimmied to his seat behind the bench, waving to the crowd that was already going crazy high up in the second balcony.

"Judge, yoah honah," the prosecutor sang out, doing his own crazy-legged dance. "Got a boy heah who can't dance."

"Can't dance?" the judge cried out, the band banging away for all they were worth in back of him. "Can't *dance?* Thirty days Boog-a-loo." *Wham!* Down came the judge's gavel against the bench, the drummer underlining the gesture with a wicked rim shot. "Thirty days Shing-a-ling!" *Wham, wham,* a double backbeat that set everyone on stage and in the house twitching in time. "Thirty days Funky Broadway!" *Wham, wham, wham.* As

156

the victim was dragged screaming into the wings, the entire audience exploded with laughter. People were doubled over, fighting for breath. The skinny old man sitting next to me actually had tears in his eyes as he moaned, "*Damn!* Ain' seen nothin' *that* funny since the cat died."

I ask myself what any of this has to do with Yom Kippur, the day on which we have pledged to abstain from all work and afflict ourselves forever more as an everlasting statute of our covenant with God. Today, as Nat Weiss would be only too glad to tell me, dancing, of any kind, is out of the question.

I think about Lesley, Rob, Anita, Cole T. Walker, and Norris. I even think about E.C. Now there is a man who has sinned. *Repeatedly.* Yet he is making it pay. I wonder what any of this has to do with them, or me.

As a child, I would stand in shul on Yom Kippur morning filled with awe, overwhelmed by a sense of God that was thrilling and complete. Back then, I even thought I knew exactly what the Book of Life looked like. Lots of gold leaf on fine old parchment, bound with the finest red morocco leather. Probably cost a fortune to throw together. Down each page, I could actually see the crooked celestial finger moving slowly past the names. Next to each and every name, He would make a mark. Check. Check out. Check, check, check. Check out. God was never more real to me than at that moment.

Only this year, it is just not happening for me. There is something inside my heart that keeps getting in the way. Something smaller than a breadbox and harder than a chunk of granite. If life is sin, and the wages of sin are death, then why bother? All you can do is shout out the six saving words of the *Shema* as you go, and hope for the best. Begging for forgiveness on Yom Kippur has to finish a poor second to the way you live throughout the year. At least that is the way I feel about it. Now that I am old and fully grown.

Rushing through the last line of *Ovenu Malchenu*, I look up from the *Mahzor*. Nat Weiss has assumed a watchman's position at the very back of the center aisle. Impatiently, he taps the big ring on his pinky against the edge of the bench beside him. The rhythm is insistent, and very familiar. Check. Check. Check. Check out.

Then the rabbi comes through the back door. Nat flashes him a cold, hard smile. Taking the rabbi by the arm, Nat leads him down the center aisle as though this is a wedding and he is the father of the bride. All the while, Nat is talking away in a rumbling monotone. The rabbi keeps nodding his head in agreement. It is not all that hard to see who *really* runs the shul. All you have to do is look.

Solomon comes slouching over to our corner. He is once again wearing the suit he had on last night. That bulge is visible just above his heart. I am about to ask him what he has hidden in there when the rabbi's hand comes down hard against the wooden lectern at the front of the shul.

"Friends," the rabbi says. People go right on talking, stretching the muscles in their arms and legs as they prepare for the ordeal of *Yizkor* that is to come. "Friends," the rabbi says again. The back doors suddenly fly open. A crowd of people flood down the center aisle. "Friends, *please,*" the rabbi begs, getting in a couple of really impressive belts with his hand against the wooden lectern.

A wave of indignant shushing runs around the room. Marvin himself joins in enthusiastically, a fine spray of mist issuing from his mouth. "Friends," the rabbi says, as the shul finally gets quiet. "We have just completed the first portion of the Torah for *Yoam Ha-Kee-Poreem.* We have heard of the deaths of Aaron's two sons. Why? Because the death of the righteous brings about atonement for Israel. Those moved to tears by the death of the righteous will also win forgiveness.

"My friends," the rabbi continues, his voice rising and falling as only a rabbi's voice can when he is posing questions that he knows no one else can answer. "The righteous are dying still, even as we pray. Why?"

The back doors fly open again. More people push into the shul, talking away to beat the band. The rabbi's stormy face darkens. Fighting to maintain his self-control, he says, "Will the *gabboim please* tell all those standing outside to come in and find seats? What I have to say is for them to hear as well."

A couple of men get to their feet. Opening the center door, they motion those outside to come right on in. The group that enters is made up almost exclusively of women. Some have small scarves draped over their heads. Others wear little black hats with dotted veils that fall over their faces, making them look somehow Parisian and very glamorous despite the solemnity of the occasion. Every last one of them has come to shul to cry. In their hands, they hold tiny handkerchiefs that are already damp from having been rolled and unrolled a hundred times. Inside their pockets, they carry little bottles of blue and green smelling salts, to be shoved under someone's nose at the first sign that they may pass out.

After they have all taken seats, it grows quiet in shul once more. Sensing that he finally has the attention of the entire congregation, the rabbi leans forward. He stretches his neck up and out from the collar of his shirt so that he seems to grow taller. "We hear so much about man's inhumanity to man these days," he says, "but what about man's inhumanity to God?"

It seems a fair question all right. I myself certainly cannot answer it. The rest of the congregation seems just as puzzled. In itself, this is a very good sign. Since they do not understand, they may actually have to listen for a little while before they begin talking among themselves again.

"We read over and over in the *Mahzor* today about men who died for their faith," the rabbi says. "Martyrs for the cause. Rabbi Amnon of Mayence, who composed the *unesanah tokef* in shul on Rosh Hashanah even while dying from his wounds, his hands and feet cut off by a cruel tyrant because he would not renounce his faith. Rabbi Ishmael and Rabbi Simeon ben Gamaliel, after whom I myself am named, each begging to be allowed to die before the other so as to be spared the sight of a dear friend's death.

"Great Simeon, his head cut off. Rabbi Ishmael, flayed alive, crying out only when his executioners reached the place of his *tephillen*. Rabbi Akiba, lacerated with combs of iron. Rabbi Hananya ben Teradyon, wrapped in a Torah and placed on a pyre of green brushwood with his chest drenched in water to prolong his agony . . ."

The rabbi shakes his head in sorrow. He pulls his long *tallis* up and over his shoulders. The corners of his mouth are white with caked saliva. He looks truly awful, as though he himself is experiencing every one of these terrible deaths and feeling the pain.

"Over the centuries, my friends, how our oppressors have fed on us. They have made us swallow poison. They have stood by the side of the road laughing as we rode in wagons to the grave in the Middle Ages singing *Olenu*, then the death song of the martyrs. The events of the last World War that so many of us lived through need no review. A war unparalleled for the sheer, unremitting persecution and destruction of a single people for one reason and one reason only . . . *religion*. The faith of our

159

fathers, as expressed in the *Shema,* which we say over and over today to affirm our belief that God is one.

"My friends. You may well say, 'If God is One, then am I one too?' Why have *my* people been selected for po-groms? For massacre and mass murder? For pain, injustice, suffering, and death? For years, our great scholars wrestled with this very question. The chosen people. Chosen for what? To die like flies at the end of the summer? To be shoveled into mass graves like so many bits of broken pottery?

"For far too long, my friends, we have looked within ourselves for the answer, the cause, the reason. We have *clupped* our hearts on *Yoam Ha-Kee-Poreem,* begging forgiveness for all the wrongs we have done. And we have died. Oh, my friends, how we have died. Permit me to read to you in English a passage from the *Mahzor.*"

Clearing his throat, the rabbi looks down at the lectern. " 'They were lovely and amiable in life,' " he reads. " 'And were not parted in their death. They were swifter than eagles and stronger than lions to do the will of their Master. . . .' Beautiful words, no, my friends? Fit for any headstone in a graveyard. My friends, let me tell you something."

The entire congregation leans forward. Their mouths come open. I cannot ever remember hearing it this quiet in shul, even on Yom Kippur. My grandfather stands beside me with his right hand hooked over the bench before him. His eyes are closed. He nods his head as though he has heard it all before, yet still agrees with everything that is being said.

Punctuating each word with a *zetz* of his hand against the lectern, the rabbi says, *"It . . . will . . . not . . . happen . . . again."* He pauses for breath and looks around. "Not at the hands of the rulers of Mayence or Emperor Hadrian or the assassins who threaten *Eretz Yisroel* even now. For in the *Mahzor* it is also written, 'May our God remember them favorably among the other righteous of the world; may he avenge the blood of his servants which has been shed. . . . And it is further said: He will execute judgment upon the nations and fill the battle-field with corpses; he will shatter the enemy's head over all the wide earth. From the brook by the wayside he will drink; then he will lift up his head triumphantly.' "

Lifting his head up triumphantly, the rabbi says, "Triumphantly, *I* lift up my head today. Our first responsibility, my friends, is to ourselves. It *will* not happen again, no matter how many tanks they throw against us, no matter how many soldiers they send to kill our defenseless women and children. We will *never* go silently.

"Whosoever denies us the right to life, he is our enemy. The whole world stood by in silence as we died one by one in the Warsaw ghetto. It will never be so again. The struggle for life is human. In order to be hu*mane*, we must first be human. Man's greatest humanity is to himself, to serve God in *life*, and not from some shallow grave. So we will *fight* to live, to uphold our dignity here in America, as well as in *Eretz Yisroel*. Today, on *Yoam Ha-Kee-Poreem*, my friends, I say once more to you, with all my heart: Man's greatest humanity to God, and to Man, is to make very, very sure . . . it will not happen again."

Closing his *Mahzor*, the rabbi steps back from the lectern. "I give you now the president of our shul, Nat Weiss," he says. Then he is gone, back in his chair beside the Ark. Nat Weiss charges towards the lectern. Since he is a good head and a half shorter than the rabbi, he has to stand on tiptoe to be seen above it. Looking around the shul, he starts to smile. Then he slams his hand down so hard that everyone in shul, myself included, jumps.

"Never in my *life*," he says, "have I ever heard such a speech. Rabbi Hakveldt, you have moved us once again. You have stirred and shaken our consciences, scrambling them like eggs in a bowl. Most remarkably of all," he confides, "Rabbi Hakveldt had an entirely different talk prepared for us today, one that I hope we get to hear some time soon. At the very last moment, in response to certain late-breaking developments from overseas, he was able to deliver the talk you only just heard, without notes. And what a brilliant talk it was! What a phrase he has left us with this morning! *It will not happen again*. The thought rings on in the mind, like a broken doorbell. It *will* not happen again. That I can assure you. But what will stop it from happening? What can *we* do?"

I know the answer to that one right away. Not that I am about to raise my hand and call it out. "In-creased giving," Nat says, taking the words right out of my mouth. "Through the kind of enthusiasm we used to generate here in shul on *Kol Nidre* night back when we still made our appeal by calling names, a practice we discontinued some years ago. Only when we hear stories like those that have come to us today, we realize that never in our long history have we been so alone, so isolated, so dependent on

161

only our own resources to pull us through. In such times, extreme measures are justified. . . ."

Putting a pair of tiny half-glasses on his nose, Nat rustles some papers before him. "Aaronsen," he says, singing out the name. "Irv Aaronsen. The builder. A good friend of the shul, and of mine. I know this takes you by surprise, Irv. But who told you to be so double-A rated that they put you right at the top of the alphabet, hah?" Nat laughs generously at his own little joke. His half-glasses bob on his fleshy nose. "We thank you in advance for what I'm sure was your generous *Kol Nidre* gift, Irv. Only that was then and this is now. So here comes the sixty-four tousaint dollar question. Irv. What can you do for us today?"

Irv Aaronsen sits near enough to the front of the shul to definitely have some money. A builder, a friend to both the shul *and* Nat Weiss, at the moment Irv looks nervous. With his head down, he calls out, "Two hundred, Nat."

"Wonderful," Nat says. Then he rolls his shoulders beneath his *tallis*. He puts both of his elbows on the lectern. "Israel, Irv," he says conversationally, as though the two of them are all alone in here today, "have you thought about it? A desert where now trees grow and flowers bloom, watered by the blood of our people. A father like yourself, Irv, you can imagine what it must be like to see your children lying dead before you. . . ."

"A hundred more in honor of my son, David," Irv calls out quickly. "And a hundred more for my daughter, Sherry."

"Four hundred," Nat says. "God bless you, Irv. Much *naches* from David's bar mitzvah in a couple weeks. Some of you younger members of the congregation may not remember the man whose name used to follow Irv's in the roll of honor, as I like to call it. Saul Abrams, our first rebbe here, a *gudten neshuma* of the first order. In memory of his hallowed name, I pledge five times *chai*, five years since he left us, ninety dollars. My regular gift, I'll announce later. Sol Bender," Nat announces. "Our excellent dentist, his suite of offices on the avenue is always so crowded, you're lucky if you can get a foot in the waiting room door. Solly, the gold inlay in back is a little loose. But never mind. I know you'll take care of it when I come in next week. Solly, how much? Talk to me. *Gelt*."

"Five hundred, Nat," Sol calls out. "And in honor of our rabbi, who made such a wonderful speech, another five hundred."

"May you live to be a hundred, Solly," Nat responds. "If it pleases the *Rabboina Shaloilum*. And why should it not, with so generous a gift? Morris Benson, the lawyer. Believe me, friends, you got Morrie representing you downtown, your case is already won. *Nu*, Morris? We're waiting. Don't keep us on pins and needles here.''

Morris Benson calls out his pledge. Nat acknowledges it with a grin and a nod. Then he goes on to the next name. I have to give the man credit. He has it all down to a fine art. First Nat calls out someone's name. There is a split second of silence as each member of the congregation makes his own rapid mental calculations as to what this man may give. Tension mounts as Nat kibitzes with the giver, *shtipping* and probing like some expert surgeon at work in the operating room. The thrilling moment when the gift is announced is followed immediately either by a soft, collective sigh of pleasure or a short, sharp intake of breath, indicating that Nat has yet more work to do.

Every now and then, someone in a far corner of the shul cries out, ''*Nat!* You missed me.'' With these people, Nat takes extra care. As soon as he bellows out their names, they are trapped. Everyone turns to look at them. They have to dig down extra deep to come up with a gift worthy of all the attention.

On the holiest day of the year, they are raising money in Ahavath Mizrach to avenge the dead, erecting a mountain of cash that will never bring anyone back to life. Blood money, of the first order. Yet I cannot bring myself to leave. I am plagued by technical questions. How are they ever going to remember who has given what? To make a promise in front of the Torah that you do not intend to carry out is a sin of the highest degree. Still, once the actual heart-throbbing moment of giving has passed, some people will just naturally fail to remember their pledges. It is only human.

Then I notice Solomon. As people shout out their gifts, he whirls in their direction. The man is spinning like the label on a forty-five. ''Solomon,'' I whisper, ''what gives, man? You can tell me.'' Solomon rolls his eyes and shakes his head. Then he pulls back his coat. Strapped to his chest like the automatic weapon I thought he was carrying last night is a small pocket tape recorder. I lean towards it and take a look. Sure enough, the tiny wheels are turning.

''Nat?'' I ask.

Solomon nods. Leave it to Nat Weiss to think of everything. He has armed Solomon with the means of recording just who gave what. I have finally had it. I mean, today *is* Yom Kippur.

Up on the pulpit, Nat steps back from the lectern. He looks down into the front row. "Patience, Sol," he calls out. "I'm coming to you. I wouldn't leave you out today even if you *weren't* my brother-in-law."

"Stryker," my grandfather whispers in my ear, "*gibt a fortune.*"

I do not doubt it for a second. I just have no desire to be around to see it happen. "Listen," I tell him, "I'm going out. For some air."

"*Gae gezinta heit,*" he says. Then he grabs my arm. "After *Yizkor, ich gae duchenen.*"

I know that. There is no way in the world I am going to miss it. Only at the moment, I just have to leave. See you later, gator. Loo-ka-poo, all through. Giving Marvin a wide berth, I make my way through the crowd hemmed in along the back wall. All the air at the rear of the temple has long since been used up. Pulsing waves of heat come at me from the wall of *Yizkor* lights above my head. A whirling rush of dizziness shoots up my spine. Little brown specks that almost are not there start swimming madly before my eyes. My lungs fill with fluid.

My big moment is about to happen. I am going to have an attack in shul, on Yom Kippur, no less. Women by the score will fight for the right to shove smelling salts up my nose. Battling it every step of the way, I edge slowly towards the door. I am standing with the handle in my hand when I look towards the opposite corner of the shul. Whatever telepathic messages my mother has been sending me have gotten through. Immediately, she starts coming towards me.

Pointing to the door to let her know that I will be outside, I just keep right on going. In the hallway, it is a good ten degrees cooler. A gentle breeze blows in from the street. I follow it right out onto the front steps. I am standing there breathing through my mouth when I see the old man. He is the one who is responsible for all of this. Him and his lousy radio with the built-in antenna that pulls in stations from out of town and all around the world when atmospheric conditions are just right.

"You look good," he says, coming up to me and making a face to let me know that he means just the opposite. He wears his only suit. Up and down his wide striped tie, blue and red pheasants are bursting into flight. "Maybe you ought to grab yourself a little drink of water," he suggests.

"Shout it a little louder," I tell him. "So the rabbi himself can hear you."

"What *hear?*" he says, annoyed. "They're so busy counting money in there that they haven't seen yet, they don't have the time to *hear* anything. Much less worry about Yom Kippur."

"How do you know? You been in there?"

"Peeked in," he says. "Now I'm out. That tell you anything?"

"Yeah. You couldn't afford a seat."

"How come you walked out before Stryker's gift?" he asks, ignoring my remark. "That's the big event of the day. They have him stand up and take a bow from the audience, like Ed Sullivan used to do with celebrities at the end of his show. That's right, huh?"

What can I say? I have already heard him do this routine a million times before. It is not as though it is a new topic with him or anything.

"How's Pop?" he asks. "Holding up okay?"

"He's great."

"His name you won't hear mentioned once in there today. A man like him. That's fair, right?"

My head is killing me. All I want to do now is take my little *Yizkor* walk in peace. Only the old man cannot stop. He has big news for me. I can see it in his face. "Let's see how much of it they collect when all the big givers go home tonight and read the *Post*," he says. "This incident in the Negev they're all so cox-cited about?"

"The one they found out about from you? That one?"

"A crock," he says, tossing off the word as though the situation no longer concerns him at all. "I went back home to check it out after I talked to Nat. First thing I said to him was that the report hadn't been confirmed. Not that he listened. Flew right off the handle before I could finish what I had to say. Turns out some radio operator in Beirut got his English mixed up. Nobody got killed. Nobody but Arabs. They wiped the floor with them. All those big givers in there," he says, pointing with his thumb, "they made their pledges for nothing. You know what else?"

"What?" I say, no longer certain of anything except that I have to get away.

"You look lousy. Go take yourself for a walk or something. The fresh air will do you good."

Then he goes inside the shul for *Yizkor*. I stand by myself on the front steps. The faint smell of burning leaves comes floating to me on the breeze from somewhere far away. It is autumn in the city all right. The time when everyone gets to start all over again from scratch, with a completely clean slate next to their name.

One thing I know for certain. The kid who once walked through the big oak doors behind me on Yom Kippur morning, wanting only to sit next to his grandfather for as long as they would let him, is definitely dead. Instead, I am here in his place, gasping for breath and holding onto the porch railing for support.

It is time for me to take my little walk all right. On the way, I can recite what little of the *Kaddish* I remember by heart. I will be the first person in history ever to say *Yizkor* for myself.

CHAPTER SEVENTEEN

BEFORE I CAN move out of range, my mother looms up on top of me. Like some top secret, heat-seeking missile of which the Pentagon is particularly proud, she is programmed to seek out her primary target no matter where I happen to be at any given moment. Although she and Morty no longer even speak to each other if they can possibly avoid doing so, the two of them are still a team.

Esther is large and explosive. Morty is thorough and deadly. He comes in first, softening up my resistance. Then she follows, making certain that the devastation is complete. Together, they are the ultimate weapon. The always weird Chinese pre-engineering students in Cambridge should throw away their slide rules and study my parents instead.

"Dear?" she asks, her voice low and funereal. "How are you feeling? You *look* awful."

"Thanks for the compliment."

"If you have a headache, you know that you don't *have* to go on fasting. A sick person does *not* have to fast. The rabbi himself told me this."

"I'm fine," I tell her, knowing that this is what she wants to hear.

166

"Good for you," she says, completely reversing her position without batting an eye. "I can't stand people who walk around all day on Yom Kippur as though they're going to *plotz*. Just because they haven't *shtipped* themselves with food for a couple of hours. Believe me, there isn't anyone here today who can't afford to go a day without eating. I know better than anyone."

I do not argue the point with her. I know how sensitive my mother is about her weight. For years now, I have been urging her to go see a doctor about it. It does me no good to urge. I could just as well be talking to a wall. Trying to reason with parents can be frustrating. It is the way they pay us back for what we did to them as children.

"Paulie," she says, fingering the material of my jacket with a look of pure disgust on her face, "whatever happened to the camel blazer?"

"What camel blazer?" I ask, playing dumb.

"The one I sent you for your birthday, dear."

"Oh. *That* camel blazer. I left it up in Cambridge, ma. Along with my heart."

"And this beautiful suit," she asks. "You found in some trash can?"

"That's it. In a dumper right outside Morty's apartment. The one where Meshuggener Marvin always shops." The look on her face makes me stop. "Lesley bought it for me," I say, telling the truth. That she bought it for me at a church rummage sale, I do not mention. Why make a bad situation even worse?

"Whatever they charged her for it, dear," she sniffs, "it was too much."

I can just see her telling Lesley this. World War III would start immediately. "And the tie?" she demands. "One of Morty's?"

"That's it. From Braunstein's, everyone's favorite discount outlet."

"What *Braunstein's?*" she demands. "Old Man Braunstein sold it more than a year and a half ago. See the nice looking gentleman on the steps? Don't turn around and stare, dear. It's not polite."

I do my best to look sideways without moving my head. "What about him?" I ask.

"Jerry Kahn. He runs it now. A very sharp cookie, if you ask me."

My mother is talking about a man who stands no more than ten feet away from us. He is thin and pasty faced. A pair of yellow

167

tinted aviator glasses hides his eyes. His expensive blue mohair blazer goes perfectly with his gray wool pants. His loafers are black and highly polished, with little gold chains across the front.

As though he knows we are looking at him, he runs the tips of his fingers through the manicured little waves in his salt-and-pepper-colored hair. Then he slowly opens his jacket. Reaching into his side pocket, he takes out a heavy gold watch attached to an old-fashioned chain fastened to one of his belt loops. He squints at the watch. Then he sighs heavily. Slowly he goes up the stairs and into the shul for *Yizkor*.

"He certainly dresses nice," I say.

"You think so?" my mother asks. "A little *too* nice if you ask me. His wife died a year ago last month. Cancer of the colon, *uf dir nisht ugedacht*." My mother always throws in this phrase when she is discussing fatal illnesses so that if God is listening, He will know that she is not wishing a similar fate on anyone. It is her corporate disclaimer.

"I must say, dear," she notes, "he is always *very* nice to me. Why, I don't know. Whenever he calls the shul on business, we talk. About everything under the sun."

What business Jerry Kahn, who now runs the discount outlet down the avenue, could have with the shul, I do not know. "Yeah, well," I say, "for a man his age, he really does dress very nice."

"Better than you do, dear," she agrees, "it goes without saying."

Turning away from me before I can answer, she looks up at the porch. She waves to someone standing up there. My mother knows everyone. "Steffi," she calls out, "why are you standing up there when I'm down here? You're avoiding me? All of a sudden, I'm not good enough for you to talk to anymore?"

"Oh, Esther," a girl about my age sighs, "you know it's not that. I just didn't see you. Without my glasses on, I'm blind."

Down the steps the girl comes, heading our way. The sheer force of my mother's incredibly magnetic personality is strong enough to draw tenpenny nails right from the rafters of the building itself. Immediately I realize what is going on. Esther is working. Even on Yom Kippur, she cannot rest. This is definitely a fix-up. For all I know, my mother called this girl on the phone and ordered her to be here at a specific time so that we could meet. Not that there is anything so wrong with this girl. As always, my mother has excellent taste in nearly everything but husbands and sons.

"Steffi Weiss," my mother says softly, "my son, Paulie." She puts her hand on the girl's dress. Lightly, she fingers the material of the sleeve. I can see that it gives her pleasure just to feel such fine workmanship. "The original wandering Jew," she adds, "who somehow found his way home for the holidays. Paulie . . . Steffi. It's high time you two finally met."

I nod hello. Steffi is a racehorse all right, long, tall, shiny, and smooth. Her fine oval face sits atop an elongated, almost tubular, neck. Her chestnut colored hair falls to her shoulders in a single curl, framing her angular features in a perfect halo. Were it not for her eyes, which are large and soft, the girl would look positively two-dimensional.

For some reason, I glance down at her hands. Every last fingernail has been bitten right down to the nub. One thing I know for sure. Never in her life has Steffi ever sat at the dinner table long enough to finish everything on her plate. In the neighborhood, this is known as being "not an eater." Maybe that is why my mother likes her for me. She will be cheap to feed.

"Pleased to meet you," Steffi says sweetly. "Esther has told me *so* much about you." She licks her cracked lips with the tip of her tongue. Her head sways gently on her neck. A single strand of hair falls into her eyes. She leaves it there. What a heartbreaker.

"Forget it," I say. "None of it is true."

"Steffi used to go to school up by you," my mother says quickly, shoveling some dirt into the hole I have opened in the conversation. "By where you *used* to live," she makes a point of adding.

"Where was that?" I ask.

"Connecticut," Steffi says simply, leaving it at that.

Not a bad answer. Had she supplied me with the actual name of the school in order to let me know immediately just how well off her parents are, I would have been forced to disqualify her immediately from further competition. As it is, she now advances to the second round of questioning. "Where do you go now?" I ask.

"Hunter. Downtown. My father drives me in each day. On his way to work."

The buzzer sounds loudly in my ear. Red lights flash. The duck comes down with the secret word, then flies right off again.

Steffi will not win the grand prize. Not as long as she lets Daddy drive her to school each morning.

"Steff," my mother says familiarly, "they started already in there?"

"Not yet, Esther. Any second now. That's why I came out."

"Then I better go in." She sighs with her entire body. "God," she mutters. "How I hate this part of it."

"Just take it easy in there, huh?" I plead, knowing it will do me no good at all. "It's really hot, there isn't much air, and . . ." Morty is also there, lying in wait. Although I do not spell this last part of it out for her because of Steffi, she gets the message nonetheless.

"Don't worry about me, dear," she says. "I'll be fine. Thank God, neither of you have to go in with me. You should *never* know."

Now that she has brought the two of us together, my mother seems unwilling to walk away and just leave things to chance. She has to put in one last word for me. "You be *very* nice to him, Stephanie," she calls out over her shoulder as she begins slowly moving away. "He's all I have in the world."

"Great, ma," I tell her. "Fabulous thing to say."

"Tell the truth, Steff," my mother demands. "You talk to your father this way also?"

"Never, Esther," she answers. "But then I'm bigger than he is."

Esther laughs. Then she disappears through the middle door of the shul for what I know will be an hour of absolute agony for her. I stand there for a moment, trying to think of something cute to say before I disappear myself. I wrack my brain. Nothing. Living with Lesley has rendered me socially impotent. I no longer can come up with the lines. Fortunately, Steffi has one ready.

"You *do* know who my father is, don't you?" she asks.

"Do I?"

"Nat Weiss," she says.

"Aha," I say. "Right. You're Nat's daughter. Figures. I mean, your last name is Weiss and so is his. . . ."

Poor Steffi. All her life she has been apologizing in advance for her old man. During Open School Week, when parents came to sit quietly at the very back of the classroom so they could watch their brilliant children in action, Nat probably stalked right up to the blackboard, cigar in hand, to say a few heartfelt words.

170

Then he made an appeal, calling names in alphabetical order. All the while, she had to sit there with her head down on her desk, wanting only to go somewhere and die.

Still, from this sorry accident of nature, Steffi has come away a winner. From Nat, the scaly lizard of the desert, she has inherited only the bones in her face. The eyes have come from someone else entirely.

"My father," she says, making me wonder if we are going to spend the entire morning discussing the man, "is really very kind and good-natured. Only sometimes . . . he just gets carried away. It's because he's nervous. I take after him that way."

"*Nat?*" I say. "Nat *Weiss?* He's nervous? What does he have to be nervous about?"

"You try being married to Sol Stryker's younger sister and spending your entire life working for Sol. See how much sleep you get at night." Steffi bites her lower lip. She has been waiting for years to tell someone all about it. The family complaint. For some reason, I have been elected. "They all treat him like *shit*," she says bitterly. "Like he should get down on his hands and knees to thank them for all that they've done for us." Steffi speaks in a low, urgent whisper. Even out here, the Strykers may have people listening. The royal family is never without its spies.

I do admire her for sticking up for her old man. Of course, Nat has probably never denied her a thing. *Clothes?* Certainly, darling. *A nice, expensive, out-of-town college?* Name one, sweetheart, and I'll get you right in. *A diaphragm?* Of course, precious. I'll ask your mother to pick one up for you on the avenue while she's out shopping.

Steffi will be Nat's little baby girl until the day he dies. That is why he drives her to school each morning. He wants to make sure that no one on the subway gets to handle the merchandise. When the time comes, he will make certain that she marries someone headed right for the very top rung of the ladder of success. Yet the two of us are talking as though we have known each other for years. America, as the old man likes to say so bitterly. It is one hell of a country all right.

"I really shouldn't stand here like this," Steffi says. Then she puts her index finger into her right ear. She shakes her head from side to side as though she has only just come from the pool with half a gallon of water still lodged in her semicircular canals.

"Why not?"

"My mother. She'll be out in a second, wanting to know why I'm not keeping Aunt Sylvia company. . . ."

"Sol's wife, huh?"

Steffi nods. Then she goes to work on her ear again. It is certainly a very odd habit. Disconcerting, I would call it. "Steffi," I ask, "is there something wrong with your ear?"

"You don't hear it, do you?"

"Hear what?"

"It's just . . . don't laugh at me, please. Promise you won't."

"I won't," I say, holding up the first two fingers of my right hand. "Scout's honor."

"Sometimes I hear this tone. . . ."

"What do you mean, a tone?"

"A buzz. Like there's a phone off the hook somewhere or it's time to change classes in high school."

"How long have you had this condition?"

"*Years,*" she says, her face brightening as she warms to the topic. "The doctor up at school told me that it would go away if I wanted it to, but it hasn't."

"There's a lot medical science doesn't know these days," I note solemnly. Did I say that? Did I?

"I don't really worry about it anymore. Know why?"

"No," I say cautiously. "Tell me."

"I read in a magazine that Barbra Streisand had the exact same problem when she was young. And look at her now."

How do I find them? I should hang out a shingle and open an office. P. Bindel—Girls with Problems My Specialty. The more neurotic they are, the better I like them. Lesley, who does stretching exercises before going to bed at night, preparing for the career she will never have. Stephanie, who hears a buzzing inside her head but does not mind because Barbra Streisand once had the very same problem.

"Want to walk?" I ask, blurting out the question before I change my mind.

She nods and smiles. She would like nothing better in the entire world. Why, I have no idea. Together we set off for the corner. Gliding along on those long legs of hers, Steffi has no trouble at all keeping up with me. Although it may sound crazy, Lesley and I were never able to walk this way in the street. She would zig when I would zag, the two of us constantly bumping into one another. Then we would argue furiously about whose fault it was.

172

Steffi and I do not have this particular problem. We move together well. Whether this is good or bad, I cannot say. "Listen," I say, throwing caution to the winds on this, the holiest day of the year. "Tell me some more about this tone. What does it *really* sound like to you? A buzzing or a humming?"

Even before she answers, I know that it does not matter what she says. I cannot stop looking at her. Buzzing or humming, what does it matter? To me, she looks good.

CHAPTER EIGHTEEN

BY THE TIME Steffi and I get back to Ahavath Mizrach from our little walk, the sky is completely gray. The bright blue canopy that has been hanging over the temple all morning long is gone. It has been elbowed roughly to one side by thick mushrooming clouds. If I did not know better, I would almost say that it looks like rain. In the neighborhood, it *never* rains on Yom Kippur. It is not permitted.

Leaving Steffi behind to go in through another door so that no one will see us together and start to talk, I push my way into shul. Although the sun is definitely finished for the day outside, in here it is warmer than ever. The air is heavy with the sticky, sour odor of bad breath. Nameless little gases seep from bodies that have not been washed or fed in eighteen hours. If I could scrape my fingers across the smell, it would cake up all white, dry, gritty, and disgusting under my nails. It is just that intense.

Miracle of miracles, the old man is still around. He stands in the corner next to my grandfather as though there is nothing at all unusual about him being here once *Yizkor* is over. Although he is not wearing a *tallis*, he does have a yarmulka on his head. He holds a *Mahzor* in his hands. Who knows? Maybe, as my grandfather likes to say, it *is* going to be a good year, for all of us.

When I come up beside him, Morty tilts back his head. He shoots me a suspicious look. "What'd you do?" he asks. "Walk all the way to Coney Island and back?"

173

I would love to tell him that I have been with Stephanie Weiss, daughter of the *president* of Ahavath Mizrach. But I am too much of a gentleman. Instead, I just nod. To Coney Island and back. Right. "You really missed it, kiddo," he crows. "What a *stink!*"

"Yeah?" I say. "What happened?"

A great wave of *clupping* and shushing runs around the shul. They are starting *Musaf*. They want it so quiet you can hear a pin drop. This fazes the old man not at all. He has something to say. "Stryker walked out," he whispers hoarsely, so excited by the news that he is actually bouncing up and down on the balls of his feet.

"How come?"

"Who knows? Just before it came time for Weiss to call his name, Stryker gets up and marches down the center aisle. Couldn't have been no coincidence. The whole shul saw him do it. What a *stink!*" he says gleefully. "Stayed out *all* during *Yizkor*, then came back only minutes before you. Should have seen Nat's face. White, like a ghost."

"How about Esther?" I ask. "You seen her?"

"Excuse me," he says. "But what does this have to do with the price of tea in China? I'm talking to you about Sol Stryker."

"I know you are. You seen her?"

"Seen her, yeah," he concedes.

"You *talk* to her? Wish her a Happy New Year and an easy fast? Or is that too much to ask?"

The old man stares at me as though I have completely lost my mind. It is not as though I am harboring any secret dreams of Morty and Esther getting back together. That I know is impossible. I just want them to be civil to one another. Polite, which in time may even lead to friendly. What better time and place for them to start than today, here in shul? But the old man does not quite see it that way himself. Frederick of Prussia probably had a whole *slew* of ex-wives he made a point of not speaking to.

Giving up on my previous question, I ask, "So how come *you're* still here? *Yizkor* is over, right?"

"Maybe I'd like to hear *my* father *duchen* on Yom Kippur," he says. "That all right with you?"

"Fine," I say. "I just want you to know . . . I forgive you."

"*You* forgive *me*? For what?"

During the ten days between Rosh Hashanah and Yom Kippur, if you are really religious, you are supposed to ask all of those

174

you know to forgive you for anything you may have done to them during the previous year. "You know," I tell him. "Everything. Anything. Like you're supposed to forgive me. *And* Esther."

He shakes his head. "If you don't mind my saying so, Paulie, this is your problem right here. If you would pay more attention to what is going on around you instead of flying off half-cocked in a thousand different directions at once, you might find it a whole lot easier getting things done."

I cannot argue with him. Concentration and focus have always been my weakest points. "You mean, you *don't* forgive me?" I ask.

"I forgive you, I forgive you," he snaps. "Enough already."

Right in front of us, Sidney Meyers wheels around with a look on his face that says, "How come you two can't afford seats, yet *you're* talking?" It is a question I cannot answer. So I shut my mouth. The old man, however, is not quite finished. "While you're here, Mr. Chief Rabbi," he says, "go find yourself another *Mahzor*. I'm using yours."

I take down another High Holy Day prayer book from the shelf. Flicking quickly through its pages, I find the afternoon service for Yom Kippur. As those around me start mumbling softly to themselves, I try to concentrate on what I am supposed to be reading. Only I cannot. It is just as the old man said. Next to focus, concentration is my number one problem.

Today, the men of the family Bindel have finally assembled, three generations strong, in a single corner of the shul. I stand between my father and my grandfather, unable to understand why either of them have chosen the lives they now lead. My grandfather will not tell me. My father cannot. All around us, people just keep right on praying. I do not know what any of it has to do with me.

Then the cantor begins the *Avodah*, the devotional part of the service that describes the way in which Yom Kippur was celebrated back when the Temple still stood in Jerusalem. From the tribe of Levi, son of Jacob, son of Isaac, son of Abraham, they would choose a man to serve as High Priest for the day. During the week before Yom Kippur, he would be secluded so he could make himself familiar with the service.

Elders were commissioned to read to him the prescribed details of the day, saying, "Lord High Priest, read by yourself; you may have forgotten; or perhaps you have never learned." On the day before Yom Kippur, the High Priest would be taken to the Eastern Gate, so he could view some of the beautiful offerings of the day as they were made to pass before him.

At sunset, the older priests would warn the High Priest to change nothing of what they had instructed him. Then the High Priest would turn aside and weep, for having been suspected. The elders would also shed tears for having had to remind him of his sacred duty in this manner. After staying up all night long, the High Priest would begin Yom Kippur by bathing. Standing in the east, facing west, he would confess his sins.

When the priests and the people standing in the court of the Temple heard God's glorious and revered name clearly expressed by the High Priest with holiness and purity, they would fall to their knees, prostrate themselves and respond: "Blessed be the name of His glorious majesty forever and ever."

Then the High Priest would make the sacrifice, selecting from a pair of goats the one tied with a crimson thread to symbolize the sins of the people of Israel. The people would fall upon their faces in awe. Then the High Priest would enter the most holy place, knowing that if he did not concentrate his mind on what he was about to do, he would fall dead and the atonement of Israel would not be attained.

Having already slaughtered his own bullock, the High Priest now sprinkled the blood once upward and seven times downward. He came out and slaughtered the goat, sprinkling its blood as before, once upward and seven times downward. Then he mixed the blood of both sacrifices and used it to clean the gilded altar. Then he hastened to the scapegoat and made confession of the unintentional and the intentional sins of the people.

Then the High Priest made confession for the people, who prostrated themselves, falling on their faces to intone: "Blessed be the name of His glorious majesty forever and ever." The High Priest then sent the scapegoat into the desert to bear the stain of Israel's iniquities into the wilderness. The scapegoat was driven over the edge of the rock, its bones shattering like a potter's ware. The High Priest opened the he-goat and the bullock and offered their inward parts on the altar. He recited aloud the portions of the Torah concerning Yom Kippur, washed his hands and feet, and took off his linen garments.

Bathing a third time, he put on the golden garments. He made further sacrifices, bathed a fourth time, put on the white linen garments, and entered the most holy place to remove the vessels used to offer incense. Then he took off the linen garments and put them away forever. He bathed a fifth time, put on the golden garments, presented the daily afternoon burnt offering, burned the incense, and lighted the lamps. Then he washed his hands and feet.

In all, he had bathed five times and sanctified his hands and feet ten times. Elated, his face beaming with sunlike radiance, he put on his own clothes. Then the people conducted him to his home, knowing that the crimson thread of wool had turned white and all their sins had been washed away. The people were now washed and purified, their hands clean. They were guiltless, perfectly pure, and wholly renewed. They sang, triumphed, and rejoiced.

Having entered the most holy place and left it safely once again, the High Priest declared a holiday and made a feast for his friends. He prayed: "May it be Thy will, Lord our God and God of our fathers, that the forthcoming year shall be for Thy people, the house of Israel, a year of abundant prosperity; a year of generous decree declared by Thee; a year of grain, wine, and oil . . . a year of dew, rain, and warmth. . . ."

Today, money has taken the place of blood. The sacrifice that once was real is now symbolic. The flashing blade of the knife is nowhere to be seen inside Ahavath Mizrach today. I think they call this progress.

Because the Temple in Jerusalem is no more, thousands of synagogues like Ahavath Mizrach now exist. Once, a single building was enough. Thousands of years after its destruction, we are still mourning that structure and all that it represented, saying *Kaddish* for a building and a way of life that none of us have ever known.

Nor can we ever know it. Not even my grandfather will ever get to see the crimson thread turn white. He will never hear the High Priest pronounce God's glorious name with holiness and purity. Ever since the destruction of the Temple, even the correct pronunciation of the name of God has vanished. With the building has gone the knowledge. The house of Israel has been shattered, its children cast asunder. The words of the *Mahzor* are all that remain. The words, and a single wall of the structure I know will never be rebuilt, at least not in my grandfather's lifetime.

Slipping off his *tallis*, my grandfather grabs me by the arm. "Come," he orders. *"Handt vashen."*

I follow along behind him. All over the shul, men are quietly getting up from their seats and moving toward the back door. There has been no announcement from the pulpit telling them to do this. Anyone not familiar with the order of the service could just go right on praying without noticing a thing. Yet it is happening all the same. The *kohanim* are gathering once again, as they have for nearly six thousand years.

Downstairs, the door to the big kitchen where Solomon usually takes his naps is wide open. The room is filled with men of all ages. Some are even older than my grandfather. Others look as though they have only just been bar mitzvahed. All priests, as I am as well, descendants of the tribe of Levi. Leaning against the wall, they bend forward to undo the laces of their shoes. One by one, they join the curving line that is slowly moving towards the sink. There, Solomon stands proudly filling one shiny metal pitcher after another with water from the tap. Then he hands them out to anyone who can get close enough to take them from him.

"Make room," someone says as my grandfather sweeps through the crowded kitchen. "Here *kommt* Mendel."

As though the order has come directly from some higher authority, those waiting in line obediently fall back to let my grandfather through. Smiling and nodding as though it is only natural that they treat him in this manner, he goes directly to the sink. Bending over with his back braced against it, he undoes the laces of the old high white sneakers that I gave him years ago to wear on Yom Kippur. Then he straightens up again. *"Mein einekel,"* he announces, pointing to me with a single finger. *"Er gaet vashen meinen handten."*

I stare at all the faces staring back at me. To them, I am Mendel Bindel's grandson, and nothing more. Yet it is enough. Nothing I can ever do in my own life will ever mean more to them than the simple fact that I have his blood in my veins. I am accepted by them all without any questions. At long last, I am finally home.

Then I realize that they are all waiting for me to do something. Someone nudges me forward. Solomon shoves a water-beaded metal pitcher into my hands. It is icy cold to the touch. I stand with it by the sink. Silently, I am praying that I do not spill it all over myself. Impatiently, my grandfather hikes up the sleeves of his long white robe. He thrusts his thin wrists forward over the edge of the sink. Then he nods with his head, motioning that I should begin to pour.

I lift the pitcher up over the edge of the sink. Carefully, I tip it towards him. A forked cascade of water, split in two by the pitcher's divided spout, spills out onto his hands. Rubbing one over the other, he snorts through his nose. "More *vasser*," he orders. "*Alles*. Pour it out. *Daf ganz* clean *veren*."

I upend the pitcher over his hands. The water covers both of his wrists in a thick, translucent stream that has both weight and power. I become the pitcher. I am pouring out everything left inside of me. Soon, I will be empty. Finally satisfied, my grandfather grunts and steps back from the sink. He shakes his hands. Tiny droplets of water fly in all directions. Someone claps me heartily on the back. Someone congratulates me in Yiddish. The pitcher is taken from my hands. A new person moves towards the sink. The pace quickens, the assembly line of men moving through the room in a definite hurry now. I search for my grandfather in the crowd.

He is already gone, out the door and on his way upstairs. I go right after him. He walks with his hands folded carefully before him so that he will not accidentally touch something and have to wash them all over again. The laces of his sneakers flap wildly as he mounts the steps one by one. Following along, I catch up to him just as he reaches the door leading back into shul. Without being told, I know enough to open it for him so he will not have to use his hands. I cannot be certain that he even remembers who I am at the moment. Not that it matters. He has far more important things on his mind.

Going directly into the corner, he lifts his *tallis* up from the chair. Kissing its collar, he swings it into a big, billowing circle. Smoothly, he steps inside its whirling orbit, letting the shawl wrap itself neatly about his shoulders. Picking up his *Mahzor*, he places the book between the curled fingers of his right hand and his heart, cradling it tightly against his chest. Then he slowly begins walking up the center aisle from the cheap seats to the podium.

Pausing at the bottom of the red carpeted steps that lead to the Ark, he manages to pry off both sneakers without using his hands. Looking even smaller than usual in his stocking feet, he pads silently up the steps. Just to be allowed near the Ark on Yom Kippur is an honor of the first order, reserved solely for the sons, nephews, and cousins of the big givers who sit down front.

If my grandfather knows this, he gives no sign. He yanks confidently on the cord that hangs from the Ark. The beaded, starry white curtains fly open before him.

Stepping back, he shakes the rabbi's hand. The rabbi nods. Moving to the lectern, he loudly clears his throat. *"Friends,"* he croaks, his voice filled with rocks, gravel, and sand. The rabbi looks at least twenty years older than he did this morning. All the blood has drained from his face. His eyes float helplessly in dark sunken pools. His skin is the exact color of melted wax.

"The *kohanim* will perform the priestly blessing," he intones. "When the Temple still stood in Jerusalem, this prayer was said every morning and evening. Now we get to hear it only a very few times a year. It is a very great *mitzvah* indeed to receive this blessing. I think all of us know that it is not proper to look directly at the *kohanim* when they *duchen*.

"But please, do not, as I have seen so many do, despite what I tell them year after year, turn your backs to the Torah during the prayer. This is *very* disrespectful. Instead, look down into your *Mahzor* or stare at the floor. Avert your eyes by all means. But please . . . *not* by turning your back."

He pauses to lick his lips. For a moment, he looks as though he is going to say something more. Then he changes his mind. "Page eight hundred and sixty-eight in the *Mahzor*," he announces instead. "The *kohanim* recite the priestly blessing."

Slowly, he comes down the steps to join the rest of the congregation. "You see?" Morty whispers loudly in my ear. "He ain't even a *coin*. He's *gotta* step down. You or me, kiddo, we could be up there right now, if we wanted."

"So how come we're not?" I ask.

The old man shrugs. Instead of answering, he pokes me in the arm so that I will look towards the center aisle. All the men who were down in the kitchen having their hands washed are now making their way up to the Ark. They arrange themselves before it in a ragged line. Like a drill instructor inspecting a company of raw recruits, my grandfather carefully looks them over. Then he nods. These men will do. With his right hand, he rolls open the wooden doors of the Ark. The Torahs come suddenly into view. They are gorgeous in their gold-embroidered robes and silver breastplates. They sparkle in the light, like warriors from Biblical times.

I take a quick look at the women's section. My mother is standing at the very back of the shul. She has this really strange

180

expression on her face. At any moment, she may burst out crying.

The congregation lets loose with a rapid-fire burst of prayer. Then the *kohanim* begin the introductory blessing. I stare down at my *Mahzor*. Looking at the *kohanim* when they *duchen* is absolutely forbidden. All around me, men twice my age have their heads down. Their eyes are glued to the floor. They are as scared as I am to take a peek. Despite the rabbi's plea, more people than I can count have turned their backs to the Ark. With their eyes shut and their *Mahzors* closed before them, they stand facing the back of the shul. They are not being disrespectful. At least not on purpose. This is the way they have always stood during *duchenen*. It is too late for them to change now.

On the page of the *Mahzor* before me, the letters of the Hebrew alphabet begin to swim one into the other. The words wriggle across the paper like so many tiny black tadpoles stroking madly in every direction at once. The *kohanim* begin to *duchen* in earnest. Their hoarse voices rise and fall in a confused, tumbling river of sound. Except for my grandfather. His voice I hear above all the rest.

He is not so much singing as wailing, in that manner known only to people of the desert. Giving out with a single long continuous note, he holds it for longer than seems humanly possible. Then, suddenly, he goes even higher, crying out from down deep inside. The sound echoes and wavers across the rows before slowly dying away. Then it starts right up again. Actual chills run down my back. The hairs on my neck stand straight up. Goosebumps form on my arms. It is not just me, either. Across the entire shul, people feel it. His voice runs through everyone like an electrical current.

This is his single moment. This is the act he has been put on earth to perform. As he blesses the others, the power passes directly through him to those assembled below. Always, my grandfather knows precisely to whom he is praying. With him, it is entirely personal. *Kvitching* and carrying on, he appeals to God just as he heard *kohanim* before him do in those little *shtetl* shuls where those who *duchened* with a full heart often were carried out afterwards into the street on the shoulders of the congregation, great heroes who had won God's forgiveness for the entire community.

Again and again, his voice cuts through the silent shul like a knife. I *have* to see him up there, no matter how dangerous it may be to look. Gazing up out of the corner of my left eye, the one I figure I can always do without should God suddenly pluck it from my face in anger, I catch a quick glimpse of the *kohanim* standing before the Ark.

They face the Torahs with their *tallisem* drawn up over their heads. They sway like an endless caravan of black-and-white striped canopies moving slowly through the wilderness towards the Promised Land. Then they turn to face the congregation. By all rights, I should stop looking now. But I cannot turn away. The power is too great.

Holding their *tallisem* up over their heads on the very tips of their fingers, which are spread in the secret manner known only to them, they rock slowly from side to side. They keen and wail and moan. They plead with God. They implore Him to take pity on us. They ask Him to permit us to live in peace.

The *kohanim* glimmer softly in the pale gold light of early afternoon. They shimmer like incandescent souls from another age and another time. Relentlessly, my grandfather drives them on. Whenever they begin to falter, his voice rises even higher, forcing them to keep up. Where he gets the strength, I have no idea. But he is always there, pushing them on to greater heights.

I have spent the entire day fasting. The shul is hot and airless. Quite possibly, I am not exactly in my right mind. But I swear that I can feel my soul being pulled from my body. It rises up out of me towards my grandfather's voice. One self is being separated from the other, the one that is left behind purer and more real. All the various, miserable events of my recent life have conspired to bring me back here for only one reason. So that I can hear my grandfather *duchen,* and respond.

This small, quiet man, who never asks for nor ever gives any explanations, is passing on to me the understanding he was given by his father, who got it in turn from his father before him. *Kohanim* all, our line stretches all the way back to when the Temple still stood in Jerusalem. As long as one of us is left alive, the Temple still stands.

On the holiest day of the year, with the Ark open before me and all the Torahs clearly visible, I am having my own little revelation. Silently, I make a solemn promise. Before I leave again, I will give him something in return to acknowledge my acceptance of this great gift. It seems only fair.

Up on the podium, the *kohanim* take their *tallisem* down from their heads. They drape their heavy shawls across their shoulders once again. One by one, they slowly begin moving off the platform, shaking hands as they go. My grandfather alone remains behind. He shuts the curtains on the Ark. Then he turns towards the congregation. The ceremony is now complete. The High Priest has entered and then safely left the most holy place. My grandfather's face beams with a sunlike radiance. He is new, clean, and wholly remade, an old man no longer. His work for the day is done.

The moment passes. As he steps down into the center aisle, he is once again just the *shamus* of Ahavath Mizrach, a man who cannot even afford to pay for his own seat in shul on Yom Kippur. The power has passed through him completely. He has manifested and become. Now he is once again just who he was before. Silently, I thank God for my grandfather.

Men wait for him right at the very edge of the steps. Eagerly, they press forward to shake his hand. They slap him on the back. With big smiles on their faces, they offer him their heartiest congratulations. Feeling dazed and shaken, I stumble along the back wall towards the center aisle. I am not alone. All the men from the cheap seats are standing there to welcome back one of their own who is returning in triumph, like a king. I cannot help but wonder if he will even remember who I am.

"*Yasha ko-ach*, Mendel," Murray Friedberg calls out, wishing him strength and health as he enthusiastically pumps his hand.

"*Biz a hundredt and tsventsig yuren*," Sidney Meyer adds. For a hundred and twenty years.

"Next year, Mendel," someone behind me calls out, "you'll *duchen* again on Yom Kippur, God willing."

Shaking hands and smiling, my grandfather comes towards me. His small face is bright with pleasure. Nervously I put out my hand to him. He shakes it like all the rest. Then he stops dead in his tracks, looks at me, and smiles. His clear blue eyes sparkle. He *knows*, without my having to say a thing.

The two of us have a contract all right. It is not written down on paper. There are no terms to be negotiated later. Yet it exists all the same. The funny thing is that I have only just found this out. He has known it all along.

CHAPTER NINETEEN

IT IS GETTING late. All around me, men with herring breath so strong it should be put into jars no longer even bother to look up at the clock. Their bodies tell them that it is almost over. Most of the men have long since pulled their ties away from the tight collars of their stiffly starched white shirts. Under their *tallisem*, beneath the rich fabric of their fine three piece suits, the muscles ache and throb. Down in the legs is where the pain is worst. Although it is nearly over, it has not yet ended. We still have a way to go.

"So, Mendel?" Murray Friedberg asks. "What are we looking at today in terms of going home? Seven-thirty?"

"What seven-thirty?" Morty demands. Amazingly he is still around, having said not a single word about heading back to the apartment to put up some coffee even though the sun has already definitely set behind the bank across the street from his apartment. "It's almost five now, right? You got *Maftir Yonah*, then *Ne'ilah*. When did they *ever* get through *Ne'ilah* here in less than an hour and a quarter?"

"They want to speed up," Sidney Meyers observes. "They can *fly* through *Ne'ilah*. Those last thirty pages, they go like . . . zzzzt! No, Mendel?"

My grandfather shrugs, making a sleepy face. He reaches up slowly with his fingers to massage the very edge of his nose. "*Efsher*, seven-thirty," he says, venturing a guess. "Depends *uf um rebbe*."

To me, it makes no great difference when we finish. I am here for the duration. I feel no need to be anywhere else. For the first time in longer than I can remember, I am actually calm. At peace, you might say. When the service ends, it ends. Not a second before.

"*Gib a kuk*," my grandfather says, gesturing towards the front of the shul. "*Er gaet* auctioneering."

Up on the podium, the rabbi stands holding on to the lectern like it is the only thing still keeping him on his feet. A dense layer of five o'clock shadow has arrived right on time to take possession of his face. He does his best to smile. Then he says, "Friends, we now come to the reading of the second portion of the Torah for *Yoam Ha-Kee-Poreem*. The *Maftir Yonah*, the Book of Jonah. As I am sure you know, it has always been a tradition here at Ahavath Mizrach to auction this section of the service off to raise funds for the shul. First the *aliyahs*, then the *Maftir Yonah* itself."

"Tradition," Morty mutters. "They never did it before he got here."

"*Er hat gebrungen it mit im from* his *anderer* shul," my grandfather explains. Then he sits himself down, resting his chin against the flat of his palm. "Is *nisht natig*."

"You bet it's not necessary," the old man says.

Up at the lectern, the rabbi does his best to smile. "Perhaps this year," he suggests. "Some of you younger men . . ." He makes a vague gesture with his hand toward the back of the shul. I realize that he is talking about *us*, all of those in the cheap seats. "Could form a cart-*el* and buy together, as a group."

"Why not a holding company while we're at it?" the old man asks.

"For the first *aliyah*," the rabbi announces, opening the bidding. "This is for the blessing over the Torah said by a *kohen*. But a Levite or a Yisraelite could buy it for a friend. A woman could purchase it for her husband or son. For the first *aliyah*, starting at four times *chai*."

Chai, the eighteenth letter of the Hebrew alphabet, represents not only the number eighteen but also "life" as in the Hebrew word *l'chaim*. At seventy-two dollars, or four times *chai*, the first *aliyah* is a steal. Even I know that. A real bargain.

"Four times *chai*," the rabbi repeats, looking around the *schul* for a bidder. "For the first *aliyah*, four times *chai*."

No sooner are the words out of his mouth than a hand shoots up from the aisle seat in the second row. The big diamond ring on the pinky catches the fading light of late afternoon without breaking it up into colors. Nat Weiss is making his opening bid. The rabbi nods, acknowledging the offer. "For the first *aliyah*," he says, "*five* times *chai*." He has seventy-two dollars. Now he is looking for ninety.

Murray Friedberg throws his hand up into the air. It takes the rabbi a while to find him, but where money is concerned, the man's eyesight is perfect. Twenty-twenty, all the way. He nods.

"Six times *chai*," he says, boosting the price again.

"Murray," Sidney Meyers whispers loudly, "since when do *you* buy *aliyahs* on Yom Kippur?"

"Who's buying?" Murray answers, snorting through his nose. "Nat wants it so bad, let him pay *top* dollar. He can afford."

As if on cue, Nat's hand rises in the air once more. "Seven times *chai*," the rabbi calls out. In his chair up by the Ark, Judah Benjamin leans forward. Loudly, he clears his throat. The rabbi turns to look at him. "Eight times *chai*," the rabbi says, nodding.

"He'll *never* get it," the old man whispers in my ear. "First *aliyah* always goes to Nat. He buys it every year to impress his brother-in-law."

"Eight times *chai*," the rabbi says again. Nat's hand goes up into the air. The rabbi nods. "Nine times *chai*," he says. Scanning the rows with his eyes, he seeks the buyer who may be tempted to take a sudden plunge at this price. "For the first *aliyah*," he repeats. "Nine times *chai*."

Drawing out the suspense, he steps back from the lectern. The first *aliyah* hangs in the balance. Anyone who suddenly reaches up to scratch his nose while the rabbi is looking at him will find that he has been saddled with a hundred-and-sixty-two dollar first *aliyah*. It definitely could happen. I make certain to keep both my hands at my sides.

"Nine times *chai* for the *ersta moul*," the rabbi chants. "Nine times *chai* for the *tsveita moul*," he says slowly, drawing out the suspense. "Nine times *chai* for the *dritta moul*," he announces definitively, bringing his clenched fist down hard on the lectern as though it is an auctioneer's gavel. "Nat Weiss, president of our shul. The first *aliyah*. How many years in a row is it now, Nat?"

"Five," Nat calls out modestly from his seat on the aisle. I guess this is certainly something to be proud of, especially if you have Nat's money.

Nat Weiss buys the second *aliyah*. He buys the third and then the fourth. The rabbi makes a big production of refusing to sell the fifth one to him, pointedly ignoring Nat even as he waves his hand wildly in the air from the second row. Instead, it goes to Sol Bender, the dentist. The sixth *aliyah* Nat buys, just for a change of pace.

"This is right?" the old man demands, talking in my ear once

186

more. "That one man should be able to buy them all? The rich buy, and the poor cry?"

I have no answer that I can give him. Making a rough calculation in my head, I figure that Nat has already laid out nearly five hundred dollars just for the honor of distributing the *aliyahs* on Yom Kippur. On Shabbos, when he does this without having to pay for the privilege, he probably has to beg men to go up and say the blessings over the Torah. No one wants to make a mistake up there, embarrassing himself in front of the entire shul. Today, though, it is a great honor to be given such an opportunity. Today is Yom Kippur.

"Now, my friends," the rabbi intones, "we come to the *Maftir Yonah* itself, a very, very special *mitzvah*. Because I feel that we are going to have some *extremely* spirited bidding this year, I would like to weed out the competition a little by starting at eight times *chai*."

A little gasp runs across the shul. *Eight* times *chai* to start with. This is definitely heady business all right. Very heady. Only the big givers and the real plungers, the large money boys who sit down front, will be able to withstand this kind of pressure. No five-and-dime operators need even apply.

"In honor of my lovely wife, Leah, and my two wonderful children, Daniel and Rachel," the rabbi says. "*I* say eight times *chai*. Nine times *chai*? Nat? Fine. Ten times *chai*. . . ."

To my amazement, a woman sitting in the very same row as my mother puts up her hand. Her face is pale and fine, like bone china. The expensive gold encrusted cameo made of ivory on her burgundy dress immediately establishes her credentials. In a voice that rings through the temple like a solid silver fork being struck against a cut crystal decanter, she says, "Ten times *chai*."

"Huh-*ho*," the old man exclaims, letting his breath out all at once. "Sylvia Stryker. Sol's wife. A *great* woman, Paulie. Always has a 'Hello, how are you doing, Morty,' for me when she comes into the post office. You know," he says, looking slowly around the shul, "this could be good. She can buy and sell Nat. With her left hand."

Just then, Murray Friedberg raises his hand again. "Eleven times *chai*," he calls out.

Sidney Meyers nearly keels over in his seat. "Murray," he hisses from between clenched teeth, "you lost your mind altogether?"

187

"Twelve times *chai*," Nat calls out quickly from the second row.

"I'm crazy all right," Murray says, congratulating himself for having boosted the price without putting down a single cent of his own money. "Like a fox."

"Thirteen," Sylvia Stryker says in a dignified manner, her voice carrying across all the rows just the same.

"Fourteen," says the cantor from his oversized chair by the Ark.

"Uh-oh," the old man says. "Here comes trouble."

Nat Weiss is headed down the center aisle towards our corner. His head is down. His shoulders are hunched together. "Where the *hell* is he going?" Murray Friedberg asks, not really expecting an answer.

"Fifteen times *chai*," the rabbi sings out, looking for a buyer.

Nat rounds the corner of the last row. He passes directly in front of Marvin. Marvin has long since left the land of the living. Slumped against the back wall with his arms crossed over his *Mahzor*, he is either asleep or unconscious. Marvin does not have to worry. God will surely inscribe his name in the Book of Life for the coming year. Who else will take care of him?

"What's the big hurry, Nat?" Murray Friedberg asks pleasantly. "You gotta call your broker?"

Nat ignores him completely. He has far more important business on his mind. Before he can get to my grandfather, Morty puts his hand on Nat's arm. "Nat," he says, "so how come you missed an *aliyah?*"

"Ah," Nat says from out of the side of his mouth. "They shut me out. I got the first, the second, the third, the fourth, and the sixth," he says, ticking them off on his fingers. "So who was running in the fifth? Not some horse you were on, was it, Morty?"

Then he laughs. Nat is not exactly having the greatest Yom Kippur of his life. First, his brother-in-law walked out of shul on him. Then they shut him out of the fifth *aliyah*. Now he is engaged in a bidding contest for the *Maftir Yonah* with his very own sister-in-law. I almost feel sorry for the man. Really, I do. Almost, but not quite.

"Mendel," he says, shaking my grandfather by the shoulder. "The kid. Can he say *Maftir Yonah?*"

For a single terrifying second, I think he is talking about me. A bolt of pure fear courses through my entire body. "Who?" my grandfather asks, looking a little glazed. *Duchenen* has really taken it out of him. He needs to go home right now and rest.

"The *kid*," Nat says impatiently. "The kid. *Marvin*."

"Marvin?" my grandfather says, his eyes opening wide. "*Der Maftir Yonah?*" He shakes his head slowly from side to side. "*Es zer* long, Nat."

"He told me he could," Nat protests. Exactly when Marvin did this, Nat does not say. Somehow, I cannot imagine the two of them ever having sat down to discuss this particular question. Of course I could be wrong. "I wanna buy it for him," Nat says.

There is no way Marvin will ever get through the Book of Jonah in one piece up there before the Ark. Instead, he will make a complete and total fool of himself, stumbling over words that he cannot pronounce, stuttering and *fumphering* and fumbling. Every last mistake that he makes will be corrected out loud as well, for everyone to hear. So the law decrees when a person reads before the Torahs.

"*Er kan*," my grandfather says, more to get Nat out of his face than because it is true. "*Efsher*," he adds. It is the single biggest "maybe" I have heard in my entire life. Not that Nat picks up on it.

"I *knew* he could," Nat says quickly, straightening back up. "That's why I'm gonna give him his chance. I mean, it's only right. Let the kid have it, I thought to myself. As a *gesture*, you know?"

I know all right. Nat Weiss is going to buy the *Maftir Yonah* and then make himself look good by giving it away to a totally helpless case like Marvin. Nat's sister-in-law will not be able to say a word about it either. Not without looking bad. Nat has figured out all the angles. In his twisted mind, this is what passes for charity.

"Listen," I say, desperately grabbing for the old man's arm as Nat goes back toward the front of the shul, "we can't let him do this."

"*We?*" he says. "What you mean '*we*,' Kemo Sabe? What am I supposed to do about it? Make a citizen's arrest?"

"Stop him."

"Stop him? How?"

"Listen," I say. "Nat forced the rabbi to make that appeal this morning because he thought that they had wiped out half of Israel? Only they hadn't, right?"

"Right. So far."

189

"Then he called names. . . ."

"So? There's no law against it."

"How about Nat having Solomon in here with a tape recorder under his coat so he could make certain that anyone who made a pledge would come up with the money later on?"

"Go-*wan*," the old man says, unable to believe what I am telling him.

"I swear on my life. Ask Solomon if it's true. Nat *is* president of the shul, right? He pays Solomon's salary, right? Solomon does whatever Nat tells him to do."

"A tape recorder?" Murray Friedberg says, turning around in his seat. "This I *never* heard of," he says sadly. "Not even in Beth-El."

"And they're Reform," Sidney Meyers chimes in.

"Hold your horses here for a second," the old man mutters, as though what I am telling him has only just struck home. "A *little* tape recorder? Like a pocket model? American made, not Jap?"

"How do I know?" I moan. "I didn't see what brand it was."

"Fifteen times *chai*," the rabbi calls out. Up goes Nat's hand from the second row. The *Maftir Yonah* already is in his pocket.

"Could be the truth," the old man allows. "I know that Nat owns one. He told me so himself."

"He's buying the *Maftir Yonah* to make himself look good," I say, the words tumbling so rapidly from my mouth that I cannot keep track of them. "He's going to give it to Marvin so his brother-in-law won't be able to say anything to him. How is Marvin going to look up there, in front of everyone? Huh?"

Having heard his name mentioned, Marvin straightens up against the back wall. His eyes open slowly. Grinning madly, he strikes himself in the forehead with the back of his hand. He is warming up for what is left of the Yom Kippur service. "Murray," Sidney Meyers says in a low, even voice. "Morty's kid has got a point."

"Fifteen times *chai*," the rabbi calls out, starting to close the bidding. *"Ersta moul."*

The old man looks off into space for a moment, as though he expects guidance to come to him from up above. The little muscle in his jaw is twitching like crazy. Then he leans forward, grabbing Murray by the shoulder. "Murray," he says, "I got a hundred bucks. Let's take it away from him."

"I'm in for fifty," Sidney says quickly.

"Gee," Murray says, counting on his fingers. "Give me a

chance here. Fifteen times *chai* is . . . a hundred and eighty . . . and ninety . . . two seventy. Two hundred and seventy bucks. I'll take seventy-five of it but we're short . . . forty-five."

"Forty-five," I blurt out. "Between my mother and me, we'll raise it. *Quick*. He's gonna close it."

"Fifteen times *chai*," the rabbi says. "*Tsveita moul.*"

"Fifteen times *chai*," Murray Friedberg sings out, his big voice filling the shul.

It is worth every penny just to see the looks on the faces of the men up front. Slowly they turn in their seats. They want to see which *pishers* from the back even have the nerve to enter the bidding at this price. I feel as though I am going to bust wide open right on the spot. *We* have said fifteen times *chai*. *We* have a cartel. Fifteen times *chai*, it is. I mean, how can they stop us now? By running a quick check on our credit ratings?

"Sixteen," Nat says, just like that.

I slump against the wall. We are finished. There is no way we can come back now. Even on Yom Kippur, one miracle is more than a person can reasonably expect. Only before I know what is happening, the old man is off like a shot. He goes across the shul to the women's section, leaning over to talk to my mother.

For a second, that cold, stony look I know so well ices up her face. Then she relaxes, actually smiling as she nods her head. Turning away from the old man, she leans across the row towards Sylvia Stryker, talking a blue streak all the while. The rabbi's wife gets into the conversation. They all start smiling. Sylvia Stryker gets to her feet. She walks towards the old man. The two of them talk for a second. Sylvia nods. Then she goes by herself to where the center aisle begins.

A tall, imposing looking woman, Sylvia would be a force in the shul even if she did not also happen to be the great Sol's wife. Slowly she puts her hand up into the air. Her blood red fingernails glow in a warm patch of dappled yellow sunlight. "Twenty times *chai*," she announces in a loud, clear voice that rings out through the entire shul. "In honor of Mendel Bindel, our *shamus* for so many years, who gladdened all our hearts today with his *duchenen* just as he does every year."

My grandfather looks up. "*Vass?*" he asks. "*Gaet saying Kaddish?*"

Nat Weiss twists around in his seat. He shoots his sister-in-law a look of pure and unadulterated hate. Then his face gives way. His body sags. Suddenly he looks completely used up, like one of those crushed metal fuel cans you see lying everywhere in empty lots.

We have him now all right. I mean, what can he do? Go head-to-head with Sylvia? Her resources are unlimited. Besides, everyone in shul knows that she is buying *Maftir Yonah* for my grandfather, who cannot possibly afford it on his own. *We* have him now all right, coming and going.

"If I am not mistaken," the rabbi says proudly, "this is a new record for *Maftir Yonah*. May it be a good year for all of us. Twenty times *chai ersta moul*. Twenty times *chai tsveita moul*. *Maftir Yonah*, bought by Sylvia Stryker, in honor of our *shamus*, Mendel Bindel."

On the very last day of the season, we have won the pennant with a two-out home run in the bottom of the ninth. The home team has triumphed. The boys from the cheap seats are on top at last. When the old man comes back to the corner, his eyes are as big as headlights. I actually grab him by the shoulders and give him a giant hug, hanging on until I feel the stubble on his cheeks rubbing the skin on my face. Incredibly, he hugs me right back. Out of the corner of my eye, I see my mother down at the other end of the shul. She is crying into her little balled-up handkerchief. It is all just too perfect. For a moment, I actually feel like I have a family again.

Only when it comes time for my grandfather to say *Maftir Yonah*, he is just not all that interested in doing it. Twice, the old man asks him why not. Both times he just waves his hand in front of his face, as though to indicate that it is just not important to him, one way or the other. He must be more tired than any of us realize.

Instead, the old man gets the cantor to do it. Which is just fine with me. So long as Nat has been denied the honor, and Marvin has been spared the ordeal. By the time they get through *Maftir Yonah*, it is nearly half past six. Murray Friedberg and Sidney Meyers are looking up at the clock and making faces at one another that say, "No *way* we'll be out by seven thirty."

Up at the podium, a new reader takes over at the Torah. He moves his head up and down on his neck a couple of times, buzzes like an electric typewriter shifting into a higher gear, and covers ten pages with a single breath. We have gotten off the local and boarded the express.

All through *Ne'ilah*, the Ark stays open. Everyone has to stand. My grandfather makes a little comeback all on his own.

When he leads the mourner's *Kaddish*, he does it as fast as I have ever heard him do it. With one hand curled over the edge of the bench before him for balance, he opens his mouth and the words of the prayer just come rolling out in that peculiar, driving rhythm he alone can generate when he really gets up a head of steam.

A lot of people who have not been in shul since *Kol Nidre* began filtering into the temple. They jam themselves against the back wall. They have all come to hear the *shofer*. With them they have brought the cold night air. Outside, it is completely dark. The streetlamp on the corner makes the big, pebbled stained glass window above my head flicker and glow. In order to go on reading from my *Mahzor*, I have to tilt the book up towards the tiny *Yizkor* lights that are still blazing brightly behind me.

The newcomers have not spent the entire day in shul. They do not know what we have been through. We are the ones who have stood and swayed and prayed and chanted since early morning, remaining in one place as the day moved on around us. We are the team. *We* have survived yet another Yom Kippur. Soon it will be over. For all of us.

During *Ne'ilah*, the phrase "seal us" in the Book of Life replaces "inscribe us." People relax. The decision has already been made. The weight is off our shoulders. We have done our best. "Do Thou grant us pardon/At the time of closing," the congregation reads aloud from the *Mahzor*: "Those named few in number/Raise their eyes unto Thee/And worship tremblingly/At the time of closing."

All the faces that will not see one another again for an entire year turn toward the Ark. The *Maftir* chants, "Open for us the gate of prayer/Even at the closing of the gate/Even now that the day has declined." We are almost there. We sing *Ovenu Malchenu* for the very last time. Then everyone says the *Shema* out loud, repeating "Blessed be the name of His glorious majesty forever and ever" three times in a row. Then "The Lord is God!" is repeated seven times.

Up on the podium, the man hired to blow *shofer* puts the curved ram's horn to his lips. He leans back and gives it a really strong *bluse*. A long, cold, echoing blast rings through the shul, first growing wider, then slowly narrowing into a single note that echoes through my soul.

The entire congregation thunders, *"L'shanoah haba'oah bi Yerushalayim."* "Next Year in Jerusalem." All my life, I have heard these words shouted out at the very end of Yom Kippur without ever once understanding their real meaning. Now I know. This is the gift I will give my grandfather. I will send him to Israel while he is still able to make the trip. With his very own eyes, he will get to see the last, standing wall of the Temple where once the priestly blessing was performed from a raised platform twice a day and people lived according to the laws of Moses, with God always in their hearts. No one deserves it more.

Yom Kippur is now officially over. I take off my *tallis* and shut my *Mahzor*. I have to tell my grandfather of my decision. Only before I can reach him, the crowd sweeps me towards the center aisle. I am carried out through the middle door so rapidly that I do not even have time to reach my hand to the *mezzuzah* on the doorpost. Before I know what is happening, I am outside the building, standing in the street.

The cold night air shocks me awake. I hear a loud, low pitched rumbling. A flash of jagged lightning cracks over the roof of the shul. Unbelievably, it starts to rain, something it never does on Yom Kippur in the neighborhood. Large dewy drops of rain fall into my eyes and mouth. They spot the pavement around my feet.

Even at the time of closing, a gate has opened to let me through. Before me, the new year lies like a path through the wilderness that is straight, smooth, and easy to follow. All I have to do now is walk it. Surely, this cannot be so hard. I will just put one foot after the other, again and again and again.

II
ON
THE
AVENUE

CHAPTER TWENTY

THE EYES WERE still good. Of that Esther was certain. Even now, they had the power to command people's attention from across a room, making them think twice before they dared to interrupt her when she spoke. Only with the eyes could she let him know that there was definitely someone home upstairs at all times tonight, carefully listening, considering, and evaluating everything that he said. She would engage his interest with her eyes and then hold it with the smile, her sparkling white teeth appearing slowly as her generous mouth, which some people thought was too large, widened with amusement. The overall effect would be blinding. Jerry Kahn would be riveted, unable to drift away from her for more than a second at a time.

The eyes had always been the very best thing about her face. If Esther worked overtime with the eyes tonight, there was a good chance that he would not notice all that much else about her. For although the dress she had selected for the occasion was certainly proper, black and respectable, it was nothing flashy. The shoes and the bag that went with it matched perfectly without being anything very special either.

Less than an hour ago, Toni had finished doing her hair, staying behind in the shop long past closing to make certain that Esther would look better tonight than she ever had before. Yet none of it would mean a thing unless Esther herself could convince Jerry Kahn that she was accustomed to going out in the middle of the week with a man she barely knew to a restaurant she had only heard other people rave about.

Sitting before her bedroom mirror, staring at herself in the polished glass as she clipped on her earrings, Esther could not help wondering whether she had made a mistake by accepting this dinner invitation. After all, the man's wife had been dead for only a little more than a year. Just from having seen him around the shul, she knew already that Jerry Kahn was a fussy man.

197

"Very particular" was how she had described him to Toni in the shop. Very particular about his clothes and his shoes and the company that he kept.

Unlike Dom, who had stood smirking behind the third chair all the while that Toni had worked on her, Jerry Kahn did not have to make a big show of his manhood. He was polite, courteous, and gentle, the way a *real* gentleman was supposed to be. There was something elegant and understated about the way in which he carried himself that was almost feminine. To Esther, this indicated a kind of good taste that few other men in the neighborhood even knew the first thing about.

Unfortunately, the difficult little details of this evening that she had not yet dared to call a date even in her own mind were driving her crazy. It had been so long since Esther had gone out with anyone that she had forgotten precisely how it all worked. For instance, when Jerry finally came to pick her up—and the moment could not arrive too soon now that she was ready— would he cruise down the block, blow his horn a couple of times, and then expect her to run out into the street to greet him like some giddy, overexcited schoolgirl?

Certainly not. Not Jerry Kahn. He would ring the doorbell and then come up. That would be all right. So long as he did not go into the dining room and look too closely at the awful, faded roses on the wallpaper. Of course, he would not be bringing her flowers. Men did not do that anymore. They were not going to the prom tonight. They were, both of them, old. They were fully grown adults. And yet Esther was nervous.

The house itself was immaculate. So clean that a person could eat right off the floor. Esther had taken the afternoon off from work, dusting and straightening and arranging so that everything would look perfect when he came. She was fairly certain that her father-in-law already knew Jerry Kahn from shul. So he would be no problem. Not that he ever was. Not really.

Although it was probably foolish to think this way, Esther could not help recalling the night when she had first gone out with Morty. He had taken her to Luna Park. It was the kind of cheap date in which he had delighted.

That night, the dark sky over the amusement park had been filled with fireworks launched from a barge moored out at sea. Above their heads, a series of brilliant, glowing flowers had unfolded their fiery petals, blossoming among the clouds. The overflow crowd assembled on the boardwalk had greeted each display with long drawn out "oooohs" and "aaaahs." Soon enough, the fireworks had faded away, falling back into the sea as dead gray ash and blackened cinder. The marriage that she and Morty had made together had ended up exactly the same way.

Reaching for a cigarette that she had no intention of lighting, Esther realized that after all these years she could remember only how the fireworks had looked and the outfit she had worn. A jacket with large, padded shoulders and raglan sleeves over a pleated skirt that had fallen to just below her knees. Back then, her legs had still been good enough to get away without stockings. She had been young and thin, with eyes that commanded everyone's attention even before she began to speak.

What Morty had said to her, where and what they had eaten, the things they had done on all their other dates, she no longer recalled at all. Mercifully, her memory had discarded all this information. Better that way. She did not need to know it anymore. And yet, stuck away somewhere at the bottom of a shoe box at the very back of her closet, there was a photograph of her in that very outfit, standing proudly in front of Luna Park on Labor Day, at the very end of the season.

From somewhere outside the frame, the laughing lady by the fun house had been cackling loudly, and with good reason. Less than six months later, she and Morty had gotten married. Esther sighed. The next time Paulie came over for dinner, she would have to dig that picture out and show it to him. At the very least, it would make him laugh.

"Esther," her father-in-law called out from the living room, "*er kommt.*"

Sliding the cigarette back into its pack, which she deposited quickly in the top drawer of her dressing table, Esther got to her feet just as the doorbell rang. In the living room, her father-in-law was already standing, as though *he* was the one expecting company. He seemed a bit unsteady on his feet and slightly disoriented, as though at the moment he did not know exactly where he was.

Lately, the old man had hardly been sleeping at all. A week ago, Esther had gotten up at some ungodly hour of the night to go to the bathroom only to find him emerging fully dressed from his bedroom. Half asleep and not really expecting an answer, she had asked him in Yiddish where in the world he thought he was going. "*Daf gaen en shul,*" he had explained. "*Daf* saying Kaddish.*"

199

She had accepted the explanation without questioning him any further. It was only after he had left the house and she was lying in bed unable to fall asleep again that she remembered that the first service of the day did not begin until well after sunrise. Her father-in-law was giving himself four full hours to make a jour ney that could not take more than five minutes, no matter how slowly he walked. The thought of him wandering through the neighborhood by himself at that time of night, a frail, stooped phantom who might easily slip beneath the front bumper of some speeding car without ever being noticed, had kept her awake. Instead of sleeping, she had lain in bed and worried.

Ever since then, he had been getting up earlier and earlier each night to set off for shul. In pitch black darkness, in the middle of the night, he was going to temple. Why, she did not know. What he did when he got there was another mystery altogether. If he kept it up, she was going to take him to a doctor, not only for his sake but in order to preserve her own sanity.

As though her father-in-law had sensed what she was thinking and wanted to demonstrate that he had only been playing a joke on her, he reached out for the table before him and righted himself. With a very serious expression on his face, he headed confidently towards the front door, once again the master of the household on his way to receive an expected guest. Opening the door, he stuck his head out into the hallway as Esther pressed the buzzer mounted on the dining room wall.

"Jerry?" she heard him say in surprise. *"Vas tiest du* here?"

Esther shook her head in annoyance. At the dinner table this evening she had told him more than once that Jerry Kahn would be coming to call for her tonight. To drive her to a meeting in shul, she had said. Why she had not told him the real truth, she was not certain. It had just seemed easier to lie a little.

"Mendel," Jerry Kahn said pleasantly, appearing in the doorway as though he had been here many times before and was pleased to have been asked back again, "I came to see you. What else?" Then he winked at Esther to let her know that he had said this only to please the old man. "So?" he asked. "How are you, *Zayde?"*

"Gudt, gudt," the old man replied enthusiastically. *"Ich bin zer gudt."*

"Such news I should hear only from my friends," Jerry Kahn said, smiling as with his finger he straightened the oversized yellow tinted aviator glasses perched on the bridge of his nose.

"God willing, I should be in such shape when I get to be your age." Turning away from the old man, he added, "Well, Esther, you look ready. And lovely. Shall we go?"

"Certainly, Jerry," Esther replied, grateful that it was going to be just this easy to leave the house. "I'll go grab my things."

Knowing that the two men would probably be all right by themselves for a moment, Esther went into her bedroom for her bag and coat. When she returned, her father-in-law was pinching the fleshy bulb at the very end of his nose with his thumb and forefinger, pondering some especially difficult question that Jerry Kahn had only just posed.

"I was a cobbler," he said finally, obviously having given the matter a good deal of thought. "Shoes I made. Black leather, with high tops that laced up the front. *Zer gudt.*"

Jerry nodded as though he had known this all along. "A craftsman," he said. "I could tell from your hands."

Unwilling to interrupt them just when they seemed to be getting along together so well, Esther remained where she was for a moment. Then she began moving towards Jerry Kahn with a questioning look on her face. He acknowledged the look with a nod, stepping back so she could precede him out into the hallway. Jerry Kahn was a gentleman all right, from the old school.

"The television is already on the channel," Esther told her father-in-law. He was now staring at them carefully, as though he had only just grasped what was really going on tonight. "All you have to do is turn it on. When you get sleepy, shut it off. The *schissel* is already under your bed."

The old man grunted. Then he turned and went back to his favorite chair in the living room. He still was not walking as confidently as Esther would have liked to see him do. For a moment, she wondered whether it was safe to leave him here all by himself tonight. Then she realized that no one would deny that she deserved a night out on her own. She had it coming.

As soon as Esther stepped out into the street, closing the front door of the house behind her, all fears about her father-in-law's well-being slipped from her mind. She was actually going out to dinner with a man, on a *Wednesday* night no less. Somehow this seemed incredibly sophisticated to her, far more exciting than if they had been doing the very same thing on a weekend. Jerry Kahn had style all right. Real style.

Not until they were both seated inside Jerry Kahn's long shiny mother-of-pearl colored car and headed towards the avenue did either of them speak. Then Esther murmured, "You have a lovely car, Jerry." Running her hand along the rich leather upholstery that seemed to melt like butter from the padded dashboard right on to the seats themselves, she added, "A *very* lovely car. What is it? A Buick?"

"It's a Brougham, Esther," Jerry said, keeping his eyes on the road as he slowly turned the steering wheel in circles with his small, capable hands.

A Brougham. Desperately, Esther tried to remember what little she had learned about cars from Morty over the years. Cadillac, Oldsmobile, Pontiac, Chevrolet, and Ford. That was how Morty had ranked them, from top to bottom. A Brougham was something else again. Morty had never mentioned this particular make to her. Since Esther knew that some of the well-to-do men in the congregation drove Imperials, she decided to take a chance.

"Is this a . . . *Chrysler*, Jerry?" she asked hesitantly.

"It's a Cadillac, Esther," he told her with a smile. "A special model, with custom features built in right at the factory. Actually works out cheaper that way, in the long run."

For a man like Jerry Kahn, who surrounded himself only with the very best of everything, certainly it worked out cheaper. Had Morty ever been able to afford such a car, he would have bought it stripped down to the bare essentials just to save a couple of dollars. The two men were at absolute opposite ends of the spectrum, as different as night and day. A Cadillac. Jerry had to be doing far better running that discount outlet at the end of the avenue than anyone knew. In Esther's opinion, anyone smart enough to make a living the way Jerry did and still remain a gentleman deserved respect.

"It may be foolish of me to ask, Jerry," she ventured. "But how is business at your place these days?"

"These days," Jerry said, turning the question over in his mind, "business is good. If you can stand the *yachnas*."

The car passed under a streetlamp. Jerry Kahn's face appeared suddenly in a shaft of brilliant light. His skin gleamed as though he had shaved himself extra carefully tonight. Then the car moved on. Like a lantern extinguished by an unexpected gust of wind, Jerry Kahn's face disappeared once again. Esther felt a fleeting pang of regret. It certainly was a very nice face. Pleasant to look at, she would have called it.

"For a nickel," Jerry noted, "they'll cut your heart out, every time."

"Oh, but those people are *everywhere* these days, Jerry," Esther said. "I don't know if you've heard what's going on in the shul. But it's frightful."

"Tell me, Esther," he urged encouragingly. "Tonight, I've got nothing but time."

"Well, we just can't seem to get people to honor the pledges they made to us on Yom Kippur. The rabbi made an appeal, well, don't ask. It was a disaster. He blames it all on Nat Weiss, but even with the list of names that I had to compile from a *tape recorder*, if you can believe that, we're *still* in trouble."

"Actually," Jerry said softly, "I heard that myself."

"Really? You heard? How can that be?"

"You run a store like mine, Esther, you hear everything, sooner or later. I even know where you get your hair done on the avenue."

"But how could you know that, Jerry?"

"Dom Cerullo."

"You know *Dom?*" Esther said, truly shocked.

"He buys his shirts from me. At discount, of course."

"Incredible."

"As far as the shul is concerned, Esther, I wouldn't worry. Sooner or later, something will turn up."

"Let's hope so," Esther said, suddenly eager to drop the subject completely. Already she had probably said more about the temple's problems than was proper. "Because I've seen this month's financial statement. Don't ask."

Jerry laughed. For the first time, Esther noticed how delightful the fragrance of his after-shave was—clean, pungent, and much lighter than the cheap stuff Morty had doggedly slapped on his face each morning through all the years of their marriage. "You know, Esther," Jerry said, "you should come by the store sometime. I think you'd get a real kick out of watching the *yachnas* shop. They buy a four dollar item, marked down from ten, they still don't want to pay any tax. 'Look,' I tell them. 'I pay tax, you pay tax.' No good. They want to go home with the money in their pocket."

"So what do you do?" she asked, truly curious.

"Simple," Jerry answered. "I don't charge tax any more. Only I bumped the price of everything in the store ten percent. That way, everyone goes home happy and I pocket the difference."

Esther was about to tell Jerry just how brilliant a solution she thought this to be when he turned the steering wheel in her direction. With great care, he nosed the car into a parking spot directly in front of a green-and-white striped canopy "Napoleon's," the name of the restaurant where they would soon be eating dinner, was written on the canopy in curving white letters. Esther realized that they had driven nearly the entire length of the avenue, passing directly below the front window of Morty's apartment, without her even noticing it. She felt certain that the ride had gone just as quickly for Jerry as well.

After they had gotten out of the car, Jerry graciously held the big front door of the restaurant open for her. No sooner had he joined her inside than a waiter wearing a black suit and a starched white shirt dotted with glittering buttons down the front presented himself

"Mr. Kahn," the waiter said, the ends of his brisk little mustache positively quivering with delight, "we no see you here in too long a time. I got the corner table for you tonight. Like always."

Pivoting smartly on his heels, the waiter stepped off in front of them, leading the way. "Jerry," Esther trilled, genuinely impressed. "They know you here."

"A friend of a friend," Jerry said casually, as though he was accustomed to receiving such service everywhere.

"Mr. Balbano was in only last night, Mr. Kahn," the waiter noted, moving a chair back from the tiny table so that Esther could sit down. "Ate right here at this very table, too."

"I'm sure you fed Tony well, Vincent," Jerry said.

"Always, Mr. Kahn, always. That's our business. Now, how about a drink? Anisetta or a Cinzano and soda? Tell me what. On the house, of course."

Jerry looked at Esther, silently soliciting her opinion. Esther nodded. Whatever was being offered, she would have. It was the reason she had come out in the first place tonight, to treat herself well.

"Cinzano and soda for the lady," Jerry ordered. "I'll take a Cutty. No ice, no water. Large antipasto and two orders of baked clams oreganata to start with. Then we'll decide what we *really* want to eat."

Looking intensely pleased, as though Jerry had not disappointed him in any way whatsoever, the waiter nodded and moved away. "Are you sure that isn't too much food, Jerry?"

Esther asked distractedly, far more interested in looking around than by what they might be having for dinner.

Her first impression of the restaurant was of a series of tiny, gleaming tables set back into perfect little nooks, crannies, and corners. Every table was covered with a starched white cloth on which a single candle sat. Although the holiday season had not yet officially begun, strings of red and green Christmas lights blinked merrily from above a white wooden latticework strewn with green plastic vines so lifelike that the pale, waxy grapes dangling from them looked good enough to eat. Between long, pendulous clusters of bulging white bulbs of garlic, empty straw-covered bottles of Bertolli, Ruffino, and Soave chianti swung. Their graceful, elongated green glass necks reflected the light back into Esther's eyes.

To her, it seemed as though everything was in constant motion, flickering, shifting, and changing shape even as she looked at it. Napoleon's was more than just a beautiful little restaurant. It was easily the most romantic place that she had ever gone for dinner. To think that it had been here all these years, less than a mile from the house, without her ever seeing it before, was further confirmation of what Esther had already suspected. For far too long, she had been denying herself a life. Now the time had finally come for her to enjoy. It was only right.

Talking all the while, they picked their way through the antipasto. Esther sipped tentatively at her drink. Although it was far too sweet for her taste, she could not deny that it went well with the atmosphere. The clams they devoured in complete silence, for good reason. Such food deserved respect. Every last clam tasted even better than Esther had been told they would. Lightly breaded, the clams had first been spiced with thyme, rosemary, oregano, and just a hint of bay leaf. Then they had been baked to perfection in a sauce that defied description. Napoleon's was famous in the neighborhood for its baked clams, and rightfully so.

"Heaven," Esther pronounced after she had put the last shell back on the plate. "Absolute heaven."

Delicately, Jerry wiped his hands on his starched white linen napkin. Then he sucked at a front tooth, grinned, and asked, "And now, Esther? What would you like for dinner?"

So far, no one had even brought a menu to the table. The evening had progressed in a smooth, elegant manner, generating its own momentum so that everything seemed to flow naturally. Esther herself had not been forced to work to make any of it happen. The very last thing she wanted to do now was to ruin everything by asking for something truly ordinary like spaghetti with meatballs or veal parmigiana. Those were the only dishes Morty ever ordered when he ate Italian food. Tonight, though, they simply would not do. Everything had to be special.

"You order for me, Jerry," Esther said impulsively, putting herself completely in his hands. More than anything, Jerry Kahn was a kind man. A kind and capable man who would always catch her long before she even began to fall. Jerry knew instinctively what was best for her, as Morty never had. Of this Esther was certain.

Nodding as though he had expected nothing less than to be granted this great honor, Jerry crooked his finger at their waiter. Before Esther could even ask what was especially good here for a main course, the waiter appeared. Like the clams, the service at Napoleon's was legendary.

"Two veal piccata," Jerry ordered, naming a dish that Esther had never before eaten in her entire life. "What vegetable is fresh tonight, Vincent?"

"All fresh," the waiter replied without blinking an eye. "Says so on menu. Only some are fresh frozen."

"Which would you eat, if you were me?"

"*Me?*" the waiter asked innocently, enjoying the byplay nearly as much as Esther. "I take the escarole."

"Two escarole," Jerry said. "Some pasta, Esther?"

"Oh, I don't think I should, Jerry," she said, shaking her head.

"Come on," Jerry urged. "Live a little. It's an occasion." To the waiter, he said, "A couple sides of tagliatelle."

"*Si,*" the waiter agreed, making the three-ring sign with his fingers. "You like to see a wine list?"

"No wine list," Jerry said. "A nice Verdicchio. I leave which one up to you."

The waiter nodded respectfully and moved away again. Esther watched as Jerry reached up with his right hand to remove a bit of breaded clam that had been clinging stubbornly to his lower lip. For a long moment, she stared at his hands. Then it hit her. Jerry Kahn got *manicures*. His nails were perfectly filed, very even, and coated with clear polish. Although she had never once permitted herself this luxury, Esther found it a very positive sign that Jerry cared enough about his own appearance to pay someone to do his nails for him. It was funny how exciting a man's hands could be. Esther had never before noticed.

Soon the waiter brought their food. In silence, they fell to it and began eating. After they had both finished, the waiter brought two small finger bowls filled with warm water along with tiny towels. He then replaced both the towels and the bowls with miniature green-and-white-edged cups of espresso. Jerry drained his cup in three quick swallows and pushed himself back from the table. Uttering a small sigh of utter contentment, he reached into the inside pocket of his jacket, bringing forth a polished black briar pipe.

"Do you mind?" he asked politely.

"Of course not," Esther said. "I love a pipe."

From his other pocket Jerry withdrew a richly grained leather pouch. Zipping it open, he began extracting tiny pinches of black tobacco mixed with lighter shreds that seemed almost golden in the light. Tamping the tobacco into the bowl of his pipe, Jerry carefully evened it up with his thumbnail until he was satisfied that it was packed just so.

Deciding that the pipe was finally ready to be smoked, Jerry stuck it absentmindedly into the corner of his mouth and forgot about it, as though he had never had any intention of lighting it in the first place. "Not too full for dessert, I hope?" he asked. "They make their own zabaglione here. Pure rum delight."

"Oh, I couldn't, Jerry," Esther protested. "Really."

In fact, Esther did not feel full at all. What they said about fine food was true. You could eat as much of it as you liked and still have room for more. Instead of being stuffed, Esther was almost hungry, as though she had not eaten a single thing all night long. Watching as the waiter set a large bowl of shimmering, pastel colored zabaglione on the table, Esther followed Jerry's lead. First she dipped her spoon into the bowl. Then she put the spoon into her mouth.

The lightly whipped, feathery taste of the sweet pudding was so overwhelming that Esther was forced to close her eyes in order to savor it fully. When she opened them again, she saw Jerry juggling his spoon and the pipe, as though unable to decide which one to put in his mouth first. She had to laugh.

Jerry laughed right along with her. "A terrible habit," he said. "Having to smoke right after dinner. Used to drive Pauline crazy. To satisfy her, I would just hold the pipe in my hand until I got outside."

207

"Pauline," Esther said softly. "That was your wife, right, Jerry?"

Jerry nodded. "I lost my mind a little when she went, Esther," he said.

"It's only natural. Such a tragedy. Who wouldn't?"

"I kept thinking. Why her and not me? Who knows? Maybe if I had loved her more, she would still be alive."

Esther did not know what to say. Although this man ran a shlock store for a living, he was a sensitive, vulnerable soul. Reaching out with her hand, she placed it lightly on his arm, just to let him know that she was there if he needed her. "Don't blame yourself, Jerry," she said. "These things happen."

"Why her, and not me?" he asked again, blinking his eyes rapidly as though to stop the tears from forming. "Ah," he said, waving his hand in the air. "There I go again. Let's talk about something else. Let's talk about business at the shul."

"What business, Jerry? We're a temple."

"Your business is the same as mine, Esther. To *stay* in business."

Although she had never before thought of it this way, it did not take her long to understand the truth of Jerry's remark. "See, Esther," Jerry went on. "I buy from all kinds of firms. Any time someone has merchandise they want to close out, it's water damaged or a season out of style, I get a call. Ever seen my kiddie wear?"

"It's been a long time since I bought children's clothing, Jerry. Whenever someone I know has a baby now, I just send cash."

"Stryker Togs," Jerry confided. "Top of the line. And I get it for below cost. So I know how certain people feel about certain things that might surprise even you."

It suddenly struck Esther that Jerry was talking about Sol Stryker. Only a week ago, at a temple business meeting, Sylvia had confided to Esther that Sol was none too pleased with what had happened in shul on Yom Kippur. For someone who was not a regular in temple, Jerry Kahn was certainly in the know when it came to the latest gossip about Ahavath Mizrach. The man was definitely connected.

"I can't deny that at the moment things at Ahavath Mizrach are a little slow, Jerry," Esther conceded. "But they'll pick up. They always do."

"When, Esther?" Jerry demanded. "After Chanukkah? With

208

that long, dry stretch until Purim and then Passover?'' Jerry shook his head. ''What with utility bills, staff salaries, and mortgage payments, I bet your yearly nut over there has to be around a hundred thousand, no?''

Esther did not answer. Jerry was closer to the actual figure than even he knew. Currently, expenses at the shul were running right at ten thousand dollars a month. ''Any time your donations lag,'' Jerry said, ''you've got a cash flow problem. It's only natural. That's why the annex drive Nat ran did so well for you last year. It filled a hole. Only this winter you've got nothing. You know what, Esther? I think I can help.''

''You, Jerry? How?''

''Las Vegas Night, Esther,'' Jerry said. ''Now, I know you've heard of other temples running them but Ahavath Mizrach never has. As an Orthodox shul, let's say you're a little behind the times. The secret to running one that is successful is to bring people in to play the tables. And the way you do that is to hold a raffle. . . .''

''We already do that, Jerry. Every year.''

''Not some lousy buck-a-chance thing for some holiday like L'ag B'omer, Esther. A grand raffle. Five hundred tickets at, say, twenty bucks apiece. With a real prize.''

''Like for instance, what?''

''Well, a very good friend of mine runs a travel agency on the avenue. Say I get him to donate a trip to Jerusalem for two, all expenses paid. That's your big grand prize right there. For twenty bucks a pop, people figure, 'Why not? I'll take a chance.' After all, it is tax deductible, right? They show up on Las Vegas Night for the drawing. Once they're there, they gamble. Like crazy. And the shul gets all the proceeds.''

''It certainly is an exciting idea, Jerry, but the board, well . . . they'd never go for it.''

''You'd be surprised what people will go for when money is involved, Esther. If it's the law you're worried about, I can tell you that all the churches in the area already do it. The cops don't care. It's for a good cause, see?''

''Gambling for money, Jerry?'' Esther said dubiously. ''In shul? Somehow, to me, it doesn't seem right.''

''Not real money, Esther. Scrip, like in Monopoly. They pay real money for it, then they redeem it afterwards for merchandise. Merchandise that people like myself will donate. No expenses, only income. You think the board might go for that?''

"I don't know, Jerry," Esther said. "Honestly, I couldn't say."

Jerry waved his hand for the check, which appeared on the table as smoothly as everything else had all night long. "I bet I could sell them on it," he said.

"I bet you could," she said admiringly. Jerry eased an expensive looking wallet from his back pocket. From it he took a credit card that he casually placed on top of the check without even bothering to look at the total. Morty would have added up everything twice before paying, just to make certain that he was not being cheated.

"You think you could take me to a board meeting, Esther?" Jerry asked.

"Why do you need me? They're open to everyone."

"It's always nicer to go with someone who is part of the temple. . . ."

"Certainly."

"When?"

"Tomorrow night?"

"All right then." Jerry agreed. "Let's call it a date. I'll pick you up and we'll go together."

Getting to his feet, Jerry moved the table back so that Esther could get up without difficulty. "Besides," he said flashing her a smile that pinned her to her seat so that for the moment she could not have moved even if she had wanted to do so. "It would give the two of us a chance to see one another again. In, you know, what you might call *different* circumstances."

CHAPTER TWENTY-ONE

THEY HAD NEVER, ever loved him at Ahavath Mizrach. This the rebbe had known right from the start. Never had they taken him into their hearts, inviting him to their homes for seeded coffeecake with raisins, freshly baked *hamantashen* at Purim, and tea with preserves, making him feel as though he was a friend as well as their spiritual adviser. Of course, they had been only too glad to do all this for his predecessor, the fabled Saul Abrams. But then Saul Abrams had been lucky enough to die while visiting Israel, long before they had gotten tired of him. Now that Simeon Hakveldt was growing weary, the vultures were circling round, eager to pick his bones clean once they could be certain he was dead.

Ever since Yom Kippur, and that *shrecklich* appeal he now regretted having made with his entire heart, the pressure on him had been constant and unrelenting. Inside the shul, the men of the congregation were giving him the cold shoulder, staring goggle-eyed when he approached as though they were seeing him through the wrong end of a telescope. Outside the walls of the temple, their wives watched his every move. No longer could he even go to his favorite market on the avenue to buy his beloved special pickled herring. For although the herring itself was kosher, they also sold ham there. And now, as at no time in the past, Simeon Hakveldt had to be completely above suspicion.

Still, the rebbe could not help but feel that soon enough, they would catch him. He would be trapped in some unavoidable lie or commit an unpardonable social blunder, and then it would begin in earnest. Straight to the board they would go with their complaints, claiming that he was no longer fit for his post. Once the board would have laughed such claims away. Now there was no telling what they might do.

They had hired him in the first place only because they had been in desperate need of a rabbi who could step in and take over immediately so that the congregation would not bolt, switching their membership to some other shul. He had been both eager and available, not to mention a bargain at what they had paid him for that first, terrifying year.

Four separate times since then, the board had rehired him. Grudgingly, they had boosted his salary each time in accordance with the constantly rising cost of living without ever giving him the overwhelming vote of confidence to which he felt he was entitled, based on his unflagging efforts to bring the shul into the twentieth century.

The partnership of rebbe and congregation was much like a marriage. At certain specified intervals, emotional crises just naturally seemed to occur. Simeon Hakveldt had spent the last five years of his life at Ahavath Mizrach. If the board let him go now, his term of service would become no more than just another chapter in the ornately bound history of the temple, which would be compiled on the twenty-fifth anniversary of its founding.

But if they renewed his contract for another year, he would have every reason to believe that the marriage was still strong. Conceivably, he might be here for another five years, and then another ten beyond that. He would become a fixture. When the temple celebrated its twenty-fifth anniversary, Simeon Hakveldt would be present to accept hearty congratulations from all assembled. He would be the only rabbi they even remembered.

Unfortunately, in today's world, Simeon Hakveldt knew better than anyone that a rabbi could only be as effective as the businessmen behind him, the ones who kept the shul alive with their volunteer efforts and large cash contributions. He had done his level best to keep these men happy, Nat Weiss and Sol Stryker foremost among them. It was Nat who had pressured him into making that blood drenched, mad dog appeal of which he was now so ashamed.

Yet when Nat himself was questioned about the appeal at a recent business meeting, in light of the pitiful stream of Yom Kippur pledges that had been trickling slowly into the shul, he had cleared his throat and croaked, "Certainly, it was ill advised." That day, Nat Weiss had been the rebbe's only adviser, when it was to God instead that he should have turned for guidance and direction.

What nearly everyone at Ahavath Mizrach seemed to have forgotten was that Simeon Hakveldt was first a man, and then a rabbi. Within him, he had all the faults and failings that made one human. Not even the great Moshe Rabbenu, who had come down from the mountain with the twin tablets bearing the Ten Commandments in his hands, had been perfect. For failing to obey one of God's many commands, Moses had been harshly punished, denied the right to ever set foot in the Promised Land for which he and the tribes of Israel had searched for over forty years. Where Moses himself had failed, how could he, Simeon Hakveldt, ever hope to succeed?

Only last night, the rabbi had opened his heart to his mother in her apartment in Brighton, telling her of his impossible situation at the shul, then asking plaintively for her advice. Even in her eightieth year, Rebeccah Hakveldt was still an invaluable source of strength and guidance. Time had aged only her body, sucking the marrow from her bones so that for all the world she now looked as though she had been cut from stone. Her mind was still as sharp as it had ever been.

"Even as a child," she had told him, "you could not bear being judged, Simeon. When you brought home what the *melamed* had written about you, you would run into the other room and hide until I had read it. . . ."

Now it was not his teacher who was about to judge him, but the board—the board on which Nat Weiss and Sol Stryker sat like the highest judges of the land. "If you do nothing, Simeon," his mother had told him, "then you can do nothing wrong."

This piece of advice the rabbi was certain had come to him directly from God through his mother's mouth. If he put himself into a holding pattern, circling and circling on every issue, never committing himself until he was certain which way the wind was blowing, he would survive. First, he would determine precisely how the board *and* the congregation wanted him to act. Then and only then would he take a position. Since at all times he would be acting in accordance with *their* desires, they would not be able to find any further cause to be displeased with him.

The simple brilliance of this strategy was beyond dispute. It was the single weapon he needed to confound his adversaries. Once again, his mother had brought light to the darkness, illuminating his way clear. Despite her age, or perhaps because of it, she knew much that he himself still had to learn.

So it was that when the rabbi swept into the walnut paneled boardroom of Ahavath Mizrach for the regular Thursday night business meeting, he did so with a look of complete and utter confidence on his face. He was determined to let nothing affect his brand new attitude.

Everything at Ahavath Mizrach was just as it was meant to be. The temple had never been more prosperous. And he was its first and most favored son, without whom nothing, not even this deadly boring meeting, could begin.

Like his mother before him, Simeon Hakveldt was a survivor. If they really wanted what he had worked so hard to build for himself, they would have to take it from him. From now on, he would be giving nothing away.

The very first person the rabbi laid eyes on in the crowded, smoky room was Esther Bindel. Esther seemed to be everywhere these days, most especially where she was needed least. The woman just took her job too seriously. Constantly, she was extending her responsibilities into areas about which she knew nothing at all. Lately, she had even become a regular at these meetings, staying right to the bitter end, week after week.

As soon as he had weathered the current storm, and the board had renewed his contract for another year, the rabbi was going to very quietly let Esther Bindel go. Then he would find himself someone a little younger and much more manageable to work with as the recording secretary of the temple. Until that happened, it was only in his own best interest to be nothing but very pleasant to the woman, distasteful as he found this chore to be.

"Esther," he said, acknowledging her presence with a nod.

"Rebbe," she said boldly, stepping in front of him. Obviously, she felt that she alone had the right to monopolize his valuable time whenever anything was on her mind. "I'd like you to meet a good friend of mine, and the temple. Rabbi Hakveldt, this is Jerry Kahn."

The rabbi stared past Esther at a pale, very well dressed man who perhaps should have left the wearing of oversized, banana colored spectacles to someone ten or fifteen years younger. "Mr. Kahn," he said nevertheless, cheerfully extending his hand to him in greeting. "Esther has told me *much* about you." Precisely what she had told him, if anything, the rabbi could not recall. Not that it mattered. People only wanted to be told that they were somebody.

"Thank you, Rabbi," Jerry Kahn said sincerely, accepting the compliment as though it was coming to him. "You couldn't have a better person than Esther on your side."

Just what side that happened to be, the rabbi did not know. Before he could ask, Judah Benjamin waved furiously at him to come over to the other side of the room. Judah was a short, pudgy man of exceeding good humor who constantly got on the rabbi's nerves with his cheerful, never ending banter. But then Judah was fortunate. Born with a voice that was perhaps better suited for the stage of the Metropolitan Opera House than the podium of a shul, Judah had only to perform brilliantly on *Kol Nidre* night each year and the board automatically renewed his contract, with a generous raise in pay.

At the moment, Judah was standing with a circle of board members who had gathered around Nat Weiss in the far corner of the room. Although the rabbi thoroughly resented being summoned in this manner, he knew that this was neither the time nor the place to make a scene. From now on, he would let no one, not even cheerful, pudgy Judah, annoy him.

214

"If you'll excuse me, Mr. Kahn," he said politely stepping past the man.

Nodding to everyone as he made his way across the room, the rabbi looked automatically towards the big, padded leather armchair where Sol Stryker always sat at these meetings. On the wall above the chair was an expensively engraved brass plaque bearing Sol's name as chairman of the shul's construction committee. Above the plaque hung a framed photograph of Sol himself holding a shovel tied with colored ribbons at the temple's ground breaking ceremonies so many years ago.

As it had been every Thursday night since Yom Kippur, Sol's chair was conspicuously empty this evening. In the rabbi's opinion, Sol's continuing absence from all temple functions, meetings, dinners, and even services on Shabbos was a judgment on them all. That the man who had almost single-handedly built the shul was now completely estranged from it was an intolerable state of affairs.

After tonight's meeting, the rabbi resolved to speak to Leah about inviting the Strykers over for dinner at their house a little earlier in the year than usual. The two families could then sit down together to dine in peaceful splendor. Afterward, he and Sol would adjourn to the living room for a session of serious fence mending over brandy and dessert.

Drawing abreast of the circle of men surrounding Nat Weiss, the rabbi greeted each one of them in turn. Morris Benson, the lawyer, first vice-president of the shul, stood at Nat's shoulder with an expression of pure boredom written all over his patrician face. Morris was the only member of the board that Nat did not have tucked safely inside his pocket. Morris alone dared to argue with Nat on important issues. If and when Nat ever stepped down, giving up the gavel, Morris Benson was a sure bet to be elected shul president.

Next to Morris stood Irv Aaronsen, the builder. A bluff, big-shouldered man, Irv had long ago assured his position in the temple by personally supervising construction of the shul without taking a fee. He had brought in the entire building under cost as a favor to the community. Irv's single great vice was his obsessive love of football. From September to January, Irv hurried home from temple each Saturday so he could watch his money in action on the college gridiron. Unfailingly, Irv voted the way that Nat told him to.

Leaning against the wall behind Irv was Sol Bender, the

dentist. As third vice-president of the shul, Sol rarely spoke at meetings, preferring to lean back in his chair and study the ceiling while constantly stroking the absurdly thin, villainous mustache on his upper lip. One night soon, the rabbi hoped, Sol might actually wipe that mustache off his face.

The circle was completed by Murray Friedberg. Only a month ago Murray had *fumphered* his way onto the board as acting treasurer, replacing Milton Bernstein. Milton's wife, Rose, had been seriously ill for almost a year and was now very near death. Friedberg seemed to know instinctively that he was completely out of his league here. Instead of speaking during meetings, he fumigated the boardroom with his obnoxious black cigars, rolling them around his mouth before he smoked them as though they were made of bittersweet chocolate.

"Twenty-*two* tousaint, six hundred," Nat Weiss said, biting off the end of each word as though it was causing him pain to speak. "Right, Murray?" Murray Friedberg nodded without taking the cigar from his mouth. "We never before had a deficit of more than six or seven," Nat continued. "Only now, all of a sudden, we're up over twenty."

Shifting his eyes to the right, Nat said, "Evening, Rebbe. Now that you're here, I guess we can start."

"Oh, am I late, Nat?"

"No more than usual," Nat noted sourly.

"I saw my mother last night, Nat," the rabbi said pleasantly, as though he had not heard a word of what he had just been told. "She mentioned that in her shul they look at us and wonder how we do it. This building, our large congregation, our new annex, they envy us. And they wonder how we do it."

"Got a long agenda tonight, gentlemen," Nat muttered, moving towards his chair at the very head of the table. In a far louder voice he announced, "Shall we start?"

Immediately, everyone in the room stopped talking and began taking seats so that the meeting could get underway. No matter what else you might say about Nat Weiss, and the rabbi himself could have spoken on the subject for hours without completely expressing all of his feelings, whenever Nat opened his mouth, people jumped. It was the kind of respect that Simeon Hakveldt had never been able to command.

Settling into a chair by the wall, the rabbi consoled himself by thinking about what was yet to come tonight. An endless round of the very same reports he had spent the entire day reading, accompanied by testy criticism, vague backbiting and boring asides. The routine never seemed to vary one iota from week to week.

As soon as Nat intoned, "Meeting called to order at eight-fifteen . . . report from the Women's Club on their proposed expenditures for the coming quarter," the rabbi stopped listening. He had heard it all before. Paralyzed by boredom, all he could do to pass the time was watch as the second hand of the clock on the wall crept slowly towards ten thirty, the magical hour when the meeting would finally be adjourned.

After two interminable hours that to the rabbi seemed like an eternity, Nat Weiss's voice shifted in timbre, causing the rabbi to look up. "Any new business?" Nat demanded, this question being the usual signal that the meeting was nearly over.

From the very back of the room, Esther Bindel enthusiastically began waving her hand in the air, as though begging permission to leave the room. The rabbi groaned silently to himself, hoping that perhaps Nat would fail to recognize her. "Esther?" Nat said.

"Nat," Esther said, getting slowly to her feet as though what she was about to say was of the utmost importance. No doubt, the rabbi thought, they were now going to be treated to another of the woman's regular heartfelt pleas that board members take better care of the stencils in the duplicating room. Instead, she said, "For those of you who have not yet met him, I would like to introduce Jerry Kahn."

In back of Esther, the man wearing those foolish yellow spectacles got slowly to his feet. All this choreographic introducing of people from the back of the room with flowery courtesy was extremely unusual for a regular business meeting. It made the rabbi feel that something definitely was afoot. Just on the off chance that he might be involved in it before the evening was over, the rabbi forced himself to pay attention.

"Jerry has a proposal that he would like to put before the board," Esther said, sitting back down again.

In what the rabbi recognized as the classic suppliant's position ever since the time of Solomon, hands clasped respectfully at waist level, face serious and composed, eyes grave, Jerry Kahn began to speak. What he said was completely astonishing, a mad plan that would have the shul sponsor some kind of grand raffle, with the actual drawing to be held at a Las Vegas Night of all things. The event itself was to take place on Christmas Eve no less, in the downstairs ballroom.

217

Clearly, the idea was absurd. In a moment, the board would table it for further discussion at next week's meeting and then never bring it up again. Still, the rabbi could not help admiring the way in which Kahn presented his case. Speaking directly and to the point, he delivered his pitch like a practiced salesman. Apparently not everyone was subject to the same kind of nervous disorientation he himself had felt the first time he had come before the board.

"If there are any questions," Kahn said, completing his presentation with a big smile on his face, "I'll be more than glad to answer them."

As always, it was Nat Weiss who spoke first. "Very interesting, I must admit, Mr. Kahn," he said. "But tell me. What kind of figures are we talking here?"

"Figures?" Kahn asked.

"Numbers," Nat clarified. *"Gelt."*

"From the raffle, five hundred tickets at twenty dollars each, minus what printing and advertising will cost, say nine thousand. Then, maybe twice that much from the night itself."

"How can that be?" Morris Benson asked curiously, drawing from behind his ear a long, yellow Number Two pencil on which the rabbi could make out the words Dixon Ticonderoga.

"Five hundred people show up on the night, maybe more," Kahn explained. "They're good for, say, an average roll of twenty bucks apiece. Some may only go for a fiver and leave, while others will walk around all night long without putting down a penny, but your high rollers, your plungers, as I call them, well . . . the sky's the limit."

"Excuse me for asking, Mr. Kahn," Judah Benjamin said quietly. "But how is it that you are so well versed in the details of such an event?"

"My old shul," Jerry Kahn answered without a moment's hesitation. "I was fund raising chairman there. Ran a whole slew of these things."

"Where was that, exactly?" Morris Benson inquired, pursing his thin lips so that his entire face took on an inquisitive, faintly Oriental air.

"Kol Eloheem of Bethpage," Jerry answered, naming a suburb on Long Island so prosperous that even the rabbi was impressed. "My wife, Pauline, and I lived there . . ." Jerry Kahn paused for a moment. "Until we needed to be closer to the city for . . . care."

Just from the way the man struggled with the word, the rabbi knew immediately that Jerry Kahn's Pauline had suffered from the same disease that would soon claim Milton Bernstein's Rose. "Mr. Kahn," Nat said abruptly, "so how much *total* are we looking at here?"

"Say . . . twenty-five thousand?" Jerry Kahn said quietly. "At the very least. Maybe more."

"Frankly, Nat," Judah Benjamin interjected, his usual good spirits nowhere in evidence tonight, "to be honest with you, I can't for the life of me see a shul like ours getting involved in such a thing."

"Murray Friedberg," Nat sang out, "our current deficit, please?"

Murray Friedberg nearly swallowed his cigar. Then he began fumbling through the papers piled up before him. Pulling an oversized accounting sheet with blue lines running across it from the bottom of the pile, he handed it to Nat. Nat squinted at it for a second, then announced, "Twenty-two tousaint, six hundred. *Dollars*," he added, just in case anyone thought that the shul still honored its debts with shekels. "Which, according to this gentleman, we could wipe out in a single night. Anyone have any other questions?"

"Certainly," the rabbi said, feeling that it was time he made himself heard. "Morrie? Is this legal?"

Morris Benson leaned back in his chair, making a little steeple of his long, fine fingers so he could consider the legal ramifications of such an event. Before Morrie could speak, Jerry Kahn began telling the board how every church and synagogue in the neighborhood had already sponsored a Las Vegas Night with the full cooperation of "the boys from the precinct on the avenue, most of whom I already know on a first name basis from my store."

"Perhaps, Mr. Kahn," Nat suggested after the man was through, "you could give us half an hour or so to discuss this amongst ourselves. Then we could come back to you with a definite response, one way or the other."

"My pleasure," Jerry Kahn said easily. "You need me, I'll be right outside, in the hall."

The rabbi watched Jerry Kahn walk to the back door. With interest he noted the extremely significant look that passed between Jerry Kahn and Esther Bindel before Kahn left the room. Whatever was said in here in the next half hour, Esther would carefully record and then repeat to Jerry Kahn. The two of them were definitely in cahoots on this project. Why, he could not say.

"This is too much, Nat," Judah Benjamin said angrily as soon as Kahn had closed the door behind him. "Making him wait outside. And what if we need more than half an hour? Morris?"

Slowly, Morris Benson readjusted his pencil in his thatched silver hair, moving it up and down until it rested comfortably against the top of his ear. "It *could* be shifted to next week's agenda, Nat. That would give us all a little more time to think about it."

"Time is just what we don't have, Morrie. We're borrowing to meet our payroll now each month as is, donations from the Yom Kippur appeal aren't coming in, they're charging us as much interest as the market will bear, and you're asking me to put it off a week? *Morrie,*" Nat pleaded, putting both hands in the air in a gesture of complete helplessness, "Come *on.*"

"Morally," Judah Benjamin insisted, "it's not right."

"That I think the rabbi should tell us, and not the cantor," Nat said icily, swiveling around in his chair. "Rebbe? Would you like the floor?"

Without getting to his feet, the rabbi said, "There has been much discussion of this very question throughout the ages, my friends. I can tell you that. With many opinions on every side."

"Could you possibly enlighten us as to *some* of those opinions, Rebbe?" Nat demanded, his patience obviously wearing thin.

"Well, although there is nothing in the Talmud that makes recreational gambling a crime, one who plays at cards, dice, or pigeon racing cannot serve as a witness. . . ."

"We're not talking traffic court here, Rebbe," Nat interrupted. "We're talking Las Vegas Night."

"On some festive occasions," the rabbi noted, "Chanukkah among them, restrictions on gambling were lifted in ancient times."

At the moment, the rabbi's mind was littered with random bits of the law that he had gathered together during his many years of study. Much like the Talmud itself, none of the information was indexed or cross-referenced in any coherent manner. For every opinion on the subject pointing in one direction, the rabbi could think of at least three others which leaned the other way. All in all, the issue of gambling in shul for charitable purposes was a problem that in his view definitely required further study.

"Are we mobsters?" Judah Benjamin demanded passionately,

"who run casinos where people throw away their hard-earned money on games of chance? Irv? Sol? Say something."

"They're gonna gamble," said Irv Aaronsen, "they might as well gamble by us. At least we'll put the money to good use."

"No minors," Sol Bender said quickly. "No one under the age of eighteen admitted. Ab-so-lutely not."

"Murray," Judah said desperately, appealing to the only member of the board who had not yet spoken. "How do you feel?"

Murray Friedberg removed the big cigar from his mouth. Slowly he twirled it in circles in his hand. "You want my opinion?" he asked. "It stinks. From the word go."

"It's strictly a one shot thing," Nat said angrily, his face growing red. It was the first sure sign that Nat was ready to scream, bang his hands against the table, and if need be, keep the meeting going until everyone's tongue was hanging out, in order to get his way.

As president of the shul, Nat alone had the power to adjourn a weekly business meeting. It was a clause that he personally had railroaded into the temple's constitution. If the president so desired, he could keep them all here until long past midnight discussing this issue. Nat had done it before. The rabbi did not doubt that he would gladly do it again tonight.

"A one shot," Nat said again so everyone would know for sure exactly how many Las Vegas Nights he was planning to hold. "A quickie. Wham, bam, thank you ma'am, and we're out of debt."

"Elegantly put, Nat," Morris Benson noted drily. "As always."

"Have we all gone mad?" Judah Benjamin demanded. "Gambling in *shul*? What's next? Money lenders in the front hall?"

"Actually," the rabbi said, primarily to take some of the wind from Judah's billowing sails and to remind him who was the *real* expert on the law here tonight, "there *is* a long history of gambling in synagogues for charitable purposes. Some rabbis have even stated that he who wins a lottery should say a *brucha*, thanking God for his good fortune."

Flashing the rabbi a withering look, the cantor put both of his elbows on the table and turned towards Nat Weiss. "Nat," he said. "That you yourself feel no shame in having roulette wheels, keno tables, chuck-a-luck cages, and who knows what else downstairs, where young boys have celebrated the joyous occasion of their bar mitzvah and couples have danced the first dance of their married lives . . . I am shocked. Really I am."

"What am I trying to do that is so bad?" Nat asked the room at large. Suddenly, he had become a young and eager child who wanted only the best for everyone concerned, his parents included. "Raise some money for our shul?"

"Nat," the cantor said, leveling a finger at him. "I won't stand for you ramrodding this through without giving us sufficient time to think about it. I warn you."

"*You* warn *me?*" Nat Weiss cried out, getting to his feet.

All over the room, men who recognized the danger signals began calling out, "Nat? *Nat!* Take it easy. It's just a meeting. We're all still friends here."

"All right, all right," Nat snapped, making a visible effort to calm himself. "How's this for an offer, Cantor? If it offends you to have it downstairs where couples have danced their last fox trot at some young snotnose's bar mitzvah, we'll move it out of the temple altogether."

"Where to, Nat?" the cantor demanded, firmly standing his ground. "The park?"

"The *annex*," Nat said, his face glowing with satisfaction. "We string some crepe paper over the handball court, set up tables, and we're in business. Look, it's all for a good cause, right? The *best*. I say we vote. Morrie?"

Morris Benson nodded. "As president of the shul, you have the right to call for a vote, Nat. That's what the constitution says."

"So let's vote," Irv Aaronsen urged.

"Why not?" Sol Bender agreed, seconding the motion. "We all have homes to go to tonight."

"All right," Nat said. "We vote. Morrie?"

"No," Morris Benson said. "I'm opposed, in principle."

"Irv?"

"Yes. We need the money."

"Solly?"

"Why not? Let's give it a try. Yes."

"Murray Friedberg?"

"No."

"Two yesses and two no's," Nat noted. "A deadlock. As president, I vote yes. Cantor?"

"No, Nat. No tonight, no next week, no any time the question comes up. *No.*"

"You're voting 'no' then, I presume?" Nat said, his eyes winkling. "*If* I heard you correctly?" Looking down at the sheet of paper before him, he said, "Three yesses, three no's. Another deadlock. Rebbe? Care to cast the deciding vote?"

All eyes turned in Simeon Hakveldt's direction, just as they had on the night when he first came into this room with hat in hand five long years ago, seeking a job. Looking right back at them, the rabbi slowly cleared his throat. "As I have already told you, on this point, the law is not absolutely clear. Since I am responsible for the spiritual welfare of the temple, rather than its financial affairs, I feel that it is not proper for me to express an opinion."

"Yes, or no?" Nat demanded.

"Neither," the rabbi said. He had told them what the law said. In order to protect himself, he could not possibly take sides on this issue. Although the idea of holding a Las Vegas Night in the annex gave him no pleasure, if the money it brought into the shul made it possible for him to keep his job, then he could well afford to look the other way. Greater rabbis than he had been faced with the very same problem. Their responses had been collected in the Talmud for all to read. Not a single one of them had indicated that it was Simeon Hakveldt's duty to break new ground on the question.

"*Rebbe,*" Nat persisted, "will you vote?"

"I already have," he answered. "I abstain."

Smashing the wooden gavel he held in his right hand so hard against the wooden table that it nearly splintered, Nat said angrily. "Three in favor, three opposed. One abstains. A deadlock. In such cases, as president of the shul, I am entitled to poll any of the remaining officers of the synagogue who happen to be present at this meeting. Esther Bindel," he called out. "As recording secretary of Ahavath Mizrach, how do you vote?"

From the very back of the room, Esther eagerly called out, "*Yes!*"

"Motion carried," Nat said quickly, a smile of triumph breaking out on this face. "Meeting adjourned."

Down came the gavel on the table once more. Everyone got to their feet and began talking loudly about what had just transpired. Wanting only to get away before anyone could pin him down as to his real feelings on this issue, the rabbi made straight for the nearest door. Before he could escape through it, Judah Benjamin appeared, planting himself squarely in the rebbe's path.

"Simeon," Judah said bitterly, "before you go, let me congrat ulate you personally. Because of your great show of courage Ahavath Mizrach is now in the Las Vegas Night business."

Before the rabbi could respond, Judah spun angrily on his hee and walked away, leaving him standing there dumbly all b himself. But then how could Judah even begin to understand One brilliant performance a year and his family would be we fed for the next twelve months. Simeon Hakveldt alone had t bear the awful, oppressive, daily weight of being the spiritua leader of a temple that had fallen on troubled times.

Long ago, his mother had taught him that it was far better t live to fight another day than to throw away everything in a battle that he could not possibly win. Those who were without sir could cast the first stone. The rabbi knew he would have no problem living with his conscience. His business was to survive. At the moment, nothing else really mattered.

CHAPTER TWENTY-TWO

IN A MOMENT of almost human weakness, E.C. had once told Paulie Bindel how he had acted on the one and only first date of his life. Arriving some two and a half hours late, he had been greeted at the front door by the girl's grim and disapproving mother. E.C. had panicked. Sliding past the woman with his left leg bent at a right angle beneath his right knee and one hand pointing to the sky, he had looked up and asked sincerely, "Excuse me, ma'am. But did I beat the throw from right field?"

Tonight, a simple baseball slide just would not do. In order to neutralize Nat Weiss, he would need something far more dramatic. A dark blue New York Giants football helmet and a full set of pads. When the front door came open, he would crab-block Nat in the hallway. Then, with head down and knees pumping, he would shove Nat, against his will of course, all the way to the back of the house. Removing the helmet, he would put forth his hand, smile, and say, "Paulie Bindel, sir. Perhaps you remember browbeating me in shul? *Kol Nidre* night? How *is* your knee there? Not too badly damaged, I hope?"

Substituting sheer spectacle for physical violence, something in the Andalusian mode might do just as well. When the front door came open, he would be standing on the stoop resplendent in a tight fitting suit of lights flown directly from Madrid by Iberian Air just for the occasion. In one hand, the twin-eared cap. In the other, a full and flowing scarlet cape. Unfurling the cape slowly so that it billowed in the breeze, he would advance step by mincing step into the living room, barking, "Hi, *toro. Toro*, hi." All the while, he would be performing various fabulous and intricate passes with the cape, forcing Nat to retreat until he was trapped in the middle of the living room, furiously pawing at the carpet as plumes of hot, steamy anger poured forth from his flared, taurine nostrils.

Having given a good deal of thought to these and many other options earlier in the day, he had rejected them all on a cost-effective basis. Instead, he had decided to go with the Fifth Amendment. Claiming his constitutional right against self-incrimination, he would refuse to answer any and all questions relating to the current status of his mother and father's divorce, their aggregate total yearly income, and his own prospects of finding gainful employment in the very near future.

Having come only to take Steffi with him into the night, he would proudly stand his ground in silence even as they peppered him with inquiries and raked his face with looks more piercing than grapeshot. Once she had been given over to him, he would leave, having told them nothing that they could use against him. Death before dishonor, every time.

Finally he rang the doorbell. Miraculously, it was Steffi herself who opened the door. Her long brown hair was freshly washed, smelling of sudsy shampoo. Her face was devoid of any makeup whatsoever. Still, it gleamed. All this just for him. The elevator in his heart dropped several floors all at once. For the moment he could think of nothing to say. In itself, this was unusual.

"Paulie," she said, smiling sweetly, "I didn't expect you for another half hour."

Looking past her into the house, he asked, "Mom and Dad gone off to bed? After an early supper?"

"They're at a meeting in shul," she explained, giving him cause to let his breath out fully for the first time all day long.

"Daddy goes every Thursday but tonight she had to be there too."

"What a shame. I was *so* looking forward to seeing them."

"I'll bet. . . ." She laughed, shaking her pretty head. Like the curtain on a Broadway stage, her hair closed over her eyes for a moment. Then it opened back up again. Neatly, he stepped past her into the living room.

Having taken the fortress without firing a single shot in anger, he looked around the room in which he now found himself a prisoner. It had been decorated to within an inch of its life by someone with absolutely no taste whatsoever. Between two identical overstuffed couches encased in thick, clear plastic, a large bronze horse stood with its front hooves high in the air. A clock with Roman numerals on it had been inserted into the stomach of the horse. Nearly everything in the room seemed to be either white or gold or a combination thereof, these being the primary colors of what in the neighborhood was known as the French Provincial style.

"Lovely plastic," he noted, rubbing a finger along its icy surface. "From France?"

"Fortunoff's," Steffi said. "Mommy's kind of a frustrated interior decorator. She won't even let Daddy smoke in the house because the smell gets into the throw pillows. He has to walk around the block at night after supper with his cigar."

Poor Nat. At home, the scaly lizard of the desert, the prowling lion of Ahavath Mizrach, was but a man. A man who had to slink through the streets of the neighborhood in darkness to smoke his lousy after dinner cigar. For a moment he almost felt sorry for Nat. Almost, but not quite.

"Where are we going tonight, Paulie?" Steffi asked, reaching for her coat. He noted with pleasure that she had already folded the coat over the back of a chair so that there would be no delay when he declared it to be officially time to leave. "Is it a mystery?"

"Call it a surprise," he told her. "Somewhere you definitely have never been before. Trust me. We'll have big fun."

"In the city?"

"Nowhere else."

Steffi sighed with pleasure, obviously thrilled to be going out with someone who really knew the ropes. At the moment, she looked so completely sweet standing there that he was flooded by a sudden desire not to go anywhere at all tonight. After all, the house *was* empty. The couches beckoned. Covered in clear plastic, they could be wiped clean afterward with an ordinary kitchen sponge. How thoughtful of Mrs. Weiss to have done them up this way.

Then he decided to proceed as planned. All first dates, E.C. had also once explained, were military in nature. The moment you diverted from your original battle plan, you were asking for trouble. You could be seriously outflanked without ever knowing it.

Together they went out into the street. For days he had wrangled with the old man for the keys to his car and permission to use it tonight. At the moment, he was thankful that he had parked it beneath a tree. Sandblasted by time and weather, the original paint job on the car had faded so badly that now you could almost see the bare metal beneath. Still, it ran. When he turned the key in the ignition, the ancient engine fired right up. Considering where they were headed tonight, this was all that mattered. If it came time to make a sudden getaway, the old man's car would do just fine.

Heading out of the neighborhood on a street that led directly to the parkway, he busied himself with the radio. Dialing past the quiet, middle-aged stations on which Frank Sinatra still was king, he carefully tuned towards the far end of the dial, searching for the mad young disc jockey with soul who had kept him going ever since his return from Cambridge. "The Dapper Rapper in the City," the deejay called himself. He was the brand new number one. Whatever he put down *had* to be picked up on right away, or they would revoke both your license to drive and your right to live.

Swinging the car onto the parkway, he headed towards Manhattan in the outside lane. Off to his left, Staten Island loomed like a dark smudge on the horizon. The gauges on the dashboard before him glowed a soft, eerie, iridescent green. The car's heater hissed softly in time to the throbbing sound of Gene Chandler doing "Nothing Can Stop Me." Rapidly he began passing one car after the other.

Down went the music into the background as The Dapper Rapper began earning his paycheck. "If you can't dig what I'm putting down," he purred, caressing the entire city all at once with a voice as soft as velvet, "then you got a hole in your soul and you *don't* eat chicken on Sunday. *Push*, girl!" The Dapper Rapper urged. He was the real thing all right. Cole T. Walker,

227

eat your heart out. "Tall and tan, young and bad. I ain't never had enough of nothin', most especially your sweet thing, mama. And I *wants* to get next to you," The Dapper Rapper moaned. "Tighter than whites on rice," he crooned, coming back hard. "Tighter than coals on ice. Tighter than hams on a country hog. That's how tight I want us to be. You and me. And it *will* be so. For *I am* The Dapper Rapper, getting it all together on a Thursday night in the big city for all the hip cats and pretty kitties. Where the soul *never* shuts down and the sound comes down from uptown to the Batt-a-ree. Bad as I want to be and don't it sound good to you, mama? Go on, Gene. Tell the tale. . . ."

Back came Gene Chandler doing "Nothing Can Stop Me." The Dapper Rapper sighed, "Just so nice, I *had* to do it twice. Watch me work, New York. And remember . . . you just can't lose, with the stuff we use." Then the music took over for good. Looking over at Steffi to see whether she was enjoying this as much as he was, he saw that instead she was staring fixedly at the floor of the car. "Steffi?" he said softly, as much to get her attention as anything else.

"You're ignoring me," she said in a low, flat voice that he could barely recognize as belonging to the girl he had picked up earlier tonight. "Please don't do that. I can't stand it."

"I'm just driving," he said, puzzled by her sudden and inexplicable change in mood. "See?"

Like a high school kid trying to impress his date, he took both hands off the wheel to illustrate his point. The car shimmied violently to the right, both tires on that side being worn right down to the rim. Immediately, he grabbed for the wheel again.

"If you want to take me home," Steffi offered, still not looking at him, "it's not too late."

"Steffi," he said, "people can't talk *all* the time. . . ."

For a second, she said nothing at all. Then she bit her lower lip and sighed. "This is the first time I've gone out since I came back from school," she whispered. "Maybe you should know that."

Suddenly he saw her as she had once been, sitting at a desk in home room on the very first day of junior high school, wearing a little girl's tartan skirt that fastened with an oversized brass safety pin in front and a pair of dark, mysterious woman's stockings with long, laddered runs up the side. Leaning forward, she was laboriously filling out every last square of a tiny blue-and-white Delaney card. Between the ink-stained middle fingers of her hand she held a leaky fountain pen. Just the tip of her little sweet pink tongue was visible between her teeth. Even after the teacher called out for her to stop, Steffi just went right on filling in all the squares. The little card ran blue with damp and shining ink.

"You want me to take you home?" he said, having absolutely no intention of doing so. "There isn't enough gas in the car. I don't have the time to fill it up again and still get where we're going. So you're stuck. Okay?"

"Okay," she said in a halting voice, reaching out to touch his arm with her hand. "Just so you know. I haven't been out with anyone . . . in a very long time."

Instead of answering, he stared through the dirt specked windshield of the car. Across the water, the skyline of Manhattan gleamed brightly against the dark night sky. The reflection of all the great neon dappled buildings trailed towards him on the rippled surface of a river that was completely different from the Charles, one as busy and troubled as the city itself. New York, New York.

Just then the parkway curved away from the water, throwing the car onto the approach to the Brooklyn Bridge. The road then coiled back the other way. For a second, he was granted a single, unforgettable glimpse of the bridge itself, its keystone arches supporting the narrow ribbon road that led into Manhattan. The harbor twinkled brightly down below. There was no greater bridge in the entire world. There never had been and there never would be, no matter how many of them they built. The original was still the greatest. Whenever he saw the bridge at night like this, a sudden feeling of pride surged through his entire body, as though he himself had personally supervised its construction from an apartment in the Heights with a telescope at his side.

On the Manhattan side of the bridge, he drove up a narrow one lane stretch of badly patched asphalt onto the West Side Highway. Taking his chances in the road race that was constantly being waged on its treacherous curves and short, sudden straightaways, he began passing cars with wild abandon, seesawing from lane to lane. He was definitely making great time. Making great time was all that mattered when you drove in the city, and the only way to make it was to avoid all the cars with New Jersey license plates that seemed to wallow right in the middle of the road like cows mired in mud up to their knees.

When he passed the midtown exit without giving it a backward glance, Steffi evidenced definite signs of being upset. "Paulie," she said plaintively, toying with the lank ends of her long hair, "where are we going?"

"Uptown," he said succinctly, doing his best to cut off a blue Dodge panel van with those hated Jersey plates.

"How *far* uptown?"

"All the way."

"Oh. Do you have a friend who lives up there? In Riverdale?"

He shook his head. He had no friends living anywhere in the city, most especially not Riverdale. Besides, at the moment, he was driving. "You'll see," he said, leaving it at that.

Guiding the car off the parkway at a Hundred and Twenty-fifth Street, he headed crosstown along the great boulevard that some people referred to as "the last frontier." One Hundred and Twenty-fifth Street was certainly where it all really began, although those who lived on neighboring downtown streets also had some claim to being part of it as well. Hogging the inside lane near the curb, he began looking for a place to park. Fabulously, one opened up right in front of him. So far, things were going his way.

Shutting off the engine, he rolled his window all the way up. Then he checked to make certain that Steffi had done the same. "Okay," he said. "Now we run."

"Why?"

"No reason. Just to get the blood moving before we sit down again inside."

In the street, he took her hand. Making certain to keep his head down so that he would not have to look anyone in the eye, he led her towards the theater. He had timed it perfectly. They were arriving just early enough to avoid the line that would soon be forming behind the wooden barricades on the sidewalk. Slipping six crumpled dollar bills to the girl who sat punching out tickets behind a thick glass window, he accepted two tickets in return. Then he gave them up again to the huge black man at the door.

Inside, the lobby smelled of burnt popcorn and melted butter. The red damask walls were covered with fading blowups of all the greats who had played here in the past. There was no time to inspect them closely. The point now was to get a seat. In the darkness, no one would trouble them. "Can we sit upstairs?" Steffi asked innocently, completely unaware of what went on in those tilting tiers at night. "I just love the loge." "Actually, no," he said, leading her into the downstairs section to a pair of seats right on the aisle. "Down here is better." That it was also safer, he did not mention. Why make the girl any more nervous than she already was?

After they had sat down and he had helped Steffi off with her coat, making a big production of putting it behind her so that she was more or less sitting on top of it, he sat back and let out his breath. Congratulations were definitely in order all around. They had made it in unscathed. Getting back out again might well be an entirely different story, but he would worry about that when the time came.

On the ragged movie screen that had been lowered over the stage, they were showing a scratchy, epileptic print of *West Side Story*. Having been here many times before, he knew that this made as much sense as anything else. The movie was just a throw-in, designed to keep the people occupied until the real business of the evening began. Steffi, however, was definitely upset. He could tell.

"Paulie," she whispered, "I've already seen this movie in the neighborhood. *Twice*."

"That's okay," he advised, speaking from experience. "It probably won't be the same up here."

Snuggling in next to him, Steffi quickly settled down, giving *West Side Story* her complete attention. He too had seen it more than once. So had everyone else in the world. That was why they were showing it tonight. To control the crowd through boredom. Ten minutes passed. Totally engrossed in the tragic conflict raging between the Sharks and the Jets up on the big screen before them, Steffi leaned his way and confided, "You know, this really isn't so bad at all. Besides I *always* cry when Natalie Wood and Richard Beymer kneel down together in her bedroom to sing 'One Hand, One Heart.' "

"Me too," he said quickly. "Only try not to cry *too* loud, huh?"

Doing a quick survey of the people in their immediate vicinity, he decided that no one would mind if Steffi did some polite and quiet sniffling from her end of the row. No one actually seemed to be watching the movie, anyway. Instead they were talking, eating candy bars and popcorn, and continuously passing large cardboard cups of orange soda from hand to hand while seeing who could make the most interesting noises with ice in their mouths. Compared to this, the movie finished a poor second.

Sitting right in front of Steffi was a tall, disjointed dude who might well have been Norris Rice's twin brother. He was slouched all the way down in his seat with his high black Converse sneakers stuck out into the aisle so that everyone had to step over them. A tiny ditty-bopper's hat was perched at the very back of his head like a soulful yarmulka. Talking loudly to no one in particular, he was keeping a running conversation going with himself that was impossible to ignore.

The movie wound on, one scene following the other just as he remembered them. Sure enough, when Tony and Maria knelt down once again on the floor of her bedroom to sing "One Hand, One Heart," Steffi began to sob softly into the crumpled but clean tissue he had pressed into her hand only a moment before. "Isn't this a *wonderful* scene, Paulie?" she whispered. "It just gets me, every time."

Before he could tell her that he felt the exact same way, the tall dude sitting in front of them crumbled under the pressure. Unable to take Hollywood's Technicolor version of life in the ghetto for another second, with choreography and a score to match, he sprang to his feet, turned to face the entire house and cried, "Quit singin', man. Fuck her. *Fuck her!*"

The entire audience collapsed with laughter. Several people actually took the trouble to lean over so they could slap five with the tall dude. The tall dude bowed gracefully from the waist to acknowledge that, yes, he had indeed delivered the single best line of the night so far, on screen or off. It was then that Steffi began to cry in earnest.

"I don't think I like it here, Paulie," she noted, wiping her eyes with the tissue. "Everyone is *so* rude. If they didn't want to see the movie, why did they come in the first place?"

"For what comes next," he explained.

"Then maybe I should go to the bathroom right now," she said, getting to her feet.

"Wrong," he said, pulling her right back down again.

"What do you mean 'wrong'?"

"No one goes to the bathroom here, Steffi."

"That's ridiculous. People have been doing it all night long."

"No one from *our* neighborhood goes. Not unless they want to buy a watch. Can I make myself any clearer than that?"

"I don't think I understand you, Paulie."

"Just wait till the lights come up. Then see if you still want to go. Okay?"

Steffi nodded. She would remain in her seat a little while

longer. It was the kind of simple courtesy that Lesley never would have extended to him. Instead, she would have gone off all on her own, returning with a whole circle of brand new friends, all of whom had already taken her phone number and would soon be calling to find out just when she might be able to take a little ride with them so they could "talk."

The version of *West Side Story* being shown up here tonight had already long since been scissored to ribbons in a hundred other theaters. The last half hour was entirely gone. A few sudden and abrupt cuts, several frames of pure white light accompanied by the sound of film clicking loudly through the projector, and the words "The End" appeared on the screen. There was a good deal of hooting, hissing, groaning, and some scattered applause.

"Nex' time," the tall dude in front of them drawled, "save that shit for the Army."

"Air Force and Marines, too," the heavyset girl next to him chimed in.

"But doan never show it here," the tall dude added.

"*Ever,*" the heavyset girl shouted.

"*Again,*" the dude yelled, their impromptu little chorus of abuse ending just as the lights came back up.

"Well," he asked Steffi, looking around at a theater that was now *very* crowded, every last seat taken as yet more people jammed themselves down all the aisles. "Still want to go?"

Steffi looked around for a moment. As promised, he had definitely taken her somewhere she had never been before. "Paulie," she said quietly, "are we the *only* white people in here tonight?"

"It's possible."

"Do you come here . . . *often?*" she asked, searching for the clue that would unlock the mystery of such strange behavior, especially on a first date.

"I used to. Of course, back then, if you were crazy enough to be here, everyone figured that you just naturally had to be all right. Lately, though, it has gotten a little tense in the community. But only for folks like us."

"Then why come at all?"

Certainly, this was the sixty-four thousand dollar question. He could not have answered it had his very life depended on it. Instead of even trying, he just said, "You'll see. Wait till it starts."

After an interminable intermission made all that much longer by the constant stream of people coming down the aisle who made a point of stopping by their row to ask if anyone was actually sitting in the seats that they were occupying at the moment, the lights suddenly went down without warning. Immediately he was seized by the same kind of expectant tension that he had last felt in shul on Yom Kippur just before the *kohanim*, with his grandfather among them, had *duchened*. Would all that had been promised be delivered? Would he feel the power, and be moved?

For although he could never have explained it to anyone who attended Ahavath Mizrach on a regular basis, and he was reasonably certain that the rabbi himself would have considered it blasphemy even to discuss the topic with him, it was the single moment that he worshipped in this theater and the shul as well. The instant when everything false seemed to flow out of him and nothing was left behind but what some called God and others called soul but that he knew to be his very essence. Only then were there no lies or pretense left behind to cloud the issue. Unfortunately, once that moment had passed, everything again became just the way it had been before.

From out of the darkness, a deep voice boomed, "Ladies and gentlemen, it is now . . . Showtime at the Apollo Theater." The crowd howled its appreciation. The holy moment was finally at hand. "Tonight," the disembodied voice continued, "the Apollo Theater is proud to present the one and only . . . Mr. *Dynmite*."

From behind a translucent scrim that had been lowered across the stage, the band of men sitting with instruments in their hands hit everything in sight, brass, bass, and drums combining to underline the announcement with a mighty thump, as though some large part of the building itself had only just collapsed into the street.

"Mr. Outta Sight," the announcer boomed, the excitement mounting in his voice. *"Soul Brother Number One. The King of Rhythm and Blues. The King of Show Business . . ."* Impatiently the crowd called out his rightful name, knowing that he would not appear until it was sounded in the hall.

"The man who made 'Night Train!' " A blaring ovation from the band, hunting horns held high heralding the beginning of the chase. " 'Think.' . . . 'Try Me!' . . . 'I Found Someone!' . . . 'Please, Please, Please!' " The band blasted out one long and continuous note as the entire audience got to their feet to greet im. "Ladies and gentlemen, the Apollo Theater is proud to resent . . . *The Hardest Working Man in Show Business* . . . *aaaaames Brown!"*

Up went the translucent scrim, revealing the band as they tood frozen in place with no sound at all coming from their nstruments, the golden saxophones poised, the drummer holding his sticks high above his head to fashion a rugged cross, the agged cat at the piano waiting with his hands in the air, diamond ufflinks gleaming brightly at his wrists, all of them holding the ose for longer than seemed humanly possible.

From the wings, legs pumping like pistons to a beat that only he could hear, hair swept up in an audacious pompadour that challenged the basic laws of physical gravity, wearing a wicked houndstooth-checked jacket over a purple shirt with a floppy velvet bowtie at the collar and a matching checked cummerbund around the waist that would have looked absurd on anyone else but was just fine on him, sharkmouth James with the barracuda smile came churning towards the microphone. His skinny legs knotted around themselves as he did an impossible mashed potatoes, a leaping jump back jack, a fall-to-the-floor see-you-later-alligator.

"There he is," he cried, pulling Steffi to her feet so she could see James above all the bobbing heads. "That's *him*."

Seizing the microphone from the stand, James put it to his mouth. He nodded and the band came suddenly to life. Then it began, a boiling cauldron of witches' brew stirred by the killer brass. The ack-ack punch of bass and drums kept putting holes in everything as galvanic, electroshock James marked out his territory for the night.

Patrolling back and forth across the very edge of the stage as though it marked the only boundary that he respected, James screamed, letting fly with a high, piercing shriek that came from the very depths of his soul where it was always night, and very cold. The band scrambled desperately to keep up as James whipped the microphone wire back and forth, skipping rope in time. The microphone stand teetered dangerously first one way and then the other, falling almost all the way to the floor before James wheeled in a turbulent circle to catch it backhanded, neatly flipping it back up to a standing position once again.

James. He was the gutbucket. The bottom line. The first cause and the final solution. Sheer, raw funk from the street. The hardest working soul brother in the world. He *had* to give the drummer some, again and again. Bantam rooster James, working

235

from the soul, the heart, tearing himself to pieces as he wore his wizened body down, shredding his sandpaper voice into tattered remnants. Throwing away what he could not use, James surged forward with what was left, discarding first the bow tie and then the jacket as the sweat came pouring off his body, soaking the purple shirt a darker, bloody hue. The audience let him know just how they felt with constant high-pitched screams of *"That's right, baby!"* and *"You tell 'em, James!"* and the simple, all inclusive command, *"Testify!"*

Blue, red. Blue, red. The lights went blue, then came back red. James turned in spinning circles on the stage, preening and prancing like a back alley bully. Then, suddenly, he was humble once again, a helpless child trapped in a world he had never made. The world went blue, red, blue, around him. All the while the band pounded on, an elemental beat, a primitive jungle rhythm, why get fancy when the truth was being told, the talking drums calling to the echoing bass as the brass cried out for mercy on top of everything. *"Huh!"* the crowd grunted whenever James exhorted them to feel what he was feeling. He called, and they answered, *"James! Hnnh! Baby James! Hnnh, hnnh! Bad, sweet James! Hnnh, hnnh, hnnh!"*

"Good God!" screamed James, as though his very soul was breaking and he had caught sight of the devil himself. "Good God!" he howled, as though there was no one else he could call upon in his moment of need. Sliding the entire length of the stage on his knees with both fists clenched above his head, James fell suddenly to his side, lying there in a crumbled heap. Then, miraculously, he rose. Yet more penance was due. "Watch me work!" he cried. "*Good God!*" Across the stage he shimmied on one skinny storklike leg, grinning madly to let everyone know he had taken far worse punishment in his time yet was still around to tell the tale. Above all else, James was a survivor.

Pausing for a moment before the microphone as the band quieted down in back of him, James stood silhouetted by several brilliant spotlights. He brushed a speck of dirt from his pants. "Ah may be tired," he admitted, pronouncing the word "tarred," "but ah'm *clean*." Then he was off again, racing his shadow towards the wings as though both of them were fleeing the devil's grasp.

Down James went to his knees, one hand pointing to the sky, pleading for forgiveness. Three counts, and he was back up again. *"New Breed Boog-a-loo!"* James hollered, throwing back

236

his head and holding on to the microphone stand with one hand as his legs swirled like deadly, coiling snakes on the wooden floor beneath his feet. Bending at the ankles, bending at the knees, bending yet never breaking, James bobbed and weaved and ducked. Then he came off the ropes with a sudden flurry of soulful rights and lefts to survive another round. He might be knocked down, but never out.

James pushed the crowd to the very edge. Then he brought them back again. The time was not yet right. People cried out to him, shouting his words back at him, their eyes big and goofy in their heads. Then James cried, "Lawd have mercy! *Lawd have mercy!* Bay-bee, take my hand . . ." and the band began the slow, rolling break that led into "Please, Please, Please."

On the far side of the stage, the Famous Flames, three in number, assumed their rightful place behind a microphone of their own to slowly moan in harmony the single, insistent refrain, *"Bay-bee . . . please . . . don't . . . go."* The drummer pounded everything to death in double time as James screamed on top, flinging himself about the stage like a man possessed. Afflicted with the fever and the sweating fits, James was sick all right but certain that he could heal himself. All he needed was time.

When they came for him, gently placing a cape over his shoulders so they could lead him to the hospital bed that had to be waiting just behind the curtain, James resurrected himself, fighting off his saviors with a look of grim determination on his face. Flinging away the cape with a gesture of complete disdain, he high stepped furiously toward the microphone for yet another verse. One more time, yeah, they cried from the audience. One more one more. And then one more time again.

Three separate times they came for him, each of the Flames advancing in turn with a cape of a different color in his hands and a look of soft compassion on his face, pleading, begging, entreating James to let them take him home. Thrice James rose, fighting for his life, his soul, his very existence. Thrice he did deny them all. As soon as they helped James up, he was right back down again. Down, and then back up again, wracked with fever yet chilled to the bone, hot and cold all at the very same time.

Inside the music was where James lived, between the chorus and the backbeat, just before the bridge where his trusty sidekick Maisie-o could always be counted on to blow and pull him through. In order to get down, James screamed, he had to get in deep. In order to get *down*, he *had* to get in deep. There just was no other way.

Now James was on his knees at the very front of the stage, the congregation reaching up with eager hands to clutch for a souvenir, a bit of flesh, a button, or a cufflink. From out of the wings came four men in expensive suits with vicious razor scars on their cheeks. The look in their eyes was fearsome. Dedication to the cause was all they knew. As James leaned forward to shake all the hands he was being offered, two followed and two preceded.

"Paulie, Paulie," Steffi cried wildly, "what are they doing?"

"The Flames? Which one? Bobby Byrd or Bobby Bennett or . . . shit, I can't remember the third one's name. . . ."

"Not them. The bodyguards. . . ."

"The mean dudes right at the edge of the stage? They're the handshake breakers. See how they never look at James himself? Anyone gets too strong a hold on him, they break the shake. Otherwise, they'd *kill* him. . . ."

Now James was at the microphone, thanking everyone in an emotion-choked voice for the five wonderful days and the five wonderful nights he and the boys in the band and all the Famous Flames as well had enjoyed right here in their wonderful, wonderful city. It had all been just so fine, so nice, and so right. He had never had a better five wonderful days and five wonderful nights anywhere. Remember, he told them all with a triumphant smile, James Brown *will* be back. When you expect him least and need him most. Maybe next week, maybe next year. But definitely some time soon.

Then the heavy red curtains swept across the stage and it was over, just as suddenly as it had begun. No amount of cheering in the world, no standing on the seats while clanging garbage can covers together like cymbals could bring him back again tonight. Having given his all, James was finally through, tired *and* clean.

"Steffi," he croaked, having lost his voice some time ago, "that's it."

"No," she insisted, her damp hair falling into her glittering eyes, her mouth wide open. "He's coming back again. I *know* he is. . . ."

"Baby," he said hoarsely. "I've seen the show before. Once they do 'Please, Please, Please' and the handshake breakers come out, it's over. He's probably halfway back to his house in Queens by now. Look, can we discuss this in the car?"

Remembering where they were, Steffi nodded. Swallowing

238

hard, she let him take her hand and lead her up the aisle. "God, Paulie," she gulped. "What time is it?"

"One o'clock?" he said, squinting at the illuminated clock over the back door as they filed out into the street with the rest of the crowd, all of them having been so thoroughly stewed in their own juices that they barely had enough energy left to stand on their feet, much less walk.

"I'm really not supposed to stay out this late," Steffi said in a worried voice as they headed towards the car. "My father will go crazy."

"You want to call? Tell them you're all right?"

Steffi shook her head. "He'd have a heart attack when the phone rang. Let's just go."

As they drove downtown along the West Side, he watched in amazement as Steffi once again became Nat Weiss's daughter. The rapidly declining street numbers seemed only to accelerate the rate of change. "So tell me," he asked when finally they hit Canal Street, "how did you like it?"

"God, Paulie, I really don't know, I mean, it was so . . . *animalistic*."

Her response angered him beyond the point of reason. For one thing, it was completely dishonest. With his very own eyes, he had seen it happen. She had been moved. She had sweated along with all the others, gritting her teeth and grabbing for his hand to keep herself from being completely swept away. Yet now she was acting as though he had imagined it all on his own. Lesley would never have done the same.

"Well," he said, fighting to control his feelings. "At least James hisself worked out."

"Why do you say 'hisself,' Paulie? You're not black."

"Because it feels good."

"And why does all this mean so much to you?"

"Because it feels good, all right?"

For the rest of the ride, they did not say very much at all to each other. It was only after he had double parked outside Steffi's house and walked her up the front steps to the door that she turned to him and confessed, "I really did have a very nice time tonight, Paulie." Knowing that she would have said the exact same thing to him no matter where he had taken her, he stood there, sulking in silence. "For a first date," she added, "it was really different."

"Wonderful," he said morosely. "I'm glad you enjoyed it."

"Please, Paulie. Don't say it like that. All the time that James Brown was on the stage, I couldn't hear any buzzing at all in my ear. He made it go away, completely."

He was about to tell Steffi that she could apply directly to James himself for further treatment of her condition when she suddenly stepped forward. Boldly, she kissed him right on the mouth. Then she shuddered as though a chilling breeze was blowing right through her. Once again, she kissed him. Then she shuddered some more.

"You cold?" he asked.

"No," she whispered in a husky voice. "Why? Are you?"

Then she put her key in the door and disappeared into the house before he could say another word.

CHAPTER TWENTY-THREE

LYING FLAT ON his back with his eyes wide open, Morty stared up at the ceiling over his bed as though at any moment it might tell him something that he did not already know—specifically, where his kid might be at this godforsaken hour of the night. Quite possibly, Paulie had wrapped the front end of the car around a light pole out on the Long Island Expressway and even now was sitting helplessly behind the wheel with his head cracked open and blood streaming down his face as police sirens wailed in the distance.

Rolling over onto his side so that he could check the time by looking at the illuminated hands of the little Big Ben clock near his bed, Morty realized to his great horror that he was once again thinking exactly like Esther, driving himself crazy for no good reason simply because he did not know what else to do. Tuning past the subject in his mind like some out-of-town radio station that was coming in too faintly for him to hear, he forced himself instead to concentrate on what he would be having for breakfast.

Since today was Friday, it would be Frosted Flakes. Although they were a little sweet for his taste and he had long since grown

240

tired of Tony the Tiger fiercely growling *"G-r-r-reat!"* at him every time he turned on his television set, Morty had no choice in the matter. Since he always bought the Kellogg's Variety-Pak when he shopped in the market on the avenue, he had to take the good with the bad. Actually, all their cereal was pretty decent, considering the price. His favorites, Corn Flakes, Raisin Bran, and Rice Krispies, Morty made a point of eating early in the week. By the time Friday came, he was always down to the sweet stuff once again.

Still, the Variety-Pak was so damn handy. In order to make himself breakfast, all Morty had to do was select one of the little foil-lined cardboard cartons, split it open down the middle along the perforated line with a fork, and he was in business. After adding powdered milk that he had carefully mixed to his own exacting standards with a soup spoon in a water glass over the sink, his morning meal was ready to be eaten. Afterward there was no bowl to wash, nothing. He could just throw the carton away and go to work.

More times than he could remember, Morty had urged his son to sit down and eat with him, saying, "It's good, it's *good*. Try it." The kid always refused point blank to even taste the stuff. Paulie was one fussy eater all right. Always had been, even as a kid. The fussiest. Only the other morning, Paulie had asked him, "Why *powdered* milk? Why not the regular kind?" Unwilling to get into a big discussion with him about it at that hour of the morning, Morty had just said, "Because it's cheaper, okay?" He had let it go at that.

In truth, if Morty had known where to find powdered eggs for sale, he would have eaten them for breakfast as well. The flat, gritty taste of prepared food in his mouth each morning served to remind him of his Army days. Most of the guys he had been in with back then had bitched like crazy about the food. The stuff was nauseating. They could not eat it without rushing right to the latrine to throw up. Their mothers had never served them such slop.

Not Morty. His mother had never once cooked him a decent meal in America. Instead, he had fed himself right out of the icebox most nights, standing there with the door open and the light bulb on as he picked through shelves that more often than not were empty. During his first six months in the Army Morty had actually put on fifteen pounds, filling out in the chest and becoming a man. Go explain to Paulie that this was the reason he still ate breakfast each day as though he was on bivouac.

On course, there was no denying that powdered milk *was* a hell of a lot cheaper than the real stuff. Every penny that Morty saved on food went right into his stamp collection, the one that he had been compiling for Paulie ever since the kid's bar mitzvah.

No other clerk or carrier in the entire station, and there had to be at least twenty of them who saved stamps on a regular basis, crowding in front of his window whenever a brand-new first-day issue came in, had a collection that could rival the one he had assembled.

The stamps were more than just an investment for the future. They were also the past. Each peppermint-striped looseleaf folder stored in the hall closet marked not only another year of Morty's life but the history of the country to which he had been brought as a boy. Amelia Earhart, Franklin Delano Roosevelt, Adlai Stevenson, Walt Disney, and Andrew Carnegie, the greatest figures America had ever produced, were in there. Men and women who had lived the kind of life Morty had always wanted for his son. It was a life he was only now beginning to realize that Paulie might never have.

Even more strongly than Esther, Morty had been the one who had urged Paulie to stay in college and get a degree. Wholeheartedly, he had agreed with the kid's decision to go on to graduate school. He had chipped in each month with as much money as he could afford in order to keep him there. Only then Paulie had dropped out without getting a degree and moved to Boston. Ever since, it had all been going downhill for the kid.

Better than anyone, Morty knew that what a boy could run and hide from, a man had to face every single day of his life. If you had been born with a penis between your legs, that *shmendrick* that as a kid you used to piss with in vacant lots only to later discover that it was in fact a baby-making machine, with a purpose other than pleasure, you had to go out in the world and bring home a paycheck each week.

If Paulie had chosen, for reasons that Morty himself still did not clearly understand, not to find himself a profession so that he could spend his days behind a desk, then there were far worse places for him to make a living than the post office. People would never stop writing letters and sending packages to one another. Although the work was dull, it was steady. No one ever got laid off. With all the big shots that Morty knew, he was confident that he could get the kid an appointment to the GPO downtown, where the bosses worked.

In a couple of years Paulie could move up, becoming a route inspector or a station superintendent, pulling down a solid five figures a year. The kid *was* bright. Always had been. *Too* bright. That was his problem. Once Paulie got started in Avenue Station as a Christmas temp, at two thirty-six an hour, maybe he would see the light. The work itself might straighten him out.

Morty heard the front door of the apartment come open, followed by the noisy jangle of car keys being thrown on the kitchen table. Sitting up in bed, he reached out with his right hand to shut down the alarm before it went off in his ear. "Paulie!" he called out. "You leave me enough gas to get to work?"

"Half a tank," the kid called back, obviously exhausted from his big night on the town. The kid had been out on a date. With whom, Morty had not asked, figuring that it was just none of his business.

"Half a tank won't get me through the weekend," Morty muttered, swinging his bare feet on to the cold floor. "I'll have to stop by Frank's on my way in, get it filled all the way up."

Rubbing the sleep from his eyes, Morty padded into the living room. Carefully he looked his son up and down, just to make certain that he had in fact come home with most of the clothing on that he had worn the night before. "Where *you* been?" Morty asked. "On your date?" Paulie nodded. "*This* late?" Morty said. "What kind of a girl stays out this late on a weekday night?"

"I took her home a couple hours ago. Then I just drove around. . . ."

"Oh. *That* kind of date, huh? Listen. You hungry? I mean, after burning up half a tank of gas driving around the neighborhood in circles?"

Paulie considered the question for a moment. "I could eat," he said finally. "Not Frosted Flakes, though."

"Not here, Mr. Fussy Eater," Morty told him. "I thought . . . if we leave now, we could go by the Greeks' for breakfast. You interested?"

"Yeah?" the kid said. "What could I get there?"

"What could you get there?" Morty repeated, wondering if his son wanted him to recite their entire menu before he made a decision. "You could get whatever you like. They got it all."

"Sure. I'll go."

"Let me get dressed then. Only take a minute."

After Morty had slipped into his blue uniform pants and long sleeve regulation shirt with the postal emblem on the shoulder, he made certain to button his yellow Perry Como sweater all the way up. In Avenue Station, it would be freezing cold until early afternoon. Then Morty went back into the living room. His son now had on a different shirt than the one he had worn the night before. "For the Greeks', you changed your shirt?" Morty asked in disbelief. "Believe me, they would have let you in with the other one. Come on, let's go."

Out in the street, it was not yet day. The darkness had given ground around the buildings on the avenue so that with all the streetlamps still on, the shadows had vanished, absorbed into the fuzzy gray predawn light that seemed to hang over everything like an old Army blanket. It was quieter than usual out here today, a solitary milk truck slowly making deliveries to the little grocery stores scattered on various corners. More than once, Morty had come out to go to work at this ungodly hour only to be greeted by someone lying on the sidewalk more dead than alive or a police car standing in the middle of the gutter with its red lights flashing as a cop put the cuffs on someone who had been shopping for bargains before the stores opened for business.

By noon, what Morty had seen in the street at this hour often seemed no longer real to him at all, as though he had dreamed it while still asleep. At this time of the morning the respectable people of the neighborhood were still lying safe and warm in their beds. In a few hours, they would all clog the streets at once in their mad morning rush towards the city, where they worked at higher paying jobs than the one he himself had held for the past twenty-three years.

Like some barely human creature emerging from a cave after a long period of hibernation, Morty alone had to go to work each day in this primitive darkness. Never was he actually certain that the sun would in fact rise later in the day. Winter and summer alike, he was out here before anyone else had even rolled over for the first time, hoping that his car would start so that he could make it down the avenue to punch in on time.

Deciding to go directly to the Greeks' and take his chances getting gas after breakfast, Morty took a right off the avenue and drove down the block on which the synagogue stood. As they went past the temple, the kid suddenly jammed his face up

244

against the window on his side of the car. Then he began frantically waving his hand. "You see him?" Paulie asked.

"Seen who?"

"Pop."

"Where?" Morty asked, immediately taking his foot off the accelerator. "In the street?"

"In shul. Sitting in the window of the Talmud Torah. I waved but I don't think he saw me."

"Oh, yeah," Morty said, giving the car gas again. "He does that."

"Does what?"

"Sits there."

"At a quarter to five in the morning?"

"That's it. He sits and he waits."

"What for?"

"You tell me," Morty said. "The Messiah?"

"You ever ask him about it?"

"Sure I did," Morty said angrily. "Plenty of times. You think that just because he lives with your mother I don't care about what he does?"

"What did he say?"

"What did he say?" Morty repeated. "He never talked to me as a kid growing up on the other side. So why should he start now?"

"Why would he be here so early?"

"Maybe he can't sleep. *Hey*," Morty said, having already grown tired of the subject, "after what he lived through, it's amazing that he can still walk to shul at *any* time of day. Let him be, I say. He's happy as he is."

From the look on his son's face, Morty could tell that the kid still was not satisfied. When it came to grabbing hold of a topic and going round and round on it until you felt sick to your stomach and wanted only to throw up behind a door somewhere, Paulie definitely took after his mother. "You know," Paulie said slowly, "I been wanting to do something for him."

"You already did. Washed his hands for him on Yom Kippur, didn't you?"

"*Give* him something, I mean. Something special."

"Get him a carton of cigarettes for his birthday. He'll appreciate it."

Sensing that his son still was not happy, Morty added, "Look, Paulie, as long as he's got a bed to sleep in, food to eat, and a

245

shul to go to, he's happy. Believe me. His mind don't work like yours or mine. It never did. I mean, he was a shoemaker on the other side, right? Any time they can't let a shoemaker live in peace, you know there has to be something seriously wrong in the world. When the Nazis came, he got his whole family out, one by one. Not just me and my mother, but all his brothers and cousins, everybody. Only him they caught, the bastards.''

"How come he never talks about her? His wife, I mean. Your mother.''

"That woman? Listen. I say `Kaddish` for her once a year on Yom Kippur and that's it. She was worse than the SS, believe me. Hitler let her escape because he was afraid of the competition. She was older than him, see? An arranged marriage. When we came over here, she liked it right away. 'My America,' she used to call it. Had me bar mitzvahed only because she thought he was already dead. When he finally showed up after the war, she lived with him for six months, then went off to Florida with her sister, where she died. That's why you never knew her. Your mother, well, she took him in right away. When I left, he stayed.''

"How come?''

"She was the one who cooked.''

"Yeah, right.''

"I'm serious. After what he went through, why should he ever have to worry about where his next meal is coming from? Your mother's good at taking care of people. I give her that. Too good. But him, *hey*. The first time he saw me after he got out of the camp, I'd already been in the Army three years, I'm a *man*, right? 'Ziendel,' he says to me, 'you read your *haftorah* like you were supposed to? Then you made *Kiddush* after?' Unbelievable, huh?''

"The high priest,'' the kid said softly.

Morty shook his head and made a face. Paulie was resisting him every step of the way. Deciding to give it one last try, he said, "You take my advice, Paulie, which I know doesn't happen all that often anymore, the best thing you can do for him *and* yourself is to work out how you're going to make a living in the world now that you're through with school and maybe come home a little earlier at night with the car so I can get some sleep. That would be the *best* present you could give him. *Fershtayst?*''

"I guess,'' the kid answered, making Morty wonder whether any of it had gotten through.

"All right then,'' he said nevertheless. Pulling the car around in back of the Greeks', where it was easier to park, Morty shut off the ignition. "Let's go in," he said. "Otherwise the carriers are going to have all the good tables to themselves, the animals."

Pulling open the aluminum frame plateglass door, Morty confidently led his son past the long pink Formica counter behind which the three dark haired brothers who owned the place were hustling like crazy, sliding one thick china cup after the other filled to the brim with scalding coffee onto little saucers without ever spilling a single drop.

Behind them, several of their many cousins and nephews stood tending the long, sizzling griddle with crusty spatulas in their hands, waiting for the precise moment when an order was ready so they could scoop it on to a waiting plate. Morty had to hand it to them. When it came to running restaurants, no one could touch the Greeks.

The place itself was jammed, cigarettes burning down in tinmetal ashtrays on all the tables so that the air was blue with smoke. Carriers in thick blue winter uniforms sat talking in loud voices to one another. Whenever the bullshit really started to fly, one of them would lean all the way back in his chair and begin laughing until he choked. Then he would cough, reach for his coffee, light up a fresh cigarette, and it would all start over again. Behind the counter, the old cracked Bakelite radio standing on the narrow shelf that ran below the mirror was turned all the way up. Frank himself, the Chairman of the Board, was singing "Come Fly With Me." In every way it was a typical morning in the Greeks'.

Looking around, Morty realized that the only place left to sit was in a booth against the far wall that already had four men in it, Mo Tannenbaum among them. Before Morty could look away again, Mo caught sight of him and waved him over. "Come on," Morty sighed, indicating to Paulie that he should follow him. "You might as well meet the worst of them now. You remember Mo Tannenbaum, right? Say hello. Most likely, you'll be working alongside him when you start."

"Since when are you eating here again, Morty?" Mo demanded when they got within shouting range.

"Starting now," Morty told him. "Mo—I brought my kid in with me."

"*Paulie?*" Mo said in disbelief. "Jeez. Been a *long* time since I seen you."

Feeling relieved that his son actually had enough sense to put out his hand for Mo to shake, Morty slid into the booth. He

247

motioned for Paulie to do the same on the opposite side of the table. "What goes, Morty? What goes?" the man sitting next to Mo demanded. "To a fellow clerk you introduce your kid but not to the carriers?"

"I was getting around to it, Monte," Morty said quietly. "Monte Serrano, my son, Paulie. Come next month, Monte, he's going to be working with us as a temp. *Inside*."

"Too effin' bad for you, kid," Monte said, squinting his right eye shut against the smoke from his cigarette, which was curling up directly into his face. "Who'd you have to fuck to get the job? Abe Stark?"

"How about taking it easy on the language, huh, Monte?" Mo asked before Morty could get the very same words out of his mouth.

"Yeah, right," Monte said. "I'll do my best."

"Paulie," Morty said. "Tommy O'Connor."

"Tommy Oh, we call him," Monte explained, taking over the introductions as though it was only right that he do so. "As in, 'Oh *shit*, Tommy, not again.' "

The thick shouldered man in the far corner of the booth nodded. Then he slowly blinked his eyes. In nearly every way Tommy resembled a nearsighted camel, one that *knew* there had to be water somewhere in this desert without ever quite being able to find it.

"Shut the fuck up, huh, Tommy?" Monte said good-naturedly. "You're givin' me a headache with all that conversation. This big good-looking sonofabitch over here is Russ Balbano. Russ wins *every* beauty contest he enters because not only is he pretty but he's got . . . personality."

Morty watched Paulie shake Russ's hand as Monte launched into an annoying version of a song that had once been popular, wailing, "*Wawk* with personality, *tawk* with personality . . . *strike* with personality."

"Enough, Monte, huh?" Russ said softly. Immediately, Monte turned his attention back to Paulie. "Bee-yoo-ti-ful kid, Morty," he crooned. "His hair was any longer, I'd go out and buy him a violin myself."

Knowing that it was always better to make jokes with such people than to get angry at them, Morty said, "Forget it, Monte. He can't carry a tune."

"Besides," Mo chipped in quickly, "nobody here can remember the last time you bought anybody anything."

248

"Fuckface To-masso," Monte hissed, poking the big man in the corner with his finger. "Shove your fat Mick ass over so Morty's kid the violinist here can grab a cup of coffee without having to juggle it in the air."

Tommy did just as he was told. The effort caused him to lose what little control he had been exerting over his oddly shaped head. Slowly it fell forward onto his chest. "Fuckface Tomassa," Monte cried, banging his cupped palms against the tabletop to simulate the hollow sound of pounding hoofbeats. "Leaves the gate at five to one, catches a banana ride around the first turn, and fades badly in the stretch."

Tommy's head continued to fall at an alarming rate towards the very edge of the table so that it seemed certain he was about to split his skull open right to the bone. At the very last possible moment, Monte jerked Tommy's coffee cup out of the way. Then he slid a rolled-up copy of the brand new *Playboy* still encased in a brown mailing wrapper in its place and threw up both his hands in surrender.

"And . . . he's *out!*" Monte announced proudly as Tommy's head plopped down softly onto the magazine. Reaching into the side pocket of Tommy's uniform jacket, Monte rummaged around with his hand for a second before withdrawing a green glass pint bottle. Unscrewing the cap, he turned the bottle over. A single drop of whiskey fell onto the tip of his finger. Rubbing the finger across his gums, Monte laughed out loud. "Cheap, but Tommy likes it all right. He heard that Scotch was good for the heart. Right, babe?"

Tommy did not answer. "Christ, Monte," Russ said. "He do the *whole* pint? Already?"

Monte nodded. "This is what we're talking about right here," Russ said.

"He needed a *fifth* before they put him on his new route," Monte said. "But if you're talking union, Russ, don't let me stop you."

"Not union," Russ said. "Postal employees can't have no union. It's illegal."

"Strike then," Monte said. "*With* personality."

"Not a strike either," Russ said. "Work-to-rule, with no guys taking overtime. Soon as Christmas mail starts piling up all across the country, you'll see how fast they'll meet our demands. Only we need the clerks to stand with us."

"Russ, *please*." Mo Tannenbaum protested as Morty himself

249

dodged the entire issue by waving at one of the Greeks behind the counter to come over to the booth for their order. "It's apples and oranges. Clerks and carriers are two different ball games. Always have been. Right, Morty?"

Morty shrugged. "I got to live on my salary," he said simply. "Come Christmas, overtime is half my check."

"Minus what you hand back to Messer to get the time, right?" Russ demanded. "Now, that is *completely* illegal."

Morty shrugged once more. "It's a terrible world all right," he said. "But I didn't make it that way. Sometimes, to get, you have to give first."

"Think about Russ then a little, Morty," Monte begged. "He's got the big future in the national association. Or you want him to go bad and follow in his brother Anthony's footsteps?" Bending his nose to one side so that he resembled a gangster, Monte began loudly humming the theme music from "The Untouchables." Russ shot Monte a withering look that shut him right up. "So what's with your kid, Morty?" Monte demanded a moment later, unable to keep still. "Deaf mute?"

"Wait till he has something to say, Monte," Morty said. "Then even *you* won't be able to shut him up."

"Hey," Monte said, the idea having apparently only just occurred to him, "how about you let me have him on the route? I could use a good *Yiddishe kopf* with me out there to keep those animals on Six Route in their cages. Six Route," he said bitterly. "The all-time fucking number one ballbreaker in the entire station. All stoops. Up and down and up and down and the ghinnies living there are so tight that come December, they plug their friggin' Christmas lights into each other's outside sockets just to try and save on the electricity bill. Oh, excuse me, Russ," Monte said, as though he had only just noticed him sitting there. "I didn't mean to insult your people or nothing."

"My people come from Naples, Monte," Russ said easily. "You know that."

"Yeah, right. And Six Route is all Siciliano. Skulls eighteen inches thick and pure concrete. *Tips?* They never heard of the animal till I got there and showed them how to live. So how about lettin' me have the kid on the route, huh, Morty? No one needs him more."

"Up to Mr. Messer where he works, right, Monte?" Morty asked innocently, knowing that the fix was already in. He him-

250

self had personally paid Messer off only last week. Come Christmas, Paulie would be working *inside*, where he belonged.

"Yeah, right. And his heart ain't in his diamond horseshoe money clip or nothin', right, Morty? Forget it. I'll go ask the Kraut bastard myself. Speaking of which. For two years now, I been tryin' to get my oldest, Philip, to come work with me at Christmas. Two thirty-six an hour and he gets to help take the load off his old man's back. Does he want it? No fucking way. Studying to be a priest, he's too busy making novenas to get his hands dirty. 'Philip,' I told him the other day, 'pray *real* good for me. 'Cause Christ in Heaven himself knows I'm gonna need *someone* to put in a good word for me up there when I croak.'"

It was completely quiet at the table for a moment. Then one of the brothers from behind the counter came over to take Morty's order. "Three scrambled eggs," Morty told him without looking at the menu. "Potatoes, rye toast with no butter and a large orange for my son. I'll have Rice Krispies."

"That's *all* you're eating?" Paulie asked.

"That's it. You eat. This one's on me."

Without having written down a thing, the Greek nodded and moved towards the counter. Already he was shouting out the order to one of his brothers. "What a memory," Morty said admiringly. "Never forgets a thing. If you asked him, he could tell you right now how much money is in the register, down to the very last penny."

"Which is how comes *he* lives in Bayshore," Mo noted.

"Yeah, right," Monte grunted. "And I'm walking Six Route every day."

"Morty," Russ said, cutting Monte off before he could get started again, "you know I deliver the synagogue now, right? The one where you belong?" Morty nodded. "Well, since this is my first year on the route, I wonder . . . do they come through at Christmas?"

"Chanukkah, Russ," Morty corrected him. "No reason they shouldn't. What with all the special delivery and packages they get. I could ask around for you," Morty offered, as the Greek reappeared with Paulie's breakfast on one plate and a foil-wrapped packet of Rice Krispies in a bowl next to a carton of milk on another plate for him. "Find out what they gave in the past. My ex-wife handles these kind of things for them."

"Appreciate it, Morty," Russ said. "See, I already know

251

Esther. The other day, she sounded me out. Would I be able to sell any tickets for her, if and when they held a raffle there?"

"Raffle tickets," Monte repeated. "Bee-yoo-ti-ful move, Morty, all the way. The ex-wife gets young, good looking Russ with the Neapolitan eyes to move some tickets for the shul on his route while the kid is pulling down two thirty-six an hour as a temp. No wonder you won't stand with us on work-to-rule. You already got your entire *mispocheh* on the time clock."

Ignoring Monte completely, Morty said, "I haven't heard anything about the temple running a raffle, Russ."

"Mom said they might," Paulie muttered, his nose buried in food.

"How much a ticket?" Monte asked.

"She didn't know yet," Russ said. "Maybe twenty."

"*Twenty!*" Monte yelped. "Christ. They giving away a Coupe de Ville?"

"Trip to Jerusalem," Paulie said from over his plate. "That's what she told me. It's already been donated."

"Forget it," Monte said, losing all interest. "I want to see that many Yids all in one place together, I can always take myself for a walk down the avenue any time they got a discount sale goin'."

"Plus Las Vegas Night," Russ said.

"Now, in that I might be interested," Monte noted.

"How many tickets did she make you promise to buy *personally*, Russ?" Morty asked quietly. "If and when they actually hold this thing."

"Two?" Russ said hesitantly. "That's why I asked you if they come through at Cha-noo-kah, Morty. So I could afford them."

Monte crossed his eyes, did his best to hold it in, then just gave up and busted out laughing. A fine brown spray of coffee misted up before his face, then settled gently on to his pale-blue uniform shirt. "Bee-yoo-ti-ful move, Morty," he chortled. "I couldn't have played it any better myself."

Having completely lost what little appetite he had sat down with, Morty looked over at his son and said, "Eat up, Paulie, eat up. I got to get gas, then run you home before I clock in for the day."

As soon as the kid had polished off what was on his plate, Morty stood up. He made a point of saying goodbye only to Russ and Mo Tannenbaum, knowing that Tommy O'Connor was too asleep to care. After paying the check, he led Paulie back outside

252

to the car. It was only after he had let the door to the restaurant slam shut behind him that he turned to his son and said, "See, Paulie? This is the lowest kind of animal God ever put on the face of this earth. Monte Serrano. All he knows how to do is take. How about that nerve? Asking me to let him have you on his route. To him, everything is a joke. Doesn't respect his religion or ours. With that kind of attitude, how can a man ever get anywhere in the world?"

"I don't know," his son said, looking right at him. "I kind of liked the guy. He was funny. What would happen if I worked with him on his route?"

"What would happen? You would wind up doing all his work while he got *shikker* in some bar. This is a bum, Paulie. From the word go. Besides, I got Mr. Messer all set up to give you a nice job sorting special delivery inside the station. What do you need being out in the weather for every day, with your health?"

"For the raffle," the kid said, as if that explained it all.

"What raffle?" Morty demanded, starting to lose control. "All of a sudden, this raffle is all anyone can talk about. A raffle I never heard of before."

"Well, if they have it . . . I would want to sell some tickets."

"For what possible reason?"

"For Pop."

"How does he stand to get anything from this? This is a Nat Weiss production, all the way. I can smell it."

"Well, every ticket I would sell, I could ask the person who bought it to donate it back to the shul. Then I would put Pop's name on it. Maybe he would win the trip. Mom thought it was a great idea. . . ."

"Win the trip?" Morty said, stepping back to take a good look at his son. "Have you completely lost your mind, or what? This is an old man, Paulie. What does he need with a trip to Jerusalem? And what if he won it? Who would go along to take care of him?"

"Maybe you. . . ."

That did it. Pulling his car keys from his pocket, Morty said, "I don't have the time for this. Okay? I'm living in the *real* world. Selling raffle tickets to send an old man to Jerusalem is not real. It's from out of some storybook you read as a kid. And what really surprises me is that someone with all your education can't tell the difference between the two."

Yanking open the door of the car, Morty threw himself behind

253

the wheel and drove off, leaving Paulie standing behind him with a puzzled look on his face, as though he still did not understand what he had done that was so terribly wrong. Not until he had gone nearly all the way down the avenue to Frank's gas station did Morty begin to feel like a complete and total jackass. Instead of going back to look for his son so that he could apologize to him right away, Morty promised himself that he would make it up to the kid tonight, after he got home from work.

Not that he had really done anything that was so terrible. Ever since Abraham and Isaac, fathers had been sacrificing their sons for one reason or another. That was not his intention. It never had been. All he had done was leave his kid stranded ten blocks from home without a ride. So what? It wouldn't kill Paulie to walk a little. He could use the exercise. Besides, if his son was so damned eager to go out and work the streets with an animal like Monte Serrano, the very best thing Paulie could do for himself was to start walking everywhere right now.

Come next month, Paulie was going to be doing more of that than he had ever thought possible. For all Morty knew, maybe being out there on the street all alone, without either of his parents to protect him, would teach the kid the terrible lesson that he himself had learned so long ago and done his very best to keep his only son from finding out about on his own. In America, the land of opportunity, nothing was free. You had to pay for everything they gave you, if not with money, then blood.

OVERS

CHAPTER TWENTY-FOUR

WITH JUST TWO more shopping days left until Christmas, snow is in the air. This is what all the carriers tell me and I have to believe it is true. To do anything less would be a first class betrayal of the faith. Sitting with Russ Balbano, Monte, Big Frank Mancuso, and Tommy O'Connor at noontime in yet another of the anonymous little corner luncheonettes where we meet each day to eat, I watch the storm take shape in their eyes. I see the soft white flakes start to fall in late afternoon. They come down faster and faster all through the night. Finally, the storm mushrooms into an authentic howling monster with teeth that shuts down the entire city, much like the legendary 1947 blizzard that Monte claims kept mailmen off the street for *weeks*.

Snow is definitely in the air. The carriers have been telling one another this for a week. I hope that they are right. For nothing short of an all-out disaster will help them now. Their work-to-rule struggle fell apart before it could even get started. It died slowly as in turn, each and every carrier shuffled forward at the end of the working day to take the overtime being offered them by Martin Messer, supervisor of Avenue Station.

With the possible exception of Hungry Louie Schwartzman, whom no one can stand, neither Russ nor Monte seem to blame any of their fellow workers for what they have done. Guys like Tommy O'Connor have kids at home to feed. They have wives who are always in and out of hospitals. They have Christmas bills to pay. As Monte insists over and over, driving home the point until everyone is sick of hearing him talk about it, snow is their only chance.

A sudden, swirling storm that will bury cars and obliterate all the sidewalks will keep the carriers off their routes. In Avenue Station, as well as other post offices like it all over the city, the mail will pile up even higher than it stands right now. In order to get it all delivered before Easter Sunday, the big bosses in

Washington will have to come through with a raise. Or so Monte insists, over and over again.

Having worked straight through since the fifteenth of the month with no days off, Saturdays and Sundays included, the carriers are long past making much sense about such matters. Instead, they are sleepwalking. Out on the route they stumble suddenly off curbs into the gutter. They slam storm doors shut on their frozen fingers. Loudly, they curse the day they ever took the Civil Service exam. They forget waiting sacks of mail in relay boxes and have to go back to get them. Day after day they scramble madly to keep up. Never getting far enough ahead to actually relax, they know only that tomorrow will be even worse.

The rest of the neighborhood is completely oblivious to their plight. Everyone else is slowing down to take the one big, deep breath that the city permits itself each year at this time. Even I have a fat soft spot in my heart for Christmas in the city. It is still the magic time, when anything seems possible. So long as you do not have to take out the mail each day.

The mail is an endless river. Much like the inscrutable Charles up in Boston, it moves and changes, yet is still somehow always the same. At the very back of Avenue Station, automatic sorters operate twenty-four hours a day. They spit out from forty-five to sixty pieces of mail a minute, depending on whether Monte or Messer has adjusted the setting last. The pieces are boxed by hand into sloping gray rubber trays that the night clerks pile high on the carriers' desks. By morning, the trays nearly block out the route cases themselves.

For at least three hours each morning, the carriers stand sorting mail from the trays into the cases. Then it all comes back out again to be bundled. Wrapped with coarse manila twine, it is shoved deep into heavy canvas sacks that waiting trucks carry to relay boxes scattered along the routes, not to be seen again until well after noon. No matter how much mail is taken out, still more always remains behind. Mail and more mail, piled up into ragged, sloping mountain ranges.

Getting the mail out at Christmas is the be-all and end-all for those who punch the clock in Avenue Station. The mail moves from machines through pigeonhole racks into sacks. Then it is shoved through tiny, hinged slots in doors out on the route. If it is then thrown immediately into the garbage can, no one cares. It *has* been delivered. The mailman has discharged his sacred duty one more time.

258

Nearly all the carriers have begun drinking earlier and earlier in the day. Each morning I watch as they pour short shots of Scotch into their coffee before the sun is even up. After lunch they grab a quick snort from someone else's half-empty pint. On their way back to the station in late afternoon, they stop off in some bar for the refill that keeps them going until they clock out. Then they go home, falling into a deep and dreamless sleep by the television set long before supper is even on the table.

All of them seem to be standing up to the strain fairly well except for Tommy O'Connor. Tommy Oh looks a hundred years older than when I first met him. At times, he seems to be positively on his last legs. Tommy drinks from the moment he gets up each day until he passes out again at night. He uses the stuff like antifreeze. Tommy's face is now the color of raw liver. The little veins around his eyes are cracked and broken. His lips are blue, his hands chafed and red. For Tommy Oh, the snow cannot possibly come too soon, if it comes at all.

Each morning, the cold gray promise of the storm that everyone insists is definitely on the way hangs over our heads as we go to work. The sky above Avenue Station is dark and sinister. A few faint rose-tinted patches of light in the distance are the only sure sign that the sun will in fact soon rise. When we all come back out again after having put in our eight or ten hours on the clock, the sun is already gone. It has vanished into the woolly gray mist that draws all the color from the bright, metallic chains of tinsel and holly that swing across the avenue in the breeze. The mist turns the warm cheery reds and flashing friendly greens of the season into yet two more shades of endless gray. Both morning and evening, it feels like snow. It really does. It even smells like snow. Soon, it has to snow.

Day after day, at five in the morning, while nearly everyone else in the neighborhood is still asleep, Avenue Station works, buzzing and humming like some great cathedral devoted to the perpetual adoration of Our Lady of the Mails. With steam knocking loudly in the paint caked pipes that run along the ceiling and cylindrical cones of bright yellow light pouring down through a blue gray haze of cigarette smoke, the sound of Sinatra caroling "Have Yourself a Merry Little Christmas" rings out from the station's radio.

The powerful smell of coffee grounds that Monte has dumped on purpose into the big wastepaper basket by Messer's desk in order to annoy him floats over all the cases, spiced with the tang of sweet, sharp whiskey. From behind the rows, Monte starts the shouting. *"Messer!"* he screams in a high-pitched girlish voice that penetrates. *"Shmesser!"* someone screams right back at him. *"Suck-a-me-off!"* Monte screeches, completing the litany.

Sometimes, Monte varies the routine by breaking into his own inimitable version of Lotte Lenya singing "Mack the Knife" in German, something he picked up from watching the Ernie Kovacs show on Thursday nights. Madly, he trills, "Oy, Mack-*ee* Messer, Mack-*ee* Messer . . ." as everyone hums in harmony behind him.

The post office is not yet open to the public at large. No customers stand in line before the windows waiting to buy stamps. We are safe in our own little world. It is just us and the mail. When finally we hit the streets at 10 A.M., having already put in half a day's work, we shout and carry on like children set free from elementary school by the three o'clock bell.

At this time of day, the streets belong entirely to us. We are the landlords, watchmen, and guardians of the entire neighborhood. Since we pass the same way each day at the exact same time, only we know at just which corner the dog shit lies piled high by the curb. Only we know all the telephone poles, shop windows, and sewer covers. All are different yet exactly the same. We alone know on which street the fire hydrant that has been leaking like crazy for the past three days has finally frozen solid, a wild phantasmagoria of ice having done what the city would not do to stem the never-ending flow of water. But we have no time to stand around. Out there somewhere there is money, waiting to be made.

The season cannot be distinguished from the money it brings. The tinkle of loose change jangling in all the carriers' pockets has replaced the sound of sleigh bells in the snow. The envelopes we deliver are stuffed thick with currency and checks. As we work, our time cards lie in little gray metal slots back at the station, the hours piling up. Quite possibly, the very next house we come to will be the one where the occupant whose name is printed above the doorbell will suddenly remember that yes, it *is* time to finally take care of the friendly mailman who has served everyone on the route so faithfully all year long.

A shouted invitation through a still locked door, a quick drink at the dining room table inside an overheated house, and yet another envelope changes hands. This one too is stuffed with cash for the postman to take with him back out into the cold. At

Christmas each year, some men make as much in tips as they earn in salary for a full three months.

It is no wonder then that each and every carrier has his very own special methods for mining a route to its ultimate potential. Monte, naturally, is an absolute master of the art. He can extract cash simply by slamming a storm door extra loudly or by boldly ringing a doorbell whenever he has too much mail to fit through the door slot. Of course, he never mentions that he has been saving letters up for a week for just this purpose.

For reasons known only to him, Monte has decided that this year even Old Man Pappalardo will come through for him. Old Man Pappalardo is the shortest, fiercest, deaf when he wants to be, hair sprouting black mole on the cheek, dead cigar chewing Sicilian of them all. Never in history has he been known to tip any mailman, sanitation worker, or cop. Once he even went so far as to fail to thank the ambulance driver from Coney Island Hospital who restarted his heart for him on the sidewalk in front of his house. Old Man Pappalardo has become an obsession with Monte, his very own version of the Holy Grail.

"I get this guy to give, Paulie," Monte told me only last week out in the street, the whites of his eyes gleaming like headlights in the gloom, "they'll have to put my name on the honor roll in the carriers' hall of fame. I'll move ahead of Big Frank, who, as I already told you more than once, sits down to dinner every night over a finished basement filled with tens of thousands of sample-sized Prell shampoos, Alberto VO-5 hair sprays, and Zest soaps, as well as every other product that ever came through the mail addressed to 'Occupant' which Frank, in his sick mind, actually thinks is his last name."

"Monte," I told him, "you'll never top Hungry Louie, so forget it."

"That animal. What'd he do now?"

"He printed up little paper wallets that say 'Season's Greetings' on one side. There's a flap in back for the money. He delivers them with the mail."

"You're shitting me," Monte said, stunned. "This is completely illegal. Who said?"

"Kevin Delaney told me about it the other day in the station."

"Well, he *would* tell you," Monte simpered. "You're his type. All this means is that I *got* to nail that old man." Pausing for breath, he added, "Fuck cards. Cards cost money, right? To trap a ghinny, set a ghinny. Besides, look what I found."

Reaching into the cracked leather sack that hangs over the handlebars of the three-wheel tricycle Monte uses to deliver Six Route, he took out a government check with Old Man Pappalardo's name on it. I noted with interest that the old man's first name was "August." "With this," Monte hissed, "I'm gonna flush old Augustino right out of that house of his. The Fortress of Calabria."

Even I have to admit that Old Man Pappalardo's house is completely forbidding. No one has ever seen a window open in it, winter or summer. The storm door at the front of the house is rusted shut. Day after day, we have to leave the mail lying on the little porch in front of it. Although there never seems to be anyone home, Monte assures me that Old Man Pappalardo is in fact always there, watching from behind the curtains. As soon as we turn the corner, he rushes out to get his mail before anyone can steal it from him.

Every morning for the past week, as we delivered the house, Monte has muttered, "Soon. It's gotta be soon. Any day now. He's gonna ask me about it. You watch." Sure enough, as we passed by his house this morning, Old Man Pappalardo just happened to come strolling towards us. Without bothering to say hello, he went straight up to Monte. Grabbing him by the sleeve of his uniform coat, he demanded, "You seen my check? That's-a my money. I work all my life for it."

"Check?" Monte said, scratching his head as though this was the first he had heard about it. "Gee, Pop, I don't know. What's it look like?"

"Govern-a-ment check," Pappalardo told him, wiping his mouth with his thick, twisted fingers. "Govern-a-ment enve-a-lope. Come every month. Like clockwork."

"Oh, *that* check," Monte said sympathetically, the spirit of the season flowing right through him. "Tell you the truth, Pop—this year, the mail is so fouled up, you'll be lucky if you see it by Good Friday."

Pappalardo's eyes narrowed. His chest started going up and down as though he was going to have another heart attack right there in the street. From the look on the old man's face, I could tell that he was watching his precious Christmas money sink from sight. Monte clapped him heartily on the back. "Don't you worry about it, Pop," he told him. "Me and my special assistant here will keep an eye out for it. Even better. We'll search for it."

"Doan do nothin' special for me," Old Man Pappalardo said

quickly, alarmed that he might have to pay extra for this kind of personalized service.

"*Special?*" Monte said. "We're gonna put a red tag tracer on it. We're gonna go through that mountain of mail in the station with a fine tooth comb. We're gonna look until our hands bleed and our eyes go blind. As Mary was the Holy Mother of Jesus, Pop, we *will* bring you that check before Christmas."

And that was how we left him, staring after us in the street with an expression of sheer terror on his face. When Monte told Russ the story at lunch, all Russ could say was, "Monte, you are sick. The sickest." While I cannot argue with Russ's judgment of the man, neither do I agree with him completely.

Monte Serrano is not yet dead. Despite all the hard time he has put in at Avenue Station, he still marches only to the beat of his very own special drummer. Monte cares, passionately. He is not afraid to show people how he feels. Because of him, I have been accepted completely by the other carriers. Figuring that anyone who can work for Monte Serrano has to be at least a little bit crazy all on his own, they have made me one of them. For the first time in longer than I can remember, I feel as though I actually belong.

Of course, the real reason I am working with Monte is so that I can sell raffle tickets. Whenever he disappears into someone's house out on the route for a quick drink and that ritualistic exchange of money, I am on my own. So long as I never tell anyone where Monte actually happens to be at the moment, insisting that the last time I saw him he was working the block up ahead, I am free to sell anyone I can find a raffle ticket.

Most of my customers are old men who are not all that different from August Pappalardo. Born somewhere in the wilds of Sicily long before the century began, they could not pronounce Ahavath Mizrach if they tried. And yet, some are actually willing to come up with the twenty dollars for the ticket and then hand the stub back to me so that I can put my grandfather's name on it.

"This for your church, right?" they ask, their garlic breath perfuming the air as they squint one eye shut against the cold. "Go on. Take the ticket. Long as it's for a good cause, what do I care?"

It is the kind of real charity I had nearly forgotten about. That it exists along Six Route, where no one seems to have very much money to spare, especially at Christmas, is but another of the miracles of the season. Every day, one or two of those fierce old men proves that in some brave hearts the Christmas spirit still lives.

So far, I have sold eighteen tickets. Sixteen of them have my grandfather's name on them. As soon as I sell the two remaining in my second book, his name will go on two more bonus chances. Sixteen plus two, plus two. Twenty chances to win a trip he deserves to take more than anyone else.

Monte has Old Man Pappalardo and I have the raffle. "Shall I build you a castle with the tower so high / It reaches the stars?" the great Smokey Robinson once asked. Answering his own question, Smokey sang, "And if that don't do . . . then I'll try something new." Which is just the way I feel about it myself.

All this is running through my head as Monte and I finish Six Route today. After the last letter has been slipped through the final slot, we head back towards the station, passing by the fruit store where Russ always waits for us so we can all walk in together. Only today there is no Russ. We wait for a while, then Monte says, "C'mon, c'mon. Let's go." Impatiently, he stamps his feet against the sidewalk. He blows into his gloved hands as though his breath will warm them through the wool. "My shorts just froze up into my asshole," he notes.

"Why not wait?" I ask.

" 'Cause. I just remembered. Russ got *other* business today."

"The national association?"

"Get outta here," Monte snorts as we start walking once again, our breath misting up before our faces. "Today's the day he makes his house calls. He sees his number one."

"Number one what?"

"Jeez, kid. You can't be a Yid and act *this* dumb. His number one woman. Out on the route. What do you think I'm talking about?"

"You're kidding," I say, unable to believe that the stories I have heard about what goes on between some carriers and the women who live on their routes are really true.

"Am I? Ask him about it. On second thought, don't. This woman is beautiful, kid. I seen her myself once, from across the street. What a face. What a body. One look from her and the ice we saw on that hydrant this morning would melt. . . ."

I turn this bit of information over in my mind. Young and good looking Russ, the Lancelot of Avenue Station, has his very own Guinevere stashed somewhere out on his route. By the window of her two-story brick house, she waits for him to come to her. Neither snow nor rain nor gloom of night can stay him from the swift completion of his appointed rounds. It is story-book stuff all right, happening under everyone's nose and at Christmas no less.

"Who is she?" I ask eagerly. "Do you know her name?"

"How would I know her name?" Monte says. "Russ won't tell me it. He calls her The Contessa. *The Contessa*," he repeats, shaking his head. "Can you believe that?"

Before I can interrogate him any further on the subject, Monte leads me back inside the station. For the next hour we work together in silence, sorting mail. At this time of the day, the station is fairly subdued, as close to normal as it ever gets. Then the disgusting daily ritual I have come to dread begins once more.

At the very center of the station, Martin Messer positions himself in front of his desk with his hands clasped behind his back. Standing at parade rest, he inspects the troops as they make their way past him to the time clock to punch out. All Messer needs is a riding crop, a pair of jodhpurs, and a helmet with a crest on it and he could pass for an authentic member of the SS.

As always, Hungry Louie Schwartzman is the very first one to go towards him. Not that Louie wants to go home. Around the station, it is well known that Louie will do anything to make sure that his time card stays on the clock until long after all the others are gone. Today, Messer looks right through him. The skin on Messer's face is pink and smooth. It glows in the dull light of late afternoon. The man is an absolute fanatic on personal grooming. He has his very own private bathroom at the back of the station so he can wash his hands without having to mingle with the help. At noon each day, his number one tool and all-purpose assistant, Kevin Delaney, brings a little hand mirror to his desk so that Messer can eat lunch and shave all at the same time without ever missing a phone call from the bosses down-town who are his pals.

Hungry Louie looks as though he has been sleeping in his uniform for years. His blue long sleeve regulation shirt is spotted and stained. A thick layer of stubble covers his face. Louie's eyes shift nervously from side to side in their deep, bony sockets. "So what is it, Mr. Messer?" Louie asks plaintively. "Some trouble on my route? Just tell me. I'll go back out right now and take care of it."

Messer paces away from Louie. Big Frank Mancuso ambles past them both, heading for the time clock. Catching Big Frank's eye, Messer holds two fingers in the air. Big Frank nods. Messer motions with his head to Kevin Delaney. Kevin writes something down in the oversized accounting ledger he always carries around with him, even into the john. Precious overtime is being doled out in the unique Messer manner. Big Frank has just been granted a generous two hours.

"I already chipped in to the station collection, Mr. Messer," Louie whines. Messer makes a sudden U-turn in mid-stride, nearly knocking Louie over. "The wife is baking you one of those fruit cakes you said you liked so much last year and . . . the Chivas I ordered for you is on the way. Should be on your desk by tomorrow morning."

Messer stops pacing. Reaching into his pants pocket, he takes out the diamond horseshoe money clip that carriers in his last station gave him as a going-away present, no doubt out of sheer gratitude that he was leaving. Lovingly, Messer strokes the clip with his hand. His left eye flutters madly. The man has an authentic nervous tic. When they make the movie of his life, I hope that Erich von Stroheim is available to play him.

Behind Messer hangs his lousy immaculate white raincoat. In the side pocket of the coat is where the regulars put their money so that he will give them overtime. Some days there is so much cash in the pocket that the damn coat actually seems to glow, as though it is radioactive or something. Louie himself is well known as Messer's most dependable contributor.

Louie's forehead is now damp with sweat. He licks his lips constantly. His head jerks back and forth on his neck in an insistent, compulsive rhythm. For all the world, Louie looks like an oversized rat trapped in a maze from which there is no escape. One by one, carriers begin walking to the end of their rows to watch. Everyone likes to see Hungry Louie sweat for his money.

Oblivious to everything save where his next drink is coming from, Tommy Oh lumbers past Messer's desk. Blinking his large, myopic eyes, he hacks away with that dry whiskey cough of his. Messer holds a single finger in the air. Delighted, Tommy nods. Then he rushes right back to his route case where trays of mail are stacked so high that it will take him at least an hour just to clear enough space to even begin racking letters into the slots.

"Fucking Tommy Oh," Monte whispers, his lips barely moving as he speaks, as though we are both in the yard of some

266

maximum-security prison. "Don't know enough to grease Messer with a fiver in the old raincoat pocket. Waits for overtime every day like a kid at Christmas hopin' for a bicycle, and when Messer throws him one lousy hour, Tommy, the *shmuck*, is *grateful*. . . ."

"It's the grounds, ain't it, Mr. Messer?" Louie asks desperately, a slick ring of anxious concern having formed around his mouth and chin. "I smelled 'em myself when I came in this morning. To Mancuso I said, and you could ask him yourself if you don't believe me, 'I wonder what horse's ass went and put the grounds in Mr. Messer's wastebasket again.' That *is* it, right?"

Regally, Messer nods his head. Louie lets out his breath. "*Never* happen again, Mr. Messer," Louie swears. "I'll see to that. I catch the guy who's been doing it, I'll kill him myself. Even if I have to stay here till midnight to do it."

Monte laughs softly, the sound just barely making it to my ear. "Let him try," Monte whispers so that only I can hear him. "Soon as Louie goes home, this black kid who's workin' midnight to eight will put 'em right back in there again. I told him that's where they belong. . . ."

Messer holds up the thumb and first two fingers of his right hand, giving Hungry Louie a big three hours of overtime. Louie's entire face lights up. He grins as though he has just won the Irish Sweepstakes. The guy is in seventh heaven. Once again, no one in the station will go home this week with a bigger paycheck than him, even if he did have to wipe the floor with himself to make it happen.

Messer sits back down at his desk again. The ceremony is over for the day. Monte and I go back down our row. "Funny," I say. "Six Route didn't get any time."

"Noticed that, did you?" Monte asks, squinting as the smoke from the cigarette in his mouth, easily his thirtieth of the day, curls up into his eye. "Gee, I wonder why not. . . ."

"What is it with Messer, Monte? He's got it in for you special?"

"That's it. Go talk to him in his executive washroom sometime. He'll show you how to wash your hands without gettin' any water spots on your shirt. The man is a friggin' nut case if you ask me."

"You giving him something for Christmas? Kevin Delaney's collection for his present?"

"*Zingotz*," Monte says. "That's what I give him. And he

267

knows it, too. That's how come we can't get *near* my desk. It already disappeared under the mail. You start givin' Messer, it never stops. Believe me."

Messer appears at the end of our row. In itself, this is an event. Mr. Messer does not like to mingle with the carriers. With good reason. He feels far safer behind his desk, close enough to touch the white raincoat. "Serrano?" he calls out. "I been getting calls from someone on your route." He looks down at a little piece of paper in his hand. "A Mr. August Pappalardo? He says you haven't brought him some government check."

"That's it, super," Monte agrees. "Me and the kid here, we been kinda swamped lately. What with one thing and the other. You know how it is. Come Christmas, all them good Eye-talians on Six Route got their relatives on the other side sending them cards and letters, not to mention parcels wrapped in that funny paper from the old country, *zazeech* and goat cheese, salamis, bottles of homemade dago red, and who the hell knows what else?"

"Are you asking me for overtime?" Messer says, loud enough for everyone to hear. Monte can have the overtime if he asks for it. Only he has to ask for it so that everyone will know he has folded under the pressure.

"Huh?" Monte says. "I didn't hear you, supe. It was so cold out there today, I froze my semicirculars. Canals those are. In the ears. You know? That's why I can't walk so good neither. My balance is all shot to shit."

"Overtime, Serrano," Messer repeats, his X-ray eyes shooting out beams of light that can penetrate right through solid steel in no time flat. "Are you asking me to give you some?"

Grabbing hold of his balls with both of his hands, Monte starts hopping up and down like an oversized jack rabbit with a hernia. I bust right out laughing. Then I swallow it when I see the look on Messer's face. Monte hops all the way to the far wall. He starts coming back towards Messer, closing the distance between them in huge, loping strides. Messer steps back, not sure if Monte is going to hop over him, punch him out, or what. Behind him, carriers from other rows stand, watching the action.

Monte hops right up to Messer. Then, just like that, he drops the act and starts walking like a regular human being again. "Sorry, supe," he apologizes. "But I sweat so much going up and down all them stoops out on Six Route today that the crotch of my uniform pants shrunk up on me.

All down the row, carriers stare into their route cases, laughing. Monte has done it again. "Get them Sanforized, Serrano," Messer says, nothing moving in his face as he speaks. "You'll feel better when you do."

Then he moves away, no match at all for the only man in captivity crazy enough to take out Six Route day after day without begging for overtime. Monte is once again the winner, and still champion. About an hour after Monte leaves for the day, Russ comes dragging into the station. He looks much the worse for wear. I tell him the entire story of what Monte did to Messer. Russ is so tired that when I finish, it is all he can do to laugh once before he punches out and goes home. The Contessa has taken all that he has to give and then demanded more. Tomorrow I am going to *have* to ask him all about her.

With an inked pad by my elbow and a neat row of rubber stamps before me, I sit myself down and start doing the overs. All the mail that did not go out today and may in fact never go out because of the illegible manner in which it has been addressed must be sent somewhere else. First, I cross out the original address with a pencil. Then I stamp "Return to Sender" or "No Such Known Address" across the front of every envelope in big, blurred, inky purple letters. Doing the overs is a task for which I am uniquely suited, both by temperament and birth.

I am hard at work when Kevin Delaney cautiously sticks his head around the far corner of the alleyway. Carefully, he checks to make certain that I am alone. Then he starts coming towards me. Within the station, no one has a good word for Kevin. The list of charges against him is endless. Kevin walks funny. He lisps and stutters whenever he gets excited. He still lives with his mother in a four-room apartment on the avenue, taking his entire paycheck home to her instead of drinking most of it up with the carriers after work. Worst of all, he is Messer's number one boy.

Monte insists that Kevin is in fact a homosexual, or as he puts it, "a fucking queer." Myself, I am not so sure. To me, Kevin looks as though he still expects the nuns from the parochial school that he attended as a boy to descend upon him again at any moment, beating away all his impure thoughts with long wooden rulers. He is so nervous that he makes me feel calm. So maybe that is why I always try to be nice to him. The very first thing Kevin says to me is, "Monte gone?"

"Gone, Kevin," I tell him. "Left nearly an hour ago. So it's okay for you to talk to me."

Kevin twitches a little in place. He consults the oversized ledger that he is never without. At any moment, he may suddenly flit away, a tiny bird winging rapidly towards the next nearest branch. "Can I put you down for a couple bucks on Mr. Messer's gift?" he asks, flipping through the pages of his book. "Tomorrow is the very last day."

"I'm really glad you asked me that, Kevin," I say, stamping the envelope in front of me so hard that he actually jumps. *"No."*

"Everyone is chipping in," he notes, "except for Monte. And I wouldn't exactly call him the best example for anyone to follow."

"Let's not get el seven about it, huh, Kevin? The other temps aren't giving, right?"

"Of course not."

"Then why ask me?"

"The overs," he says, pointing to the stack of mail I have not yet done.

"What about them?"

"Ask your father," he suggests, backing away from me even as he speaks. "He'll tell you."

"He already left for the day, Kevin."

"Then ask him at home."

I can see that it gives Kevin great pleasure to be able to say this to me. As far as he is concerned, we are two of a kind. He lives with his sainted mother and I am boarding with my old man. Of course, in my case, it is strictly a temporary state of affairs. Still this makes Kevin think that I am his friend. Boldly, he steps towards me again. "I'm not, you know," he says.

"Not what, Kevin?"

"A f-faggot . . ."

"Who said you were?"

"They do. Someone even wrote it on the bathroom wall."

"You shouldn't pay attention to what other people say, Kevin. It'll drive you crazy in no time flat. Just look at me. I'm living my own life and loving every moment of it."

Kevin looks me up and down, wondering if I am telling him the truth or putting him on or what. Then he moves away. Kevin Delaney has problems that only a transfer to another station will solve. Here, they have already passed final judgment on him. Nothing I do is going to change that. Concentrating on the pile of envelopes before me, I go on working in the silent, empty tomb the station has become.

After I finish, I go and pull my card from its slot by the time clock. I cannot help but notice that of all those who work in Avenue Station, my card is the only one still left on the clock. Why this is, I have no idea. I will have to ask the old man about it at dinner. That way, I will have my answer ready if someone brings the matter up tomorrow morning.

It is just as Monte once told me. Whenever the carriers chip in for a bottle of Scotch here, someone always stands outside the circle of those who are drinking, carefully keeping count to see who pours the most whiskey down his throat. In Avenue Station, where I now work, this is just the way of things.

CHAPTER TWENTY-FIVE

THE OLD MAN and I are now fellow workers. At long last, two separate generations of the Bindel family are finally putting their big shoulders to the wheel in tandem so that the mail will be delivered before Christmas. Yet things between us have never been worse. At home, inside the dark cave of the apartment, we are navigating blind. Like a pair of maddened bats fighting to get into the sky at twilight, we slam constantly into one another. Squeaking loudly, we flutter our hairy little wings in protest. Then we settle back onto our rocky little roosts, baring our teeth in what we pretend to be a smile.

Simply, everything I do is wrong. If I happen to tune his precious radio to the far end of the dial at night so I can hear what The Dapper Rapper is up to during the midnight hour, Morty takes it as a personal affront. The next morning, he charges over to the couch where I lay with my eyes still closed. "What is it with you, Paulie?" he demands angrily. "You want to *be shvartz?*" More asleep than awake, I mumble, "I just like the music. Okay? Why make such a big deal out of it?" Naturally, this does not satisfy him. "First, the *shvartzes*," he grumbles, turning away from me in disgust so he can go get dressed for work. "Now, the Italianers. You got something *personal* against the *yeeden?*"

What can I tell him? I have made a fatal error by throwing in my lot with the men that he despises. At home, just as in the station, he is a clerk and I am a carrier. The gap between us grows wider each day. Tonight, as we sit down to yet another miserable Morty dinner of broiled liver and lumpy mashed potatoes, he starts right in on me before I can say a word.

"So tell me this then," he says, continuing the only conversation we ever seem to have any more. "The Negroes have it even worse than we do, right? Yet they feel better. How come?"

"How should I know?" I tell him. "I'm not their ambassador. I don't represent them. Black people don't talk to white people. No one knows what goes on in their lives."

"A-*ha*. I'm glad to hear you finally admit this," he says triumphantly, as though he has just won a major victory. "You *don't* know. Neither do I. But the difference is . . . I don't pretend. I take care of my own."

Even as the old man talks, he is wolfing down his food. It is the only way to eat such a meal. But then supper can never end soon enough for him. Once he is through, he will collect the dishes from the table and put them into the sink. Then he will come back to the living room. Sitting himself down in front of his lousy brand new television, he will watch for hours, waiting for something to come on that will make him laugh. Long before the eleven o'clock news begins, he will already be fast asleep in his chair, snoring loudly with his mouth wide open. Tomorrow morning, in darkness, his alarm clock rings and it all begins again.

"You want my advice?" he asks, although I cannot recall having requested it. "Take care of your own. When you need them, they're the only ones who will take care of you, *if* you're lucky."

The old man is not telling me anything that I do not already know. As I have patiently explained to Steffi Weiss more than once since our first date, I do not want to *be* James Brown, putting my hair up in a do-rag before the show as nervous assistants run into my dressing room, saying, "Ten minutes, Mr. Brown . . . Five minutes, Mr. Brown . . . *Showtime*, Mr. Brown."

The responsibilities that come along with being Soul Brother Number One would overwhelm me. I do not want to cool urban riots by appealing for calm over the radio. I do not wish to appear at high school assemblies, urging kids to be cool and stay in school so they can get that diploma and become a part of the great American work force lined up at the nearest unemployment office.

I am not even a fan in the usual sense of the word. I do not want to meet or greet James or even grab for his hand as he leans over the front of the stage at the end of the fifteenth thousand chorus of "Please, Please, Please." I just want to feel what he must feel on a really good night when the band is cooking, the lights flash in his face, and people sway before him in ecstasy. It is then that the magic takes over and all the ordinary bullshit of daily life is left behind. This is the real meaning of soul, the feeling that makes everything else worthwhile.

But how can I explain this to the old man? Either you understand it or not. There is no middle ground. It is for this reason that I am reluctantly giving up on Steffi. Steffi is one sweet girl all right. In many ways, the sweetest. Only she has problems that even I cannot solve. The buzzing tone that rings constantly in her ear is a busy signal. Someone else is always on the line. I cannot get through to her no matter how hard I try.

Steffi is saving herself for the husband I hope she finds. On our second date, she told me the real reason that she came back home to live. At her out-of-town college, she was going with a boy who was definitely Mr. Right. Pre-med *and* a member in good standing of the best fraternity on campus. Only late one night, he went for a drive through the local ghetto. He was changing a flat tire in the middle of the street when someone shot him through the head at close range. Because he was out looking for what Steffi would not give him, she blames herself for his death. Not that she has changed her policy on the matter of sex. A ring on the third finger of her left hand must come first. Death before dishonor, every time. I wish her luck. The two of us just happen to be crazy the wrong way around for one another.

"You know," I say, pushing the food around on my plate so that I will not have to eat any of it, "Kevin Delaney hit me up for Messer's present today in the station."

"You didn't open a mouth on him, did you? The way only you can?"

"Why? Is he somebody I should be scared of?"

"*Scared?* You shouldn't be *scared* of anybody. Only anything

273

you say to Kevin Delaney, Messer hears about it before the day is over. Kevin even calls him at home at night sometimes.''

"I *am* impressed," I say, making a face to let him know otherwise.

"Go on, laugh. For your information, Paulie, within six months Kevin will be in the GPO downtown, taking home twenty-two thousand a year as an assistant route planner. . . ."

"Yeah? Tell him to plan Tommy Oh's route six blocks shorter. The way it is now, he couldn't deliver it all on horseback.''

"This is you talking now, or Monte Serrano?"

"What difference does it make? Monte doesn't take shit from anybody. He doesn't pay off cockroaches like Martin Messer to get work, either."

"That he's your big hero now," the old man says, sarcastic as hell, "this I know already."

"How much did it cost you to get me the overs?" I ask. "Plenty, I bet."

"So what?" he answers, not even bothering to deny the charge. "The money goes into *your* pocket, right? Not some stranger's. That's all that really counts."

"I wish you had at least told me about it. *Before*, you know? I mean, I wish you had extended me the courtesy of consulting me about it."

"Why? You think you would have gotten those hours without me? You think it's a beauty contest in there? A democracy? Like you learned about in college and then the graduate school where you never finished up? Besides, I don't *have* to consult with you, buddy boy. I'm your father. Or maybe you forgot that as well out there in the street with those new friends of yours."

"How could I? When you're yelling it right into my face over supper?"

"Look," the old man says, balling up his paper napkin and throwing it on to his empty plate in disgust, "you'd rather let Monte Serrano help you than your very own flesh and blood? Fine. Fine with me. Play by his rules. See how far it gets you."

Before I can say anything more, he is up and out of his chair. Actually, the old man does not get *really* angry all that much. When he does, I know enough to stay out of his way. Stomping into the kitchen, he takes a half-empty carton of ice cream from the refrigerator. Then he heads into his bedroom to eat it in solitary confinement. He slams the door shut so hard behind him that the whole apartment shakes. Without having to ask, I know that I will not be seeing him again until tomorrow, if then.

Sure enough, it is the alarm clock that wakes me the next morning and not the old man. Although he is now officially not speaking to me, he has gone to the trouble of bringing the little clock from the side of his bed into the living room so that I will not oversleep. None of it makes any sense. Not when you think about it. But then I guess no one can understand the joys of fatherhood until they have a kid of their own. Myself, I am not exactly rushing towards the experience.

The day itself just keeps on getting worse. All morning long, Monte rushes the two of us through the route as though he has to see someone out at the far end of Long Island by noon. After we eat lunch together with the rest of the regulars in a luncheonette where the waitress gets only my order wrong, Monte takes me outside and tells me that he is lending me to Russ for the afternoon as a personal favor.

"What gives, Monte?" I demand, backing him right up against the brick wall of the luncheonette as we stand there, freezing our faces off in the cold. "I'm your Christmas present to Russ, or what?"

"Hey," he says. "I'm doing this for *your* benefit, *shmuck*. Russ delivers the *shul*. His whole route is Jewish. You'll peddle those raffle tickets of yours like they were French postcards. Besides, I *do* owe Russ. Good enough?"

I nod, wanting to believe that what Monte is telling me happens to be the truth. After Russ and I walk down the avenue to where the second half of his route begins, he flashes me this big grin, slaps me on the shoulder, and says, "Nice and easy now, Paulie. One house at a time. Anything you can't deliver, just bring back to the station with you and I'll take it out myself tomorrow. . . ."

"Where are you going to be while all this goes on, Russ?"

"Didn't Monte tell you? I got an appointment to see somebody."

"Who?" I ask, deciding to take a chance. "The Contessa?"

"So he *did* tell you, right? Me and Monte'll be waiting for you by the fruit store so we can all go back in together. That way, Messer won't be any the wiser. Right?"

I nod my head. Right, right, right. As far as these guys are concerned, I am another Kevin Delaney. I have become their number one tool. One thing I know for sure. No matter how many storm doors I slam loudly, no fine looking older woman is going to ask me inside. Things like that happen only to other people, like the lunatics who write those long and graphic letters to *Penthouse* magazine that Monte likes to read out loud over breakfast in the Greeks' until everyone stops eating so they can groan out loud while reaching for themselves under the table with both hands.

The very first house I deliver for Russ happens to belong to the rabbi. Actually, he does not own it. He just lives there, rent free. I know this because the old man complains about the situation at least two or three times a week. The rabbi *must* be popular with someone. Today, there is a whole bundle of mail in the sack just for him, one so thick that I cannot shove it through the door. Instead, I have to ring the bell and then stand there in the cold so I can hand it personally to whoever comes to the door.

The rabbi's wife appears. For some reason, I did not expect to see her here. She wears a housecoat on which the top three buttons are open. Her hair is knotted in a long braid that hangs over her shoulder. *Penthouse* magazine, here we come.

"Mail," I say, holding the bundle up in front of me.

"How nice of you not to just leave it on the step," she says, taking it from my hand. The storm door starts to close in my face.

"Listen," I say, "have you bought a ticket for the raffle yet?"

"You know," she laughs, "I haven't. Do you think I should?"

"Ever been to Jerusalem?"

"You know, I never have. . . ."

"Then this is your big chance."

"I'll have to get some money from my handbag. Would you like to come inside for a moment? It's warmer."

I push the storm door open and follow her into the living room. The place smells like a museum. Bookcases with hinged glass doors that no one has opened in years stand between overstuffed chairs that give off the sickeningly sweet odor of sweat stained upholstery. For all I know, the Angel of Death himself is crouching in the far corner waiting to claim his very next victim. It could be me.

Coming back into the room with an expensive looking black leather pocketbook in her hands, the rabbi's wife looks at me and says, "I'm afraid I don't have enough cash. Can you take a check?" I nod. "Will you promise not to mention who you got it from?"

"They'll know at the shul, won't they?"

"Oh, I'll call Esther and tell her not to say anything to Simeon about it. She *is* your mother, isn't she?"

"That's right."

"I thought I recognized you. That's why I asked you in. You were in shul with your grandfather on Yom Kippur, weren't you? Standing in the corner with him? Or am I mistaken?"

"No mistake," I say, watching as she signs the check. She has really nice fingers. The arm they are attached to is also pretty good.

"I knew it was you," she says, handing me the check. "You have a very distinctive look, if you know what I mean."

"Listen, Mrs. Hakveldt," I say. "Most people I sell to, I ask them for the ticket back." The steam heat in the house is making me sweat. Suddenly, all the wool on my body begins itching like mad.

"Really? Why, dear?"

"I put my grandfather's name on it. Maybe he'll win the trip."

"Why, what a *wonderful* thing to do," she cries. "No one deserves it more. *Here.*" I am now holding her ticket *and* her check. It is definitely time to leave. "I wonder," she says, apparently feeling that now she has the right to ask me a few questions, "how does your grandfather feel about . . . the rabbi?"

"Huh?"

"Well, so many people in the congregation misunderstand Simeon completely. Not that he doesn't have his faults. I mean, no one knows that better than I do. A certain single-mindedness of purpose that often tends to put people off. But at heart he really is a *very* good man."

Sure he is. As far as I am concerned, the rabbi, Martin Messer, Nat Weiss, and E.C. all graduated from the very same school. Not that this is the time or place to get into it. "I have never heard my grandfather say a bad word about him, Mrs. Hakveldt," I tell her, which actually happens to be the truth.

"Oh, but he wouldn't," she sighs. "He's like that. A saint, really."

"Yeah. I feel that way myself."

"You're a lot like him in a way, aren't you?"

"Uh, not really," I say, edging nervously towards the door. "Actually, I take after my mother, Esther. I'll probably be seeing her when I deliver the shul in a few minutes. So don't bother calling. I'll tell her myself about the check."

"Then don't let me keep you a second longer," she says. "With both my children in school, I'd probably waste the rest of your day, if you let me."

Where? Down here, or upstairs? This is the all-important question. I mean, I know that I am in way over my head here. Although I am pretty certain that God would not waste an entire thunderbolt on me for just having a conversation with the rabbi's wife, why take chances? Slowly I keep backing up until I am out the door, down the stoop, and in the street once more, pushing my little three wheel trike as fast as it will go in the general direction of Ahavath Mizrach—and safety.

Going around in back of the shul to the door marked "Tradesmen's Entrance," I take out the huge bundle of third-class mail that the temple probably receives day in and day out. Most of it seems to be circulars, religious newspapers, and advertising flyers. Pushing open the door with my shoulder, I go inside. The door slams shut loudly behind me. A moment later, Solomon comes out of the downstairs kitchen, looking as though I have only just interrupted the very best part of his regular afternoon nap.

"What could I do?" I say. "I had my hands full, Solomon," I ask, before he has a chance to get away from me. "Bought a ticket for the raffle yet?"

"Naw, I ain't," he admits, yawning as though it does not matter all that much to him one way or the other now that he is up. "I been waitin' for someone to put the bite on me, though. So it might as well be you. Come on down here while I unlock my cash." Then he cackles loudly to let me know that he needs no safe to guard his money.

Today, the kitchen is just a room again. All the wondrous magic that swirled through it on Yom Kippur is gone. Instead, Solomon has already begun unstacking large round wooden tables so they can be set up in the annex for Las Vegas Night. As he reaches into his side pocket for his money, I cannot help but wonder how he feels about all this. Solomon has nothing, at least that I can see. Yet he is the one who is entrusted to stand guard over the temple each night. He has been at Ahavath Mizrach for so very long that the place practically belongs to him by now.

"Solomon," I say, "you were here when I was bar mitzvahed. Remember?"

"Was I? When was that?"

"Ten years ago?"

"Must be then. Been here fifteen, no sixteen years come June."

"Solomon, are you religious?"

He laughs. "You mean, 'Am I a Hebrew man just 'cause I wears a yarmulka on Shabbos?' Un-*uh*," he says. "I jes believe a little in everythin' and a whole lot in lettin' people be. You know what I mean?"

Sure I do. Only I cannot believe that Solomon would have said the same thing to Norris. I mean, it is just too jive. We all workin' hard down here, boss. Doin' what we sposed to do and feelin' fine. I want to grab Solomon by the shirt and scream, "*Talk* to me, man. Tell me something I *don't* already know." Not that it would do me any good. Solomon and my grandfather are two of a kind. Which is probably why they get along so well. All that they have learned, they keep strictly to themselves. No doubt, this is why they have both lived so long.

Handing me a series of ancient, crumpled dollar bills that look as though they have not seen the light of day in years, Solomon says, "You got your money now. So how come your hand is still out?"

"Right," I say, giving him the ticket. "This is yours. Only, Solomon . . . you ever *been* to Jerusalem?"

"Oh yeah," he says. "I go maybe five, six times a year. Naw, I ain't. Why? Ain't it no holy place, like they say?"

"See, what I usually do with these tickets is put my grandfather's name on them. That way, maybe he'll win the trip."

Solomon looks at me as though I am the dumbest white boy he has ever had the misfortune to come across in his entire life. Then he shakes his head. "You think it works like that?" he says softly. "I kin tell you it don't." Before I can argue, he says, "Go on now. Take that mail upstairs to your mother. Esther already been down here three times today to ask about it."

"How about the ticket?"

"How about it?" he says. "I bought and paid for it, right? Guess I ought to be able to write anyone's name I please on it, Mendel included."

Not knowing if Solomon will actually do this or whether he just wants me out of his frizzy gray hair so that he can go back to sleep, I nod and head up the stairs. Fortunately my mother is not at her desk. Putting the mail where I know she will find it as soon as she comes back, I lay all the raffle tickets that I have sold right on top. My grandfather's name is written on nearly every one.

Then I wander down the hall to the Talmud Torah classroom where my grandfather maintains his eerie all-night vigil. Sure enough, he is standing there now with his back towards me, staring out the window into the street. His left hand is shoved all the way down into the side pocket of his spotted brown suit pants. With his right hand, he is carefully feeling along the grooves of the blackboard by his side. Slowly, he fingers each of the tiny crumbs of chalk that lie there, rejecting one after the other as though he is searching for the single diamond hidden among them.

"Pop?" I say softly. He turns my way. His eyes seem very clear in the failing gray light of late afternoon.

"*Vas tiest du* here?" he asks in surprise. Coming towards me, he rubs and rubs at the single crumb of chalk between his fingers until it shatters noiselessly into a pale layer of dust that covers the side of his thumb, turning the skin a milky white.

"I'm working," I say, showing him the letters in my hand that I still have to deliver for Russ to houses farther down the block.

"Ah," he says. "*Andt* Morty?"

"In the station. Also working."

"*Du hust gezayn* Esther?"

"She must be out somewhere getting coffee or something. You'll tell her I was here, right?"

He nods. Whenever we see one another, this is how we begin our conversations. Together, we check to make certain that we know where all the members of our immediate family are at the moment. That way, we can find them quickly should the need suddenly arise. Having run down the entire list, we stand looking at each other in silence.

When I was younger, these silences of his always defeated me. No matter how much I would pester him to tell me what it had been like in the camps, my grandfather would always just shake his head and refuse to answer. I know that he cannot have forgotten. But he will not talk. Instead, I have to hate by proxy, never knowing exactly who I should blame it all on. That he has not forgiven them, I know for certain. "Forgive?" he said to me once. "Never. Why should I? Those bastards. What I ever did to them? To forget is easier. . . ."

"*Der vaist,*" he says to me now, "*Ich hat gevillt der eppes talen. . . .*"

"You wanted to tell me something? What?"

He licks his thin, dry lips, concentrating on the problem. Even as I stand before him with the mail in my hand, I can see it slipping from his mind. *"Ach,"* he says, snapping his fingers in frustration. *"Ken nisht mir demannen. . . ."*

So that he will not feel too badly about not being able to remember, I say, "I just sold my last raffle ticket. For Las Vegas Night."

"Nat Weiss's big *geshichta,* eh?"

"That's it. They're going to raise a lot of money for the shul."

"Macht kein difference," he says.

To him it certainly makes no difference. Las Vegas Night will not change his life one single bit. Not unless he actually wins the trip. That will be something he will not be able to shrug away with a sudden, upward movement of his shoulders and that ensuing sideways glance that defies all interpretation.

"All the tickets I sold," I blurt out, wanting him to know, "they have your name on them."

"Fa voos?" he asks.

"So you can go. To see the Wall. . . ."

I can tell from his face that what I am saying is not getting through. *"L'shanoah haba'oah bi Yerushalayim,"* I say, repeating the final words of the Yom Kippur service. "The Temple. In Jerusalem. Where the *kohanim* used to *duchen. . . ."*

"Uf Yom Kippur, ich hab geduchened," he says. "You forgot already? You washed *meinen handten."*

"Not here," I say patiently, trying to explain it all to him so he will clap me heartily on the back and tell me what a really wonderful grandson I am, as nearly everyone else has already done. "In Israel. *Eretz Yisroel. . . ."*

Carefully, he considers this information, rubbing his face with his hand. A tiny chalk white blossom appears by his nose. I reach out with my hand to brush it away. Like an infant, he offers no resistance. Then he blinks and says, *"Ich ken nisht gaehen,* Paulie. *Ich bin shamus of der shul. Daf* saying *Kaddish fir der anderers. . . ."*

"They can find someone else to do it while you're gone. The shul will still be here when you get back. . . ."

"Zah nisht kein nahr," he says forcefully, his tiny face darkening like the gloomy sky outside the window. Don't be an idiot. *"Ken nisht gaehen,"* he repeats. Then he starts moving slowly back to the window, putting a definite end to the conversation.

Whether he will even remember it an hour from now, I do not know.

Once again, I have been judged and found wanting. I am now and forever more the boy who cannot do the Shing-a-ling, the Boog-a-loo, or the Funky Broadway. It is just as Morty said. No one really knows my grandfather. He is as much a mystery to me as he is to his very own son. I should have listened to the old man. The very best thing I can do for my grandfather is to give him a carton of cigarettes for his birthday and then go to work straightening out my own life.

Jerusalem is half a world away, too far from the life he has made for himself here at Ahavath Mizrach ever to be real to him. Sending him there is something I have dreamed up all on my own, without even having had the courtesy to consult him about it beforehand. Of course, if he does win the trip, everyone will urge him to go. The men of the temple, Murray Friedberg and Sidney Meyers foremost among them, will make him their very own special emissary. They will entrust him with tiny scraps of paper on which their names are written to be inserted into a crack in the Wall so they will all be blessed with luck for the coming year. Perhaps for the sake of the others, he will go.

First, he has to win. The raffle books with his name on nearly every stub are already on their way into the hopper. Come Las Vegas Night, we will all of us be gambling on several levels, taking chances that perhaps we should have left for others. The odds are definitely against us. The outcome itself is in doubt. From now on, it is all strictly up to God, or whoever it is that looks after the fortunes of old men in lotteries where fate itself hangs in the balance.

I wish my grandfather all the luck in the world. No one deserves it more. Whether this is the best that I can do for him, I do not know. It is a question that I will never be able to answer. Not until my grandfather finally tells me what he has so far stubbornly refused to ever talk about, as though it is better for me not to know.

CHAPTER TWENTY-SIX

FOR THE PAST twenty minutes, I have been standing patiently in front of the fruit store on the corner waiting for Russ and Monte to show. In order to keep my toes from going dead inside my shoes, I have been stamping my feet constantly against the pavement. My breath swirls up into lovely ice-white curls of vapor before my face. I decide that I can wait no longer. I will just go back into the station by myself and take a chance that neither Messer nor Kevin Delaney is waiting by the door to pull the time cards of all those poor and unfortunate carriers who are still out on their routes.

As soon as I get inside, I know that something is wrong. All the regulars are at the very back of the station by the old red Coca-Cola machine. Monte stands toe to toe with Messer himself. Their faces are no more than six inches apart, Monte making up for Messer's height advantage by propelling himself forward on the balls of his feet.

"*Flowers?*" Monte screams. "You're gonna send him flowers? On *your* grave, you bastard."

"This is none of your concern, Serrano," Messer mutters, his voice very low, and colder than death. "Butt out. Now. While you still can. And *no* jokes. I warn you."

"*Jokes?*" Monte says. The big vein in his forehead pulses rapidly, as though he is sending Messer a message in Morse code. Dit-dot-dit-dot. Messer's left eyelid flutters right back at Monte in response. Dot-dit-dot-dit. "*You* warn *me?*" Monte bellows. His mouth moves with nothing coming out but saliva. Then he says, "Maybe I should file a grievance on this, huh? So your rabbi in the GPO downtown can wipe his ass with it."

"Maybe you should," Messer answers, his eyelid doubling up to keep time. "But if I were you, I'd clean up my language first."

"Grievance this, you cockeyed motherfucker," Monte shouts.

Grabbing his right forearm with his left hand, he pumps it up and down in that unmistakable motion that can mean only one thing. All the while, he is howling "*Ah-bah-fungoo!*" right at the very top of his voice. Messer looks as though he is going to fall backwards from the sheer force of the sound alone.

It is now time for the fight to start. Everyone else knows this as well. The carriers drop back a couple of steps to give Monte and Messer enough room to really get into it. At the front of the station, all the clerks, the old man and Mo Tannenbaum among them, quickly pull down the wooden shutters that cover the windows of their cages. That way, none of the civilians waiting in line outside will be able to watch what is about to happen. My money is on Monte, all the way.

Messer, though, is too slimy smart to start throwing punches. Inside the adding machine he has for a brain, Messer knows that there is no percentage at all in taking on a maddened Italian whose face is now two shades redder than the Coke machine. Instead, Messer turns towards Kevin Delaney. "Kevin?" he says. "Pull Serrano's card from the clock. The man is drunk. I want him off!"

That tears it. With both hands extended before him, his fingers curled into claws, Monte leaps for Messer's throat. He screams like a banshee. Before Monte can actually make contact, Russ vaults in front of him. Looping both of his arms around Monte's chest in a rough half nelson, Russ wrestles him up against the wall. Monte bucks and snorts and curses, completely out of control and going wild. Messer is really scared. I can see it in his face. His lower lip trembles as though he is about to break out crying.

"*Kevin?*" he calls out. His voice vibrates in the upper register for a moment. Then it breaks completely, becoming a high-pitched falsetto that I know Monte will be imitating tomorrow morning. "Call the precinct. I don't have to put up with this nonsense. Not in my station."

Russ has been talking softly to Monte in both English and Italian, crooning away in that lulling, repetitive rhythm that fathers use to put their kids back to sleep in the middle of the night. Suddenly, he jerks his head around. "No cops on this, Martin," he says in a quiet, commanding voice. "*No* cops."

For some reason, this gets through to Messer. "All right," he says, countermanding his last order to Kevin by waving the little creep away from the phone. "Just get him out of here then,

Balbano. All the rest of you men, back to work. Clerks, open those windows. This is still a United States Post Office here, not the G ward at Kings County." Then he moves away, headed back to his desk where for all I know he keeps a pearl-handled revolver stashed in the top drawer for protection in just such emergencies.

Still steaming, Monte lets himself be half pulled, half pushed towards the back door by Russ. Russ keeps right on talking to him, saying, "Come on now, Monte. Monte, come on. Come on." Although my card is still on the clock and I am technically supposed to remain inside the station until told to do otherwise by someone in authority, I do not have to think twice about where I really belong. Heading for the back door, I go out once more into the cold. Neither Russ nor Monte is anywhere to be seen.

Figuring that they can have gone to only one place, I walk down the block to the Antler Inn. The Antler Inn is a gloomy Irish bar where the beer is mostly water and the regulars sign their Social Security checks over directly to the bartender so that they will not have to get off their stools to keep on drinking. Sure enough, Russ sits in the back booth by himself. Sliding in across from him, I say, "Jesus, Russ. What the hell happened? I thought you and Monte were going to meet me by the fruit store."

"We were. *Shit*. I wish we had."

"So?"

"You mean you didn't see it?"

"I saw the main event, yeah. But not what led up to it."

"Tommy Oh," he says, as if that explains it all.

"What about him?"

"Keeled over right by the Coke machine. Blue in the face and hardly breathing. Big Frank came running out of the station to get a doctor. Me and Monte saw him so we ran right in. They took Tommy away in an ambulance, the poor bastard. . . ."

"Dead?" I say, unable to believe what I am hearing. "He's dead?"

"Nah. Not dead. Close to it, though."

"Where is he now?"

"Monte? In the crapper. Washing up."

"Tommy."

"Emergency Ward, Coney Island Hospital. It's his ticker," Russ says ominously, tapping the pocket of his uniform shirt just once, above the heart. "Christ. I *never* seen Monte blow up like that.'' Russ grins, letting out his breath all at once. For a mailman, he has tremendous teeth. "For a second there," he says, "I thought he was going to wipe the floor with Messer. Can you believe that ghinny? At his age? Bastard is strong as a horse. And all because Messer pulled Tommy's time card. Said he wasn't about to pay no overtime to a guy in the hospital . . .''

Holding up both of his hands to show me that they are still shaking from the effort of having held Monte back, Russ says, "What we need is a drink. Hey," he calls out to the old, balding bartender, "three Scotches. No ice and no water. Make 'em doubles. And not that cheap shit you usually pour. *Dewars*. Open a fresh bottle. Where I can *see* you do it.''

The bartender nods. By the time Monte comes back to the table, the drinks are in front of us. Nodding hello to me, Monte picks one up. *"Salut,"* he says heartily, knocking it back in a single gulp. "One more, the same," he orders, waving to the bartender with one hand while using the other to wipe his mouth.

"Think you should, Monte?" Russ asks.

"Why not? I ain't workin' no more today, am I?''

"Right," Russ agrees. "And while you're at it, maybe you ought to call in sick tomorrow as well. You can relax right through Christmas and then the weekend. Come Monday, you coast back in all nice and smooth. No heat, no friction. It'll all be ancient history by then.''

"Ancient history, my ass," Monte says. "Starting tomorrow morning, *early*, I'm goin' on the warpath.''

"Monte," Russ warns, "the best thing you can do now is just cool down some. What with all the connections Messer has downtown and all . . .''

"Cool down some, huh?" Monte snorts. "Like Tommy Oh? Layin' in Coney Island Hospital with all them tubes goin' up his nose? *No way*, Russ. No *fuckin'* way. From now on, I'm comin' at them. Like the fucking Marines taking the beach at Tarawa. Gang Busters, all the way.''

Lifting the glass before me in tribute, I look through its thick double bottom at Monte's face. The swirling liquid makes all his features run together. From the middle of his forehead, a single large and bloodshot eye glares back at me. Actual tongues of bright orange flame spew from his mouth. The string of cheap tinsel behind his head dissolves into a streaky red green halo. Across the booth from me sits Monte Serrano, the avenging Christmas Angel.

"So what can you do, Monte?" I ask, putting the glass back down. "*Shoot* Messer?"

"Shooting's too good for him, kid. I'm gonna take his white raincoat and shit in all the pockets. I'm gonna ram that diamond money clip of his so far up his rectum, he'll make change every time he sits on the bowl. Like I said. From now on, Monte Ger-o-ni-mo Crazy Horse Sitting Bull Serrano is on the warpath. Officially."

Grabbing the brand new drink that the bartender has just set down before him, Monte drains it in a single swallow. Then he burps loudly. "For Tommy Oh," he proclaims. "And God. And Country."

Slowly, he looks from me to Russ and then back again so there will be no doubt as to whom he is now addressing. "You two ladies don't feel like helping, *fine*. But you better stand *way* back. Otherwise, you might get your dresses wet, just from the spray."

Slamming his glass down on the table, Monte stalks angrily from the bar. "He leave anything for you to say?" I ask Russ after Monte has left.

"I don't think so," Russ says wearily. "Let me pay for these, Paulie. Then we better head back inside before we're missed. Maybe if I talk to Messer some, I can head off whatever Monte already has planned inside his head."

"Russ," I say sincerely, "I wish you all the luck in the world. Not that it's going to help you any."

"You never know," Russ says, reaching into his pocket for some money as we both head towards the bar. "Sometimes Messer can be reasonable. He likes to trade. So long as you give him something he really wants, you can usually get something back in return."

The rest of the day passes without incident. I alone stay behind after all the other temps have gone home to do the lousy overs for the very last time. As I work, Kevin Delaney makes a point of staying away from me. No doubt, the old man has told him to do this so that I will not be able to ask Kevin just how much he gets for letting me work later than anyone else. When I get back to the apartment, the old man is not there. Instead, he has left a note on the table telling me to get my own dinner tonight because he has gone bowling with Mo Tannenbaum. The old man likes to bowl about as much as I do, which is not at all. So I know that he has done this in order to avoid talking to me. I am still being punished. For exactly what, I am no longer certain.

By the time Morty comes back home, I am asleep. When I wake up the next morning, he is already gone. Thank God, there is but one more shopping day left until Christmas. In nearly every way the season is wearing thin. Getting dressed in a hurry, I walk down the avenue without bothering to stop for breakfast. As always, the sky over my head is dark and gray, filled with the promise of snow that must come soon.

Inside the station, everyone is sleepwalking with cups of coffee in their hands. If Big Chief Serrano, leader of all the Indian nations, is in fact on the warpath, swinging the blooded tomahawk high above his head so that it gleams in the sunlight for a moment before falling onto the scalp of his next victim, he certainly does not look the part.

On a stool in front of his route case, Monte sits hunched over. He rolls a mug of hot coffee between his palms, trying to warm himself against the cold. A half empty pint of Scotch stands by his elbow. Monte's eyes resemble a pair of bloodshot egg yolks. Without having to ask, I know that the drinks I saw him down yesterday afternoon in the Antler Inn were only the beginning. Monte probably spent the rest of the night improving his mood in a similar manner.

I mean, the man has to be either very hung over or completely drunk. Why else would he be talking a blue streak to Kevin Delaney, his next-to-least favorite person in the entire world? Every now and then, Monte actually reaches out to tap Kevin's arm in a comforting manner as he talks, a kindly parish priest instructing a brand new altar boy on how to act during Mass.

"I'm not shitting you, Kevin," Monte says casually, crossing one knee over the other as he crushes his cigarette dead in the metal ashtray by his elbow. "I'm driving home last night after lifting a few when this cop pulls me over on the avenue. 'Drunk driving,' he says." Kevin laughs with his mouth closed. It is a fairly repulsive gesture all right, suggesting that as far as Kevin is concerned, Monte is almost always subject to conviction for such offenses. Monte, however, does not seem to notice.

" 'Drunk drivin',' I say to the cop. 'No way. Smell my breath.' " Reaching for the pint by his elbow, Monte dumps a good inch and a half of Scotch into his cup. He sips at the mixture. Then he sighs in approval. "To make a long story short," he goes on. "The cop don't wanna smell my breath. So I drop a few names, guys I know from the precinct. Nothin' doing. He's already starting to write me up. Then I get him. Know on what?''

Kevin thinks about it for a second. Then he bites. ''What?'' he asks.

''The Constitution, Kev. The fucking American Constitution. *Habeas corpus* and all that shit. 'You say I'm drunk?' I tell him. 'I say I ain't. Now, to save us both the trouble of spendin' a day in court, give me the test.' ''

Kevin blinks his eyes rapidly three or four times in a row. He is definitely interested. So are the rest of the carriers in the alleyway. Nearly all of them are listening as they rack in the mail for the very last time before Christmas.

''What test is that, Monte?'' Kevin asks, having apparently decided that the spirit of the season has gotten to everyone, Monte included. It is time to forgive and forget. Peace on earth, good will to all mankind. Jingle bell rock and jingle bell roll. Snowflakes falling on an open fire and Jack Frost nipping at your nose. Any second now, Santa Claus himself will be coming to town.

''You don't know the *test?*'' Monte says in horror. ''Here. Let me show you. Might come in handy someday if you ever find youself in the same situation.''

Getting quickly to his feet, Monte grabs a stack of third-class mail. Carefully, he lays it out in a line down the middle of the alleyway. ''See that line?'' Monte asks Kevin. ''That's what the cop asks me. 'Hell, yes, I see it,' I tell him. 'Well, *walk* it,' he says.''

Kevin stares at the line. Then he looks at Monte. ''That doesn't seem very hard to do, Monte,'' he says.

''*Hard?*'' Monte says. ''An infant could do it. *Blindfolded.* Only the cop don't just let me walk it. No way. He does this. C'mere, Kevin. Let me show you.''

Moving Kevin over to where the line of mail begins, Monte takes Kevin's right hand and puts it behind his ear. Delighted to finally be accepted as one of the boys, Kevin just lets him do it. ''My other hand,'' Monte says, ''the meathook I use for grabbin' sacks, he makes me stick into the side of my belt. To fuck up my balance, see? Like this . . .'' Monte places Kevin's left hand at his side, the fingers fanning out so that they point towards the floor. ''Then he says, 'Go on, walk it.' So go ahead, Kev. Walk that line. See how easy it is, dead sober . . .''

Taking care not to step on any of the mail, Kevin starts to walk. Monte steps back. He flashes someone at the far end of the alleyway the high sign and the overhead lamps go out. The next thing I know Monte is standing on top of his stool with a big flashlight in his hand. Training the light on Kevin as he tiptoes down the alley with one hand on his hip and the other behind his ear, Monte starts singing, *"Here she comes . . . Miss America."* He really wails, hamming it up like Bert Parks does every year from Atlantic City when they crown the new Bess Myerson.

At least twenty carriers, no doubt tipped off in advance by Monte as to what was going to happen, have gathered at the far end of the alleyway. "Is he a *piece,* or what?" Big Frank Mancuso shouts.

"What an ass!" someone howls.

"What tits!" someone hollers.

"A pretty girl is . . . like a melody," someone sings.

"Lovely to look at . . . delightful to hold," someone else croons, totally off key.

Guys are bent over double, their faces turning purple as they hold their stomachs and laugh. Big Frank grabs madly at his crotch. He was on his way to the bathroom when this all started. But there is no way he can tear himself away. Not now. This is *rich*. This is too freaking much. When the lights come back on, I take a good, long look at Kevin Delaney's face.

For all intents and purposes, Kevin Delaney is now dead in Avenue Station. He can take a rusty razor blade, go right into Messer's private washroom, and slit his throat from ear to ear, and it will be no more than a bloody little footnote to the story of what happened when mad Monte went on the warpath before breakfast, wiping out Big Chief Messer's number one brave just to start his day off right.

Messer will *have* to get Kevin Delaney that soft and cushy job in the GPO downtown now because no one who works here will ever be able to look Kevin in the face again without busting right out into hysterics. Myself, I feel sick to my stomach, as though I am the one the joke was played on, and not Kevin.

After Kevin has slowly walked away with his mouth open and his hands hanging limply at his sides, Monte stands in front of his route case accepting congratulations from nearly everyone. He has just pulled off the event of the season. "You feel good now, huh, Monte?" I ask him, unable to forget the look on Kevin's face when the lights came back on.

"I feel better," he says, forgetting about his coffee to swig down a belt of straight Scotch directly from the pint. "That's for shit sure. Why? Didn't you think it was a picture? Kevin swivel hippin' down the aisle like Miss Fruit America?"

"Yeah, it was really something, Monte. You ought to feel proud of yourself."

"Serves the little prick right, if you ask me," he says. "Do me a favor, will you, kid? Pick up all that mail before Messer sees it. I don't want him getting *too* hot and bothered. At least not yet. His time is still coming."

Although I know I should just tell Monte what he can do with the mail, I bend over and gather it all together. When I straighten up again, I see Kevin standing in the middle of the station talking to Martin Messer. For all the world, Kevin looks about twelve years old. He is telling his father how the *girls* beat him up after school. It is enough to make me puke. Messer himself does not say a word. He just keeps on nodding, his face growing harder every time he moves his head.

Knowing that I am going to need all the help I can get just to make it through the day, I slip over to the alleyway where Russ stands racking in his mail. Before I can open my mouth, Russ holds up his hand and says, "Don't talk to me about it, Paulie. I tried. I swear. The man is out of control. Completely."

"Russ," I plead, "I got to go out on the *route* with him."

"You got my sympathy, kid. But I'll tell you one thing. When he gets like this, you can't worry about him. You got to look out for Number One. That's what I'm doing and I'm his friend. Understand?"

I nod. There is definitely something hard and cold inside of Monte that no one can understand or control. The old man did his best to warn me about it but naturally I was too busy to listen. Still, what with Tommy Oh having gone down by the Coke machine yesterday afternoon and tomorrow being Christmas, I figure that Monte does have more than a few reasons to be off his rocker today.

"You hear anything about Tommy?" I ask. "How he's doing?"

"Hey," Russ says. "He's sitting up and taking solid food already. A moderate heart attack, they call it. Tommy plays his cards right, he can retire *now* on full pension. This could be the best thing that ever happened to him."

"Monte knows this?"

"He's the one that told me. He visited Tommy at five A.M. this

291

morning. Waltzed in the back door of the hospital with a bottle of Tommy's favorite Scotch in his hand like he was the doctor in charge or something. So it ain't like that is what is on his mind or nothing. Monte's got a hard-on for the entire world. Always did and always will. You're smart, you'll concentrate on getting yourself back here tonight in one piece. Understand?''

Russ means well. I can see that all right. Only he does not have to actually go out into the street with Monte. I alone get to do that. By the time the mail for Six Route is all bundled and tied out, Monte's pint is empty. He makes a big show of dropping it loudly into Messer's wastebasket as we head for the front door. Neither Kevin nor Messer is anywhere to be seen.

Not that Monte cares. For him, what happened this morning is already old news. He is too busy thinking about what he is going to do next. I take a deep breath as we hit the street. One thing I know for sure. It is going to be one very long and difficult day.

CHAPTER TWENTY-SEVEN

ALTHOUGH I KNOW in my heart that soon disaster will strike, out on the route everything goes pretty quietly for the first few hours. It is colder than hell, and damp. Even I can smell snow in the air. From his old leather mail sack, Monte produces yet another pint of Scotch. He nips at it constantly, toasting his own good fortune whenever we finish a block. Aside from wobbling a bit every now and then as we cross to the opposite curb, he seems to be holding up okay. Then we get to Old Man Pappalardo's house.

Right away, Monte starts singing that old song by Ruby and the Romantics. Only he changes around the lyrics to "*Your* day has come, Augustino. When you give everything. Your day has come. It's-a your check I bring. . . ." Reaching into the side pocket of his uniform jacket, he takes out the old man's precious government check. "Time to *co*-llect," he announces. "Postage due. *With* interest."

Grabbing hold of a wrought iron railing that is rusted orange from years of neglect, Monte starts hauling himself slowly up Pappalardo's steep red painted stoop. When finally he reaches the heavy aluminum storm door, he rattles it so loudly that even a deaf person could hear the noise.

Old Man Pappalardo himself is nowhere to be seen. As always, the shades are down on all the windows. The house is completely silent. It occurs to me that maybe the old man saw us coming down the block and had enough sense to clear out. "Monte," I say, "maybe he isn't home."

"The hell he ain't," Monte snorts. He leans his shoulder against the bell. Even from where I stand, I can hear it blasting away inside the house.

"Why don't we come back later?"

"Because. We're here *now*, ain't we?" Then he slams the flat of his hand so hard against the glass panel before him that the entire door quivers for a full minute after he is through. For some reason, this really infuriates him. "Open up, you rat sonofabitch!" he screams. "Your fucking check has come!"

"Monte, *please* . . ."

"From the Axis powers," he howls. "From El Doo-chay himself. Benito Fuckin' Mussolini, your *God!*"

"Monte, shit. The neighbors . . ."

"Remember that fuckin' day when they hung him by his heels in Rome? You cried your fuckin' eyes out, you Fascist prick! Remember how you went home and dyed your black shirt red, white, and blue so the GIs wouldn't string you up like a Genoa salami? *Open this door!*"

The two aged sisters who live in the house next door stick their heads out of adjoining windows on the second floor. Like always, they are both dressed all in black. Both of them have their thick black-and-gray-streaked hair drawn back into a tight bun. "What's-a the big *co*-mmotion?" the one nearest to me asks. Since they have already tipped Monte for Christmas, a big two bucks, they figure they have the right to know. Besides, they also hate Old Man Pappalardo with a passion. Last year, he called the cops on them for making wine in the basement without giving him any.

Before I can explain that everything is just fine out here, Monte sees them. "Special fuckin' delivery, girls," he hollers. "Get the whole freakin' neighborhood out for this. Old Man Pappalardo is getting himself a *big* check. He's gonna buy everyone a drink for Christmas. Fat chance, huh?"

One of the sisters looks as though she is going to faint right on the spot, falling two stories into my arms in a perfect swan dive. The other puts the first finger of her right hand to her ear and revolves it in a circle. *"Pazzo,"* she says. Then both windows come down hard, followed immediately by the shades being drawn tightly against the sill. Although both sisters hate the old man, this is more than even they can stand. Respectable people of all creeds, colors, and religions are washing their hands of us today.

"Monte," I plead, going halfway up the stoop to get him away before the sisters call the cops on us for disturbing the peace, "maybe he's in Bruno's, on the avenue."

"Maybe he's cuttin' out my heart with a dull knife to save a dime!" Monte shouts. "You cheap ghinny fuck. You penny-pinching dago tightwad. Here's your fuckin' check. *Take it.*"

Throwing the envelope against the door, Monte watches as it flutters in the breeze for a second before falling into a patch of rotten leaves and old dirt on the third step. For good measure, Monte kicks the check off the stoop into the arid little garden where nothing ever grows. "Go dig for it, Pop!" he bellows. "Buy yourself a nice fat turkey for Christmas and stuff it with dollar bills. Then you can eat yourself sick while your relatives starve to death in Sicily. I hope the wishbone gets stuck in your throat! I hope you choke on it! And when the ambulance comes this time, I hope they start your heart in *reverse!* Merry Christmas, motherfucker, and a Happy New Year. . . ."

So much for Old Man Pappalardo's check and the spirit of Christmas, past, present, and future, along Six Route. It is not yet two o'clock. At the rate we are now working, we will not even reach our second relay box before dark. Primarily this is because Monte insists on personally inspecting every last piece of mail before allowing me to shove it through the door. Holding the card or letter close to his face, he squints one eye shut, examines it carefully, then mumbles, "This fuck didn't contribute. He don't need no mail today." Then he throws it back into the sack. Soon we will be carrying around more mail than we left the station with this morning.

"Monte, listen," I say, stopping in the middle of the street to reason with him. "Why don't *you* go to Bruno's? Go see Bruno, grab yourself a little nap in the back room, and then, in a few hours, I'll come get you. . . ."

"You think I can't finish this route by myself?" he demands, completely missing my point as he polishes off the rest of his pint. "I done it *blind*. Lots of times."

"We'll *both* finish it. Only let me give you a head start."

"Yeah?" he says slowly. "You would do this for me?" I nod. No favor is too great if it gets Monte off the street for a couple of hours. "You know," he says, suddenly overwhelmed by emotion, "you are fucking okay in my book, kid. A real gentleman, in spite of your old man and the way he raised you. Go on. Take out the route. Learn what it's like to serve these . . ."

Monte stops talking. Apparently he has forgotten what he wanted to say. He looks around in confusion. The street is completely deserted. The strings of red and green Christmas lights tied around all the houses blink brightly on and off. The houses themselves look like presents that will not be opened until tomorrow morning.

Tipping his head all the way back, Monte opens his mouth so wide that I can just about see his wisdom teeth. He howls, "UNGRATEFUL BASTARDS WHO TAKE AND TAKE AND TAKE AND NEVER GIVE NOTHING BACK. NOT EVEN ON CHRISTMAS."

Having gotten it out of his system at last, Monte shuts his mouth and winks at me. In a normal tone of voice, he says, "Go on, kid. I'll meet you in Bruno's." Shoving his hands into the side pockets of his uniform coat, he turns and begins walking towards the avenue. Suddenly Monte looks very small, as though it was someone else entirely who was making all the noise.

As soon as Monte disappears around the corner, it is once again very quiet on the route. For the next four hours, I do nothing but work. With all my heart, I hope that Bruno will have enough sense to pour some strong coffee down Monte's throat, make him eat something, and then put him to bed on the cot in the back room. That way, the two of us will still be able to go back into the station together, ending my term of service as a Christmas temp on a distinctly honorable note.

By the time I get through delivering most of the mail that we brought out with us today, it is really late. Although Monte and I are now a good four and a half hours behind schedule, we are not yet completely dead. Slowly I drag myself up the last block toward Bruno's. Shoving open the door with my shoulder, I go inside.

The wooden floor is covered with a thick layer of coarse sawdust. The store itself smells the way Italy must. Sharp, pungent, and delicious. For all I know, Bruno keeps a goat tied up in the back room. Big rounds of Parmesan, provolone, Bel Paese, and gorgonzola hang over the counter, waiting to be sliced into sections with the string cutter.

Bruno has soft cheese and hard cheese and sausage of every kind for sale. Thin, spicy *zazeech* and thick Italian salami. Ham stuck through with spicy black peppercorns. Trays of stuffed peppers, artichokes, and cherry tomatoes. Tubs of soft, creamy ricotta. Boxes of wide lasagna noodles with serrated edges. Big tins of imported olive oil. Plastic gallon jars filled to the brim with shiny black olives floating in their own sinister oil. Sacks of roasted coffee beans and dried *ceci*. Bottles of homemade vinegar with herbs inside. I can never come into the store without wanting to throw myself face down into the food.

Bruno himself nods to me as I come through the door. "Bruno," I say, "Merry Christmas."

"Same to you," he answers, slicing some ham thin with a big knife.

"Monte here?" I ask.

"Oh, yeah," he says. "In back. Go on in."

"He take a nap?"

"Nap? What nap?"

"He came here to get some sleep, no?"

"Maybe he did. But he only pulled in like ten minutes ago. Jeez. Has he got a load on?" Bruno whistles softly. Then he says *"Whoo!,"* answering his own question before I can say another word.

Having heard his name, Monte himself comes wobbling from the back room. He waves his hand in front of his face, as though trying to clear away cobwebs that only he can see. All that Monte has put inside of himself today has finally taken over. Monte Serrano is drunk the way people get drunk only in movies. He is eyes rolling north, face going south, soft, mushy, fall down, tongue flopping drunk. His hair is mussed. His face is creased in fifty brand-new places. The man is just a mess.

"Kid," he says, lurching in my direction, "that was some trick you pulled. Leavin' me out there all alone like that. I coulda drowned in some sewer and no one woulda been the wiser."

"I didn't leave you, Monte. You walked away. Under your own steam.

"Hey. I waited for you by the second relay box for *days*. You never showed. . . ."

"Monte," I say, looking him up and down, "where's your leather bag? You didn't lose it, did you?"

"Nah," he says. "Locked the fucker up. In the second relay box." He grins. Then he burps. "Did lose my keys to the box, though. Ah. What difference does it make, huh? I mean, who really gives a flying fuck anyhow?"

Monte starts coming towards me once again. He is actually making headway when his back foot slips in the sawdust. Suddenly, he pitches forward into my arms. I manage to catch him all right but he is a lot heavier than he looks. Together, we go sliding backward towards the towering pyramid of vinegar bottles heaped by the front window. Bruno nearly has a heart attack. At the last possible moment, I manage to regain my footing. Using all the strength left in my arms, I haul Monte back into a standing position.

It occurs to me that we should leave before we do any damage that neither one of us can afford to pay for. Nodding goodbye to Bruno, I drag Monte to the door. I pull it open. Then I stand back to let him through. He half staggers into the street. As always, I bring up the rear. All the streetlights that line the avenue are now on. The dark night sky glows purple around them. Something soft and wet hits me in the face and I look up.

Sure enough, it is finally snowing, big fat flakes coming down slowly in the light as though God himself is shaking out a feather pillow in heaven up above. Here and there the stuff is already starting to stick, clinging to gleaming automobile hoods and the woolly hairs of my gloves and scarf. "Monte," I say, "it's snowing."

"Yeah? Where?"

"Right here. Look up. It's coming down. For Christmas . . ."

Monte looks up. What he sees is anyone's guess. Shaking his head, he looks me right in the face and says, "Who'd I hurt, huh? You tell me."

"I don't know, Monte. You want a list?"

Monte is not listening. Putting my hand up under his arm, I steer him slowly towards the gutter. "Who'd I hurt?" he demands once more, pushing himself away from me so that he spins in a tight little circle before coming to a stop right at the very edge of the sidewalk. The only surfer left in town, he stands perfectly balanced on the curb. His feet are spread wide apart. His hands are out with the palms pointing down. With eyes closed, he is waiting for a wave.

297

"Nice woman," he says. "A *nice* woman. Divorced. So who'd I hurt, huh? You tell me."

"Monte, I don't even know what you're talking about."

"Toni," he whispers. Then he puts his finger to his lips as though this will be our little secret from now on. "Runs a beauty parlor. Beautiful woman."

"What about her?"

"*The Contessa,*" he says. Then he grins. His entire face is lopsided, completely out of whack. "*I'm* the one that sees her, kid. Not Russ." Reaching for my arm, Monte squeezes it so hard I want to cry out from the pain. "I figgered you wouldn't like hearin' that so we played the old switcheroo on you. Right? I mean you understand why I did it, right? What with your old man bein' in the station and all . . . ."

"Look, Monte. What you do on your time is your business."

"Not any more," he says, the words catching in his throat. "Went to see her today. Brought her that nice bottle of Courvoisier someone gave me, and flowers. I brought her *flowers*. For a gift. When I come in, she's crying at the kitchen table. Messer called her *house*. The sonofabitch. Does she know a carrier can't spend no time in anyone's home when he's on the route? Like it's a fuckin' Federal offense or something, right? This is a *nice* woman, kid. Business woman. Respectable. Crying right at the kitchen table when I come in. She can't see me no more. She don't want no trouble. Because people talk, and all. The one decent thing in my life, kid. And now it's gone. For Christmas. Understand?"

I understand all right. Messer has gotten back at Monte for what he did to Kevin this morning, the scene at the Coke machine yesterday, as well as all the mornings of abuse shouted from between the route cases. "How could he know about her?" I ask, unable to think of anything more comforting to say at the moment.

"That Kraut bastard has spies *everywhere,* Paulie. He musta had one follow me or somethin'. 'Cause I only told Russ. And now you."

Monte is too drunk to make the connection himself. But I get it on my very first try. Even though Russ is Monte's friend, he has looked out for himself. He has taken care of Number One, just as he told me to do. What Messer will give Russ in return for his information, I have no idea. Maybe Russ Balbano and Kevin Delaney will both be working at soft and cushy jobs in the GPO downtown when the new year comes. It is just as the old man

298

said. Out here, they routinely cut one another's throats and then just keep right on walking.

By now, the snow is really coming down, as it only can in the city right at the start of a tremendous storm. All the buildings on the avenue are being dismantled a single brick at a time. Soon they will vanish completely into the haze. The snow will cover all, and the neighborhood itself will disappear, becoming once again the gentle, rolling farmland it once was.

None of the carriers will be able to finish their routes in this kind of weather. All I have to do is get Monte back to the station and punch him out. Then he can go home and sleep it off. What he will do when he wakes up tomorrow morning only to discover that it is in fact Christmas day, I do not know.

"Monte," I say, "if we walk back to the station, you think someone would drive you home?"

"Drive *me* home?" he says. "This is Monte Fucking Serrano you're talking to here. Monte Fucking Serrano always drives himself home. No matter *what*, understand? Drank seventeen Dewars-and-water once, drove myself home. Two bottles of White Horse, drove myself home. J and B, Thousand Pipers, Glen Rossie. You name it, I done it, and drove myself home."

"How about walking to the station?"

"That," he admits, "is something else. Kid, I ever tell you about the Stadium?"

"No, Monte, you never did," I say, pulling him away from the curb. Out in the gutter, cars are slipping and sliding like crazy as their drivers rush to get home before all the good parking spots in the neighborhood are gone and the streets themselves become impassable. "You walk and we'll talk."

He nods. Together, we start moving slowly down the avenue towards the station, taking it one step at a time. "This is years ago," he says as we cross the street. "Series is Dodgers and Yanks, like always. I ride the subway all the way up to the fuckin' Bronx, stand in line for three solid hours, and come away with a grandstand seat. I was young, right? What did I know? I thought it mattered. . . .

"DiMaggio is finishin' up in center for the Yanks. His wheels are bad, his arm is gone, he's all gray at the temples but they gotta have him out there because he's class. *Class*. All the way. Shit. Berra, Raschi, the Scooter, none of 'em can compare with Joltin' Joe. The fuckin' Yankee Clipper. 'Cause there never was a ghinny like the great DiMag. The greatest, right?

"I'm there watchin' the game when it hits me. Nah, I think, this is nuts. But it won't leave me alone. I can't think of nothin' else. I don't know what the score is, who's up, nothin'. All I can do is stare at DiMaggio and think about it. Comes the seventh inning, I start moving down. It's like I'm in a fuckin' trance or something. I don't even know who's pitching. I just got this thing workin' in my brain.

"Comes the top of the ninth and I'm all the way down by the low fence in right. Guys are standin' and hollerin', waiting for the game to end. I can't take it no longer. I get up on a chair, grab the rail, swing over, and *bingo*, I'm out there on the field, runnin' for all I'm worth. . . ."

We come to the end of the block. The traffic light goes from green to red, the colors of the season. Monte takes a deep breath and closes his eyes. I can tell that there is no way I am going to move him until he finishes. So I just let him talk.

"I can still smell that grass, you know? It's like a fuckin' carpet under my feet. Thick and green. Seventy thousand fans. They get one look at me, they go fuckin' bananas, screaming and hollering. Me, I'm just stretchin' it out nice and easy, doin' my home run trot on that rich man's lawn they got out there.

"I get close to DiMag. Crowd's howlin' so loud that they got to stop play. Umps come runnin' from the infield to stop me. I just keep on movin'. Now I'm right on top of him. He's wearin' those pinstripes. *Jesus!* He looks like a million bucks, even if it is the top of the ninth right at the very end of his career. I can smell his after-shave, the shit he'll be slappin' on his face soon as he starts climbin' into the rack with Marilyn at night. That big Number Five is sticking right into my face. I can see the black hairs on his forearms pokin' through his uniform shirt.

" 'Joe, Joe,' I say. 'You gotta tell me. *Joe!* How's a ghinny to live?' "

"That's what you asked him?" I say.

"That's it."

"Why?"

"How the fuck should I know? It's what came into my head. Like if I could get out there and ask, he'd tell me, you know? Like he knew and I didn't. And he'd tell me if I asked."

"So what did he say, Monte?"

"Well, I can see right away that he likes what I asked him. He's given the matter a lotta thought all on his own and he's got it all worked out in his head. He's just been waitin' for someone like me to pop the question so he can explain it all. He starts to answer.

"*Boom!* This cop blindsides me. I fall like a ton of bricks. They're all over me then, giving me the bum's rush to the wall. One I deck with a good right hand. He falls down. Crowd goes completely nuts. Next day my picture is on the front page of the *Daily News*. In the post office where I worked back then, I'm fucking 'Queen for a Day.' 'The Fan Who Wanted to Chat with DiMag.' Judge gives me a big lecture in court, lets me off with a warning. Of course, the Yanks win the Series, like always."

"Monte, look, it's getting really late. . . ."

"I tell you, Paulie. Sure as shit and I'm standing here today, he *wanteda* talk to me. I could see it. He *knew* what I was askin'. But those cocksuckers wouldn't gimme a chance. They never do. The fucks . . ."

"Monte, if we stay out much longer, they'll have to send a dog sled to bring us in."

I hook my hand into the side pocket of Monte's jacket and start tugging him towards the gutter. Monte is having none of it. Jerking himself out of my grip, he spins around crazily in the snow. His feet slip on the wet pavement. In the lamplight, his eyes glow like big white saucers in his face. He looks like a West Virginia coal miner who has just emerged from an all-night shift underground.

Flinging his arms into the air, he cries out, "*I don't wanna live. I don't need to live. I wanna die. Right here and now. So help me fuckin' God.*"

Then he looks around wildly in all directions, trying to remember where he is. Doubling over as though someone has caught him with a sucker punch to the gut, he throws up violently into the street. The stuff slops all over his shoes and the cuffs of his uniform pants. Monte gags and spits. He makes noises in his throat. Like an animal in pain, he stays down there, refusing to let me help him up.

When finally he lifts his head again, he actually looks better. His color has improved and his eyes are clear. So maybe he is making a comeback. "Kid," he says quietly, "I think I also just shit my pants."

"Let's get back inside, Monte."

"Why? You in some kind of hurry or something?"

"Yeah, well . . . I got that drawing to go to tonight. . . ."

"Then go."

"What do you mean, '*Then go.*'?"

"Who's kidding who, huh?" he says, pulling me close to him. "*Huh?* You belong out here walkin' a route with me about as much as I did with DiMag in center field. So go take care of your business and I'll take care of mine."

I do not want to leave him out here like this. But there is not all that much I can do for him if he will not let me help him. Besides, in the annex of the shul, they are getting ready to draw the winning raffle ticket. I *have* to be there to see them do it. "Monte," I tell him, "the station is dead ahead. Six blocks. Your house is about twice as far to the right, then turn left and keep going till you see the door."

"Right," he says, breathing heavily through his mouth. "I couldn'a said it better myself."

Grabbing my arm, he pulls me close to him once again. The smell of sour vomit and whiskey comes right into my face. "Merry Christmas, kid," he groans, as though they are breaking all the bones in his body one by one. "I hope you and your grandfather there win that fuckin' raffle. You deserve it. . . ."

Then he pushes me away. I stumble sideways off the curb into the gutter. A car with its brights on comes sliding down the street right toward me. The driver is blowing his horn like crazy to let me know that even if he wants to, he cannot stop. Forced to make a quick decision, I bolt instinctively for the far corner.

When I look back, I see Monte standing all alone under the streetlamp with his arms spread out wide. His mouth is open and his head is thrown all the way back. Snow clings to his face in great, soft white flakes. It sticks to his eyebrows and the grizzled stubble on his chin like powdered sugar. For all the world, he looks like Jesus on the cross, waiting for the nails to be driven in.

Six blocks dead ahead, Avenue Station lies before him. His house, where his wife and kids are probably waiting for him so they can sit down to dinner, is just about twice as far in the other direction. Any way you look at it, with no more shopping days at all left until Christmas, Monte is still only halfway home.

CHAPTER TWENTY-EIGHT

BY THE TIME I slip through a side door into the annex, a good three hundred people are already there. Gathered about tables covered in green felt, they are intently playing games of chance. The loud babble of their nervous voices washes over me, pinning me up against the back wall. Half a foot above everyone's head hangs a foul, eye-watering, dead yellow haze. It is composed in equal parts of cigar ash, cigarette smoke, and body heat. No one seems to notice. They are all too busy having fun. There has not been a turnout like this at Ahavath Mizrach since *Kol Nidre* night.

Despite the snow, the congregation has come out in force this evening to answer the call of the clicking chuck-a-luck cage, the rolling dice, and the tiny white ball that skips merrily across the turning numbers at the roulette wheel. Tonight they are gambling only for money. That little *shtip* they feel in the general region of their hearts whenever it looks as though they may actually lose more than they can afford to part with is in itself worth the price of admission. For how else can they be certain that they are not yet dead? So long as it still hurts, they know for sure that they *are* alive, and in the game.

People hold stacks of play money in their hands. They squint their eyes tightly shut against both the smoke and the overwhelming odds. They sigh and murmur as the wheels go round. Inscribe us in the Book of Life for the coming year, O Lord, they pray. Make the red ace fall perfectly on the black king for an automatic twenty-one. Grant us a year of dew, rain, and warmth in which the dealer will always stand on seventeen and hit on sixteen, come what may. Grant us. Inscribe us. Give us. For our need is great, and never ending.

I search the crowd for a familiar face. Slowly, it dawns on me that some of these people have never been inside the shul before. Not that it matters. Tonight, their money is just as good as

303

anyone else's. So long as they can afford to play, they are welcome. Since it all goes to a good cause anyway, there can be no losers. Not really. Besides, with a little luck, some of them may even leave with more than they brought. As always, this is still the very best cause of all.

Before I can find myself a place to hide until the grand prize drawing begins, my mother corners me. Her eyes dance and sparkle in her face. Although she wears a billowing lime-green outfit that does absolutely nothing for her, she looks happier than she has in longer than I can remember. So maybe some good has already come from the evening.

"Isn't it *wonderful*, dear?" she cries, kissing me on the cheek as she extends her hand in a sweeping, indiscriminate circle. "All these people. All this activity . . ."

"All this *gelt*," I say.

"All this *gelt*," she repeats without missing a beat. "Come," she urges, tugging at my hand. "Let me take you around. I want you to meet *everyone*."

We have only just begun to hack our way through the crowd when the rabbi's wife motions us over. She happens to be standing with none other than Sylvia Stryker herself. If we are going to meet *everyone*, I guess we might as well start at the top and then work our way on down. "Sylvia," my mother calls out, "you look lovely tonight. But where's Sol?"

Sylvia manages to smile while at the same time staring down her nose at the crowd. It is no mean feat. In a moment, she will politely ask everyone to please quiet down so she can deliver a small talk on how people *should* behave when their money is on the line. Instead, she says, "Sol is not here, Esther. He wouldn't come. I tried to make him. But you know Sol."

"What a shame," my mother says brightly. Right away, I know that she considers this a personal insult. "And how are you, Leah?" she asks the rabbi's wife. "Have you ever met my son, Paulie?"

"As a matter of fact," the rabbi's wife says, "we spent some time together only the other day."

"You know, Esther," Sylvia remarks casually, "you really shouldn't let the fact that Sol stayed away tonight upset you. The man is just becoming a hermit in his later years. Personally, I think you have a *raging* success on your hands."

"Especially when you consider the weather," the rabbi's wife puts in.

"Upset?" my mother says. "Who said I was upset?"

"Besides," Sylvia adds, "you know that Sol *never* gambles. He feels that having Nat for a brother-in-law is quite enough of a risk all by itself."

For a full second, the three women look at one another. Then they all start laughing at once. The girls. They do have timing. It is something they were born with. "Myself," Sylvia adds, "I just can't seem to lose tonight, Esther. I already cashed in my chips once, for some children's clothing if you can believe that, with Sol's label right on it no less and gone back to the tables, and I'm *still* winning."

"Knowing you, Sylvia," my mother notes, "I don't doubt it for a second."

"So-o-o-o," Sylvia says, stretching out the word to give herself time to examine me in microscopic detail, "*you're* the one who has been taking my niece to all those strange places."

I can feel my mother start to sag at my side. In a second, she will turn to me and plaintively demand, "*Paulie*. Why am I *always* the last to know?" Before she can do this, I squeeze her hand, hard. All I need is for her to start giving me the third degree in front of these two women. "To night court they went," Sylvia says. "On a date. Can you imagine? Sol never took me anywhere like that when we were dating."

I keep nodding my head and smiling. I am not about to tell Sylvia that her niece and I are no longer an item in anyone's column. "You make sure and take *very* good care of Stephanie, young man," Sylvia orders. "She's special."

"And my son isn't?" my mother demands, bristling like a large, lime-green porcupine about to loose all her quills right in Sylvia's face.

The two women glare at one another. It is now my responsibility to step between them and order them to opposite corners so they can come out swinging at the bell. I would sooner step in front of a city bus. Knowing that she is evenly matched, Sylvia decides to concede the round. "Oh, Esther," she sighs. "You're *so* sensitive. That's not what I meant at all. . . ."

"Come, dear," my mother says pointedly, taking my hand. "Let's circulate. I'm sure we'll see you both again later on."

As soon as we are out of earshot, she whispers, "Do you believe the *nerve* of that woman?" Steering me toward the corner of the room where people stand shoulder to shoulder in front of a

305

large spinning wheel covered with numbers, she nudges me in the side with her elbow. "That's him, dear," she notes.

"That's who?" I ask.

"Jerry Kahn," she says. "Who else? He put this whole thing together single-handedly. Brought us all the wheels and the tables for next to nothing. He even printed up all the play money at his own expense."

"What is he? A close personal friend of the late Bugsy Siegel?"

"He, dear, is a very nice, lonely man. Because of him, I'm actually going to see a doctor about my weight on Monday. A specialist no less."

"It took you long enough. I've been after you to do it for years."

She holds up her hand to silence me. "Please, dear," she says, "don't nag me. You sound exactly like your father when you do. Come. I want you to say hello to Jerry."

Jerry Kahn stands behind a board covered with play money. His right hand rests on a red-and-white painted wooden wheel that looks as though it has come directly to the shul from the midway of some carnival out in the Midwest. Jerry himself wears an old-fashioned green sun visor pulled down low over his forehead. His eyes are covered by the same yellow tinted aviator glasses I remember his having worn on Yom Kippur. The sleeves of his expensively tailored white-on-white shirt are rolled perfectly just above his elbows. I can tell that he has done this kind of work before.

Stepping back from the wheel, he carefully primes it for another spin by rolling it backwards. The tiny nails around the outer edge click loudly against the red wooden arrow that will soon point to the winning number. A flurry of play money is dumped on the board before him. Then Jerry Kahn gives the wheel an enthusiastic push. The wheel turns in a smooth and effortless circle. All the numbers meld rapidly into a single whirling blur. "Lucky seven, lucky seven, double heaven," Jerry Kahn chants. The wheel begins to slow down once more. The numbers gradually reappear as separate digits. For all the world it looks as though lucky seven will indeed come up, the number with more money riding on it than any other because it pays double.

The arrow clicks over the first nail into the "7" slot. It hangs there for a moment. Then it softly hits the second nail, trembles, and falls over into double zero. The house collects. Jerry Kahn rakes in the money with a big grin on his face. "It only hurts when you laugh, friends," he spiels, trying to make the people believe that they *can* still beat the odds. "Take it from a man who knows. Now, who wants to go again? Let's go again. . . ."

"I'll meet him later," I say, starting to move away. "When he's not so busy."

"*Esther?*" Jerry Kahn calls out. "This your son?" Reaching out, he grabs for my hand. He shakes it briskly. At the very same time, he presses a thick roll of play money into my palm. "Go on," he urges. "Take. Who knows? Maybe it's your lucky night."

"Thanks," I say. "I can buy my own."

"Take, take," he says. "Don't stand on ceremony. You win, you can pay me back. You lose, the shul collects. Either way, we all come out ahead."

"Paulie, *please*," my mother hisses.

"Right," I say, accepting the roll of funny money with the intention of losing it all back as fast as I can. "After all, it's not the real thing, right?"

"That's the spirit," Jerry Kahn says, winking at me.

Sensing that my mother wants to stay right here, I nod to her and start moving towards the other side of the room, where they are selling food. I join the long, winding line that has formed in front of a fat man with no hair on his head. Rapidly, he is slicing a whole corned beef. The meat tumbles forward perfectly beneath the blade of his knife, a thin skein of pearly-white fat holding all the tiny red brick bits of corned beef in place. With both hands, he begins shoving slices of meat between thick pieces of rye bread. Someone grabs me by the elbow. The old man is standing behind me.

"So?" he demands, having apparently decided that he is now talking to me once again. "What happened to your good friend Monte today? He never came back in off the route, did he? Missing in action, hah?"

"I had to leave him out there," I confess, still feeling guilty about it.

"Dead drunk, I'm sure it goes without saying," the old man says. "You couldn't have done anything about it. It's the way he is."

"Look," I say. "I want to apologize for . . ."

"No need," he says, cutting me off before I can begin.

"No, I want to . . ."

307

"Forget it," he orders, getting me really annoyed. "You learned something out there today? Fine. That's better than any apology."

"So what are you doing here tonight?" I ask, just to get back some of my own. "You came to gamble?"

"Me?" he says. "Never. For family, though, I make an exception."

"Meaning what?"

"I sell an entire book of raffle tickets, I got a right to watch them draw the winner, no?"

"*You?*"

"A whole book. To the clerks. Mo himself took four, the big spender. He's over there right now playing craps. You should see him roll those bones and rattle those chip-*kes.* He's cleaning up."

The old man is so happy tonight that I barely know who he is. He has a big grin on his face as though he, and not Mo, the big Mississippi riverboat sharpie, is the one raking in the jackpots. Wearing the very same suit he had on for Yom Kippur, the old man looks strangely natty tonight. It is the only word that describes him. He is definitely natty, except for that lousy Perry Como sweater that he has on under his jacket, for protection against the cold no doubt.

"So what are you eating tonight?" he demands.

"Corned beef," I tell him. "They only just sliced one up."

"Forget it," he says. "Overcooked and overspiced. Falls apart inside your stomach and lays there like cement. My advice would be . . . take the brisket."

"I don't like brisket."

"Brisket on rye with a pickle and a bottle of that good cream so-*day?*" he asks, his eyes twinkling. "Sounds pretty good to me."

Before I can tell him that if it sounds so good, *he* should eat it, he shouts, "*Hey, Mac!* Two briskets on rye. Seaboard. To go." On the off chance that the guy behind the counter is hard of hearing, the old man throws two fingers right into his face. Blind also, he cannot be. Although this may be a terrible thing to say, I realize that I prefer my father when he is slightly depressed. He is easier to handle that way.

The fact that the old man has actually sold an entire book of raffle tickets on his own gives me no pleasure at all. Morty has absolutely no luck when it comes to money. Any time he opens a new account in some bank on the avenue in order to get the free gift that comes along with it, that bank is sure to fail within the year. His idea of a brilliant long-term investment is saving stamps.

"Can I ask *why* you sold those tickets?" I say, watching as two steaming brisket sandwiches take shape on adjoining paper plates. Streams of thin salt brown gravy run from in between the slices of bread. Already my stomach is starting to turn at the thought of having to eat the stuff.

"I did it for *him*. Why else?"

"For him," I say. "For Pop, you mean? You *can't* be serious."

"Never been any seriouser," he answers, shaking a couple of real dollar bills in my face as he makes a point of paying for both our sandwiches. "So he can win the trip. What the hell. I got two weeks' sick leave coming. I could take it in Israel. See the Promised Land before it's too late. The Wailing Wall, everything."

"Just you and him, huh?"

"Why not?" he demands, delivering an affectionate little rabbit punch to the back of my neck. I find this gesture so frighteningly paternal that I make believe it did not happen. "I'm not too old to learn from my own flesh and blood. You were right and I was wrong. So, instead of apologizing, I sold an entire book. I put his name on every ticket. Plus of course the bonus. So, sharp guy, how many did you sell?"

"Two books," I tell him. "But his name isn't on all the tickets. I figure eighteen or twenty."

"Okay. We'll be conservative. Say your eighteen, plus my ten. That makes twenty-eight. Plus three bonus ones. Call it thirty. Out of five hundred. That's . . ."

The old man starts working it out. He is good at doing figures in his head, my father. He gets to practice all day long in his little cage at the station. "Say it's sixteen to one against us. A long shot certainly but . . . for us, *boychick*, that horse is coming in."

Handing me my sandwich and soda, he somehow also manages to press a thick roll of play money into my pocket at the very same time. What with the stake that Jerry Kahn already palmed off on me, I am now ready to break the bank. Where all this money is coming from, I do not know. They must be printing it up in the kitchen as the evening wears on.

"First you eat," he says. "Then you gamble. Comes time for the drawing, I think it's only right that we should stand together. Myself, I can't wait to see the look on Nat Weiss's face when

309

they call out the winner. He's going to turn every color of the rainbow. Then he'll *plotz*. It's going to do my heart good to watch it happen."

I now understand why the old man has sold all those tickets. He does not care about visiting Israel or seeing the last standing wall of the Temple before it is too late. He just wants to stick it to Nat. I can just see my father in Jerusalem with his little Brownie, shooting out-of-focus pictures of everything in sight. When he gets back home, he will reach into his pocket some night and wave the pictures in Nat's face.

"Seen these yet, Nat?" he will ask, loud enough for everyone to hear. "They *all* came out. Jeez, it's beautiful over there. You never been to the Holy Land, have you, Nat? You ought to go. You really should. You owe it to yourself. I can tell you all the best places to see. . . ."

This will be yet one more victory for him. He is a fighter all right, my father, dancing on his toes until he can land the single crushing blow that sends his opponent reeling to the canvas. Getting even is all that he cares about. What he does not realize is that the fight itself is already over. All the seats are empty and the fans have all gone home. Yet he keeps on dancing still, his gloves right up under his chin.

"One more thing," he says as I start to move away. "Someone called for you tonight. To wish you a Merry Christmas. A girl. From Boston. I took a number. It's on the table in the apartment. You can call her back tomorrow and tell her that our holiday is Chanukkah."

With the incredible sense for the dramatic that she has always had, Lesley is checking back in again just when I need her most. For a second, I think seriously about going into the hallway and using the pay phone to call her in Cambridge. Then I decide to wait until after the drawing. Who knows? By then, I may have some good news to tell her.

Finding a metal folding chair that Solomon has probably stashed in the corner for himself and then forgotten all about, I open it up and sit down. Putting the paper plate with the brisket sandwich on it behind the chair, I sip at my cream soda. I just do not have the strength to go out there and gamble. Instead, I am going to sit here and wait until the drawing begins.

Forty-five minutes later, a good three and a half hours after the time printed on all the raffle tickets as the magic moment when the winning number will be drawn, I watch as my mother shuffles slowly towards the single microphone set up at the far end of the annex. Blowing into it a couple of times so that the heavily amplified sound of her breath whooshes through the room like the wind, she leans forward and booms, "Can I have your attention, *please?*"

The sound is so loud that she steps back immediately, having frightened even herself. Smiling to show that she means well, she pats down the hair on the right side of her face. A few people actually stop what they are doing to look at her. Everyone else just goes right on gambling.

Since I last saw my mother, someone has pinned a white corsage to the yoke of her dress. It hangs there now like a tired badge of honor. The tiny white flowers are just beginning to wilt, going slightly brown around the edges. As soon as she gets home tonight, she will put the corsage into the refrigerator. That way, she can take it back out again tomorrow morning and look at it, remembering just what a fabulous evening this really was.

Explaining that she is, of course, completely unaccustomed to speaking in public, my mother launches directly into her own abridged version of the Gettysburg Address. This great event, she says, which seems so certain to put the shul over the top for the coming year just would not have been possible without all the dedicated men and women who worked so hard to make it happen. She would like to single out a few by name.

Credit goes first, of course, to Jerry Kahn, the mastermind behind it all. Although I am hardly an impartial judge, the round of applause that wells up for Jerry from the crowd is less than overwhelming. The real jackpot, of course, my mother goes on, will come on Monday morning when the safe is opened and the receipts are totaled. But enough of that, she says. Finally, the time has come. The moment of moments is at hand. The winner of the all-expenses-paid trip for two to Jerusalem, donated so graciously by a travel agency on the avenue whose name she mentions over and over as *the* place to go for anyone who is planning a trip anywhere in the near future, is about to be announced.

The old man comes towards me from out of the crowd. I can see that he is nervous. With the fingers of his right hand, he is kneading the pile of funny money that lies in his palm. "Won't be long now," he whispers, pinching my arm so I will look back up towards the microphone.

"To draw the winning number," my mother announces, "who

else but the lovely daughter of our shul president? *Steffi?* Where are you, dear? Now is not the time to be shy. Come right on up here so we can proceed.''

I swing my head around in a nervous circle. Sure enough, here comes Steffi. Aunt Sylvia has definitely set this up, and why not? The girl does have a voice like Streisand. She even hears the very same buzz in her ear. If Steffi *really* wants a career in show business, she has to start somewhere.

To me, Steffi looks as though she would much rather be safely tucked away in her bedroom with the stereo turned all the way up listening to Streisand sing. As she moves toward my mother, Steffi's sweet little pink tongue flickers rapidly across her dry, chapped lips. It is a gesture she got from Nat. Reaching up nervously, she pushes a strand of her long brown hair from her eyes. It is enough to make me want to rush to her side. Holding up my hand for silence, I will announce, ''Forget it, friends. This girl is under a tremendous strain. She already lost one boyfriend in tragic circumstances up at college and has had incredible trouble with another right up here in our very own neighborhood. Please excuse her if she cannot perform tonight. Your money will be cheerfully refunded at the box office out front.''

''Go on, darling,'' my mother urges, her voice booming over the loudspeakers. ''Pick us a winner.''

Closing her eyes, which I guess is what she has to do in order to remain on her feet with nearly three hundred people staring holes right through her, Steffi plunges her hand into the metal drum of raffle tickets before her. Rooting around for a good deal longer than seems absolutely necessary, she picks her way through the tickets from top to bottom, searching for one that suits her fancy.

''So enough with the suspense, already,'' the old man mutters. ''She's digging a hole in a garden up there, or what?''

Steffi finally finds one that she likes. Then she straightens back up and hands it to my mother. Steffi has not faithfully watched the Academy Awards on television each year without picking up a few moves of her own. She *knows* how to be a presenter. As soon as the winner bounds up on stage to claim the prize, she will shower him with phony sideways show-business kisses, as flash bulbs explode madly everywhere.

''And the winner is . . .'' my mother announces, drawing out the tension as she squints at the winning ticket.

''The winner is . . .'' she repeats, staring at the ticket as

312

though the name on it is written in letters too small for her to read. "Oh, my *God!*" she blurts out. "I don't believe it. The winner is . . . *Sol Stryker.*"

I do not know if it is pent-up hysteria, shock, or what. But I laugh right out loud. Everyone hears me do it as well, over the sudden buzz of excitement that runs around the room. It is just too perfect. I mean, who needs the trip less than Sol and Sylvia Stryker? What else can you give the couple that already has everything but *more?*

As Sylvia Stryker glides slowly toward the microphone, graciously accepting congratulations for continuing her incredible hot streak tonight, I catch sight of the old man. He is not laughing. Not exactly. He is grinding his teeth together so violently that I fear he will start spitting them out like Chiclets. Furiously, he shoves his pile of funny money into my hand.

"*Here,*" he says bitterly, as though it is my fault that Sol Stryker won the drawing instead of us. "As far as I'm concerned, you can wipe your ass with this stuff now. Me, I wouldn't even bother."

Then he stalks right out of the annex with his head down, looking neither right nor left. The rich just keep right on getting richer, I guess. It is the single rule to which there are no exceptions. As the old man goes out through the back door, I look up at the clock above his head. It is exactly one minute after midnight. Merry Christmas, I think to myself. And to all a good night.

TASHLIKH

CHAPTER TWENTY-NINE

FOR THE PAST week, Esther had been on a completely different schedule when it came to getting her hair done. Because Las Vegas Night had fallen on a Thursday, she had gone to Toni's on the Wednesday before for her wash and set. On the following Saturday, she had been so exhausted from the incredible excitement of the event, and the unbelievable drudgery of the cleanup that had followed, that she had slept right through her regular appointment. Giving Toni a call from home at noon, Esther had asked if she could possibly come in next Wednesday afternoon instead. Toni, of course, had said yes.

Although Esther would not have known it from her schedule, today was Wednesday. This morning, she had slept right through the alarm. Then she had taken her own sweet time over breakfast, eating *two* pieces of apple cake without thinking twice about it because of the incredible news the specialist had given her on Monday. She had gone to work late and then left early.

Tomorrow evening, the shul would be holding what the rabbi's wife was very optimistically calling "the temple's very first annual New Year's Eve Gala." The function had been on the synagogue calendar for months. Actually, it was going to be more like a get-together than a gala, which was just as well, considering that there was no way Leah Hakveldt or Sylvia Stryker, the co-sponsors of the event, could ever top Las Vegas Night.

Esther herself had always felt that New Year's Eve was easily the single most overrated night of the entire year. Still, Jerry Kahn had been nice enough to ask her to accompany him to the Gala. His invitation had given meaning to what in the past had always been for her the deadest, saddest part of the entire winter. The week between Christmas and New Year's was no time for a person to be alone. Because of Jerry, Esther found that she did

317

not mind all the annoying changes in the regular, established pattern of her life. Instead, she was actually enjoying them.

Now, as she walked slowly up the avenue to Toni's shop, the cold, bitter wind blowing right through the heavy fabric of her bulky winter coat, Esther was still in no great hurry. Most of the women who regularly jammed themselves into the little beauty parlor on the weekend would not be coming in until tomorrow afternoon.

On the final day of the year, they would all suddenly crowd into the shop at the very last minute, loudly demanding that Toni alone do them, and right away, so that they could rush right back home in time to dress for the parties to which they had all been invited. Whether any of them would really enjoy themselves as the clock ticked slowly down towards midnight was another question altogether. Their hair at least would be perfect all evening long, every last lacquered strand remaining stubbornly in place no matter how hard the wind blew.

Pushing open the front door of Toni's shop, Esther looked around in satisfaction. The beauty parlor was quieter and emptier than she had ever seen it before. Once again she had beaten the crowd, this time without even really trying. Lately it had all just been coming her way, no matter what she did. She too was on a hot streak, much like the one Sylvia Stryker had enjoyed on Las Vegas Night. Sylvia herself was about to go off on a trip with Sol. Not to Jerusalem but to some fabulous ski resort up north that was famous all over the world.

Although Esther had never once been on the slopes in her entire life, and had absolutely no intention of taking up the sport now, she had been sorely tempted to tell Sylvia that these days she too was skiing. At least that was how it felt. Ever since her divorce from Morty, Esther had slowly and painfully been making her way back up to the top of the mountain again, always holding on so tightly to the tow rope that she now imagined there to be rope burns on both her palms.

Finally she had scaled the summit. With the entire downhill run before her, the rope had vanished magically from her hands. Esther was now suddenly in motion at long last, gliding effortlessly down the mountain. All the weight had dropped from her body and she was skiing, with no sound at all save for the soft sighing of the wind in her ears and the whoosh of the powdery white snow beneath her feet.

Without having to watch where she was headed, without having to worry or plan or even think about it, Esther was finally moving in the right direction, more rapidly than she had ever thought possible. Like the young girl she had once been, she was now coasting from one day to the next, taking things as they came, and actually feeling happy for the first time in longer than she could remember. So far she had told no one about her good fortune, not even Jerry, for fear that talking about it might make the feeling disappear.

Shutting the door tightly behind her so that it would remain closed against the gusting wind, Esther looked down the long and narrow beauty parlor to the flocked red-and-gold drawstring curtains in back. The very first person she laid eyes on was Dom. On any other day, he would have put her immediately on edge, making her feel both uneasy and very selfconscious. Today, though, she did not mind seeing him one bit.

In part, this was because lately Dom Cerullo had begun looking a little old around the edges. A little old and a little worn. Ever since he had come back from the Caribbean with Toni, Dom had desperately been trying to preserve his tan with one of those artificial skin-coloring creams. At the moment, his naturally swarthy face was an odd shade of pale yellow, as though he was undergoing a serious bout of liver trouble. Like some beautiful woman who could not admit that her looks were slowly fading, Dom was not aging gracefully. What Toni still saw in the man, Esther could not imagine. She herself would not have let him put his slippers under her bed for all the rice in China.

"Esther," Dom said harshly, looking right through her with those bedroom eyes of his, "I got an hour open. Want *me* to do you?" Then he laughed, as though this was the funniest thing anyone had ever said. Esther had never liked Dom. Not ever. Today, though, she was determined to be polite to the man.

"Oh, I can wait, Dom," she said. "Why? Aren't Toni and Enid here?"

"In back," Dom said, motioning with his hand. "Filing their claws."

Esther said nothing. Dom had definitely gotten up on the wrong side of the bed this morning. Whose bed it had been was another story altogether. Not that it was any of her business. Not any longer. She now had a life of her own to worry about. "Tell me something, Esther," Dom, said. Putting his hand to his mouth as though he was holding a microphone in it, he began crooning that sad tired little song that Esther had always hated, one that dated them both as a pair of authentic old fogeys. *"What are you doing New Year's?"* he sang. *"New Year's Eve?"*

"I really don't know yet, Dom," she answered, unwilling to tell him a thing about her plans.

"Watching the ball come down in Times Square on television again, huh? With a cup of hot tea and lemon by your side?" he said cruelly, just naturally assuming that no one in their right mind would want to be seen out with her in public that night.

Stung by his remark, Esther spoke without thinking. "Why, Dom?" she demanded. "Are you looking for a date?"

"He's looking for more than a date," Enid noted sourly, pushing aside the curtains as she stepped from the back of the shop. "A job is what he needs."

"And what you need, Enid," Dom answered, "we all know. . . ."

"Tch, tch," Enid said, making little clucking noises with her tongue against the roof of her mouth. "Mustn't get nasty, Dominick. Besides, you couldn't give it to me anyway. Not from what I hear."

Moving around Dom very carefully, as though he had some kind of highly contagious disease, Enid made a funny, screw-you-too face that only Esther could see. Then she leaned in towards Esther until their faces were no more than an inch apart. "Toni caught him with his hand in the register again yesterday," Enid whispered, her voice soft in Esther's ear. "She only just handed him his walking papers. Today's his very last day. Next week, Marlene takes over his chair, regular."

Stepping back, Enid critically surveyed Esther's hair. As though she was completing a sentence that she had just begun, she announced, "No, not a regular cut, I don't think, Esther. A trim. A quarter inch off the front. But let Toni do it for you. I have to count cash. What's *left* of it. . . ."

If ever there had been a chance for Dom to open his mouth and come back at Enid with something really mean, this was it. Dom, however, just turned away. Nervously he began arranging his combs and brushes in front of the chair that would be his for only a few more hours. All the while he kept staring into the big mirror that ran the length of the shop so that he could see everything that was going on behind him without anyone noticing.

"So, Esther," Enid called out over her shoulder as she moved towards the register at the front of the shop. "From what I hear, congratulations are in order."

"Why?" Esther asked. "Someone told you I finally got my period?"

"*Esther*," Enid laughed, truly shocked. "Your mouth. For Las Vegas Night. I heard it was a great success. The shul must have made a *fortune*. No?"

"A fortune, no," Esther said. Then, because Enid was like family to her, she added, "To tell you the truth, Enid, by the time we cashed in all the money we had printed up and gave away the merchandise, well, we just about broke even."

"Broke even?" Enid repeated, shaking her head. "How can that be?"

"I can explain it," Dom said sullenly, sulking like a child by his chair. "Just say the word and I will . . ."

"Say what word?" Toni Assante demanded, coming through the curtains with a look on her face that made Dom immediately turn once more towards the mirror. "*Money?*"

Toni glared at the back of Dom's head for a moment. Then she turned towards Esther with a big smile on her face that seemed to light up the entire shop. Esther smiled right back at her. As far as she was concerned, Toni Assante could do no wrong. Although the woman was no spring chicken, she had the face of a cover girl, the body of a twenty-year-old, and the sharp, quick mind of a successful businessman. More importantly, Toni had that special something that Esther had found in only a very few people, a never-ending zest for life that made getting up each morning worth the effort. Despite Toni's taste in men, Esther had always loved her. To her real friends, Esther was loyal, no matter what.

"Jerry Kahn took care of all the details for you, right?" Dom said in a low voice, looking everywhere but right at Toni. "He was your detail man."

"He helped us run the evening, yes," Esther allowed. "In fact, he donated a good deal of merchandise from his very own store."

"All damaged, I bet," Dom muttered.

"I didn't examine it myself personally, Dom," Esther said. "No one complained so I'm sure there couldn't have been too much wrong with it."

"How about the funny money?" Dom asked. "Who took care of that?"

"Why . . . Jerry did," Esther said. "Who else? Certainly not the rabbi."

"*Dom*," Toni said sharply. "You got something to say to

321

Esther, spit it out. Otherwise, make yourself useful and go get us all some danish.''

"If you're going out, Dom," Esther said politely, "bring me back a couple of glazed doughnuts, would you?"

"Esther," Enid called out from the front of the shop, "remember the diet."

"What diet?" Esther answered, grateful that the subject had just come up in conversation so that she could tell everyone the good news. "I'm allowed. I've got my doctor's permission. . . ."

"What doctor?" Enid asked. "Sounds like someone I should see."

"A Park Avenue *specialist*," Esther said. "A *very* big man in his field. As a matter of fact, Dom, it was because of Jerry that I finally went to see him."

"Don't leave us hanging, Esther," Enid urged, coming out from in back of the register. "What did he tell you?"

"Well." Esther smiled. "I'm *not* pregnant."

"Mazel tov," Enid said.

"But I do have a gland problem."

"Esther," Enid beamed, "that's *wonderful*."

"I know," Esther said happily. "I know."

"Enid," Toni cautioned. "It's not serious, is it, Esther? Tell me it isn't . . ."

"Not serious at all," Esther said. "I go see him once a week and he gives me a shot for my thyroid. He guarantees I'll lose two to three pounds before I see him again no matter *what* I eat. Starches, sugars, whatever."

"So where does the weight come from?" Toni asked, as though she had an ounce of fat on her anywhere.

"Water," Esther said flatly, repeating what the doctor had told her. "Why I didn't go see him years ago, I can't imagine."

"This," Enid said, pressing down a button on the register so that its little bell rang loudly as the cash drawer popped open before her, "calls for a celebration. Some *real* eating." Taking out a couple of wrinkled dollar bills from the till, Enid held them up and looked at Dom. "So?" she said. "You're going out, or what?"

With a bewildered expression on his face, Dom said, "I thought we were talking about Jerry Kahn. . . ."

"We *were*," Toni said sharply, looking right through Dom once again, just daring him to open a mouth to her. "Now, we're not. Topics change, Dom. Just like people."

"You're a friend of Jerry's?" Dom asked Esther, completely ignoring Toni's challenge.

"We are social acquaintances," Esther admitted. "Working so closely together, the way we've been, it's only natural . . ."

"Of course," Enid put in. "It happens all the time."

Dom looked wildly around the shop, as though he had just realized that no one was on his side. Then he took a deep breath and said, "I don't even know why I bother. No one listens."

"Oh, we listen to you, Dom," Toni sneered. "All the time. It's more entertaining than the radio."

"I don't know why," Dom repeated. "Except that I'm headed for Miami myself in a couple days."

"Provided you make enough today for your plane fare," Toni noted.

"Oh, I'll make it, Toni," Dom said angrily, finally rising to the bait. "Don't worry about that. Because when it comes to hair, I know how to cut. I'll make enough to pay you back in full and still fly first class. Because that's the kind of guy I really am. First class. All the way. And once I'm gone, I'm *never* coming back. This beauty parlor, everyone in it, and the whole neighborhood can fall into the ocean for all I care. . . ."

"Thanks for all the good wishes, Dom," Toni said icily, staring down at her perfect fingernails. "They're certainly appreciated."

"What did I do, huh?" Dom pleaded, "that anyone else who needed a little cash in a hurry to straighten out a debt wouldn't have done? *Huh?* I was going to put it back. But did I ever get the chance? No way," he said, answering his own question before anyone else could. "Which is just what I get for mixing business with pleasure. My old man always told me, 'Never stick your dick in the cash register' and I should have listened."

"Dom," Toni said slowly, "you *are* disgusting."

"Am I? Funny you didn't say that down in Nassau. But then this is the thanks I get for putting out for a broad who can only think business, business, business all the time. Even between the sheets. She wants her money's worth, no matter what time of day or night it is. . . ."

"Dom," Toni ordered, "shut up."

"What you need, Toni," Dom said, turning to face her at last, "is a younger man. Some kid who can get a rod on whenever you snap your fingers and then thank you afterwards for being so nice to him. . . ."

323

"Thanks for the advice, Dom," Toni said. "I already got one. And he's beautiful. A real gentleman, too. With looks like a nightclub singer and manners. Which is something you *never* heard about."

"It goes both ways, baby," Dom snapped. "Or did you think Marlene and I were talking hair when you walked in on us last week in the back of the shop? I put it to her while you were out to lunch, baby. And you know what? She *thanked* me for it. Said I was the best she ever had, what with her boyfriend waiting for the priest to say it was okay for them to do it on their wedding night. . . ."

"You lowlife scumbag!" Toni shouted. "You never were any fucking help in this shop. Now, you're *fucking* the help? Forget I promised you the day."

Charging over to the register, Toni shouldered Enid to one side. Then she reached into the cash drawer. Withdrawing a handful of bills, she waved them in the air. "Here's your plane fare, Mr. First Class," she said scornfully. "Take the night coach. Do whatever you like. Only get out of my shop before I have someone *throw* you out."

"Who?" Dom demanded. "Your new boyfriend?"

"He could do it. He *works* for a living, Dom. With his *hands*."

"Hey," Dom said, throwing up his palms in a gesture of total surrender. "I'm gone." Gathering up all his combs and brushes, he began moving towards the door. Then he looked at Esther and stopped dead in his tracks. "Only before I go, let me ask you one question. Esther, you running any more of those nights?"

For a moment, Esther did not know whether or not to answer. Of course, she was totally on Toni's side in this matter. Dom was an animal all right. She had known that the very first time she had seen him. What with his expensive clothes and his elaborately curled hair, he had always looked to her like a slab of raw meat hanging in a butcher's freezer. Still, if Dom knew something about Jerry, it might be worth her while to find out about it now.

"I think so," she said. "Maybe one a month. Just until we get back on our feet financially. . . ."

"Feet?" Dom said, the word taking on a whole new meaning in his mouth. "You're on your knees right now, only you don't know it. In six months, you'll be flat on your ass wishing you never heard of Jerry Kahn in the first place. Let me ask you

324

something, Esther. You know the Sand and Sea Beach Club on Long Island?''

"The Sand and Sea?" Esther said. "Of course I do. Nat Weiss belongs. *Very* exclusive.''

"Well, a Mr. Anthony Balbano owns it. . . ."

"*Balbano?*" Toni said in surprise. "You're sure?"

"He *owns* it," Dom repeated. "Not that his name is on any of the papers or anything. Him and Jerry Kahn and a few other of your *lantzmen* from shul like to get together to play gin rummy by the pool there in the afternoon. Then maybe they all go out together to Belmont to catch the last half of the card. . . ."

"Card?" Esther said. "What card?"

"The racing card, Esther," Dom said. "The *ponies*.''

"So?" Esther said. "What a man does with his free time is *his* business. . . ."

"Ask Jerry Kahn about the week he had after they buried his wife. He went wild. Lost four in a row at Belmont five days running and did even worse at the card table every afternoon. See, he didn't figure he would ever have to pay up because all he really wanted was to crawl into the ground with her and have them shovel the dirt on his head. . . ."

"Enough," Esther ordered. "Jerry Kahn is a *fine* man. A well-respected business person in the neighborhood. Ask anyone. His store is a going concern. His personal life I won't discuss with anyone. . . ."

"Listen," Dom said, leering so Esther would know just how much he was really enjoying dragging someone who was undeniably above him in every way down to his own degenerate level, "I don't give two shits about his personal life. Jerry Kahn *owes*. That's all I'm trying to tell you. Just like I did when I grabbed that loan yesterday. Only he'd have to drive a panel truck filled with cash to pay them back. So ask him how come he all of a sudden got so active in your shul. Ask him what they think of him in that temple where he used to belong out on the Island. . . ."

"*Dom?*" Toni called out softly, as though the two of them were completely alone in the shop. "Hear this?"

Slowly Toni waved the sheaf of bills in her hand back and forth so that they rustled softly. "It's calling your name," Toni cooed. "Saying, 'Bye-bye, Dom, hope the sun in Florida agrees with the Man Tan on your face.' "

Although Esther could not imagine any man she had ever known taking this from a woman who was half his size, Dom just stood there with his mouth open and his eyes going from her to Toni and back again. Then he went right towards Toni. Boldly, Toni stood her ground. As though it was coming to him, Dom took the money from her hand. This was too much for words. Esther had now seen everything.

Grabbing his coat from a hook by the register, Dom yanked open the door. Spinning on his heel, he looked around the shop as though he was about to deliver his farewell address. Only the words would not come. For a second, he sputtered and gasped. Then he swallowed hard and said, "You ask him, Esther. About Mr. Anthony Balbano and all that funny money he printed up that you had to cash in for him. Ask Jerry where he took the proceeds the very next day. See if he tells you the truth."

Then Dom went out into the street, slamming the door shut behind him. The last Esther saw of him was the shiny, bright green flash of Toni's money dangling from his hand. "Why do I have the feeling that we'll be hearing from Dom again?" Enid asked quietly, addressing the question to no one in particular.

"Because, Enid," Toni said slowly, sighing with her entire body, "even in Florida, there are tracks where dogs and horses run in circles while people bet their hard-earned money on them. There must be at least as many women down there who are as stupid as I've been. . . ."

For a second, Esther thought that Toni was actually going to start crying. It would have been totally out of character for her to do this, especially where an out-and-out louse like Dom was concerned. The man had just never been any good. There was nothing else to be said about him. What Esther herself was going to do with the information that Dom had given her about Jerry Kahn, she did not yet know. Of one thing, she was certain. Before the week was out, she would have to sit down with Jerry for a very serious heart-to-heart talk.

If Jerry Kahn was in some kind of trouble that he had not yet told her about, she was certain that she could help. The man had barely recovered from the shock of his wife's tragic death. Perhaps Jerry had gone a little crazy when Pauline died. It was only natural. Just because Las Vegas Night had not turned out to be the raging financial success it had seemed to be was no reason to doubt Jerry's motives. Still, it could not hurt to call the temple out on Long Island where Jerry had once belonged. Probably, she should have done this before she had ever taken him with her to that board meeting.

"So, Enid?" Esther said, in order to give Toni some time to regain control of herself. "We'll get some danish? Or are we going to starve ourselves to death today for no good reason?"

"*Danish*," Enid said positively, leaving no doubt in anyone's mind that this was the only proper course of action considering the circumstances. "I'll go out and bring some back myself. Toni. You're all right?"

"Fine," Toni said, anxiously biting the corner of her lower lip, so that Esther knew immediately that she was still upset. Then Toni shook her head from side to side as though to clear her vision. "Come, Esther," she said. "Let's go in back and I'll give you a wash. I'm only sorry that you had to be in here to see all this."

"Toni," Esther said gently. "Better me than a stranger."

"Do you believe this woman, Enid?" Toni asked. Taking Esther's hand, she began walking with her towards the sink in back. "What a doll."

Esther smiled to let Toni know that she was still with her, all the way. The creamy snow covered slope down which Esther had been sailing lately was still rushing up to meet her. Perhaps the slope was not as smooth as she had once thought it to be, but so what? With the wind blowing through her hair and the trees sliding by on either side, Esther was still gliding down the path that led towards better times and the kind of real happiness that she had always deserved.

If it was true for her, then it could also be true for Enid and Toni and all the other women like them. Esther could feel it in her bones. God willing, it was going to be a good new year for all of them, no matter what.

CHAPTER THIRTY

HAVING ONLY JUST hung away the fine black wool overcoat with the thick Persian lamb collar that Sol Stryker had obtained for him at a wonderful discount some two years ago, the rabbi shut the door of the hallway closet only to be greeted by the sight of his wife coming towards him. Daniel stood by her side, clinging tightly with his tiny hand to her outstretched fingers. Both of them, he realized, were dressed as though they were going out.

"What is this, Leah?" the rabbi asked in surprise. "Over the telephone only an hour ago, I told you distinctly that I would be coming home for lunch today."

"As you can plainly see, Simeon," Leah replied, "I am taking Daniel with me so that you can eat your lunch in peace and quiet."

"Fine. Good. Thank you very much for the favor. Precisely *where* you are taking him is the question."

"To shul, dear. Where else?"

"My dear wife," the rabbi replied, "at the moment, the shul is completely empty. Except for Solomon. And if you have an appointment with him, I can tell you . . . he is fast asleep."

"Sylvia Stryker asked those of us on the steering committee to spend a few moments with her this afternoon in the downstairs ballroom."

"For what purpose, if I may ask?"

"To discuss decorations," Leah told him. "For the New Year's Eve Gala," she added, as though he should have known this already without having to ask.

"The Gala," the rabbi repeated. "The next function in our shul's never ending social calendar. Has Nat Weiss offered to bring in roulette wheels so that at the exact stroke of midnight, everyone can have money riding on the New Year?"

"Hardly, Simeon," Leah answered, dismissing the question

with a laugh. "We just have to discuss where the balloons and the crepe paper will go. You know how such things come up."

"Indeed I do," he noted. Clearing his throat, he added, "Let us hope that this affair is a bit more successful in the long run than Las Vegas Night. All that *gareider* at the board meeting. All that infighting and commotion. And what for? *Gur-nisht*," he said, breaking the Yiddish word for "nothing" into two distinct syllables. "*Gehackta leber* and *tsouris*. That's what we got from it, instead of money."

"Well," Leah said distractedly, "at least they tried."

Opening the door of the closet, she took her own very plain cloth coat from its hanger. As she drew the coat on over her shoulders, the rabbi could not help noticing how it looked in comparison to his own coat of fine black wool. The time had come for him to speak to Sol Stryker about getting Leah a quality winter garment at a price he could afford. The time had come for him to speak to Sol about many things, both personal and professional. "Maybe," Leah went on, "they'll do better at the next one."

"What next one?" the rabbi asked.

"I heard they're planning another Las Vegas Night," she said casually, dropping this bombshell without so much as the blink of an eye.

"Who said?" he demanded anxiously, having heard nothing of the kind himself.

"Sylvia. I guess she heard it from Sol."

"From Sol?" the rabbi said. "From *Sol*?" he repeated. "How is it that lately *everyone* seems to hear from Sol but us? When you yourself are such great friends with his wife. Such a *bosom* buddy, so to speak. . . ."

Having selected the phrase with care, the rabbi watched with satisfaction as Leah's left hand, the plain gold wedding band prominent on her third finger, went automatically to the yoke of her dress. Nervously, she stroked the spot where her bones met just above those breasts that he still found so eternally distracting. "Maybe," the rabbi continued, "you could ask why her esteemed husband has not yet had the courtesy to respond to our dinner invitation?"

"I already did," Leah said, stooping over to help Daniel into his small coat, one that the rabbi himself had purchased, and at cost, directly from Sol's main warehouse.

"You asked? Already?" the rabbi said. "*Nu?*"

"He's having trouble in the firm."

"Sol?" the rabbi exclaimed. "But how can this be? The man is a *genius* at what he does."

"Not money troubles, Simeon. Internal difficulties."

Before the rabbi could form another question in his mind, Leah held up her hand like a policeman directing traffic at a busy intersection. "Don't ask me any more, Simeon," she warned him. "Please. I promised Sylvia."

"You *promised* her?" he said. "This means you already know."

"Put it this way," Leah said, giving in a bit to his insatiable curiosity. "Sol may have to make some changes that will result in all our lives becoming a little easier."

"*Nat?*" the rabbi said, getting it immediately. "He'll fire Nat?"

"Nothing from me, Simeon," Leah said stubbornly, shaking her head from side to side. "Not a word."

"This I just cannot believe," the rabbi said, sinking into the chair by the closet door. The news had hit him just that heavily. "They're brothers-in-law, Leah," he said. "How can he fire him?"

Leah shrugged. "Business is business," she said simply, as if that explained it all.

"In America, certainly," the rabbi whispered, still shocked by what she had told him. "Money *is* thicker than blood. Or water. . . ."

The rabbi took a deep breath. It was just as well that he would be eating by himself today. He needed time to consider this news. The prospect of life at Ahavath Mizrach without Nat Weiss always on his back, pressing, probing, and constantly *shtipping* him to do what he did not wish to do, was far too staggering to digest all at once. Instead, like an expensive steak, it had to be cut slowly into small pieces so that the real flavor could be truly savored.

If Nat Weiss lost his job as vice-president of Stryker Togs, everyone in shul would know about it soon enough. Bad news always traveled fast at Ahavath Mizrach. This particular bit of gossip would move with the speed of light, appearing on everyone's lips at the very same time as if by magic. The rabbi sighed out loud. With the fingers of his right hand, he stroked at the corner of his mouth. Finally, it was all becoming clear to him. Now he new why Sol had stayed away from services for the past few months.

For the eminent patriarch of the temple to first have to greet Nat on Shabbos and then actually pray alongside him, while knowing that soon he would be dismissing the man from his job, would have been torture of the most exquisite kind, especially for one so sensitive and refined as Sol. The rabbi would have not wished such a situation on his very worst enemy. Poor Sol. Poor Nat. Everyone involved was to be pitied.

Of course, the power vacuum that would be created on the board when Nat stepped down as president of the synagogue would only benefit Simeon Hakveldt. Without a strong and powerful leader dictating policy, the board could hardly be expected to go looking for a new rabbi when his current contract expired. Still, at the moment, it was not of himself but of Nat that the rabbi was thinking.

Nat Weiss had to be at least his age, if not older. In other words, far too old to go looking for work with a résumé in one hand and a rolled up newspaper in the other, the available jobs circled in red on the classified pages. Besides, with an attitude like the one Nat had, what employer in his right mind would want to offer the man a job? Nat Weiss was a boss, not an employee. He could no more take orders from anyone but Sol than continue on as president of the shul once everyone had learned of his plight.

No, Nat certainly would not find it easy shopping for work in today's job market. The rabbi was sure of this. If, God forbid, he himself was suddenly forced to find a new temple to serve, he would lose his mind. Simply, there was just no way in the world he could bring himself to do it. He no longer had the burning desire that had driven him when he had been a younger man. After a certain point in one's life, holding on to what you already had was all that mattered. He himself had reached that point long ago at Ahavath Mizrach. The same was undeniably true for Nat at Stryker Togs.

The rabbi was so completely lost in thought that he barely noticed his wife slowly moving towards the door as she made her goodbyes. Absentmindedly, he nodded to her. At the very last second, he managed to flash Daniel a special smile. Then he laced his fingers together in a prayerful little steeple, got to his feet, and went into the dining room to eat his lunch.

With great satisfaction, the rabbi noted that Leah had in fact laid out a beautiful meal for him before leaving the house. All the dishes were arranged in a respectful little semicircle in front of his chair at the head of the table. Carefully, the rabbi took stock of what was waiting for him. A plate of herring in wine sauce that he himself had brought home from his mother's apartment only last week. A plate of smoked carp, each piece charred to perfection yet still slippery with its own rich oil. A nice cucumber salad dusted with spicy red paprika. A whole small round rye bread on a cutting board, with a knife beside it.

Sitting down, the rabbi dug in with both hands. As he ate, he chewed with his mouth wide open, as was his habit whenever he dined alone and there was no one present to chide him about his table manners. Eagerly, he tore apart the bread with his fingers cramming the soft, fragrant dough into his mouth to cushion his palate against the sharp taste of the herring.

After he had eaten his fill, the rabbi sat back heavily in his chair, letting out his breath in a sigh of complete contentment Only now could he relax, certain that he would make it through until supper tonight. Undeniably, a man thought differently when his belly was full. Once hunger had released its crushing grip on the brain, the mind was truly free to wander, considering matters of a more abstract, universal nature. The rabbi did not doubt that most of man's greatest insights and inspirations had come right after a meal like the one he had just devoured.

As he weighed the changes that the new year might bring to Ahavath Mizrach, the rabbi slowly began gathering together the tiny crumbs of bread that littered the starched white tablecloth before him. Moistening the tips of his fingers with his tongue, he slowly rolled the crumbs into larger balls. On the first day of Rosh Hashanah, such crumbs had served as symbols of sins and broken promises, to be cast into the waters of the bay during *Tashlikh*. Today, they were merely crumbs of bread once more, to be eaten or thrown away, as he chose.

Tentatively putting his fingers to his mouth, the rabbi dropped several of the little bread balls onto his tongue. To his great delight, he realized that even after the fine meal he had eaten bread could still taste sweet. As a dessert, it was far more pleasing to him than the fanciest flambé any rich man's cook might concoct. Bread was basic to life itself. Yet its very essence was mutable, and hard to categorize. It was a subject to which a serious scholar could easily devote an entire lifetime of study.

A serious scholar Simeon Hakveldt knew that he would never

be. Simply, he did not have it in him. So it was to Nat Weiss that the rabbi's mind returned once more. How the mighty had fallen! And what a grievous fall it was.

The more the rabbi thought about it, the more he came to see that Nat had been done in by America itself. America, the wrecking yard of tradition. America, the bitter land of exile, where a restless wind blew constantly from coast to coast, sweeping away the traditional Jewish way of life in one community after the other. Nat Weiss was not a villain. Not at all. He was a victim of the American disease. An overwhelming desire for *gelt* and the power that came with it.

The rabbi recalled again the deathless words of the *unesanah tokef,* the wondrous poem of a prayer composed by the great Rabbi Amnon even as he was dying from the wounds inflicted upon him by the cruel tyrants who had ruled Mayence. "On Rosh Hashanah their destiny is inscribed and on Yom Kippur it is sealed, how many shall pass away and how many shall be brought into existence; who shall live and who shall die; who shall come to a timely end and who to an untimely end; . . . who shall be at peace and who shall be tormented; who shall become poor and who shall become rich; who shall be lowered and who shall be raised."

On Yom Kippur, Nat Weiss had sealed his fate. That day, Nat had first judged himself by his actions, and then again by his stubborn refusal to take responsibility for them afterwards. Nat would now have to pay in full for what he had done. God was good. God was just. Although He worked in ways mysterious to man, His power was over all.

In the coming year, Simeon Hakveldt would prosper. He would be raised while Nat Weiss was lowered. Although the verdict might have seemed cruel to some, in his heart the rabbi knew that justice had been done. Gratefully, Simeon Hakveldt reflected on his own good fortune. He had his fine temple, his wife and children, and this home. And he had something more. Despite all odds, he had somehow managed to find peace of mind, even here in America, a land where that commodity was so rare as to be worth more than gold itself.

CHAPTER THIRTY-ONE

ALL MORNING LONG, an icy wind had been scouring the streets, forcing people to stay indoors. Even the post office had been virtually deserted, with practically no business at all coming in over the front counter. At the moment, the few hardy souls who had ventured from their homes to do some shopping at midday were scurrying madly for shelter against the buildings while holding on to their hats and coats as though it was March and not December.

As Morty drove slowly down the avenue, he kept one eye open for a parking spot close to the store so that he would not have to waste what little was left of his precious lunch hour by walking too far in the cold. In a halting and disconnected manner, he hummed along with the song coming from the car radio. Guy Lombardo and his Royal Canadians were playing "Auld Lang Syne" as only they could and always seemed to do at this time of year. Although the song's sad, sweet strains were supposed to evoke waves of instant nostalgia and fond memory, they served only to remind Morty that soon he would have to once again pick up a brand new calendar for the apartment from the bank across the street.

Morty Bindel would not be going out tomorrow night. He had never gone out on New Year's Eve and he never would. Much like Christmas, it just was not his holiday to celebrate. Besides, what would he miss by staying home? Nothing but a lot of noisy, drunken confusion, and then on the morning after, a splitting headache and an upset stomach that no amount of Pepto-Bismol or Alka-Seltzer could soothe.

Instead, on New Year's Day, Morty would get up bright and early, feeling fine. He would sit himself down in front of his wonderful television set with his usual breakfast and his stamps, watching as the Rose Bowl Parade came to him from Pasadena in living color, with hours and hours of football to follow.

334

Perhaps the coming year would bring remarkable changes in some people's lives. His would remain much the same. Even if his kid moved out of the apartment soon, as Morty fully expected him to do now that he had some money of his own from having worked in Avenue Station, his own routine would not change one bit.

It was not his fault that Paulie's term of service as a Christmas temp had convinced the kid once and for all that his future did not lie in the post office. Who knew? Perhaps it was better this way for all concerned. It was now clear to Morty that his son had to leave home again and again in order to become a man. Precisely why this was, he did not know. Once the kid had grown up, maybe he would then be able to come back and really appreciate the place where he had been born and raised. In any event, it was *his* struggle now, one in which Morty knew that he could no longer offer any kind of real help or advice. At least he had tried.

Pulling the car into a tow-away zone on the corner, Morty shut off the ignition with one hand while reaching under the dashboard with the other. Taking out the official looking "United States Post Office—Business" sign that Mo Tannenbaum had printed up for his friends, Morty placed it in the windshield so that no cop on patrol could possibly miss seeing it. Then he slid quickly out of the car and into the street. Carefully, he made certain to lock both doors before running towards the sidewalk with his head bent against the wind.

It was not until after Morty had closed the front door behind him and been swallowed up into the murky deep sea gloom of the store that he realized how much the place had changed since he had been in here last. It still smelled the same all right, that dense, impenetrable odor of dry goods in bulk mixed with dust that came rolling up from the scarred old wooden floor beneath his feet. But the goods themselves had been rearranged. Everything was now laid out in a completely different manner.

Menswear was heaped in tilting piles where once hardware had been. Fancy metal display racks had replaced the ancient tables on which mounds of women's clothing had perpetually threatened to tumble suddenly to the floor. The entire back wall of the store was now covered by an overwhelming display of children's clothing. Skimpy summer sunsuits, little corduroy walking outfits, and padded winter coats with tiny mittens pinned to the sleeves were hanging in disarray all the way from the ceiling to the floor.

Perhaps there had been a sudden baby boom in the neighborhood. If so, no one had told Morty about it.

Several stout middle-aged saleswomen were nervously patrolling the aisles, rushing over to customers before they could make up their minds whether or not to buy an item. Over the years, Morty had always done all his own shopping here without the slightest bit of help from anyone. Shoving aside dusty bales of merchandise with his hands, he had rummaged freely through the open cartons that had once been stacked everywhere.

Often, the treasures he had unearthed had carried no price tags at all on them, leaving him completely free to bargain with the former proprietor by offering what *he* thought they were worth. More than once, Morty had actually gone home with an item at *his* price. No more. That the changes made in here were going to cost him money, Morty knew already. While there was nothing he could do about that, he still had no intention of letting anyone wait on him, most certainly not any of these women. Given a few quiet moments in which to orient himself, Morty was positive that he could still find what he needed all on his own.

Before he could move out of the doorway, the largest saleswoman descended upon him. With her mouth closed, she was slowly chewing gum, her jaws grinding so heavily against each other that Morty could almost hear the sound of bone on bone. With a pencil stuck at a crazy angle in her thick, unnaturally red hair and a pair of half-glasses swinging from a braided silver chain looped around her neck, the woman was far too formidable for Morty to ignore. "So, mister," she demanded, her voice so cracked and hoarse that Morty wondered whether she had swallowed a mouthful of sandpaper, "what can I help you find?"

"Uh . . . something I need for myself," he said vaguely, unwilling to give her any more information than was absolutely necessary. Even a prisoner of war was required by the Geneva Convention to supply the enemy only with his name, rank, and serial number.

"Galoshes?" she demanded. "Suspenders? A bathing suit? It's a big store, mister."

"Well," he said slowly, "since I'm a man, and what I need would naturally be in menswear . . . couldn't I get a *man* to help me?"

The woman's mouth dropped open a fraction of an inch. Morty could see bright red lipstick smears on both of her front incisors. She was a meat eater all right. And a blood drinker as well.

"Mister," she said, looking at Morty as though he had completely lost his mind, "and if you were looking to buy something for a baby? Would you expect an infant to wait on you?"

Rather than answer her question, Morty reached out for one of the soft white canvas golf hats lying in a pile by the front register, marked down to the bargain price of a dollar ninety-nine. Putting the hat on his head, he pulled its floppy brim low over his eyes. Leaning towards the woman, he said, "So? What do you think, miss? Is it the *real* me, or no?"

"I'm sure I couldn't say," she answered. "Is this the item you desire?"

Morty took the hat off his head and stared at it for a second before throwing it back on the pile. "As a matter of fact," he said, "it isn't."

The woman threw up both of her hands in surrender. Spinning angrily on her heel, she called out, "*Jerry!* Front, please."

From the back of the store, where the darkness seemed to grow thicker and even more threatening, a man who looked to be about Morty's age came walking slowly towards the front register. The man was wearing a pair of tinted yellow glasses, as though the sun was even now shining brightly in his eyes. He also looked strangely familiar, although at the moment Morty could not place him.

"I can't handle them all, Jerry," the woman complained as she shuffled towards the back of the store. "I'm only made of flesh and blood, not iron."

"Then why don't I take care of the gentleman, Frances?" the familiar looking man said in a very professional way. Right away, Morty knew that he was now dealing with the person who ran the store. Quite possibly, this would save him both time and trouble, not to mention money.

"Now, sir," the man said. "Precisely what can I help you find?"

"*Gottkes,*" Morty said. "Underwear."

No amount of money in the world could have persuaded Morty to pursue this subject with the woman who had descended upon him without his having asked for her help. It was nothing personal. He had never let himself be examined by a woman doctor either. About some things, he was just particular.

"Of course," the familiar looking man said pleasantly, as if he understood. "Right this way. Please follow me."

Obediently, Morty fell into step behind him. The two of them

337

moved towards the back of the store past displays of merchandise that Morty himself could not imagine anyone ever purchasing. And yet, for every piece of shit in the world, no matter how low, there was always a buyer. Sooner or later, Morty knew, someone would come in and take all of this stuff away with them, provided that the price was right. "I think, sir," the man who obviously owned the store called back proudly over his shoulder, "you'll find that we now stock a very complete selection."

"Oh yes?" Morty said in surprise. "Well, good. *Good.* This didn't used to be, you know. Certainly, this is good news."

Both men slowed to a stop before a table covered to a depth of nearly six inches by little cellophane wrapped packages containing underwear of every size, kind, and description. Much of it was in wild pastel colors that Morty himself would never have been caught dead wearing. "Excuse me," the owner of the store said, looking Morty over very carefully, "but my name's Jerry Kahn. I don't think I've ever had the pleasure. . . ."

"Morty Bindel," Morty said quickly, shaking the hand that had been extended to him. "How is it that we know one another, Jerry?"

"From the shul. Las Vegas Night? The big drawing . . ."

"A-*ha*," Morty sighed. "The big drawing. Yes. Yes. Now I recall . . ."

"I know your father as well," Jerry said, "from saying *Kaddish.* For my late wife, may she rest in peace . . ."

"*Or-mayn,*" Morty said automatically, as was only proper. "Tell me, didn't you run that whole *she*-bang for them?" Jerry Kahn nodded. "I thought so," Morty said. "So how did you make out in the end? Financially-wise, I mean. The aggravation, I'm sure, was unbelievable."

"*Un*-believable," Jerry agreed, leaning over the table to pick through the packages until he found one he wanted. "Now, these," he said, showing the package to Morty, "have an elastic waistband, reinforced. Snug, but very comfortable."

"Never wear them," Morty said. "They leave a ring around your *pipik.* Like a tire track . . ."

"You prefer a fly front?"

"Why? They invented something to replace it?"

"These days they make them with buttons, Velcro fasteners, snaps, don't ask. Jockeys?"

"Boxers," Morty told him.

"Boxers," Jerry repeated. "Briefs or regulars?"

338

"Regulars. You know . . . droopy. The bigger, the better. I like the room. To tell you the truth, Jerry, the kind I prefer are the ones they used to sell in the Army-Navy Stores."

"You mean the World War Two models?" Jerry asked. Morty nodded. Jerry laughed and shook his head. "We're a pair of AKs all right. *Alte kackers,*" he said, as though Morty might have missed his meaning the first time around. "What division were you in?"

"First Army," Morty told him proudly. "Fourth Infantry."

"We took you guys in at Normandy," Jerry said. "First wave, right? I was a Navy man myself. LCTs."

"How about that?" Morty said. "Is it a small world, or not?"

"Too small," Jerry said. Tearing apart a package, a gesture Morty appreciated immediately as something that only a *real* salesman would have the nerve to do, Jerry unfolded a pair of shorts that Morty would have bought right on the spot had it not been for the unfamiliar material. "Jerry," Morty said apologetically, "pardon me for asking, but since we were once comrades in arms and all . . . what is this made of?"

"Dynel," Jerry told him. "Sheer stretch." Poking his finger obscenely in and out of the fly front to demonstrate its flexibility, he said, "See? When you give, *it* gives."

"To tell you the truth, Jerry," Morty said, making a joke, "I don't give all that much any more. *If* you know what I mean. Besides, next to my body, I prefer only cotton."

"Cotton," Jerry said. "Cotton. I know I got some back here somewhere." Bending over the table, Jerry began rooting around in a sloppy pile of underwear that had long since been separated from its packaging. Stepping back with the exact pair Morty wanted dangling from his finger, Jerry held it up so that Morty could survey it from every angle. Sure enough, it was the real McCoy, a pair of the very same oversized droopy white cotton drawers, starred all over with tiny multicolored flowers, that Morty had been wearing ever since he had been separated from the Army at the end of World War II.

Removing his yellow glasses to reveal a pair of eyes that to Morty looked bloodshot and strained, Jerry squinted at the label. "Just like I thought," he said. "Fruit of the Loom. Old reliable."

"Looks good," Morty said. "How's the price?"

Squinting at the little tag by the label, Jerry said, "Two and a quarter."

"*Each?*" Morty said. "How about for an old and *very* reliable customer like myself? Who you already know from shul?"

"Buck eighty," Jerry said quickly.

Morty said nothing. Even in the old days, everything in the store had always had two prices, the one they quoted you and the one you paid at the front register. So far, Jerry had not done a thing for him.

"Need a couple pair?" Jerry asked.

"Not really," Morty said.

"Take six," Jerry urged. "And I'll throw in one free. That way, you're covered for every day of the week."

"I don't really know if I need that many, Jerry," Morty said.

"Who knows if you'll even *find* them here the next time you come in," Jerry warned. "They could discontinue this style tomorrow. Believe me, it happens all the time. Tell you what. Take six, I'll throw one in free, and knock off the tax. Make it worth your while."

"Fine," Morty said boldly, deciding to live a little and treat himself right today. "You got a deal."

"Need socks?" Jerry asked, pulling six more pairs of underwear from the pile that he bundled quickly up under his arm.

"Thanks, but no."

"Shirts?" Jerry continued, still plugging. "Ties? A belt? Got them all in stock. Make you a nice price on whatever you need."

"Maybe next time," Morty said, unwilling to buy any more than he already had just because he would be getting it at discount.

"You know your own mind all right," Jerry conceded. "I give you that. Let's go up front and I'll throw these in a bag for you."

Jerry turned and began walking towards the register. Morty trailed behind, marveling in his own mind at what a *mensh* this fellow really was. To put up with what he probably had to deal with day after day in here and yet still have the time and patience to really take care of a customer was something all right. As the two men passed through the section of the store in which the out-and-out junk was piled high, Morty reached for a shiny plastic imitation alligator wallet. "Jerry," he asked, holding it up in his hand. "Permit me to ask you a question. From such shit, *kennst machen* a living?"

"Certainly," Jerry said positively. "*More* than a living."

"*Gefalich*," Morty said, shaking his head in wonder. "I give you credit. Anyone who uses his head to make a buck . . . I respect."

Jerry Kahn acknowledged the compliment with a nod of his head. Then he went behind the front counter and began ringing up the sale. Looking past the register at Morty, he said, "What a great old guy your father is. One of a kind."

"Thank you," Morty said humbly. "I feel that way myself. They threw away the mold when they made him."

"If you don't mind my asking," Jerry said, "how does he live?"

"Beg pardon?"

"I mean, who pays his way? I know he can't be getting by on what the shul gives him in salary for being *shamus*."

"No way," Morty said loudly. Jerry's remark had touched a sympathetic chord. "Not when the rebbe is always looking out for his own pocket. I help him some, when I can. He makes a little by saying *Kaddish*. That you probably knew already. Also, he gets restitution."

"Restitution?" Jerry said. "What's that?"

"Payments," Morty told him. "Every couple months, some country in Europe trying to buy back its conscience with money sends him a couple bucks. Strictly nickel and dime. Since he didn't have all that much *before* the Nazis came, he gets . . . minimum."

"*Restitution*," Jerry said again, as though he had heard the word for the very first time and was trying to define it by using it over and over in conversation. "Is that what they call it? A whole country trying to pay off what they owe, huh? *Un*-believable. I mean, it's hard enough for a man to do that. When he can't afford to. You know?"

"Not really. Myself, I always pay cash. For everything. It's easier that way."

Jerry Kahn looked at Morty for a second. Then, as though he had heard a noise in back of him, he turned and began staring through the dirty front window of the store into the street. Outside, the freezing wind was still whistling noisily down the avenue, cutting like a knife through the heavy coats of the few passersby who were still out there bravely battling the weather.

Winter had only just begun. Morty knew that there would be months and months of it before spring came once more and a person could actually walk in the street without having to fight for every breath. "You know," Jerry Kahn said, from out of the

341

blue, "what with all this lousy weather we been having since Christmas, lately I've been feeling like someone else is using up all my air. Breathing my oxygen before I can get to it. Ever feel that way yourself?"

"I know just what you mean," Morty said quickly. "It's all the shit they dump in the sewers. Not to mention the garbage they let pile up on the sidewalks."

Jerry Kahn shook his head. "I'm talking about something else, I think. . . ."

"Maybe what you need is a vacation."

"That's it," Jerry Kahn said enthusiastically, as though Morty had just solved the problem for him. "A vacation. From myself."

"To tell you the truth, Jerry," Morty said, "I'm only on my lunch hour. I'd love to stand here and *shmooze* with you but . . ."

"No problem," Jerry said quickly, coming out of the little trance he had gone into right before Morty's eyes. Throwing everything that Morty had bought into a brown paper bag that he crumpled shut at the top, Jerry Kahn took Morty's money. Then he handed him his purchases and his change all at the very same time.

"Come in again soon," Jerry urged. "The store itself will always be here."

"Certainly I will," Morty replied, not at all sure what Jerry meant by this odd remark. "And *very* nice to have met you."

"Please," Jerry said, dodging the compliment with a nod of his head. "The pleasure was all mine."

Morty smiled and made his way back out on to the avenue, where the wind seemed even colder and more deadly than it had been before. There was no denying it. This Jerry Kahn was definitely a perfect gentleman. Right to the bitter end.

CHAPTER THIRTY-TWO

ONLY A MOMENT ago, Esther had been talking on the phone, watching with pleasure as Paulie sat himself down at the table for dinner. Now her entire world had turned itself upside down. Nothing was as it had been before. In years to come, Esther would still see herself as she was at this very moment, frozen in time with the phone hanging from her hand.

"God," she muttered, finally sliding the receiver back into its cradle. "That was *so* strange."

"What was?" her son asked, leaning both of his elbows on the table as she had so often begged him not to do during or before meals.

"The conversation I just had with Jerry Kahn, dear," Esther told him. "Not to mention the little talk I had with the recording secretary of his old shul out on Long Island this afternoon."

"What were you doing, ma? Checking his credit rating?"

"Something like that," Esther admitted, not at all ashamed of what she had done. "I heard some . . . very upsetting news about Jerry that I wanted to make sure was true before I asked him about it. Only he never gave me the chance."

"His wife *isn't* dead?"

"*Paulie*," she said sharply. "Don't make jokes about such things. He's . . . going away," she said slowly, repeating what Jerry had just told her without really believing that it was true.

"Oh yeah? Where to?"

"Las Vegas."

"*Las Vegas?*" her son said, laughing out loud. "How come? So he can learn how the *real* guys run a casino?"

"I'm sure I don't know *why* he's going, dear," Esther replied, although she was fairly certain that she could make a pretty good guess. "He didn't tell me. Most likely, he just wants a little change of scene. I don't have to tell you what the Christmas season must be like in his store. A madhouse . . ."

Esther pulled a chair out from under the table. She had to get off her feet right now. She also needed a cigarette, badly. Only there weren't any in the house. The Park Avenue specialist had told her that it would be better if she cut down on her smoking until he could be absolutely certain that it was only a thyroid problem he was treating. She had sworn to quit right on the spot. So far she had been as good as her word.

Reaching towards the far end of the table, Esther pulled a yellow paper napkin from the fan shaped red plastic holder that she always kept by her father-in-law's chair. Rolling the napkin into a crinkly paper tube, she drew it slowly between her fingers, lacing it up over her thumb and then on towards her pinky. The rough feel of the wadded paper beside each knuckle served to steady her nerves. *It's all closing in on me, Esther,* Jerry had told her. *I have to get away.*

"Okay," her son said cheerfully, failing to sense her mood. "Try this one. When is he coming back?"

"Paulie," Esther said bluntly, looking him right in the face. "I didn't interrogate the man. He told me he was leaving for a little while and I thanked him for having had the courtesy to call. . . ."

"Maybe he just wants to spend New Year's Day in Vegas," Paulie suggested. "So he can bet legally on the bowl games."

Impatiently, Esther dismissed this notion by waving her hand in the air. Then she sighed. "He said something right at the very end of our conversation that was *unbelievable,*" she said.

"What was that?"

"He apologized."

"What for?"

"I don't know, dear. He said . . . if he had caused me or my family any trouble, or hurt our reputation in the shul, I shouldn't hold it against him because he couldn't help himself. His hands were tied. . . ."

"Maybe he's sorry he led you on," Paulie observed, grinning broadly.

"*Please.* He never did that. Oh, I won't deny that I had a wonderful time with him that first night we went out together. I mean, I can't remember when I enjoyed myself more. Still . . . it was *never* serious. How could it have been? A man his age, with a wife dead only a little more than a year, who talked about her constantly? Please," Esther said again, placing the palm of her hand against her throat. "For two people like us, with all that

344

we've been through, it was only . . . *companionship*. Nothing more. I never fooled myself, dear. Not for a second."

Esther stared past her son at the wall. Automatically, she began counting the faded yellow roses on the wallpaper as she always had in the past to make the time pass more quickly. She had told her son only part of the truth. Never before had she admitted that she *had* fooled herself. Not until she had heard Jerry cough, stutter, and then begin to apologize over the phone, confirming more positively than if he had actually said so himself that everything Dom had told her in Toni's shop was true.

A dark black patch had suddenly appeared on the snow white slope of Esther's perfect hill, a rugged outcropping of ragged rocks weathered by time and wind and weather. Her long, swooping descent towards the bottom, and home, had come to an abrupt halt. Once again, she was completely on her own, as she had been so many times before.

"You know, dear," she told her son, "I have the strangest feeling that I'll never see Jerry Kahn again."

"Go on," he snapped, making light of her darkest fears just as his father had always done. "He's only going to Vegas for the weekend. He'll be back."

"I mean that the person I am now will never again see the person that Jerry Kahn once was to me. Isn't that sad?"

"I guess," he said, letting her know immediately that he still did not really understand. But then how could he? Paulie was young.

"In other words," Esther joked, determined to rid herself of the mood of grim despair into which she had fallen after hanging up the phone, "I'll be so thin when he sees me next that he won't even recognize me."

"That's the spirit," Paulie said encouragingly.

"Besides," she added, "you didn't really think I was going to make a stepson out of you at this stage of the game, did you?"

"Who would want to be *my* stepfather?" he asked.

"My feeling exactly," she said, laughing in spite of everything.

The phone rang loudly from across the room. "My, my," Esther said, getting up from the table to answer it. "Isn't it busy around here this evening?"

Putting the phone to her ear, she listened for a moment before cupping her hand over the receiver. "It's for you, dear," she whispered. "A woman. You aren't still writing our home number on the walls of telephone booths in Times Square, are you?"

345

"Yeah, right. For a good time, call Esther Binder. . . ."

"A fresh mouth we know you have, darling," Esther said lightly, not at all offended by her son's remark.

"It's Lesley," he said, looking extremely guilty as he got up from the table to take the phone from her hand. "Did I tell you she's coming in for New Year's Eve?"

"No you didn't, dear. It must have just slipped your mind."

"Well she is.".

"Then at least one of us will have a date tomorrow night."

"Why? Aren't you still going to that party in shul?"

"You bet I am," Esther said, making her mind up on the spot to do just that. "Why wouldn't I? I belonged to the temple before I ever heard of Jerry Kahn. It's still my synagogue, with or without him. Now come, dear. Take the phone. It's long distance."

Handing Paulie the receiver, Esther moved quickly into the kitchen. Noisily, she began busying herself with the casserole that she was preparing for his dinner so that she would not have to listen to his conversation. That Stephanie Weiss had not been good enough for her son, Esther already knew. Instead, he preferred this strange girl from Cambridge whom she still had never met, no doubt for good reason.

As she withdrew the flat ceramic baking dish from the oven, poking at the edges of the brown and bubbling casserole to make certain that it was cooked all the way through in the middle, Esther could not help but wonder whether anything made sense any longer. Paulie had finally come back home and taken an interest in the temple, if only for the sake of his grandfather. Yet now the temple itself was in trouble. Better than most people in the congregation, Esther understood precisely what was currently going on at Ahavath Mizrach.

Five days a week, week in and week out, she dealt with the business of keeping the synagogue alive. A constant stream of bills came across her desk each month that had to be paid. Without Sol Stryker constantly *shtipping* in *gelt* whenever it was needed, the shul simply could not survive for much longer. Las Vegas Night had done nothing to solve the problem. Sooner or later in America, everything came down to profit and loss, twin columns of red and black figures running down opposite sides of neat blue lined ledger paper. No shul could exist for long if its books did not balance. Lately, Ahavath Mizrach had been unable to make even this simple claim.

If, God forbid, the temple did go under, Esther was confident that she could get herself another job somewhere in the neighborhood. Her father-in-law, God willing, would somehow find the strength to walk six or seven blocks farther down the avenue to the next nearest Orthodox shul. Esther's vital connection to Sylvia Stryker, however, would be lost forever.

It was for primarily this reason that she had asked her son to come to dinner tonight. Knowing that her father-in-law would be in shul for *Ma'ariv*, the evening service, she was going to take full advantage of the opportunity to ask Paulie for one last favor. She had already made all the necessary arrangements. Tomorrow was the day. What she needed now was Paulie's cooperation, always the most unpredictable aspect of any plan involving either him or his father. When it came to letting other people help them, neither Paulie nor Morty could exactly be called dependable. It was something in the blood.

Realizing that Paulie was now off the phone, Esther wrapped two thick dish towels around the handles of the casserole dish. Carefully, she lifted it from the oven, placing it on top of the stove to cool. Then she went back into the dining room. "Paulie," she said quickly, "there's something I want you to do for me, darling. Actually, it's more for your benefit than mine. I've set up an appointment for you to see Sol."

"Sol Bender?" he said. "The dentist? My teeth are fine."

"Sol *Stryker*, darling. Now, I know that you may not see the sense in this at the moment but trust me. I *am* older. I *have* been around. It would make me *very* happy if you would go and talk to him."

"About what? Half sizes?"

"That I leave up to you and him, dear. I've spoken to Sylvia about it and it's all set for tomorrow afternoon at five, in Sol's office in the city."

"*Tomorrow?*" he said. "Thanks for all the advance notice."

"I couldn't help the timing, dear. Sol's a *very* busy man. He has to see you tomorrow because on Monday he and Sylvia go off on a skiing trip. Then, directly from there, they fly to West Palm Beach, where they spend an entire month each winter. There just wasn't any other time available."

"What are we supposed to talk about?" he persisted. "Give me a clue."

"I really don't know, dear," Esther said honestly, having not yet thought that far ahead. "Whatever it is that men discuss when they sit down together to talk seriously. *Contacts*," she added, searching for the single word that might describe all that Sol could do for Paulie if he took an interest in him. The Strykers knew absolutely everyone, powerful people with money who sat on the boards of temples, hospitals, and colleges. Sol could do more for her son's future with a single phone call than Morty had in the last twenty years.

"You're not angry with me, are you?" she asked. "I swear to God I only did this for your own good. Believe me, it isn't easy being a mother while trying to think like a father all at the same time."

"Is Sol taking that trip?" Paulie asked suddenly, showing interest for the first time since she had brought the subject up, and for the wrong reason, which was just like him.

"Which trip? Skiing, and then to West Palm Beach? Yes. I only just told you so."

"To *Jerusalem*," Paulie said. "The big grand prize from Las Vegas Night. You forgot already?"

"I wouldn't think so," Esther said, ignoring her son's tone of voice in the hope that he would agree to do as she had asked. "How can he? With his schedule . . ."

"He'd rather go to West Palm Beach than Israel?" Paulie said, wrinkling up his nose in disapproval just as she had seen his father do at least a million times. They were two of a kind all right. A pair of *feinshmeckers*. Born with champagne taste, yet living on beer budgets.

"Dear," Esther said evenly, determined not to let him make her lose her patience, "Sol has already been to the Holy Land. *Seven* times."

"He must have his very own key to the city then, huh?"

"Answer my question, Paulie. Will you go see him?"

"Seven times," he repeated, purposely drawing out the discussion just to annoy her. "It should be someone else's turn then, no? I mean, doesn't that seem reasonable to you?"

"You want to ask Sol that question? *Fine*. Here's your chance to do it. Tomorrow afternoon at five, in his office in the city. Will you go?"

"Sure I will," he said casually, as though it made no difference to him either way. "I'll go. Maybe while I'm there, I can grab something to wear on New Year's Eve. A diaper with a banner attached to go across my chest. So I can appear at midnight with it. . . ."

"On you, darling," Esther said, her face beaming with pleasure now that he finally agreed to listen to her, "I'm sure it would look good. Sit right where you are. I made you that casserole you love so much. . . ."

"Great," he said distractedly. "But where's Pop? I thought we would be eating together. Usually, he *is* home by now, no?"

"Usually he is," Esther agreed. "But you know him. Maybe he stayed behind in shul to put away the books or something. God only knows what he does there these days. Lately, I've given up watching the clock on him."

"Is the casserole hot?"

"No, it's cold. I took it out of the refrigerator instead of the stove."

"I mean, is it *burning* hot?"

"Of course."

"Then why don't I walk over to shul and bring him back so we can eat together?"

"That's a *wonderful* idea," Esther said enthusiastically, suddenly eager to have some time to herself. "You'll probably meet him halfway, coming home. By the time you get back, your dinner will be on the table."

"Okay," he said, getting quickly to his feet and heading for the door.

"Don't dawdle, Paulie," she called out after him. "Please . . ." Before she could complete the sentence, her voice was lost in the sound of the door closing and then the muffled echo of heavy footsteps on the front stairs as her son took them two at a time. To Esther, it sounded as though a herd of cattle had broken loose from some corral and even now was stampeding wildly through the hallway.

With an awful thud, the downstairs door slammed shut. Immediately, the house became completely quiet, as it did only when Esther was here all by herself. Sitting down in her usual place at the table, she stubbornly fought the mad impulse to once again begin counting the tired roses on the wallpaper. Instead, Esther closed her eyes. She saw herself sitting here as she had so many times before. Dinner was already over. Morty was in the living room threading the projector so they could watch one of the badly shot home movies that had been their major source of entertainment before television had come into their lives.

On the cheap, fold-up screen Morty had bought on sale at Sears and Roebuck, Esther saw herself and Paulie as they had been when her son was still a child. The two of them were holding hands as they walked slowly across a broad meadow in Prospect Park on a warm Sunday in spring. Their mouths were open with no sound coming out. Their arms and legs moved spasmodically in an awkward, herky-jerky cadence. Their faces were rubbery with delight.

And for good reason. Not yet one year old, Paulie was already walking by himself. All the while, she could hear Morty the director shouting at them from behind the camera. "Esther! Paulie!" he cried, as though every moment they stood in one place enjoying the sun was costing him money. "These are *moving* pictures. So let's do some moving, huh? A little *life*, please!"

A little life was all that they had shared. A little life that was now conclusively over. Even as Esther sat watching, the film began to tear. The take-up reel started to spin convulsively in erratic, backward circles. In bulging loops, the ancient black-and-white eight-millimeter footage came spooling out of the projector onto the living room floor.

Soon only a single image remained on the screen. A mother and her tiny son laughing in a meadow filled with sunshine as though no force on earth could ever disturb the perfect beauty of the moment. Then the image itself began to flicker, shaking badly for a few seconds until it also disappeared from view.

The bulb in the projector then went dim. Even though the light had failed, Esther still sat in the exact same place, in darkness. She would sit this way forever more. Perhaps Jerry Kahn *had* been her very last chance.

For some people, such chances came and went with astonishing regularity, like subway trains rolling past empty platforms in the middle of the night, adhering to a schedule that never changed no matter what. But not for her. Esther was stranded on a station without a name. Beyond the platform's edge, she could see only darkness, and then beyond that, the faint outline of the third rail, gleaming like death itself above the pebbled ruts that lay below.

That the effortless downhill run she had been enjoying so much lately was over for good, Esther now knew beyond any shadow of a doubt. Despite that, she still possessed a fierce and undying belief that sooner or later it would all work out for the best, for everyone concerned. She would continue on and complete her journey despite the latest obstacle that had just been placed squarely in her path. For her, there was no other way.

CHAPTER THIRTY-THREE

WITH BOTH HANDS full, wanting only to reach up and give a good scratch at the maddening itch inside his nose, the *shamus* of Ahavath Mizrach was halfway down the center aisle and heading for the big walk-in closet at the very back of the shul when it hit him, a temporal throbbing in the forehead just above the left eye, a spinning whirlwind of tiny particles that were dark in color, purple black and spotted both black and purple, turning rapidly like the words of the *Kaddish* made visible in plain air, moving so fast that he alone could read them.

Blessed and praised, glorified and exalted, extolled and honored, adored and lauded. . . .

Before, he had been walking slowly with an unruly, tilting column of books in his arms. But what had come before had no meaning now. A basic, sliding dislocation in the nature of things had taken over, making it impossible for him to remember that it had ever been any other way. The big crystal chandelier was still above his head. The gray wood benches were still before him. Yet both were now utterly transformed.

There was the closet and there the floor, littered with scattered books that only a moment ago had certainly been safely within his grasp. Every last volume cried out silently to be picked up and kissed so the name of the Lord would not be profaned, yet the distance was impossible. It could not be traversed. Instead, the cold stone floor called out to him to rest. If only he could press warm skin to dead white marble for a little nap, a *bissel shlufen*, then this dream would end and everything would be all right again.

Reaching out with his right hand for the very edge of the bench nearest to him, he tried to steady himself. But the hand would not move. Suddenly, it too had a life of its own, a life curtailed by minor death, the failure of the first of the parts to function presaging what might soon be true for the greater whole. Rooted in one place, neither here nor there but definitely somewhere in between, he stood staring as the whirlwind turned before his eyes.

If he was not mistaken, he was once again standing on the narrow footbridge that led across the bay, reaching into the side pocket of his worn brown suit pants for the tiny bread crumbs that would soon flutter towards the rippled surface of the water down below. Today, the bay gleamed like a brightly polished bowl, God's very own perfect fluid mirror reflecting his future back at him, the past as both future and present now, as the sins of one year were cast aside so that a new beginning could be made for the one yet to come.

Reaching out slowly with his other hand, he took hold of the knurled corner of the bench beside him, grasping it so tightly that the edges of his hard, thick fingernails scratched through the varnish to the bare wood below. All the while, the narrow bridge on which he was standing went right on rocking, swaying from side to side as though it had been mounted atop some great ship out at sea during a storm. All he could do was ride this tempest out, hoping that soon the ship would dock and the hold would open and they would permit him to step onto the pier in yet another land with a bit of paper pinned to his lapel so that the officials could herd him quickly through, jabbering away in yet another language he had never heard before.

Someone stood before him now, a dark figure that blocked out the light while radiating a glowing, pale gold corona of its own. The figure was not some angel but someone far more familiar, a friend of whom he had not thought in years. His friend was talking, the spotted black and purple words that came from his mouth whirling through the air like specks of memory that vanished as soon as they appeared.

Schissel had grown older, like himself. Of course, it was only to be expected. Never a very big man, over the years Schissel had somehow managed to get larger and more powerful, becoming in death what he had never been in life. Schissel, with the one bad foot, sitting in the *platz* on Sunday, his pale corona of curly brown hair bobbing in golden sunshine as other people's children ran in laughing circles around him, knowing as only children can that there was something strange here, something odd, something definitely out of the ordinary.

Schissel with the one bad foot, mangled at birth when some excuse for a country doctor had crushed it by pulling him vio-

352

lently from his mother's womb, his shoulders so very wide even as an infant that he could not pass freely into the world but instead had to be dragged kicking and screaming into this life against his will. Schissel, walking slope-sided with that awful limp, wanting only to be able to sit like one of the proud musicians who gathered on Sunday with their backs against the linden and beech trees in the *platz*, strumming balalaika, playing flute, pounding on the drum.

In his old shirt without a collar, with a pair of heavy webbed suspenders holding up wool pants that were far too big at the waist, and thick Tyrolean walking socks rolled over the high topped black leather shoes that Mendel the cobbler had made for him at the cost of the materials alone, the right shoe two sizes larger than the left to accommodate his deformity, Schissel would sit slumped over in the grass, listening with his face twisted up in a haunting smile as the musicians played.

Little Schissel, who did not even own a tie, appearing each year in their fine, bright shul on the High Holy Days with his neck bare, a *shanda* of the first order for those who had left the *shtetl* behind forever to come to this great city where they were free to live like royalty, a shawl-covered piano in the living room for their daughters to play and a violin in the bedroom closet for their sons to practice with. Fanatic supporters of the Rapid Football Club, they would chant "Ra-*peed* Fertel-*shtundt!* Ra-*peed* Fertel-*shtundt!*" as loudly as anyone at the club grounds at every match that did not occur on Shabbos. Never for a moment did any of them believe that anything or anyone could ever take their fine city from them, their beautiful Wien, capital of refined culture and gentle breeding.

In Wien, these Jews were free to look like guardsmen, cutting off their thick beards to allow bristling military mustaches to sprout on their upper lips instead. Proudly, each Sunday they reviewed their wives on parade in the *platz*, laughing beneath the trees in their store bought dresses, their hair pinned back neatly into a bun on their necks as the children played with wooden blocks in the warm, soft grass.

On the High Holy Days, Schissel alone was allowed to come to shul without a necktie, for Schissel had only God, and to God alone Schissel spoke without a trace of the stutter or the halting cough that marked all his other conversations. To God alone no doubt, Schissel was wholly and perfectly made, not little, not lame, not jug-eared, hollow-eyed, and sallow-skinned, with the short, thick neck of a peasant, but just another child running in laughing circles beneath the green leafy trees.

Each Sunday in the park, the wives would gather round. Looking at Schissel with pity in their eyes, they would sadly shake their heads while silently thanking God that their own husbands and sons were perfectly made, with everything intact and functioning just as it was meant to do. "Schissel," they would say, cocking their pretty heads to one side in order to get his complete attention. "What will become of you? Listen to me seriously now, Josef, I'm concerned only for your welfare. Your mother is old. Afterwards . . . well, where will you go?"

And Schissel, who lived by sweeping out shops along the Judengasse, collecting whatever there was to be taken away, scraps of meat that had fallen from the butcher's block, spare tallow from the candlemaker, bits of leather from Mendel the cobbler, would bob his head and laugh, the protuberant Adam's apple rising in his throat like a hard boiled egg that he had swallowed whole. Watching always from the corner of his eye as the little children ran in laughing circles beneath the trees, Schissel would answer slowly, "Where will I go? To shul. Where else?" Only when the time came, he went with all the others, in the truck and then the train and then again the truck.

For Mendel the cobbler, family came first. First family and then work, and only then the shul. As a young man, he had been sent to fight in a private's uniform at Montenegro. Like all the other privates, he had seen too much death there to ever believe again in God as he once had as a young and eager bar mitzvah *bucher*. At Montenegro, in the swamps, Mendel the cobbler had contracted malaria, just like all the other privates.

Nearly twenty years later, in the little bedroom with the rose red wallpaper above his shop, he would lie under thick horsehair blankets sweating and shivering and shaking so badly that the teeth would rattle in his head as he forced himself to get up and answer the tinkling little bell over the shop's front door to wait on customers, some of whom came even on Shabbos for shoes they had to have. Mendel the cobbler waited on them all, even on Shabbos. For him family came first. Then work. And only then, the shul.

On Sundays in the *platz*, they said of him, "Mendel the cobbler? A golden pair of hands. A worker! Give him a pair of shoes to fix on Tuesday, he says they'll be ready on Thursday, you can set your watch by it. The shoes will be waiting for you."

354

As though back in the *shtetl* from which they had all come, any of them had even owned a watch, much less more than a single pair of shoes. Although all of the songs they sang when they gathered together in the park were of longing for their home town, no one ever thought seriously about going back. For whenever they chanced to look too closely at Schissel, a thin, discomforting chill ran through their bones, one not so violent as one of poor Mendel the cobbler's malaria attacks, but unsettling all the same. Even in this great city of elegant culture and gentle refinement, Schissel still walked the streets as though he was treading the rough dirt paths where chickens had pecked for bits of grain by the *mikvah*.

Of Schissel, they said only, "Josef?" Then they wrinkled up their faces like the men of wealth who stood in front of the stock exchange each day. Wanting desperately to be just like them, they whistled soundlessly through their teeth. They hooked their fingers into the fob pockets of their fine, striped vests, gazing up towards heaven through the leafy, dappled canopy of branches above their heads as though God himself might at any moment supply them with the answer. "Well . . . at least he has the shul."

Their fine, bright little shul and their wonderful rebbe, whose devotion to God was beyond question. A big man, the rebbe had a huge white beard that streamed all down the front of his chest, so that as the children ran in circles in the *platz* each Sunday, they made one another laugh by asking if he slept with the beard tucked carefully under or laid out magnificently on top of the thick goosedown quilt that the entire congregation had presented to him on the joyous occasion of his marriage.

But when the time came, it did not matter about the beard— they killed him in the street instead of wasting a place in the truck on him, a man who obviously would not work. For a while along the Judengasse, they mourned the rebbe as a martyr, not realizing that his death had been an easy one, considering what was yet to come.

In the camp to which most of them were sent, Schissel survived because of what he was and what he wasn't, not only a Jew but one born misshapen as well, the very problem they were trying to solve, the logical end product of hundreds of years of inbreeding, proof positive that if this race was allowed to continue unchecked, they would certainly pollute the world with their deep-set eyes, beaked noses, mournful glances, and stoop-shouldered piety.

An undersized, undergrown, half nourished child of a man, Schissel's very name was a joke to the guards. *"Schissel?"* they howled to one another in German, a language that never before had sounded so coarse. "This is a bowl? A bowl for only under the bed at night."

Living in a body that no man wanted, Schissel more than all the others made them feel that what they were doing was certainly right, if not actually the will of God himself, the one to whom they gave all their undying allegiance. When officials came to visit, the guards were quick to point Schissel out. With black gloved hands clasped behind their backs, the officials would stand, loudly clucking their tongues as they gazed down their noses at him until the commandant moved them on to the shops. "Here," the commandant would tell them proudly, "is where we make them work, the ones that are useful to us, like this cobbler. *You, shoemaker!* Show us what you are doing there. . . ."

Turning his head to one side, the commandant would whisper, "Limited ability of course, but in times such as these, with shortages everywhere and materials needed for the front, *useful.*"

Schissel alone was of no use to anyone. With holes in both his shoes, holes that scraps of paper and bits of cloth could never fill for long, so that in summer his feet swelled and in winter they froze, sores forming under all his toes that were so big around that Schissel's tiny body twisted yet further into itself. His limp became worse, so that he lumbered rather than walked erect, an ape with its knuckles scraping the filthy ground masquerading as a man. Because Schissel was of no use to anyone, they permitted him to survive.

Living so close to the ground, Schissel was perfectly suited for the work to which he was assigned. Becoming the camp collector, he gathered together bits and scraps, animal, vegetable, and mineral. Able to find what others had somehow overlooked in the stinking heaps and towering piles by the depot where the new arrivals were stripped of all their possessions, Schissel mined for gold. In garbage, he discovered treasure, rescuing the seared pages of sacred prayer books that had been only partially burned, ragged shreds of clothing that could still be worn, and the occasional half-rotted potato or moldy scrap of bread to eat. Things that were of no use to anyone, Schissel could always use.

Of all those in the camp, Schissel alone had a Hebrew calendar. Schissel alone knew when to say *Kaddish* for his mother, assuming as a matter of fact that she too now was dead. *Dovening* silently and from memory in barracks number nine each morning before the day began and then again at night after it was over, Schissel wrapped imaginary *tephillen* around his wrist, his forearm, and his forehead. With his thick lips going blue from the cold, Schissel mouthed the words of the *Kaddish* with a rolling cadence that was all his own.

Y'isborach v'yistabach, v'yispoar v'yisromam, v'yisnassey, v'yishaddar v'yishalleh v'yishallal . . .

There was no saying how either of them survived, not really. Mendel the cobbler, more than fifty years old when they took him, with pale blue veins already visible beneath the skin on the back of both his hands, and Schissel the collector. Having suffered so badly from malaria all his life, in the camp Mendel the cobbler somehow recovered from his illness. He was being starved into health, or so he joked. If he got any healthier, he whispered to Schissel one night in barracks number nine, he might soon be dead. And Schissel, the slope shouldered religious fanatic who was no one's idea of a traditional Orthodox Jew, yet who prayed daily without *tallis, tephillen,* or yarmulka, knowing that to do so was to risk the awful wrath of the *capo,* a Jew who hated his own kind more fiercely than any of their captors.

By the seventh autumn, the extravagant luxury of hope was gone. It interfered with what was by now Mendel the cobbler's real profession, the business of staying alive. Only the seasons themselves brought liberation, summer being so much easier than winter, each fall the time of the greatest uncertainty, for there was no telling who would be able to endure the winter soon to come. To Mendel the cobbler, a simple idea presented itself, a plan that soon became a project, providing him with work that soothed his mind now that he and Schissel were the only ones from the *platz* who were still alive.

Between the times when he was meant to be working on boots for the officers, Mendel the cobbler began sewing together scraps of leather so small that no one would miss them. With painstaking care, he extracted twelve tiny brass studs from a pair of boots too old to be saved, cutting off the soles entirely so that he could reuse them. Working in the dull light of autumn, stooped over a wooden bench with a flatheaded hammer in his hand and tacks he had straightened lined up neatly in his mouth, Mendel the cobbler solved the little problems one by one.

The last he carefully formed from memory, his skills as a craftsman having only increased in this place where nothing was new and everything had to be used again and again. Coaxing and bending the materials to fit, he tacked and mended and sewed, cutting the leather with the short, sharp blade they let him use by day provided it remained behind in the shop at night. With the blade, he trimmed the sole until it met the curve of the shoe itself so perfectly that with the naked eye he could see no deviation in the line. Each brass stud he hammered into place with a single, ringing blow. Then he set the laces so they would wrap once around the studs and then again around the ankle before tying in a knot in front.

High topped black leather shoes that were nearly waterproof, insulated against the cold with a thick rag that he first soaked in ammonia and then boiled until it was nearly white once more. Folding the rag over, he sewed it inside as lining. New shoes for the High Holy Days for Schissel, so that he could survive the winter soon to come. Shoes like the ones that Schissel had worn each Sunday in the *platz*, so that even as Mendel the cobbler worked on them, he saw once again the lacy green boughs of the trees overhead. He smelled the food that the wives were putting out on the freshly laundered clothes spread across the grass.

Such food. Platters of succulent fish and cold chicken, spicy brown goulash heaped on top of a bed of soft white wrinkled little dumplings, with freshly baked bread to sop up what was left of the gravy after the meal had been eaten. Twisted *challah* made from hand kneaded, egg yellow dough so fine that when it was held up to the light, the sun would shine right through. Loaves of tangy rye bread dotted with caraway and cumin, pumpernickel so dark it looked almost purple right at the center. Bread that had not yet grown green and moldy, bread as fresh as grass or trees. *Broidt. Broidt mit bulbas,* the little new potatoes of spring that Mendel the cobbler had eaten as a child in his mother's kitchen back in the *shtetl*. First, the potatoes were boiled. Then they were simmered slowly in heavy oil and sprinkled with parsley to be eaten cold with a whopping big hunk of cornbread in one hand to wipe out the pot afterwards.

As long as the shoes were before him, the *platz* seemed to be there as well, proof positive that life had actually once been that way. Lovingly, Mendel the cobbler rubbed lamp black carbon into the leather for color, sealing it with *trafe* pig fat and goose grease scraped from the pile of leavings behind the guards' kitchen, polishing and polishing with an old soft rag until the shoes gleamed in his hands even in the fading light of late afternoon. Shoes that looked brand new, with years of life left in them, fit for even the highest ranking officer.

On a day already smelling of winter although it was still only autumn, Schissel came into the shop as he did each week to sweep the floor. Outside, the air was blue with smoke from the officers' quarters. Leaves had already begun to fall from the trees that stood outside the wire, the first sure sign that the coming winter would be a hard one. "Schissel," Mendel the cobbler said, "bring *mir der shvartze shich. Uf der* top shelf . . . ."

Reaching up as far as he could, stretching a body that was now so thin and emaciated that the light seemed to shine right through, Schissel brought down the shoes. "*Zer shayn*, Mendel," he said, gazing at the shoes in wonder as he held them in his hand. "*Zer, zer shayn.*" After all these years, Schissel still wanted nothing so much as a trade of his own. To make something with your hands, even for *them*, was honest work. "So who are they for? Not the *capo*. Not shoes so fine as these. . . ."

"*Gib a kuk*, Schissel," Mendel the cobbler urged. "The right one two sizes larger than the left? Who *could* they be for?" On Schissel's tiny face, a look of amazement dawned. His eyes opened wide, shining like a pair of moons in his dirt-streaked countenance. "Quickly," Mendel the cobbler ordered, "try them on. So I can tell if the last is right. . . ."

With trembling hands, Schissel bent over to try them on, all the while muttering the *Shema* as though to thank God for this great gift. As though prayer alone might ever bring down the wire and overturn the barracks, causing the *capo* to fall face down into the earth, where he belonged.

Although Mendel the cobbler did his work each day, knowing that so long as they needed shoes he had at least a chance to survive, bombs were what he really wanted. Bombs and tanks and planes. To destroy the camp and all who had built it. But shoes were all that he knew how to make. Without shoes, the guards could not walk their rounds once winter came to stay.

"*Der muzzt mit shmutz der shich wngeshmearen*, Josef," Mendel the cobbler told Schissel, so that no one would know that they were newly made. "*Mit sheiss. Mit dreck.*" Instead of answering, Schissel only grinned, the cracked and rotting teeth in his mouth gleaming in the dull light like the yellow Star of David on his chest. At the corners of Schissel's blistered lips, saliva lay caked and dried like the first snow of winter that would soon be on the ground.

"*Mit neier* shoes?" Schissel said, shaking his head from side to side, "*Ken nisht*. It would be a sin." Hiding them beneath his ragged shift, Schissel limped slowly towards the door, looking back once over his shoulder to say, "*Gott tzedanken.*"

"And if not?" Mendel the cobbler asked. "You'll wear them anyway, no? Only Schissel . . . first, you *must* make them look old."

Where Schissel hid the shoes, Mendel the cobbler never asked. Schissel knew places in the camp that God himself could never have found, places to store the yellow bits of parchment with Hebrew words on them that he had found, the half smoked cigarettes that could be shared late at night, and the pieces of cloth that might yet be used for something. The shoes now belonged to Schissel. What he did with them was his business. Mendel the cobbler's work was done.

But Schissel had something to give him in return. A week later, as Mendel the cobbler lay turning restlessly on his wooden plank bunk, groaning from pains in his shoulder brought on by working stooped over a bench fourteen hours a day with no food in his stomach, a cold hand on his arm woke him. Before him, Schissel stood in a patch of dead cold moonlight, wearing a clean white cotton shift he must have taken off some body before even the *capo* had discovered that yet another one was dead. On his feet, Schissel had placed the new black leather high topped shoes. They too gleamed brightly in the moonlight.

Putting a twisted finger to his lips, Schissel led Mendel the cobbler out back to the stinking place where men pissed, shat, and vomited during the night into a narrow ditch through which muddy brown water ran whenever it rained. In the dark and silent night, Schissel's shoes glowed with a life of their own, a beacon too obvious for any guard to ignore. Gesturing towards the ditch with a shaking hand, Schissel whispered, "Running water."

In his hand, Schissel held a single scrap of paper rescued from some long destroyed prayer book. In the other hand, a crust of bread. "*Gudt, gudt,*" Mendel the cobbler said, seeing only the bread. "*Eppes essen?*"

Schissel shook his head. Instead, he croaked, "*Gaet* saying *Tashlikh.*"

Tashlikh. In a place where the only real sin was to throw away what could still be eaten, Schissel had bread to spare on God. Madness. Fanaticism that took no notice of what was real. According to Schissel's secret calendar, it was Rosh Hashanah once again. Another year. So what? What sins from the previous year could *they* discard over running water? What sins could *they* have possibly committed in this inferno where babies, some still unborn, were daily consumed by fire, balanced on the sharpened ends of the guards' bayonets, then clubbed quickly into sickening silence, to be thrown feet first into a stiffening pile?

Day by day, the sacrifice went on, without reason, meaning, or end. Why, no one knew. What sins could Mendel the cobbler atone for this year, when he had been fasting daily, against his will? What kind of new year could it be, ushered in not with the joyous cry of the *shofer* in their bright little shul with all the families gathered together, but by the muffled grunts, sleeping midnight cries, and sick smelling farts of men whose bodies had been denied for so long that they were now only barely human?

Mendel the cobbler himself had not said *Kaddish* once since they had taken him, trusting that the souls of his dear mother and father would forgive him for neglecting his rightful duty as a son here in this hell where God the Father had apparently chosen to abandon the faithful. Here, life itself was an endless *Kaddish*, for the living as well as the dead.

"Bist du teppet?" he hissed at Schissel, as though Schissel himself might ever be able to answer this question. It was like asking the sun why it still bothered to rise each morning. Of course, Schissel was mad. They all were, insane to want to go on living, insanely frightened to die.

Limping resolutely towards the thin rivulet of water trickling through the ditch, Schissel turned the crust of bread to crumbs of dust between his fingers. Scattering the crumbs over the edge of the ditch, he began speaking to God alone in his brand new, high topped black leather shoes on the first day of the New Year, performing *Tashlikh* from a scrap of paper rescued from only he knew where. With his head bowed and his body bent forward at the waist, Schissel watched his sins being carried away. In that peculiar rolling cadence in which he always prayed, Schissel intoned:

The Lord is for me, I will not fear; what can man do unto me? The Lord is for me, among them that help me; therefore shall I see my desire on them that hate me.

Yes for that, thought Mendel the cobbler. Yes for rampaging death turned back on those who practiced it daily as though it was their only religion, on those who sucked the blood of the innocent, on those who murdered casually as though it was their right. In this world, they had already been pardoned for daring to do what others had only dreamed about. Even now, in Wien, that great city of culture and refinement, they were riding down the wide, sweeping boulevards in open touring cars with their heads thrown back in laughter. No matter how it all turned out in the end, they had already won by having been permitted to get away with any of it for a single second, ignored by those who had turned their heads and looked away, insisting it was no concern of theirs.

"*Mach shnell*, Schissel," Mendel the cobbler urged, "*mach shnell*." Schissel *fumphered* on and on, forgetting who he was and where he was, conscious only that he was performing *Tashlikh*, purifying himself for the year to come by chanting in that peculiar, rolling cadence right beneath their very noses.

It is better to trust in the Lord than to confide in man. It is better to trust in the Lord than to confide in princes.

"*Shrei nisht*, Schissel," Mendel the cobbler pleaded. "If *Gott* is going to hear you, you can whisper also."

For the *capo* had ears and did not sleep, knowing that at night men brought out to eat what they had taken with them back to barracks number nine during the day. A Jew worse than any Nazi, the *capo* lived off the others, growing strong by stealing from those too weak to fight. What the guards overlooked and perhaps did not even mind that they had, the *capo* seized for himself. Following men outside when they went to piss, he would fall on them from behind with a harsh blow to the *kishkes* or a swift knee in the *eyer*, wresting away a bit of food or a forbidden cigarette without ever reporting it to anyone so that he would not be implicated.

Such a good *capo*. So dedicated and hard working. Such an efficient policeman. He made their work easier for them. Before the camp, the *capo* had worked in a ritual slaughterhouse, swinging the ten pound hammer to stun the steers, then stepping back so that the *shoichet* could cut their throats. A *bullvon* of a man, thick and stupid, with arms no longer as big around as they had once been but still powerful, he was to be feared completely because he could not be reasoned with. The *capo* was so deathly

362

afraid of *them* that to prove his loyalty beyond all doubt, he had to be ten times worse on his own.

It was the *capo*'s footsteps Mendel the cobbler now heard, coming from behind him and to the right. Footsteps and the barking of a dog, a fierce German shepherd. Wrapping his fingers around Schissel's forearm, now no bigger than a tiny stick of kindling, a thin branch torn off some dying tree to provide a moment's warmth, Mendel the cobbler tried to shake his friend back to life before it was too late.

Fumbling quickly in his pants with his other hand, Mendel the cobbler desperately searched his dry groin for what seemed like an eternity before finding his shrivelled penis in the tangled tuft of hair that was now steel gray. Bringing it out into the cold night air, he closed his eyes for a moment to say another kind of prayer, urging it to happen. At last, he summoned up a thin, watery stream of piss from a bladder which, thank God, seemed never to be entirely empty.

Opening his eyes again, Mendel the cobbler watched his urine steam in the icy darkness, glittering for an instant in the moonlight before it fell into the ditch below. With eyes closed, Schissel stood just as he had before, lost in dreams and prayers, mumbling to himself. "Schissel, *Schissel,*" Mendel the cobbler whispered urgently in that silent prisoner's undertone he had learned to use in the camp, his voice so muted it might just as well have been the wind rustling through the few leaves that still remained on the trees outside the wire or the thin trickle of water burbling through the ditch below. "*Pishen,* Schissel. *Daf gaen pishen . . .*"

Opening his eyes at last, Schissel stared back at him as though they were both still in the *platz* on Sunday with children running in laughing circles under the trees as the women put out food on the freshly laundered cloths. Only now the sighing of the balalaika and the flute was lost in the background, as the resolute pounding of the drum took over.

"*Pishen?*" Schissel said, that haunting smile twisting up the corners of his mouth. "*Uf der neier* shoes? Mendel. *Zah nisht kein nahr.*"

So that when the *capo* came, laying a heavy hand on Schissel's shoulder while saying, "This is *verboten,* Schissel. This you cannot do," in his heavily accented German, Schissel still stood with the forbidden scrap of prayer book in one hand. Crumbs of stolen bread were scattered in a circle at his feet, on which he wore the high topped black leather shoes, polished darker than the night. A clearcut case, so simple that even the *capo* knew there was no reason for him to blow the wooden whistle hanging around his neck. The charges:

Possession of illegal reading material.

Hoarding bread.

Stealing shoes intended for military use.

The guard with whom the *capo* was in deep partnership, the two of them sharing whatever they could sell or exchange for money on the black market, the guard keeping his profits in a tin box under his bed while the *capo* took his share in food, seemed not at all angry to have been shaken from his sleep in the middle of the night.

"Schissel, eh?" the guard said as Schissel stood before him, still mumbling the words of some prayer. "Some Schissel. *Capo.* Bring me the bowl from under your bed."

Hurrying off, the *capo* returned with the cracked white china bowl into which he pissed each night, proof that he was a better man than those who had to go outside and stand in filth to relieve themselves. Placing it on the ground, the *capo* stepped back. Using the sharpened edge of his bayonet, the guard slit Schissel's throat from ear to ear. The *capo* stood with his mouth wide open, as though he could not understand why he had not first been allowed to swing the ten pound hammer.

Forcing Schissel's head down into the cracked white bowl so that the blood would not stain the ground, the guard asked the *capo* for a cigarette. Lighting it up with his other hand, he remarked casually how surprising it was that so much blood still remained in one so small and crippled. And the blood spurted forth, rich and thick, like water from a fountain in the *platz.* Purple in color, it slowly turned black in the bowl, purple black and spotted both black and purple, as Schissel's eyes rolled back in his head like some steer being butchered while it was still alive.

The guard kept holding the head *down*, the level of blood rising in the bowl until finally Schissel lay without moving, his hair matted thick with blood, his skin caked with blood, his clean white shift black with blood. His eyes still were open, as though he had somehow drowned on dry land. Little Schissel, returned to his Maker at last, with no further need to beg forgiveness for his sins by scattering bread crumbs in the dark, foul-smelling slime of the drainage ditch behind barracks number nine.

As punishment for having been so careless as to let someone

like Schissel steal from his shop a pair of brand new shoes obviously intended for some officer, they made Mendel the cobbler watch it all and then clean up afterwards. When it was over, the guard emptied the bowl into the ditch. The lifeless body was carried away. The shoes were put back on the top shelf in the shop to await their rightful owner only after the *capo* had first greedily tried them on. Discovering the left one to be too small, he could only grunt, "*Hnnh*. Truly for an officer's feet."

Had the *capo* only thought to look more closely at the right shoe, or even tried it on, he would have found it to be two sizes larger than the left, a perfect fit for only one man in the camp, who was now dead. But the *capo* was a thick and stupid man through and through, so Mendel the cobbler survived.

Just one more death among the many for Mendel the cobbler, who saw people vanish around him every day. Yet it was for Schissel that he began silently saying *Kaddish* each morning and again at night in barracks number nine as the *capo* dozed, saying it as quickly as possible so that he would not be caught, in the very same rolling cadence that Schissel himself had used, remembering most of the words from memory, stumbling badly whenever his memory failed him.

For Schissel, Mendel the cobbler went right on saying *Kaddish* until the Russians came to liberate the camp. Little Schissel, who had died for a pair of black high topped shoes, a crust of stolen bread, and a yellowed bit of ancient parchment, betrayed by a *capo* who made the mistake of addressing his liberators in badly accented German and so was murdered by the Russians for the gold in his teeth. Little Schissel, who was slaughtered casually and with dispatch by a guard who climbed onto a truck before the Russians arrived with his tin box beneath his arm, riding out of sight. The guard too was now also certainly dead, the three of them finally joined together in that black and purple darkness through which only prayer could penetrate.

For Schissel and then later the others, but never the *capo* or the guard, Mendel the cobbler had gone right on saying *Kaddish* every day, morning and evening, winter and summer, as the sun first rose and then as it set again, holding onto the bench before him just as he had clung to the edge of his wooden plank bunk in the camp, sounding the prayer exactly as he had heard it chanted on a thousand frozen mornings and evenings from Schissel's bed.

Suddenly the whirlwind died down, moving off from in front of his eyes like a summer storm retreating back to sea. Things returned once more to their rightful place. The *shamus* of Ahavath Mizrach saw that he was only in shul, with his grandson before him, speaking to him in a language that he no longer understood, with a look of great concern on his face.

It was to him, the one who had washed his hands before he *duchened* on Yom Kippur, that he now wished to say something. As a *kohen*, it would be his duty to go on saying the prayer, for Schissel and all the others. Although it was all clearly formed in his mind, the *shamus* of Ahavath Mizrach could not make his tongue translate his thoughts into speech. Simply, the feeling was just too frustrating for words.

Instead, he heard himself grunt, much like Schissel had when the sharpened edge of the bayonet had bitten deeply into his flesh. It was the hoarse, guttural cry of an animal bellowing not only from pain but because it understands that the process of dying has finally begun. The words of the prayer formed an endless loop in his mind, one that repeated itself over and over, just as Schissel had done in that rolling cadence on all the cold, smoky mornings and evenings.

Yisborach v'yistabach, v'yispoar v'yisromam, v'yisnassey, v'yishaddar, v'yishalleh, v'yishallal . . . Blessed and praised, glorified and exalted, extolled and honored, adored and lauded. . . .

Rocking gently back and forth on his heels while holding onto the very edge of the bench beside him with a grip that no man would ever break, the *shamus* of Ahavath Mizrach said *Kaddish* for the final time. For Schissel, for the others, and for himself. Always, he had known that in the end it came to this, the camp from which there was no escape or liberation except through complete submission.

Letting go of the wooden bench, the *shamus* of Ahavath Mizrach looked around once, as though to assure himself that he was indeed in shul, in the presence of the holy Torahs and the one who would carry his line forth. Then he fell slowly onto the floor, his body so light that it made no sound at all as it sank on to the cold stone marble. His burden of honor he had finally laid to rest. The challenge now was for those who remained behind to somehow assume it for him once again.

STONE
ANGEL

CHAPTER THIRTY-FOUR

CONTROL IS NOW the only thing I have going for myself. Control alone will see me through. Control gets me onto the Franklin Avenue shuttle, well known to one and all as the soul train, just before the doors slam shut with a rattlesnake hiss. Although my face is the only white one in the car, everything is cool. The good brothers and sisters with whom I ride in clanking silence know immediately that I belong. I have control.

Like a magical token that is good for life, control reappears in my hand no matter how many times I drop it through the turnstiles. Should a band of street corner braves form a threatening circle around me after I get off the train, sidling over casually under the trestle in the very heart of no man's land to inquire if maybe they can hold a dime or get a really good look at the expiration date on my driver's license, I need not fear. Like the cavalry, control will come charging to my rescue, bugles blowing loudly in the distance.

Control is the hip trip. It is the happening thing, the way to go, and the only game still left in town. Control is the universal remedy, good for whatever ails you. Control goes down smooth and then comes on strong. It is highly recommended for use in what has already come to be known as "the current situation" by both Morton and Esther Bindel, famed social lions and prominent members of Ahavath Mizrach.

Control is precisely what my grandfather no longer has. Late yesterday afternoon, in shul of all places, he lost it right before my eyes. After they put him into the ambulance and drove him away with sirens screaming, I must have spent at least an hour there looking for what once belonged to him. My guess now is that he has lost it for good.

Over the phone this morning, my mother informed me that he just went right on stroking all through the night. Stroke, stroke, stroke. My grandfather is definitely on the river. The sun is just starting to set behind the buildings on the other side. As always, the very weird Chinese pre-engineering students sit on all the benches. With slide rules in their hands, they calculate precisely when he will cross the finish line.

Stroke, stroke, stroke. The coxswain calls cadence, pounding out the beat. The oars never dip beneath the surface of the pastel streaked water. The shell seems to fly forward with a will of its own. My grandfather is pulling for home at sunset. Suddenly the river catches fire. Nobody cheers.

Better than anyone, I know that there is nothing funny about the current situation. But all I can do is laugh. I know that Menashe Skulnik would understand. In the city hospital that is no more than a minute's walk from the train station, there are cops wherever I look. Transit cops, cops just off the beat, cops in plain clothes, sanitation cops, health department cops, and private security guards, hired no doubt to keep all the other cops in line. I have never seen so much heat in my entire life. Why they need all of these cops in here, I have no idea. To shoot the sick, I guess, in case they get out of hand and start emptying their own bedpans into the overcrowded hallways.

In the elevator, I nod hello to all the cops. I push the button for the eighth floor. Over the phone this morning, my mother informed me that my grandfather spent the night on the first floor, in intensive care. But the big tenement fire that was all over the front page of the *Daily News* this morning has made him second page news. The intensive care unit is so crowded that they have moved him to a semiprivate room upstairs.

After all, he is just one very old man. Ungrateful, too. All night long in intensive care, he kept on yanking the IV from his arm while trying to get out of bed. So he could walk to shul, I guess, and sit watching the sidewalk until the sun came up. Were it not for Sylvia Stryker's influence, he would not even be in this hospital in the first place. For such small favors, we are grateful.

The real reason my mother called this morning was to prepare me for the shock. My grandfather can now no longer talk at all. But he does have a bed by the window, with a swell view of the big red brick church across the street. After all, as my mother pointed out over the phone, how can they expect anyone to get better if all they have to look at is the sick person in the very next bed? It is a question I am not equipped to answer.

Despite the phone call, I nearly faint when I first walk into his room. Overnight, my grandfather has become a shrunken, withered skeleton. He is no longer the man that I once knew. Slowly, it dawns on me that I am looking at a complete stranger, a man that I in fact do not know. My grandfather is in the next bed, the one with the view. "Paulie," my mother says, rushing towards me, "thank God you're here. I need someone to help me lift him. I've been buzzing the orderly for hours. But no one comes." Lowering her voice to a whisper, she confides, "Most of them barely speak English anyway. *Mr. Lapidus,*" she calls out in a louder voice, nodding to the corpse in the first bed. "My son, Paulie. Come, dear. You'll help me."

Taking my hand, she leads me toward him. The man lying in the next bed is not him either. He looks like my grandfather all right but something is missing. The light that always shines through his clear blue eyes has gone out. Before me now is a helpless marionette without strings. A doll made of soft and doughy clay, with an ever-expanding hole right at the center of his being that just keeps on getting larger as its walls crumble slowly into blackness. My grandfather is gradually being replaced by nothingness. A single cell at a time, he is undergoing fission, the atoms within his body being scattered back to all four corners of the universe. Bit by tiny bit, we are losing him to darkness.

I can tell from the look on his face that he does not understand why he is not yet dead. Life is certainly better than death but this is neither. Death before dishonor. What a joke. Death *is* dishonor, dishonoring life in the cruellest manner possible. Yet this is even worse.

"Why move him at all?" I ask.

"Because, dear," she sniffs, wiping her nose with a tissue. "You have to move them constantly when they get like this or they develop bed sores. A nice black nurse told me that. I tried to pick him up on my own. But it's like lifting a stone."

My mother just wants to do *something*. She has to keep busy, or else. Besides, if he is not moved, my grandfather will start going bad, like a piece of fruit left for too long on top of the refrigerator. Blemishes will form on his dead white marble skin. "Listen," I say, "I'll go find someone to do it for us."

"And what's wrong with you?" she demands. "You're crippled, God forbid? Come on. Give me a hand."

There is nothing wrong with me. I just do not want to touch him. It is not what I am good at. But my mother will not relent. "Let's go, dear," she orders, motioning me towards one side of the bed as she goes around to the other. "You lift, while I push on the pillows."

Tentatively, I put my hands up under his armpits. They are strangely dry, as though all the pores in his skin have shut down in protest, refusing to pass sweat through until their demands are met. Shoving upward with all my strength, I just barely budge him off the mattress. My feet slide on the polished floor. I stumble forward with him in my arms, fighting to keep my balance. My mother nods. She is satisfied with the way he now sits. Only then do I let him slowly back down again.

One thing I know for sure. That old man is heavy. As he never was before. Lifting him was like trying to wrestle a sack of cement up a narrow ladder in a windstorm. Whether it is the part that is still living or the part that has died that weighs so much, I cannot say. He is definitely too much of a burden for anyone but God to carry now. Whether God is ready to shoulder the load, I have no idea.

"When will he be able to go home?" I ask, already knowing the answer.

"Not soon, dear," my mother says. "He needs constant attention. And then . . . there's the groaning."

As if on cue, my grandfather lets out a mournful bellow. He brays like a baby goat with its front feet caught in a coil of rusty barbed wire. It is the worst sound I have ever heard in my entire life. It is a judgment on us all, for letting this happen to him.

"I thought you said he couldn't talk."

"He can't. That's the groaning, dear. It's only normal in the situation. Or so the doctor told me."

"There's nothing they can do to help him, right?"

"Not really."

"Then why not just let him . . . you know . . ."

"The will to live," she says simply, as though that explains it all.

"The will to live," I say. "I guess that makes sense, huh?"

"Nothing makes sense, dear," she says. "That's why we have to do all we can for him without going to pieces ourselves. I'm sure you can understand that."

Sure I can. I just do not want to have to explain it to anyone else. Reaching for a tissue from the box by his bed, I blow my nose into it. Then I inspect the results with interest, expecting blood. No such luck. I have never been healthier. I will be

372

around for at least another hundred years or so, waiting for this to happen to me.

Checking me out from head to toe, my mother says, "You look very nice, dear. I'm sure Sol will be impressed."

"Yeah. I really feel like seeing him today, too. . . ."

"You *go*," she says, making it into a command. "And tonight as well. You go out with your friend from Cambridge. There's no reason for you to sit here all the time, not so long as your father and I are around."

Then she reaches for a tissue and blows her nose. Whatever I have must be catching. "Oh, look," my mother says, turning towards the door. "Visiting hours must have started already. *Solomon*. We never expected you to come all this way. Sit down, sit down. By the bed, where he can see you."

"Paulie," Solomon says quietly, nodding as he moves past me towards the bed. Once again, he is wearing the very same suit he had on for the High Holy Days, with no tie under the collar of his old white shirt. To get here from the shul, he had to take a couple of buses and then the train. Just as my mother said. Who would have expected it?

Lowering himself slowly into the chair by the window, Solomon leans forward. He taps gently on my grandfather's arm with his hand to get his attention. When he sees that this is not going to do him much good, Solomon slides his hand all the way down my grandfather's arm, taking hold of his wrist. Then he just sits there like that, holding on.

"How you doin', Mendel?" he asks softly. "They can't hardly keep it goin' back at shul without you. That's right. Nat Weiss been runnin' around like a chicken without a head tryin' to get that cottage prayer you always lead organized. Nobody else wants to do it. Not till you comes back. . . ."

I turn my head and stare out the window at the big red brick church across the street. Solomon is a *mensh* all right. I am about to thank him for having come all this way when more visitors come through the door. Back in the neighborhood, someone has opened up the gate. Chartered buses with my grandfather's name on them are leaving from the temple every fifteen minutes, arriving nonstop in the street below shortly thereafter.

The very first to arrive are Murray Friedberg and Sidney Meyers, traveling together as a team the way they always do. Sidney brings up the rear, struggling manfully under the weight of two steamer baskets covered all over with that clear, crinkly yellow wrapping paper I associate only with death and the sound of distant relatives weeping softly behind closed doors.

Sidney has to carry the baskets because Murray needs both hands free. Dramatically he clasps my mother by the shoulder, offering her his most solemn regards. Although I know that he is surprised to see that Solomon got here first, Murray does not let it show. Today, he is a visiting goodwill ambassador, all smiles and diplomatic courtesy.

"The least we could do," Sidney says apologetically as my mother starts to unload the first basket. Uttering little cries of delight, she brings out two oversized hothouse pears, three grotesquely swollen navel oranges, and a pair of dark red Cortland apples that have to weigh half a pound apiece. Carefully, she arranges them side by side on the tray by the bed.

"All out of season of course," Murray notes. "But at a time like this, who minds the expense?"

From the other basket, my mother takes out several packets of sugar coated pink and white almonds. Then some crackers. A little orange brick of cheese and a flat-bladed knife to spread it with. Dutch chocolates, wrapped in foil. Soon we will have our very own little party going here. A picnic. Catered, of course, despite the expense. At a time like this, who cares about cost?

Next through the door is Judah Benjamin, the esteemed cantor of Ahavath Mizrach. Judah's face is radiant with resounding good health and unbounded perpetual optimism. He always looks this way. I think his job depends on it. Within the shul, he is everyone's favorite uncle.

"Cantor," my mother says respectfully, "you're hungry? Go on," she urges, pressing a piece of fruit on him. "It's just a *nosh*."

Before Judah can refuse, two women from the Sisterhood surround my mother. "A terrible blow," Judah says, pumping my hand like he is running for reelection. "For all of us." Before I can agree with him, a stooped old man named Moishe who for years sat with my grandfather at the very back of the shul until he got too old to even go to temple any longer, hobbles into the room on a pair of metal canes. He is supported on either side by two remarkably plain women who have to be either his daughters or his nieces.

"Mrs. Bindel," the first one says, graciously extending her hand to my mother. "I'm Dora. And this is my sister, Tillie.

We've never had the pleasure of meeting before but when Moishe heard, he *had* to come. . . ."

"Heard?" Moishe says loudly, fiddling with the wire from the hearing aid in his left ear. "Speak up. I'll hear. . . ."

"We took a taxi all together," Dora says sweetly.

"All that way?" my mother exclaims. "Really, you shouldn't have."

"Actually," Tillie puts in, "the fare wasn't half bad."

"Moishe!" the cantor booms, turning away from me. "You're up and walking again? All the troubles gone? The piles, as well?"

"And how would you know, Tillie?" Dora snaps. "Moishe paid for it all."

"I did what?" Moishe asks, tottering forward on his canes. "Speak up," he says encouragingly. "I'll hear."

"With silver dollars no less," Tillie says excitedly. "You should have seen the driver's face. . . ."

"The *piles*," the cantor booms. "The *piles*. . . ."

"Silver dollars," my mother marvels. "Imagine that."

"God bless him," Dora says. "He saved carefully all his life. Every penny."

"Ungeshtupped," Moishe says sadly, referring to what I assume are his piles and not his bank account. Of course, there is no saying. Not for sure.

Solomon gets to his feet to let the old man sit down. Taking Moishe by the arm, I help him into the chair by the window. "It's *Morty*, isn't it?" he asks, shouting the question into my face. "At least, *you* look wonderful." Settling down before I can tell him that it is my father he is thinking of, Moishe leans towards the bed and says, *"Nu,* Mendel? *Voos macht dir?* Speak up," he urges. "I'll hear. . . ."

Morris Benson, first vice-president of the shul, comes through the door. As always, he looks resplendent. His gray sharkskin suit screams of money. His red-and-blue-striped rep tie proclaims for all the world to see that he is a lawyer. Ever the perfect gentleman, Morris takes both of my mother's hands in his, kisses her gently on the cheek, and says, "My office is not very far, Esther. So I thought, 'Why not stop by?' "

"Morris, *please*," she says, blushing. *"You* should apologize? It's an honor to have you."

Morris says something that I cannot hear. From the hallway, Irv Aaronsen, the builder, shouts, "Excuse me? I'm in the right room?'' No doubt, Irv thinks he is still on a building site somewhere with heavy equipment pounding away so loudly in the background that he has to *really* project to make himself heard. Irv's question is answered almost immediately by Sol Bender, the dentist. *''Irv,''* Sol cries out, delighted to see a fellow member of the board.

"Sol," Irv says gravely, turning to shake his hand, "tell me something. You parked in the street?"

"Of course, Irv. Where else? Why?"

"I'm driving the new Cadillac the business bought me," Irv confides. "Right out of the showroom and I don't even have collision on it yet. Some *momzer* goes to work on the paint with a rusty nail and it'll come out of my pocket. *Morrie!*" Irv cries, his face lighting up with delight as he realizes that there is actually a lawyer in the room who can represent him should any serious damage occur to his car while he is up here.

"Good to see you, Morrie," Sol says, following Irv toward my grandfather's bed. "But what a place to meet, huh? All these people . . . my God, they're *sick*."

"Yeah, well," I say. "It *is* a hospital, Sol."

"Paulie," he says, shaking my hand. "That's exactly why I became a dentist and not a doctor. I *hate* illness. It depresses the hell out of me."

"We should all only meet on happier occasions," Judah Benjamin says, joining the group to shake hands all around. "And in better places."

The men of Ahavath Mizrach stand together in the middle of the room. They are a team, a committee, a delegation. Any minute now, they will break out their pipes, cigarettes, and cigars and go off as a group to visit those poor unfortunates who are trapped inside oxygen tents and iron lungs, offering their best wishes for a successful and speedy recovery as they puff great clouds of smoke into the air.

Irv Aaronsen has brought a bottle of Scotch into the room under his coat along with a paper roll of Dixie cups. The bottle goes from hand to hand. People pour themselves little shots, then knock them back quickly, clearing their throats even as their eyes begin to water. "And the rabbi?" Irv Aaronsen demands suddenly, his voice cutting through the entire room. "He's coming?"

"He's coming, Judah Benjamin affirms nervously. "Of that I'm certain. How could he not?"

"He's coming?" Murray Friedberg says, shooting Sidney a

376

cynical, knowing look. "So then where is he? Closeted with Nat Weiss in some water closet, working on next year's budget? Without Mendel, there *is* no shul, *gelt* or no *gelt*. You should excuse me saying so, Cantor. . . ."

"Your opinion, Murray, is of course, your opinion," Judah Benjamin says judiciously, looking over at Morris Benson as though he expects him to deliver a legal ruling on the point. "You're certainly entitled to it. But I'm positive he'll be here soon."

"Nat, I think," Morris says quietly, "has some *personal* business to attend to today. Sol himself gave me a call this morning. All the Strykers send their best regards, Esther."

This is all my mother has to hear. Her day is now complete. Myself, I can only think about Nat Weiss and the rabbi. By all rights, they should have come already. It is now strictly standing room only in here. No seating at all is available in the downstairs section. The loge is jammed. Soon, we are going to have to close the first balcony. Even if the rabbi arrives, with Nat Weiss running interference for him, he is going to have trouble getting near the bed. I will see to that personally.

Only first I have to move into the hallway for a second so that I can start breathing normally again. There is just no air left in my grandfather's room. I go outside and head for the water fountain by the elevator. Before I can take a drink, the elevator doors slide open. Looking as though he has only just woken up from a nap in Bruno's back room, Monte comes walking out. "You're kidding, right?" I say, too stunned to come up with anything better at the moment.

"Hey," Monte says, closing in on me. "Who's the joke here? You or me? Real nice suit, kid. You getting married later today? Forget I asked. It's my lunch hour, right? So I said, 'To hell with the rest of the route. Let Messer take it out.' Besides, what am I gonna do? Let the clerks make *me* look bad?"

Monte presents me with a very *goyish* arrangement of flowers that I can only describe as a "spray." "The boys took up a little collection," he explains. "Your old man is on the way. Herr Messer gave him the day off, the bum. *After* Mo Tannenbaum slipped the sonofabitch a tensky right in the old raincoat pocket. Any-*hoo*," he says, turning his head to check out the ass on a nurse who clacks past us down the hall, "where's the room? I wanna say hello before I go piss. . . ."

"Monte," I say, grabbing him by the arm. "You okay? I mean, well, you know . . . The Contessa and all?"

"Hey," he says, breathing whiskey fumes right into my face. "Russ wants to marry her, I wish them both all the luck in the world. At least. Monte Serrano didn't take no sloppy seconds. Besides, I got a kid who's gonna be a priest. So how can they hurt me? *Huh?*"

"Come on," I say, shaking my head in wonder. "I'll show you the way."

Back into the madness, I lead Monte. Any minute now, we are going to have to set up some of those gray wooden barriers that line Fifth Avenue each year for the St. Patrick's Day Parade. Then we will get a couple of the cops downstairs to mount up and we will have us some real crowd control.

"Mrs. B.," Monte says, going right up to my mother with the flowers in his hand. "Monte Serrano, from Avenue Station. With our best wishes. . . ."

"Call me Esther, Monte," she says. "And thank you for the lovely flowers."

The old man rolls through the door, looking tired as hell. Nodding to Monte, he comes straight towards me. Grabbing my arm hard, he says, "You okay? I heard you tossing and turning all night long."

"And what were you doing? Working on your stamps?"

"Never mind. How's your mother?"

My mother is extremely busy. In the presence of death and/or serious illness, those of the faith just naturally develop an appetite. It is nothing that they can help. They just *have* to eat. Putting a little something into their mouths lets them know for sure that they are still alive. No one is better qualified to do the serving than my mother. Moving through the crowd like a hot dog vendor at a ball game, she demands, "Who's hungry? Don't be ashamed now. Speak up. Who wants to grab a little *nosh?*"

Coming over to me as my father moves off into the throng by the bed, she whispers, "Do you believe this turnout, Paulie? What an honor!"

"Yeah," I say, unable to understand what good it is going to do my grandfather. "It's great."

"You know," she says. "All of a sudden, you don't look so hot to me. Go stand by the window and get some air. Cantor," she calls out loudly. "Make some room for my son over there, would you?"

378

I move towards the window, obeying orders. As I go, I hear Murray Friedberg say, "*This* I don't believe." Sure enough, the party is now complete. Coming through the door, looking just as he did on Yom Kippur, in the same lousy suit complete with string tie, a big white plastic shopping bag in his hand, is Meshuggener Marvin.

Reaching out for the little black handle on the windowsill before me, I turn it in circles a couple of times. Then I realize that the window itself has been cemented shut. No doubt, the cops have done this so they will not have to fill out reports in triplicate should some patient take it suddenly into his head to make a rapid exit without using the elevator.

Joining me by the window, the cantor asks, "Seen that church across the street yet, Paulie?" In every way, we are fellow men of the world, able to discuss even the beauty of *their* temples. "Over a hundred years old, if I'm not mistaken. Wonderful building, no?"

"Yeah. All the mistakes they make in here, they bury over there."

That takes care of the cantor for a while. He is not *my* uncle. Besides, if he is so in love with the rabbi, he can point the church out to *him*, when and if he gets here. Myself, I am far more interested in watching Marvin. Carefully, he places the white plastic shopping bag between his knees onto the floor. Reaching down into it, he comes back up with a small woolen yarmulka between his fingers. He slips the yarmulka on the back of his head, holding it in place until he can bring a larger model made of white silk from the bag. He places this one on his head right on top of the first. Why he does this, I have no idea. One is more than enough for most people, and we are not even in shul.

A couple more trips into the bag and Marvin is set to go. He holds a prayer book open in his hands. He has a full set of *tephillen* wrapped around his left arm and forehead. Silently Marvin begins to pray. Rocking back and forth on the balls of his feet, he mouths words that no one can hear. All the while, he keeps on *clupping* himself in the heart with a balled-up fist. My mother does not notice him right away, but then she is a bit distracted. Once she does, however, her reaction is immediate.

"What is he doing?" she demands.

I cannot tell her. Neither can the old man, the cantor, Morris Benson, Sol Bender, Irv Aaronsen, Murray Friedberg, Sidney Meyers, old man Moishe, his two female relatives, the women

379

from the Sisterhood, or Monte, who certainly does not know. "His name is Marvin," I tell her. "Why don't you ask him?"

"Marvin," she says, moving towards him, "what are you doing?"

Blinking rapidly, Marvin respectfully inclines his head to her. "*Shmoneh Esreh*, missus," he says. "Then, *Kaddish* . . ."

"*Kaddish?*" she demands. "Whatever for?" Marvin blinks some more instead of answering. "*Morty,*" she calls out in the exact tone of voice she always used to summon him when as a kid I would go completely out of control and not even she could reach me.

"Is entirely customary, missus," Marvin reassures her. "With a *minyan*. In cases of this kind."

"*OUT!*" she screams at the top of her voice. "I want him out."

Monte starts to go right for Marvin, definitely willing and able to carry him bodily into the hall. I can just see it all happen. Marvin will go limp in Monte's arms. Then he will start singing *Olenu*, the traditional death song of Jewish martyrs in the Middle Ages. A chorus of soulful nurses will pick up guitars and join in with "We Shall Overcome." From the first bed, Mr. Lapidus will suddenly leap to his feet and begin doing James Brown splits down the hall as the cops come pouring in, busting heads right and left. We will have a legitimate riot on our hands.

"Let him be, Monte," I call out. "He means well. He just doesn't understand. . . ."

"He's not dead yet," my mother shouts, completely ignoring my advice. "And I won't have him prayed over as though he is. Morrie . . . Sol . . . Morty," she cries out, naming those that she knows will come to her aid. "Someone help me, *please*. Before I go completely insane and you have to find a bed for *me* to crawl into. . . ."

From all corners of the room, men start converging on Marvin. I have seen enough. Turning my back, I stare out the window instead. A great man is dying up here. A king. A high priest. The very last of the line. More than anything, I want to fling open the window, lean my head all the way out, and shout this into the street below. But the window does not open. They have cemented it shut, on purpose.

With sudden interest, I note the wonderful skill with which the old red brick church across the street has in fact been built. Around its slanting, red tile roof, angels of every size, shape, and description, all of them made of stone, stand poised for flight. At any moment, they may actually take off and go soaring past the buildings towards the harbor and freedom.

Just like those angels, I want to fly. I want to leave the earth behind and go careening from this room. With the cold wind blowing in my face, I will ride the jetstream away from here, never coming back down again until I am so far away that they will not be able to find me, no matter how long or how hard they look. Only, just like those angels, my feet are set in stone. All I can do is stand in one place and watch, as it all swirls madly on around me.

CHAPTER THIRTY-FIVE

ONLY SOL STRYKER can help me now. He alone can put my troubled mind to rest. Yea, though I walk through the very darkest streets of the garment center all on my own, I shall not fear. Great Sol will comfort me. His wisdom will bring me the peace that surpasseth understanding. For Sol has already climbed the mountain. He knows every rock that lies along the twisting path leading to the summit. Sol has triumphed over the minor obstacles. Now, he will show me how to do the same.

Sol's building is all gray and made of stone. Busy shoppers heading for Fourteenth Street rush right past the front door without giving it a second glance. Buildings just like this one stand everywhere in the city. They are anonymous temples of industry where people who barely speak English do piecework for a living and no one ever wears a tie. But this building belongs to Sol. So it is special.

Inside, there is no directory. There is no friendly little arrow pointing to the elevator. Instead, the hallway is dim, silent, and deserted. The only light comes from a softly glowing red-and-green Fire Exit sign over a door that is bolted tightly shut. When the final fire rages, none will escape from here. The building is sealed like the tomb of some great pharaoh.

And for good reason. Only those with *serious* business to conduct are meant to find their way in here. Casual pilgrims and salesmen out peddling their wares would do far better to make their solicitations by mail and then wait hopefully for an answer. This is Stryker Togs, Inc. Strictly the top of the line.

From somewhere above my head, I hear the deep humming of heavy machinery. At this very moment, unseen hands are cutting, piecing, and sewing together what children all over the country will be wearing in six months' time. Even for those who have already made their fortune in the city, there can be no rest.

I make my way towards a wire mesh cage. Next to it is a big red button. I press the button and then stand back, hoping that the floor beneath my feet will not suddenly give way, depositing me right back on to the sidewalk once again. A deep and sonorous clanking begins, as though ancient chains are being ground one against the other. Slowly, the freight elevator comes into view. In this chariot I will rise towards the inner sanctum, the Holy of Holies, where even now Sol himself sits, waiting to grant me an audience.

At the controls is a young Puerto Rican kid who has not bothered to shave today. Next to him stands a young girl who is definitely along only for the ride. She is sweet, with beautiful eyes, teeth, hair, and breasts. The rose that grows only up in Spanish Harlem. Both of them have gotten a head start on New Year's Eve. A little wine, a little smoke, and everything just goes up and down smoothly, again and again.

"Stryker?" I ask, pointing above my head with a single finger. There is but one way to go now. *Up.*

"Choo," the kid says.

"I've got an appointment. . . ."

"*Choo,*" he says again, giving the word an entirely different inflection as he steps back to let me on.

Jamming the car into gear, he sets it in motion again. Up we go past empty hallways stacked high with rolled bolts of cloth. Sewing machines without spindles stand next to rows of headless mannequins. The kid talks a mile a minute to his girl in rapid-fire Spanish. She just keeps nodding and giggling. Although she has heard it all before, it still sounds good to her.

Whistling through his teeth, the kid suddenly breaks into a couple of really intricate, wicked little dance steps. Slipping his hand behind his girl's tiny waist, he spins her in a tight, jittery circle. He nods approvingly whenever she gets it right. Tonight, with the lights bright in their faces, they will usher in the New Year right by doing the hot new *pachanga* in some crowded dance hall.

On the stage before them, Tito Puente will pound like a madman on his timbals. Fat Mama will do her dirty, shaking, soulful thing. All I need is a pair of high black patent leather dancing pumps and I can join them. It will certainly beat the hell out of watching the ball come down in Times Square.

On the top floor, I get off the elevator as though I have already been here many times before. I cross a huge, abandoned loft. One entire wall is made up of tiny panes of glass so filthy that the light just barely makes it through to the floor below. The floor itself has been patched in half a hundred places with different colored sections of yellowing parquet.

Once upon a time, this is where all the earnest little immigrant tailors sat hunched over their sewing machines with a bit of thread clamped tightly between their teeth. Holding up what they had made to the light, they looked first this way, then that, to make certain that the seam was perfectly straight.

Now their ghosts flit beneath the rafters, calling out news of sons and daughters who graduated from CCNY in three short years and then went on to Wall Street. Currently they are all pulling down six figures a year for putting together impossibly complicated arbitrage deals that only they, the incredible geniuses that they are, can possibly understand. And all because their mothers and fathers got the seam straight, every time.

At the far end of the loft a woman sits at a desk behind a thick glass partition. Her woolen dress leaves nothing to the imagination. Her dark red fingernails are carefully polished. Her lipstick is a perfect matching shade. When the occasion demands, those fingers can fly over the keys of a typewriter. She takes dictation in several languages, French and Greek among them. Her loyalty to Sol, of course, is beyond question.

"Paulie Bindel," I say. "To see Sol?"

Her moist tongue darts in and out of her mouth. "He's expectin' ya," she says in a nasal voice. "Go right on in."

I do not know what I expect Sol's office to look like. A mighty throne hewn from the finest cedars of Lebanon inlaid with rose-wood and ebony. A couple of ermine-trimmed pillows for Sol to lean on, with the great Stryker family crest hanging over all. Instead, Sol has an ordinary desk. Beneath a thick pane of clear glass, there are snapshots of the royal family preserved for all to see.

Behind the desk is a wall no one could ignore. Sol has been Man of the Year more times than even I can count. He has been awarded a plaque for service to the community by every last social, cultural, and fund-raising organization in the entire city. There are even awards from Catholic groups up there, proof positive that Sol's charity simply knows no bounds.

Sol himself is nowhere to be seen. I wonder if I am supposed to wait where I am. Perhaps I should sit myself right down in Sol's large padded leather armchair and try it on for size, like an eager up-and-coming somebody who knows that someday all of this will be his. Or I could just prowl around the office with my hands behind my back, inspecting plaques until Sol calls out my name. Silently, I wander towards the open door to my right.

Peering through it, I see Sol. He stands in his very own private little washroom with his back towards me. His spine is perfectly straight. His breathing is even and regular. Using his left hand to flick away the drops, Sol reaches out with his right to loudly flush. Quickly, I move back to the middle of the room.

Sol strides purposefully into his office. With him, he carries a piece of cheap brown paper toweling I associate only with elementary school bathrooms. Sol *always* washes up right after. No one ever has to remind him of the germs that lurk everywhere, even in his very own private facility. Noticing me, he smiles. "Paulie, isn't it?" he asks. I nod. *Doos bin ich*, Paulie. Now and forever more. "Paulie," Sol says, "let me ask you a question."

Anything Sol wants to ask, I am prepared to answer. I have the facts and figures at my fingertips. The capital of Nebraska? *Lincoln*. The square root of sixty-nine *Eight-something*. *Ate-something*. Get it, Sol? Just a little joke there. A little levity. The gross national product of Bolivia? Hold on, Sol, I can look it up in my Information Please Almanac. That's right. I never go anywhere without it. You mean some people do? Well, I guess I am just not one of them.

"Son," Sol says, "how many times a day do you piss?"

I stand there unable to speak. Sol has asked me the single question I cannot answer. "Uh . . . um," I stutter. "Gee, Sol, I don't really know."

"A rough estimate," he urges. "Go on. Talk to me like I was your very own family. . . ."

In my family, they do not talk of such matters. Still, for Sol, I try. "Uh. I don't think I ever counted, Sol."

"Three? Four?"

"Some days, sure. Some days, maybe more. It depends. Why?"

"Man my age," Sol sighs, lowering himself into that big leather armchair that fits him like a glove, "can't be too careful. They get you on that operating table for a prostate, kid, believe you me, you can forget about ever climbing into the saddle again. No more one on one. You're strictly a team player, from that moment on. . . ."

Sol's bald little head gleams against the polished leather. His penetrating eyes do not miss a thing. For all the world he looks like a tiny, perfect infant still waiting to be born. His hands are young and smooth, for good reason. Sol does all of his work with his brain. Every last fact he needs to know is inside that amazing *kopf* of his. Emperor Sol, the Sun King. The Wizard of Odd Sizes.

"Sit, sit," he urges. "Your mother, a tremendous woman by the way, *tremendous*, and I'm not referring to her size, tells me you got a problem. What are you going to do with your life, right?"

I nod. Sol has cut right through the bullshit. No small talk for him. No beating around the bush. Sol gets immediately to the heart of the matter, every time. And why not? He knows. Sol has been there and back again, many times over.

"*Sit down*," Sol orders, taking me by surprise. I sit right down. Sol is accustomed to being obeyed. It comes with the chair, the office, and the plaques. It is why he has never been a good team player and never will be one, no matter what they cut out. Sol leads, from the front.

I am about to start telling him all about it when suddenly he gets up from his chair and goes into the big closet behind his desk. I know that he will return with two fine Havana cigars and a cut crystal decanter filled with the finest Scotch a man can buy. Then we will sit back in comfort to kick this thing around properly.

Only when Sol comes back out of the closet, his arms are filled with tiny jumpers, pinafores, and little sailor hats with elastic bands that go under the chin. "*Take*," he orders, dumping the entire load into my lap. "Last season's line."

"Thanks, Sol," I stammer. "But I'm not going home from here and actually . . . I'm single."

"You got a baby sister or a brother?" he demands.

"No, Sol. You know my mother. *Esther*. From the shul."

"Know anyone who does?"

"Not really, no. Most of my friends aren't even married."

"Take anyway. Babies *never* go out of style. It's nature's way. . . ."

Shuttling rapidly back behind his desk as though time is money and he does not have a second to waste, Sol sits down once again. "I want to thank you for making time to see me today, Sol," I say, folding the baby clothes over in my lap. "What with your busy schedule and all . . ."

"S'nothing," Sol says emphatically, waving away the compliment with his hand as though it was a buzzing fly headed straight for his nose. In his life, Sol has been flattered by experts. He knows all the little turnings of phrase that men use to get what they want from one another. Because Sol's brain works faster, he is always a step ahead.

"Week between Christmas and New Year's is my slack season. Paulie," he explains. "So when your mother . . . Esther, right?" I nod. Esther it is, and always will be. "So when Esther, a fine woman, a *tremendous* woman, in fact, asks my wife, Sylvia, to arrange this little meeting, I'm more than happy to oblige."

Tipping back his padded leather armchair as far as it will go, Sol stares up at the ceiling as though he is seeing it for the very first time. I look up there as well. Then Sol leans forward again. He fixes me with a stare that burns right through my brain like a death ray from outer space. "So?" he says. "What do you want to know, *boychick?* I been going to shul with your grandfather for years. I feel towards him like he was my very own *zayde.* From looking at you, I can tell right away that you're just like him. A tremendous kid, in your own right. *Tremendous.* I only wish I had a son like you."

"Very nice of you to say so, Sol," I respond.

"But Sylvia gave me only daughters. Both married now. To assholes. I give them work to keep them out of jail. But that's just the way I am. You could ask anyone."

"Why should I ask, Sol? I can tell just by looking at you."

This he likes. A big smile creases his wrinkled little face. Sol is about to tell me that there is definitely a place for a young man like me in his company when he lets loose with a fart that just about blows his chair backward into the wall of plaques.

"Pardon me," he says, patting his stomach fondly. "Lately I got tremendous gas. But no heartburn. I eat only vegetarian, you know. You should join me sometime for lunch in Brownie's.

386

They got a veal cutlet in there you would swear on your life is meat. Only it's soybeans. No fatty animal protein gums up my *mugen*. My plumbing *works*."

"I'm sure it does, Sol."

"Sure, *shmur*," he says. "In this world, you got to *grab* the merchandise to know if it's any good. You got to *handle* the goods. . . ."

There it is, all right. The very first pearl of wisdom to drop from Sol's golden mouth. Whether it is a veal cutlet made from soybeans or life itself, you have to grab for it with both hands to make sure that it is what you ordered in the first place. As far as Sol's plumbing goes, however, I am willing to take his word on the subject.

"So, go on," Sol says, looking down at the thick gold watch on his wrist. I know for certain that it is a Rolex. Expensive as hell, sure, but it always keeps perfect time right down to the millisecond. Sol never has to take it in for repair. It is not some Timex like the old man wears that can fall apart on your wrist at any second.

Looking up at me again, Sol says, "You been here a good ten minutes already, kid, you ain't asked me a single question or told me the first thing about yourself. I'm a talker, Paulie. Always was. With me, you got to jump right in with both feet first."

"Okay. I was wondering, Sol, about the trip. . . ."

"Up north to ski? It's a vacation. But to West Palm Beach, the business pays. I go look in a single kid's store while I'm down there, I can write it all off. One of my son-in-laws, the accountant, takes care of it for me. If I lie, he swears to it, down the line."

"The trip to *Jerusalem*, Sol," I clarify. With him, you have to be specific. "The one they raffled off in shul on Las Vegas Night," I add. "And you won."

"What trip?" he demands. "There ain't no trip. Soon as I won, I donated it back to the shul. Nat worked it all out. They turn the ticket over to the travel agency that donated it in the first place. The travel agent pays them half price for it in cash, and everyone goes home happy. Me, I been to the Holy Land seven times. Personally, I think it's overrated. But Sylvia likes it there. She expects to find herself one of the Dead Sea Scrolls, right by the hotel pool. . . ."

"You mean, the raffle was *fixed?*"

"What *fixed?*" Sol says, spitting out the word so that I know immediately that I have made a serious error. "That's a hell of a term to use when a good cause is involved. Everything was legal and aboveboard. I had *two* hundred tickets in my name, kiddo. At twenty bucks a throw, that's four thousand clear I donated to the shul. All deductible of course. They only sold five hundred all together so it was pretty certain I would win, right? A sure thing."

A sure thing. I should have known it all along. The men who sit up at the front of the shul do it all with mirrors. That way, those of us in the cheap seats never even know that we are being fooled. "This may sound funny to you, Sol," I say. "But I was hoping my grandfather would win it."

"Funny? What's so funny about it? I think it's *beautiful*, a kid like yourself looking out for his own family. Your grandfather still wants the trip?" he asks, not letting me get a word in edgewise. "You should have come to me sooner. Maybe I could still work something out. It would be a hell of a gesture on the part of the shul. . . ."

"He won't be taking any more trips, Sol. Not now."

"Oh yeah, right," Sol says. "I sent Morrie Benson over there this morning to see how he was making out. What with one thing and another, I got Morrie running in circles these days. . . ."

Suddenly, I want to stand up, rush right out of Sol's office, and take the train back to the hospital. I belong by my grandfather's bed, not here. Sol sees the expression on my face. "You're upset about your grandfather?" he asks. "This I can understand completely. At least he got to be an old man doing what he wanted. He lived his life. Sooner or later, it happens to all of us. . . ."

Sol can see that I am not about to buy this one. "All right," he says. "So it's still lousy, any way you look at it. I'm gonna tell you something now that no one else in the entire world knows, Paulie. About my brother-in-law Nat, who will never be half the man your grandfather still is, no matter how bad off he happens to be at the moment. Of course, Nat does have a head for the business. That much I give him. Any time I need some-one to be a sonofabitch with the jobbers, they don't come any better than Nat.

"Only he likes to gamble. He likes to play gin rummy in the afternoon at his beach club. With scum like Anthony Balbano, who runs everything illegal that goes on in the garment center. You follow what I'm telling you?"

I shake my head in confusion. Sol has lost me completely.

"Nat starts chipping from the hand that feeds," he says. "We got little deficits we can't trace. The books don't balance. And why? Because *my* brother-in-law Nat is re-labeling new goods as damaged samples and closeouts and sending *my* drivers, no less, to deliver them to that discount outlet on the avenue. Run by what's-his-name. . . ."

"Jerry Kahn?"

"That's it. Another *gonif*. Kahn gives the money to Balbano and no one's the wiser. Only Kahn got too cute even for his own good. Las Vegas Night. If not for Las Vegas Night, I never would have found out about any of this. When my own wife, Sylvia, comes home with some of the goods she won at the tables. That this Jerry Kahn donated. My own stuff, Paulie! Brand new! Can you imagine? The nerve of the man. I walked into his store the next day, I nearly keeled over. My whole fall line is hanging on the back wall. So then I knew what I had to do.

"Nat I can't fire because he's family. But he's due here in an hour. With the file Morrie ran up on this for me, Nat doesn't have a leg to stand on. When I'm through with Mr. Weiss, kiddo, believe you me, he won't be able to open a mouth to me for the rest of his life. The bastard. Stealing from family. Let me tell you something else that no one knows, Paulie. The rabbi? He's gone. He should *never* have let them bring gambling into the shul. *Never*. The two simply do not mix. Like oil and water. . . ."

Because I am sitting across from Sol, the fiery sun who lights up Ahavath Mizrach's little universe, I am getting the news before anyone else. This is the inside dope all right. The real story, straight from the horse's mouth. An authentic chill runs through my entire body. So this is what it is like to be God, all of the time. Sol is paying back my enemies as I never could. He is trampling out the vintage where the grapes of wrath are stored. First Nat and then the rabbi. Sol's truth is marching on.

"You're going to just . . . get rid of the rabbi?" I say, unable to believe that it can be done so easily.

"*Me?*" Sol says. "I'm not going to do a thing. When his contract comes up, the board won't renew it. You're shocked? Don't be. You follow sports? A baseball team goes bad, they *can't* fire all the players. So they find themselves a new manager. Believe you me, it's a whole lot easier hiring a new rabbi than replacing a congregation it took years to build."

"I don't think people dislike him *that* much, Sol," I say. Why I am defending the rabbi, I have no idea. The man did not even have the simple courtesy to make an appearance at my grandfather's hospital bed. Still, he *is* the rabbi. That has to count for something. "Besides," I say, "he has a wife and two kids. . . ."

"Leah is a tremendous woman, Paulie. Make no mistake about it. A *tremendous* woman. Concerning the daughter, I hear other things. But that is not the issue. The rabbi *himself* is the problem. You like him?" Sol asks, making a face. "Strictly third rate, if you ask me," he says, answering his own question. "A *shlepper*, right from the word go. Nat thought he could work with him. Push him around is more like it. Once a year, my wife and I had to go eat dinner with him. You want the God's honest truth? It was once too much."

"He tries," I say, unable to come up with anything better at the moment. "At least, he tries."

"Running a shul is a business, Paulie," Sol says flatly. "Just like any other. If you don't produce, you're out. Which brings us right back to you. And just in the nick of time, if I may say. . . ."

Sol tips himself back in his chair. He hooks the thumb of his right hand into the belt loop of his pants. Certainly, they are custom made. Nothing but the best for Sol. All his clothes are cut by hand, carefully sewn, then fitted and refitted until every last crease hangs just so and the drape is perfect. The tailor himself comes out from in back when Sol tries on the suit. And how is the crotch, Mr. Stryker? he asks. Plenty of room? If you should ever put on any weight, please bring the suit right back in and I'll alter it for you free of charge. No trouble at all, sir. Not for a steady customer like yourself.

"So, Paulie?" Sol asks, suddenly beaming like a jovial uncle. "Tell me already. What exactly can I do for you today?"

The moment of truth is now at hand. Sol has posed the ultimate question. Certainly he has the ways and means to grant me my request. Sol is the all-powerful genie of my dreams. All I have to do is rub him the right way and I can have whatever I want, within reason. "Sol," I ask tentatively, feeling my way, "can I say *anything* now? I mean, can I tell you what I *really* want?"

"An-*ee*-thing, *boychick*," Sol says, guaranteeing me complete immunity from prosecution no matter how damaging my testimony may be. "Speak to me what is on your heart."

"Sol," I say, "I want to learn how to dance."

"Dance?" he says, his jaw dropping open. "You mean ballet? Like some *fagela?*"

"*Dance*, Sol. The real thing. The Mashed Potato. The Funky Broadway. The Jump Back Jack, See You Later Alligator. The Boston Monkey. The Popeye, Sol. The Slop, the Shing-a-ling, and the Boog-a-loo. Sol, I want to join a soul review and tour the entire country, spending five wonderful days and five wonderful nights in wonderful, wonderful cities all across the nation. I want to come on stage after the fifteenth chorus of 'Please, Please, Please' and help carry James off in a purple robe. I want to be the one who breaks those shakes when he leans over to meet and greet the crowd."

"*Bist du meshuggeh?*" Sol cries out. He is definitely upset. I can see that with my very own eyes. His little face has gone flat with bleak surprise. It is the first real reaction I have gotten out of the man. Because the rest of it is just an act, one that Sol has worked on for so many years that he now probably believes it himself. Man of the Year, my ass. Sol Stryker peddles children's clothing for a living. He did not get to the top floor of this grimy little prison by being nice to anyone.

So he likes to go to shul. So what? He can afford to have them build one to his own exacting specifications. All of Sol's money will not buy him a seat in heaven when the time comes. Myself, I pray only that I will never have so much money that I have to give lots of it away in order to avoid being struck down by God.

"You know, Sol," I say, "now that you mention it, I think I *am* crazy." Getting quickly to my feet, I reach across the desk for his hand. Before he can pull away from me, I pump it enthusiastically. "But thanks for making time to see me. I appreciate it more than you'll ever know. Especially the baby clothes. . . ."

Sol is now making little strangling noises down deep in his throat, as though he has swallowed a fishbone. I head for the door. Just before I get there, I turn like Jackie Wilson doing "Reet Petite." Swinging my right foot across my left, I plant it on the floor heel first. Then I spin in a complete circle, coming to a dead stop right in front of Sol with a big grin on my face and not a single hair on my head out of place.

"You *will* be hearing from me, Sol," I tell him. "Rest assured."

Then I go out through the door. Sol's secretary sits examining her fingernails as though she has not heard every last word of our conversation. I flash her my biggest smile. Suddenly, I *am* James Brown. Although I am soaked with sweat and more dead than alive, I am not yet through. I have enough left inside me to spring forth from the wings one last time and go sliding the entire length of the stage on my knees only to suddenly rise like Christ on Easter morning as the lights go all red and purple in my face and the band in back of me pounds away like crazy. The demonic drummer hits one wicked rim shot after the other as the entire horn section runs in whooping circles. A bolt of pure electrical energy shoots up my spine, flooding over into my brain. The trumpets madly herald my return. I *have* to do it all just one more time.

Back through the door I charge for my final score. "*Sol!*" I shout, catching him completely off his guard. For a second, he looks as though he is going to faint dead away at his desk, vegetarian diet or no. "*Get down! Get funky! Get in deep!* And remember this! James Brown *will* be back."

Then I am gone as quickly as I came, out of the silent suite of carpeted offices and on the now abandoned freight elevator riding back down towards the street below. My heart pounds like crazy, trading jungle fours with the big vein that pulses in my neck. All in all, I cannot remember the last time I felt this good, and it is not yet even New Year's Eve.

CHAPTER THIRTY-SIX

IN FRONT OF the Flatiron Building, I cut funky Broadway loose and swing on over to Fifth. Lower Manhattan gives it up and becomes midtown. The bass player nods to the drummer. He immediately doubles up on the beat as the rhythm guitarist struggles to find his groove. I begin walking faster in time to the music inside my head. I am fighting my way uptown against the current, the roar of traffic so loud in my ears that I cannot hear myself think. A big wind blows right into my face, forcing cars to leave the city whether they want to or not. In back of me, the bridges and the tunnel have already become parking lots.

All afternoon long, they have been letting people out of work early. Now they stream into the street in number, crowding the sidewalk. In order to make time, I move into the extreme outside lane. Tiptoeing along the very edge of the curb like a tightrope walker, I still have to step down into the gutter every ten seconds or so to avoid being knocked flat on my ass. As always, everyone is in a serious hurry to get where they are going.

In the failing gray light of late afternoon, in the very heart of the city in the middle of a winter I know is never going to end, they are standing three deep at every corner, waiting impatiently for the light to change. As soon as it does, they will rush right home to grab a quick shower and put on their party clothes. Then they will rush right back out again, searching for the big New Year's Eve that will finally live up to their impossible expectations.

I wish them all the best of luck. Me, I am just killing time. Trying to fill the empty hours until a certain bus comes in from Cambridge bringing a certain someone home. I am just another lousy tourist, seeing the sights here in the city of dreams that have long since been realized or forgotten.

After a certain point, Fifth itself changes, becoming the Manhattan that people only see in movies. Up here, no one looks poor. No one seems to feel the cold. Money and power stroll hand in hand, in no great rush to get where they have all obviously been so many times before.

Up ahead is the great church on the corner where anyone who likes can just wander in off the street and sit for as long as they please without being bothered. Not that I make a regular practice of visiting such places. The very first time I went inside, Lesley just about had to physically drag me through the door. Today, though, that church is the only place I want to be. A few words of silent prayer said in the presence of the competition cannot possibly do my grandfather any harm. In order to cross home, you have to touch all the bases first.

As I walk towards the church, I cannot help but think about Lesley. Pale blonde Lesley, with the dancer's body and the cartoon mind. A hundred years have passed since we lived together in Cambridge. I have changed. She has changed. I cannot even be certain that I will recognize her when she steps off the bus. Over the phone, I told her to carry a rose and a copy of *Canterbury Tales* so I would be able to pick her out in the crowd at Port Authority. Knowing it was a joke, she laughed. Why carry a book you do not intend to read?

To say that I have not missed her would be a lie. Of course, things between us can never be as they were. All I really want from Lesley now is one more night, so we can close out the year in style. It does not seem too much to ask. But then maybe it is. Knowing Lesley as I do, there will be no telling until right after I see her again for the very first time.

On the block before the church, an old blind black man is standing right in the middle of the sidewalk, singing in a high, sweet voice about angels and God's great mercy. A big German shepherd lies peacefully at his side. Every now and then, someone stops and pitches some money into a chipped white bowl on the pavement that for all I know the dog eats from at night. I take a good look at the bowl. Inside, there are two foil-wrapped pieces of Dentyne, half a roach, a book of matches from Ratner's, and a buck sixty-seven in change. Which is I guess just about all of God's great mercy that the good citizens of New York figure the old man is worth today, no matter how sweet a voice he has.

All the same, people are perfectly willing to stand around and listen for free. With no cover charge or minimum, the price is right. I am just minding my own business right at the very edge of the crowd when I realize that someone is asking me a question.

"Mister," a young kid with a black woolen yarmulka on his head says, putting his face close to mine. I stare at the little spirals of raspberry colored acne that trail from the corners of his mouth. A scraggly black beard just about covers the dead white skin on his pale, pinched face. "You're a Jew?"

"What?"

"*Du bist ein Yid?*" he repeats. "You're Jewish?"

"Why? You looking for a *minyan?*"

"*Uh*," he grunts, his head bobbing with delight. "Then you are. Mister," he says again, "you laid *tephillen* today?"

"Not yet," I tell him, neglecting to add that I did not do it yesterday or the day before either. How is it that these people always manage to find me? Although I am not wearing *tsitsis* beneath my shirt or a six-pointed Star of David around my neck, he had no trouble at all locating me in the crowd. It must be something in my face.

"You're missing a great *mitzvah* then," he informs me. "Come. Inside the bus."

Leading me by the hand, he takes me over to an orange yellow

394

school bus that is parked at the curb. Because I am still only just killing time, I follow him up the steps. Inside the bus, they have torn out all the seats, replacing them with desks covered by the same cheap blue carpeting that has been tacked down on the floor. Men of all ages, most of them Jewish, I assume, stand around the desks, grateful for this opportunity to lay *tephillen* in a little temple on wheels parked right in the middle of midtown.

Inside this bus, they are taking all comers. Given half a chance, they will bundle the old blind black man from the street up the stairs, wrap the black leather thongs around his left arm and forehead, and go ahead and say the blessings for him. That way, he too will not miss this great *mitzvah*. Just by looking, I can tell that I am in the midst of a regular crusade.

The kid who has appointed himself as my religious instructor for the day really is very pale. He has *yeshiva* skin. Never once in his entire life has he ever sat in the sun. His cheap blue suit is shiny in the seat. Snowy white dandruff lies scattered across both his shoulders. That unmistakable smell comes off him as well, the dank, musty odor of tiny basement shuls where men stand for hours wheezing and coughing and blowing their noses right into their *tallisem* as they pray, so they will not miss a single line. The entire bus smells of bad breath and unwashed underwear.

Although he is doing his very best to carry off the role confidently, I can tell that it is still a little early in the game for him to be completely convincing at it. For all I know, he already has a young bride at home who wears the *sheitl* and cooks and cleans for him. Once a month, she dutifully goes to the *mikvah*. When her time comes, she will bear him many children, thereby increasing the strength of the tribe.

Once his working day is over, he and all the others who dress just like him head back home across the Williamsburg Bridge. They sing the old melodies over and over as the city streams by outside the windows of their bus. In numbers, they find safety. They eat together, they pray together, they go into business together. At least he knows who his friends are. For that, I envy him.

Reaching under the little desk that stands between us, he takes out a really awful looking set of *tephillen* that are nothing at all like the fine set my grandfather has kept for years in a little green felt drawstring bag. More times than I can remember, I have watched him perform the ceremony in the morning. First, he carefully winds a narrow black leather strap three times around the middle finger of his left hand. Then again carefully seven times around his forearm, all the while silently reciting to himself in Hebrew.

Holding the little black box at the very end of the strap close to his heart, he drapes the leather thong around his forehead. Its little black box comes to rest just above his eyes. Then he stands and rocks gently on his heels, heart and mind joined together, at one with himself, the Lord, and Torah.

Without fail each morning, except on Shabbos and holidays, when it is forbidden to do so, my grandfather lays *tephillen*. Never once have I asked him about it. Never once has he tried to persuade me to join him. *Tephillen* is *tephillen*. Either you put it on each morning, or not. Either way, it is a simple act.

Only today, I have to know exactly what it means. I have to hear my self-appointed tutor explain the ceremony to me in painstaking detail. It is essential. Why, I cannot say. "Excuse me," I say. "Before we start. I wonder . . . what is the meaning of *tephillen?*"

"The meaning is in the *mitzvah* of laying it," he says, reaching for my left wrist so that he can begin winding the first strap around my middle finger. Quickly, I jerk my hand away. "I mean . . . the *significance*," I say.

"The *significance?*" he repeats, blinking rapidly more times in a row than I can count. "The significance is in doing it every day. You were born a Jew, you should *live* like a Jew."

I cannot argue with that. "How about the *symbolism?*" I persist, nearly pleading with him. I have to hear it from his mouth. Certainly, my grandfather can use all the help he can get today. I am perfectly willing to put on *tephillen* for him. Just as soon as I find out what it means, and not a second before. In other words, if this kid does not shout "Olley olley oxen free!" three times in a row before I count to a hundred, everyone around my base who is *it* can just stay that way forever more. It is one hell of a juvenile attitude all right. But there is not a single thing I can do about it. Not until he tells me something that I do not already know.

"Where did the practice originate?" I ask, figuring that I may at least be able to extract a little history from him.

"Ancient times," he says vaguely. "Ancient times. Thousands of years old. Come. Let's do it. Then we'll talk."

"How about the little boxes?" I demand, putting both my hands inside my pockets so that he will not be tempted to grab for them again. I can feel the sweat starting to soak through the material of my shirt under both of my armpits. "What's inside of them?"

Finally, I have asked him a question that he can answer. His pinched little face lights up with pleasure. All the while, he keeps peering anxiously over my shoulder like a traffic cop writing a ticket with one eye open for other violators so he can meet his monthly quota. "Inside," he says, "are scrolls. Parchment. Four in the *shel rosh* for your head, each in its own little compartment. Four in the *shel yad* for your arm, all together in a long, continuous roll. . . ."

"It's four prayers then?"

"Four *lignen*," he answers.

"Passages, you mean?"

"Four *lines*," he says impatiently. "Four *lines*. Sacred to the heart of every Jew, the *Shema* among them."

"The practice, though. Someone *must* have invented it, no? I mean, why do they use *leather* straps?"

"Mister," he sighs, "do me a favor. You want to discuss this with our rabbi? He'll be glad to see you anytime you like. I'll give you his address after we finish. Now, you want to lay *tephillen* today, or not?"

"Definitely," I tell him. "I want to."

Nodding in approval, he sets right to work. He winds one well-worn thong in a very professional manner around the middle finger of my left hand with three short, sharp turns. As he does it, I cannot help but wonder who had this set on before me. Do they wipe them off afterwards, or what? Rolling up the sleeves of my shirt, he bends my arm back at the elbow like a medical technician about to take my blood pressure. Seven fast wraps and the *shel yad* is in place. For all the world, I feel like I am being served lunch in a fast-food joint.

"Now, mister," he orders, "you repeat after me exactly what I say, please. *Very* important that you get it exactly right. . . ."

Smoothly he begins reciting the Hebrew from memory. I stumble along badly, a beat behind, bringing up the rear just as those who always sit near my grandfather at the very back of the shul do during *Kaddish* on Yom Kippur. Then he puts the *shel rosh* on my head. Stepping back, he gives it a quick once-over. Still not quite satisfied with the way it looks, he reaches around with a damp hand and pulls it down in back. Then he nods.

Following his lead, I mumble my way through another prayer.

All the while, I keep looking right into his eyes, hoping to see some sign that he is really with me on this. I mean, it is not as though I am looking for a legitimate religious experience or anything. I have already had one of those. I just want to feel *something*, if not for my sake, then for my grandfather. In his eyes, I see nothing. The real meaning of *tephillen*, whatever it actually happens to be, is going to remain a mystery between the two of us.

Without pausing for breath, he launches right into the *Shema*. For some reason, this takes me completely by surprise. I really mess up a couple of words before getting them right. Finally, I have made an impression on him. An adult Jewish male who does not actually know every last word of the *Shema* by heart. It will provide him with at least fifteen minutes of solid conversation for the bus ride back home.

What can I say in my defense? When my time finally comes, I will certainly regret the error of my ways. As I stare directly into death's black and gaping maw, I will open my own mouth to proclaim that the Lord is One and nothing will come out but the words of James Brown's latest hit. It is definitely a scandal of the first degree.

Reaching up, he takes the *tephillen* off my head with one hand while neatly unwrapping it from my left arm with the other. Just as quickly as it began, it is suddenly over. I cannot help but wonder what possible good it has done me or my grandfather to repeat words that I do not understand. Before I can ask any more questions, my instructor ducks out of sight to put the *tephillen* away. I note that he does not bother to wipe either of the black leather thongs clean.

"See?" he demands when he stands back up again, a big grin on his face. "Only a very few minutes of your time, mister. Yet you performed a great *mitzvah*. A *very* great *mitzvah*."

It does not feel so great. Before I know what is happening, he leads me back out into the street. The bus is still exactly where it was before, our little journey having taken us nowhere at all. Grabbing my hand, the kid pumps it enthusiastically a couple of times. "*Shalom aleichem*, mister," he says. "God be with you." Then he is gone, off into the crowd to find himself another likely looking prospect.

It is now that special time in the city, that single magic moment just after sunset when the sky turns purple, all the buildings gleam, and Manhattan itself suddenly looks newly

398

made and almost friendly. The moment passes quickly. The sky rapidly becomes completely dark, with no moon anywhere to light the coming night. Automatically, people begin walking faster, in a sudden hurry to get where they are going.

Soon, the power will be turned on full. The electricity that runs constantly through these tight, interlocking streets will peak from grid to crowded grid until it all finally explodes at midnight in a massive overload in Times Square. Not that it will make any difference to the old blind black man. He is still singing in that high, sweet voice. Apparently, no one has told him that the working day is over.

Suddenly, I am seized by an overwhelming desire to perform an act of true charity. Only I am not exactly sure how to go about it. I mean, does the person to whom I give my gift have to be truly deserving? Or is giving itself enough? As though I am in a trance, I push my way through the crowd towards the old black blind man. "Hey," I say, gently reaching out for his arm. "I got something for you. Little present for New Year's Eve. . . ."

"That right?" he says, breaking off his song to turn in my direction. His sightless eyes are hidden behind thick black sunglasses. He looks just like Baby Ray himself, the great Ray Charles. He has that innocent wildchild grin on his face, just like when Ray sits himself down at the piano with all the Raelettes gathered behind him, a cluster of throbbing hummingbirds, who maniacally warble, *Tell me what I say! Tell me what I say!* over and over, as though anyone will ever be able to answer the question for them.

"If it's a bottle," he says, breathing right into my face. "Give it to me in my hand. . . ."

"It's not a bottle, brother," I tell him, the spirit of giving having taken complete control of my mind. Carefully, I wrap both of his wrinkled, leathery palms around the crumpled bundle of baby clothes I have been carrying with me all afternoon long. "It's baby clothes," I explain. "A complete set. You know, brother. Tiny togs for tots?"

"You wouldn't be shittin' an old man now, would you, son?"

"Never."

"What in hell 'm I sposed to do with baby clothes?"

"I don't know," I say, having failed to think that far ahead. At the moment, this is the only offering I can make. I know that it is not much. I wish with all my heart that I could do better. But

399

lately things have just been kind of tough all over. "They are the very top of the line," I offer. "Maybe you can sell them. . . ."

"Mebbe I kin put'em on mah dog. . . ."

"Why not?"

For no reason I can name, I now fully expect this old blind man to suddenly whip off his sunglasses, revealing a pair of eyes that have been magically healed and can suddenly see as well as mine. Instead he says, "Well, thank you kindly, son. Thank you kindly." With a shaking, skinny finger, he beckons me closer. I step right up, eager to hear what he has to say.

"Now that you done gave me your *generous* gift, son," he rasps, "kin you do but one more thang for me?"

"Anything," I say, really meaning it.

"Git yore sorry white ass the fuck off mah corner," he whispers. "And doan *nevah* bring it back again."

God, in the person of this blind old black man, is speaking directly to me. The time has come to move on. That great church on the corner will just have to wait. There are people all over the city who need my help. The night itself is young. There is no telling how much damage I can actually do, both to them and myself, before the ball comes down at midnight. Any way you look at it, my evening has only just begun.

CHAPTER THIRTY-SEVEN

PORT AUTHORITY IS crowded. Unhappy people sit on wooden benches with string-wrapped parcels between their knees waiting for buses that will never come to take them somewhere they do not really want to go. In the harsh and ghastly light, they stare into space, so many zombies gathered around a bonfire in the warm Caribbean night. Soon, voodoo drums will start pounding from the bush. The zombies will get to their feet and sway in circles in the flickering shadows, doing dances of the dead. I am betting that they lead off with a ladies' choice.

Around the green tile walls of the station, the working girls stand. They wear purple head scarves, creamy iridescent green eye shadow, and crinkly red, black, and white satin jackets. King-size cigarettes dangle from between their fingers. For them, it is just another night on the job, servicing the dead, the dying, and the terminally weird.

Jittery young boys who have only just gotten off buses from Hoboken and Perth Amboy rush through the terminal without looking anywhere but straight ahead. They are in a desperate hurry to get to Forty-second Street before the shops close. Who knows? Maybe there is a big discount sale in progress there even now. Switchblades, gravity knives, and chrome-plated motorcycle chains priced to move before the old year runs out.

How thoughtful of me to have carefully inserted my trusty little white plastic inhaler into the side pocket of my jacket before leaving the old man's apartment this morning. How very clever. Putting it to my mouth, I fire three gigantic blasts of sour tasting spray onto the back of my throat. I am about to see Lesley once again. I need all the help I can get.

When finally I find the gate where her bus came in, she is already inside the building. She is not exactly alone either. Three very large and hard working gentlemen who are no doubt always on the lookout for new talent have her surrounded. "Fellows," I say, coming up on them from behind, "think she's pretty?"

"*Know* ah do," the largest of them answers. "Why? Y'all interested?"

"Fellows," I say again, feeling the spray start to take effect, "I am not buying. But I might be able to make you a package deal. . . ."

"You dinn't say you had no dude," the largest of them notes, spitting neatly between his teeth. Then he sighs and leads his colleagues towards the terminal bar.

"Cute," Lesley says, not the least bit amused. "But I could have handled it myself."

Lesley definitely looks good. Her hair is longer than I remember it. Her face is flushed with color. Whether it is from steam heat or vague feelings of sexual excitement generated by my presence, I cannot say for sure. I do not even know whether I am supposed to kiss her, shake her hand, take her bag, or what. Lesley solves the problem by stepping towards me and kissing me on the cheek. It is the kind of kiss you get from your second cousin who is fat.

"Don't tell me," I say. "Let me guess what those boys

401

wanted. Fiveletter word, starts with *p*, ends with a *y*. Can anyone on the Red Team take this one?'' I am rushing all right. I cannot keep my mouth shut, even though I have nothing to say. ''Sorry,'' I say, making a buzzer sound down low in my throat. ''The correct answer is . . . *puppy*. Lesley,'' I say, without pausing for breath, ''where is your luggage?

''You're looking at it,'' she answers, showing me a small suitcase just about big enough to hold two blouses and a change of underwear.

''Traveling light these days, are we?''

''I'm getting a ride back up tomorrow. Didn't I tell you that over the phone this morning?''

I shrug. Maybe I forgot. What does it matter when she goes back? At the moment, she is here. ''Why come in at all then?'' I ask.

''Oh, various reasons.'' Lesley acting coy. It is a new role for her. Still, she has definitely never looked better. Living without me suits her. ''Norris gave me an address,'' she says. ''Some of his friends are having a party in the Village.''

''Forget it.''

''Why? You *afraid* to go?''

''On New Year's Eve? You bet I am.''

''Paulie,'' she sighs. ''It's not like I'm dragging you up to Harlem or anything. The party is in *Greenwich Village*, for God's sake.''

''Oh, I get it. *Downtown* brothers. Probably speak the language and everything, right? Liberals . . .''

''Paulie,'' she says again in that tired voice I remember so well from Cambridge. ''Do we have to argue about this now? In here?''

''No, we can go do it wherever you're staying. You *are* staying somewhere, right?''

''A friend of Anita's,'' she says. ''A sublet. On a Hundred and Tenth and Columbus.''

''Lovely neighborhood. Only the best people live there.''

''Paulie?'' she asks sweetly. ''Who threw you up tonight?''

It is going to be one swell evening all right. A night of magic and mystery in the big town. Not that it has anything to do with either of us. Our problem is strictly chemical. Whenever Lesley and I get near one another, we react, causing yet more irritation in places that are already tender and sore.

Doing up the collar of my jacket, I take Lesley's bag and lead

402

her out into the street. An ice cold wind is coming straight off the river in back of us. Drunks are stumbling out of all the Irish bars on Eighth Avenue, already so hammered on Bushmill's and beer that they will never make it through until midnight. "Where did you park your father's car?" she shouts, trying to make herself heard above the wind. "At some fire hydrant?"

"I don't have it," I shout back.

"Since when?"

"Since he needs it to get back and forth to the hospital to see my grandfather."

"Oh, baby," she says, squeezing my arm tightly as she brushes softly up against my side. "I can't tell you how badly I feel about that. Let's take a cab," she suggests, her face brightening. "I want to shower and change."

"A cab?" I say. "All the way up there? What happened? The subway stopped running?"

Lesley is not listening. Stepping to the very edge of the curb, she whistles for one by placing the first two fingers of her right hand between her teeth. All my life, I have wanted to be able to do this. Unfortunately, it is just one more thing that I am not good at. Naturally, a Checker pulls up right in front of us. I help Lesley into the back seat and settle down next to her.

Lesley gives the driver the address. Then she loops her arm through mine as though the two of us are out on our very first date, with all the good times yet to come. Of course, she can afford to feel that way. I am the one who will be paying for the cab.

We head uptown. Tonight, Central Park looks romantic as hell. The taxi winds through it slowly as I stare out the window. The old fashioned streetlamps by the side of the road shower perfect cylinders of crystal light onto patches of vanilla snow starred with chocolate freckles. If I did not know that the freckles were made of dog shit, I would be completely impressed.

Desperately, I sit there trying to think of something to say. It occurs to me that this *is* our first date. Lesley and I are now actually strangers, with nothing much in common and very little to discuss. Basically, I am looking for the one indelibly perfect remark that will cause her to melt instantly into my arms. That way, we can put the sublet to good use as soon as we get inside the door. Before I can speak, she says, "Did I tell you about Anita?"

"What about her?"

"She's getting married. In June, no less. A *white* wedding. Can you imagine?"

"To Rob Rosen?" I say in disbelief. "That *putz?* That horse's ass?"

"Paulie," Lesley giggles, poking me in the side with her finger. "Not Rob Rosen. Someone she just met. And it's love, too. Did I tell you that J. Geils got a recording contract?"

"No shit!" I shout, really happy for good old Peter Wolf. Now, he will never be el seven. "This is great."

"No, it's not. They stopped playing at The Charity Ward and they had to shut the place down. But Cole T. Walker is going to manage them. . . ."

"Cole," I say. I have not really thought about any of these people since I left Cambridge. It is like hearing about the characters of a soap opera I no longer watch.

"He lost thirty pounds. You wouldn't recognize him."

"Since I never saw him before, that's probably true," I note. "How about E.C.? He pay you that two hundred and twenty-eight dollars yet?"

"Why, Paulie," Lesley says, obviously pleased, "you remember the exact figure."

"Yeah, well. Some things *do* tend to stick in my mind. Did he?"

"Not yet," she giggles. "But then you know E.C."

"Not any more," I say. "And not ever again. Not if I can help it."

"Poor baby," Lesley croons. Then she pulls my head down against her coat. I can smell the freezing fog and the cold driving rain of New England winter in the fabric. Cambridge is a place I will never see again. "You're supposed to celebrate on New Year's Eve, Paulie," she whispers. "Just relax. You'll see. We'll have big fun. . . ."

Before I can ask for her current definition of that term, the cab pulls in at the curb. Lesley slides along the seat into the street, leaving me behind to pay the driver half the money I have brought with me for the entire evening. Then I join her outside. The two of us stand without speaking in front of a ruined apartment house. The liquor store on the corner is jumping. Otherwise the entire neighborhood looks deserted. No doubt this is the calm before the storm.

Checking the address of the building against what she has written on a little slip of paper in her hand, Lesley sighs and makes a funny face. "This must be the place," she says, crossing her eyes. "Maybe the apartment itself is nicer."

The apartment itself is perfect. To get there, we walk up two flights of curving stairs soaked in old urine. Then we move slowly down a hallway that stinks of roach powder and the cheap lead-based paint they smear on the walls whenever a tenant moves out. In a building like this one, that happens *all* the time. After putting Lesley's key in the lock, I have to butt the door open with my shoulder so that we can go inside.

Naturally the steam is going full blast. I quickly open the only window in the room so that I can breathe. The room is the entire apartment. A big double bed stands against the wall across from a linoleum topped table covered with bread crumbs that the roaches probably play volleyball with at night. A tiny black-and-white portable TV sits on the table, streamers of aluminum foil hanging from the rabbit ears of the antenna.

Without ever having met the girl who lives here, I already know what she looks like. She is thin, really thin, with plain brown or dull wheat-straw hair drawn back into a severe librarian's bun at the nape of her skinny neck. She even sleeps with a pencil behind her ear. She has not had her period in three years. But she does love living in the city. It is just so *real*.

Putting my jacket on the back of the only chair in the room, I sink down onto the bed. The mattress is an exact replica of the surface of the moon, all gaping craters and steep, dusty knolls. Whenever I shift my weight, the springs creak loudly beneath me. I shut my eyes and clasp my hands together prayerfully on my chest. Insert a single lily between my fingers and call the man. I am dead.

When I open my eyes again, Lesley is gone. From the bathroom, I hear the sound of running water. At this very moment, she stands under the shower, soaping herself everywhere at once. I could stalk right in there, tear the shower curtain from its grungy plastic hooks, and take her by force, as I have never done before. Or I could stay right where I am and pillage the apartment, making myself a little CARE package to take back home with me to the neighborhood, as kind of a souvenir of the night.

My head is killing me. It pulses with a dull, heavy ache that will not stop no matter how hard I try to make it go away. Reaching for my jacket, I take out the inhaler. I hit myself up with a double dose of spray. Not that it is going to solve my real problem. Basically, I do not even know who Lesley and I are supposed to be for one another anymore. I am totally confused about everything. It is the only thing I am really good at. Not knowing what else to do, I get up and start walking around the room.

When Lesley comes out of the bathroom, she is wearing just a towel. On her, it looks good. Her hair is pinned up in back. Little droplets of water slide down her pink, scalloped shoulders onto her narrow, fanshaped back. The moment is definitely at hand. Lesley lets me know this for a fact by leaning provocatively over her suitcase. Slowly, the towel slides to her hips. Then it falls completely to the floor.

All I can do is stare. I am being paid back in full for what I did to her in Cambridge. It is no more than I deserve. "You look thin," I say.

"Do I?" she says, turning towards me so that I can see it all from a better angle. "I have lost some weight. From sheer aggravation. You don't think I'm gaunt, do you?"

Lesley will never be gaunt. Not in a million years. Instead of telling her this, I turn my head away. If I want to feel this bad, I can just go and sit in my grandfather's semiprivate room at the hospital. At least there, I will know why I am being punished. Somehow, this is worse. I cannot take it.

"Listen," I say, grabbing for my jacket, "I'm going down to that liquor store on the corner."

"Whatever for, Paulie?" Lesley asks innocently, laughing at me with her eyes as she powders herself all over.

"A bottle."

"A bottle?" she says. "Since when do you drink?"

"I don't. I mean, usually I don't. But seeing as how it's New Year's Eve and all, I might want a taste. I mean, it's better to have some and not drink it than to want some and not have any, right? If you know what I mean. Be back in a second."

I am raving all right. Before she can say anything, I am out the door and down the stairs into the street. In the liquor store on the corner, I buy myself a pint of Southern Comfort. It is the only stuff I can drink without gagging. This is because it tastes exactly like cough medicine, a substance with which I have been on intimate terms ever since childhood.

I unscrew the cap as soon as I get back out into the street. I tip the bottle to my mouth. It stings, but only for a second. Then I swallow, gagging only a little. I am practicing to be a man. No one ever said it was going to be easy. Then I do it all over again, just to get the rhythm down. I put the cap back on and slide the bottle into my jacket pocket, right next to the spray.

By the time I get back up to the apartment, Lesley is dressed and ready to go. In itself, this is a miracle. Not exactly the one that I need, but a miracle all the same. Out we go once more into the night. Lesley hails a cab in front of the building. Instead of telling the driver to take us downtown to the village, she orders him to go west, towards the river. "Relax," she says before I can open my mouth in protest. "This one is on me."

When the cab stops again, she pays the driver. Then she leads me past a uniformed doorman into an elevator. Up we go to an apartment with an open door. The door itself is a work of art. It has three different locks mounted on the frame. The frame itself has been reinforced with a plate made of solid steel. A heavy cast-iron safety bar leans against the plate. You could hit this baby with a Sherman tank and it would not give. I am impressed.

The woman standing in front of all this hardware has skin like tissue paper, large, demented eyes, and too many bones in her face. "Mirandie," she announces by way of hello, her throat pulsing like crazy. "Jack and I," she says, "are having a very loose, no-host kind of thing tonight. You are a little early but that is just fine with me. Please come in and help yourself. . . ." Then she reaches for my jacket.

Why Mirandie speaks as though she is reading from a TelePrompTer. I have no idea. Strong doses of some little known antidepressant perhaps. It may also have something to do with the way she was raised. From the expectant look on her face, I can tell that it is now time for me to introduce myself and my date for the evening.

"What a *great* door," I say instead. "I don't think I've ever seen one like it. I bet that iron bar alone weighs at least thirty pounds. . . ."

"Oh, it *does*," Mirandie says eagerly. "Jack works in metal, you know. He actually forged the bars on our bedroom window by *hand*."

"I bet they're thick," I say in a confidential tone, leering into her face.

"Carbon steel," she confesses. "We had to do it because of the neighborhood. It's changing, but slowly. We have a dog as well. A very nervous German shepherd named Ilse."

"My favorite breed," I say insincerely, grinning with only my teeth.

407

Before I can ask Lesley why the hell she has brought me here, she smiles and asks, "Is Rob here yet?

"Christ," I moan. "Is that asshole coming too?"

"Rob is one of Jack and Mirandie's closest friends," Lesley explains. "They all went to film school together. Before he decided to make therapy his career."

"Give me back my jacket," I say, taking it from Mirandie's hand.

"You're not leaving already, are you?" Mirandie asks, quivering a little around the mouth.

"Nah. I just need something from the pocket."

Slipping my inhaler and my pint of Southern Comfort into my hand, I give Mirandie back my jacket. Then I step past her into the apartment. The hallway is all white and completely empty except for a ten-speed bicycle that leans against one wall like a piece of modern sculpture. The living room is decorated the exact same way. I do not know whether Jack and Mirandie have taken out all their furniture for tonight's party or if they just never bothered to buy any in the first place. One thing is certain. As Len Barry, late of the Dovells once sang, you can't sit down.

"Evening," says a man with too little hair on top and too much on the sides. He wears old jeans and a work shirt that is too faded.

"You must be Jack," I say, failing to supply him with my name. "What a *great* floor. I don't think I've ever seen one like it." Actually, I can hardly see the one I am talking about. The reflection coming off it is so blinding that I could use a pair of shades just to look at it straight on.

"Thank you," he says proudly. "Sixteen coats of paint before I started sanding. On my hands and knees for a solid week before I saw bare wood. Almost lost the faith right then and there, I can tell you that. Stained for nearly a week as well. Twelve coats. Threw a Varathane sealer on it and haven't had to worry since. Buff it with a damp mop, and there you are."

"There you are," I say. "Lot of work just for a floor, no?"

"I looked at it as a kind of therapy. Doorbell," he notes, starting to move away. " They'll be flooding in here now. Not that they'll scuff the floor. Food in the kitchen. Help yourself." Jack disappears into the hallway. I hear him call out, "Mirandie? Delivery boy. Wants cash. Can you see to it?"

Lesley makes the serious error of drifting languidly into the

408

room. Except for the blinding glare, the two of us are all alone. Grabbing her by the arm, I hiss, "Who *are* these people?"

"I told you already," she says. "Friends. Of Rob's . . ."

"If they're going to live here, why don't they furnish the place?"

"Jack's into kind of a minimalist thing. He's actually a very talented actor. Only he hasn't worked in over a year. They're broke, I think. I thought you would like him."

"I *love* him. And her. Let's go."

"Oh, please, Paulie," Lesley sighs, more bored with me than actually annoyed. "Go get yourself something to eat. You'll feel better." Then she points towards the kitchen and drifts languidly away. I take a long swig from the pint. Then I hit myself up with a fiery double blast of spray from the inhaler. A fine, arching rainbow forms behind my eyes. The pot of gold at the very end is nowhere in sight.

In the kitchen, food has not so much been put out as arranged, in kind of a loose, no-host, minimalist way. In the middle of the room stands a butcher's block that Mirandie probably bought for peanuts down in the Fulton Fish Market. After it was hoisted up here by block and tackle, Jack the Demon Woodman sanded and sanded and sanded. Then he refinished it until he was blue in the face from the fumes.

The block is covered with a blue-and-white checked cloth, the kind you take along when you are going on a picnic in the French countryside in the spring. The food on top of the cloth I would not eat if I were starving to death. Instead, I head straight for the refrigerator. Let me look at the shelves of your icebox and I will tell you who you are. Swinging open the door, I peer inside.

Just as I expected. Imported cheese, foreign beer, non-Jewish rye bread, and a single tin of caviar. Then I spot a promising looking parcel wrapped in white paper. I shove it up under my arm and close the door. Sounds are coming from behind the bedroom door. Strange, seductive sounds. Whining followed by much passionate scratching. Pushing open the door, I discover Ilse herself.

Ilse is one hell of a big dog to keep penned up in a West Side apartment. She is also a total basket case. Her head goes in nineteen directions at once when she sees me. Her paws scrape loudly on the floor. Her tail revolves in sweeping circles.

Good old Ilse. It is only a matter of time before the dog flips out completely. She will then go straight for Jack or Mirandie's throat, sinking her razor sharp incisors right into the jugular. She will hang on for dear life until the boys from the Fire Department come to pry her off again. It is up to me to save my hosts from this awful fate. Edging into the bedroom, I start doing my Clyde Beatty routine. "Down, Big Simba," I whisper, *"Down."*

Meekly, Ilse obeys. She inserts her triangular head between my knees, forcing me backwards on to the bed. I look into her mournful yellow eyes. There is an emptiness in there that cannot be measured. The doggie void, where canine souls float forever in woofing purgatory.

Opening the white paper parcel, I take out some kind of chopped liver wrapped in dough. Ilse cannot get enough of the stuff. She runs her rough sandpaper tongue over my fingers as I shovel it into her mouth. It is then that Mirandie comes through the door. Sitting herself down on the bed, she somehow manages to keep her back perfectly straight while planting both feet firmly on the floor. She has fabulous posture.

"I wonder if you realize," she says, carefully setting each word in type in her mind before she speaks, "that what you are feeding my dog happens to be eighteen dollar a pound *pâté en croûte* from Zabar's. . . ."

"No problem. She thinks it's chopped liver."

"Ilse is a complete vegetarian. We raised her that way from a puppy."

If this dog is a complete vegetarian, then I am Joan of Arc. Ilse is wolfing the stuff down so fast that big red globules of half-chewed meat keep popping out from in between her teeth. As soon as they fall to the floor, she Hoovers them right up into her mouth again. "You're one of *them*, aren't you?" Mirandie says softly, her large eyes swimming in aberrant circles in her head. "I knew it as soon as you came through the door."

"No I'm not," I tell her. "My mother wouldn't even let me join the Cub Scouts."

"You respect nothing," she says. "You want to tear down everything people have worked so hard to build and start all over from scratch. . . ."

"Anarchist," I say, trying to help her find the word she seems to be searching for so desperately.

"Nihilism," she says instead. "That's your whole life, isn't it? The dogged pursuit of nothing . . ."

"For its own sake," I add, watching with satisfaction as Ilse the dog chugs down the last of the eighteen dollar a pound *pâté*

410

en croûte. "If I were you," I advise, "I'd watch her for a couple of days. If she starts going to Zabar's by herself or anything, call the vet."

Mirandie leans dangerously near me. Her breath smells sweet, as though she has been chewing Sen-Sen all afternoon long. "You already know what I'm thinking, don't you?" she whispers in a husky voice. "To you, I'm completely transparent."

"Like Saran Wrap," I confirm.

Suddenly, Mirandie starts sobbing into my shoulder. "You can't know what hell it's been," she murmurs. "Jack down on his hands and knees sanding that damn floor night after night while I lay here with my hand between my legs wondering why he just keeps on rejecting me. He thinks he's a failure, you know. He won't even take any more money from his family. Then you come through the door. On New Year's Eve, of all nights. . . ."

"Life *can* be a bitch sometimes," I say sympathetically.

"I swear I've done my best to make this marriage work."

"I'm sure you have."

"And now this party . . ."

"And now this party," I repeat, really starting to enjoy myself. "And *us.* . . ."

"Yes, and us. . . ."

"I can help."

"Really? How?"

"Here," I say, offering her the pint. She shakes her head. Unscrewing the cap, I push the bottle towards her again. Mirandie takes a petite ladylike little sip. I put the inhaler to her mouth. Her thin lips part. I pump three times, hard, hitting Mirandie up with spray while at the same time slapping her on the back so that she will not gag and spit it all out.

"Good girl," I say approvingly as she swallows. "Soon, the medicine will make everything better."

"Will it?"

"You bet. Just stay here," I say, slipping off the bed and heading for the door. "When you're feeling better, come join the party. I'll tell everyone you're taking a little nap."

"Oh," she sighs, already closing her eyes. "That would be lovely. I'm *so* tired. I feel as though I haven't slept since I was eighteen years old."

"Right," I say, closing the door softly behind me. "I know the feeling well."

411

Mirandie is a soul sister all right. Just like her, I could use a little sleep. A little sleep, some eighteen dollar a pound *pâté en croûte* from Zabar's, and a week or two on the quiet island watching the waves roll in, and I will feel just fine again. Fat chance of my getting any of this tonight.

People now stand all over the living room. With drinks in their hands, they are saying devilishly clever things to one another. Their faces swim before my eyes. Like a miniature deep sea diver at the end of a plastic hose, I slowly make my way across the bottom of the fish tank. Air bubbles spill from my mouth. Walleyed groupers and big mouthed bass float slowly past my fogged-up visor. I have never felt so stoned in my entire life.

When finally I find Lesley in the crowd, I grab for her arm like a drowning man. "Have to go," I say. "Have to make bye-bye to all the nice people. . . ." Lesley steps away from me as though I have some disease she does not want to catch.

"Paulie," she says, "you *do* remember Rob, don't you?"

Sure enough, there he stands. Bigger than life and twice as ugly. Good old Rob. The human doll, with no moving parts. "Have to go," I say again, ignoring his outstretched hand, his brilliant therapeutic smile, *"Now."*

"Are you ready to leave, Rob?" Lesley asks, as though it no longer matters at all what I want.

Rob clears his throat. He has dealt with much sicker people than me in his time and emerged with his reputation intact. "I do owe it to Jack and Mirandie to stay for a *little* while longer," he notes. "Why don't you two kids just run along without me? I can catch up with you downtown. We'll just move the entire party, so to speak. . . ."

More than anything, I want to tell Rob to move the entire party up his ass. So to speak. Instead, I turn away and go find my jacket. When I return, Rob and Lesley are standing right on top of one another. Lesley gets up on tiptoe. She gives him a kiss on the mouth that makes the one I got from her in Port Authority seem positively anemic. They are definitely one hell of a couple. I wish them the best of everything. So long as I do not have to stay around to watch them enjoy it.

Lesley breaks away from him and comes towards me. She takes me by the hand. I have to give the girl credit. She *is* adaptable. In the very worst sense of the word. Down we go in the elevator to the street. Yet another cab appears before us. We get in. The cab starts to roll. I feel the phlegm rising in my throat. My forehead is beaded with ice cold sweat. My chest is on fire. I open the window and stick my head outside. With deep and frantic gulps, I suck the cold night air into my lungs.

It is almost over. That I know for sure. I mean, there is not all that much left to cut out. The very next time they go in with the knife, they are going to find what they have been looking for all along. The part that feels. Once they remove it, I can hop off the operating table and go home under my own power, a brand-new man at last.

Perhaps then, like the great James Brown himself, I will be both tired and clean. My performance will be over. Until that moment comes, there is nothing I can do but just keep on dancing. It is the only way. As they like to say in the great temple of Apollo up on a Hundred and Twenty-fifth Street in Harlem, one monkey don't stop no show. Not ever. Not even if the poor dumb ape happens to be me.

CHAPTER THIRTY-EIGHT

I SMELL IT and hear it before I ever see it. Right away, I know that it is the real thing. The door is open so I move right on in. A single record goes round on the turntable. The Jackson Five doing "ABC," only the greatest single ever released in the entire history of Western civilization. No one bothers to turn the record over. After it plays all the way through, it plays all the way through again. In order to get down, you got to get in deep. Anything else is just a lie.

A big, strong line forms down the middle of the living room. People strut their stuff, looking just as fine as they please. Guys sing loudly into one another's face, trying to reach that impossible place in the stratosphere where Michael Jackson's rising falsetto screams like a police siren out in the street. No one can actually hit the note but it does not matter. In here, you can do what you like.

The counter that separates the kitchen from the living room is piled high with food. Platters of ribs and chicken done up golden brown. Red beans and rice. Salad and potatoes and sticky cake. If you do not want to dance, you can always eat. If you do not care to use a napkin to wipe your greasy mouth after you are through, that is all right too. Nobody's mama has been invited. Even if one somehow slips through the door, she will know enough to keep her funky business to herself. This is a party. The best one I have ever seen.

Grabbing a rib off the plate nearest to me, I stick it into my mouth. Hot-and-sour orange barbecue sauce runs down my chin. "Is it good?" a little guy in the kitchen demands. "Is it fine?" "Good enough to make you wanna smack your mama," an impossibly tall guy with an Afro as big around as a bush confirms. No two ways about it. It is even better than that.

The music throbs like a heartbeat. It pounds inside my chest, making my whole body vibrate in time. Lights flash pink and purple in my face. I get so excited that I swallow a mouthful of sauce and start to choke. The little guy in the kitchen hands me a bottle of Blackberry Julep, the sweetest, thickest wine around.

"Go on, brother," he says encouragingly. "That there is the wine what made the grape go ape."

I shake my head. I need water. "Give him the tea," the little guy shouts. "We onny jes' brewed up a whole new batch."

Someone shoves what looks like a laboratory beaker into my hand. It is filled with a greenish yellow mixture in which suspicious looking particles whirl in odd concentric circles. I down it in a single gulp. It has a strange ashen taste, as though it has come from somewhere inside the earth itself. "What the hell is this stuff?" I ask, picking twigs out from in between my teeth.

"That there is the *tea*, my man," the little guy says. "Cools your mind and fires up your body all at the very same time."

I am about to ask where I can buy some when I get a good look at what is going on by the stove. A guy whose eyes are all wobbly in his head is holding at least five pounds of marijuana twigs, stems, branches, and seeds wrapped in cheesecloth. Systematically, he is swishing the bundle through a large pot of boiling water. The smell is fierce. Every now and then, he inserts a long finger into the brew. Then he draws it back out and puts it in his mouth to check on the taste. The finger itself is stained a permanent yellow green.

"God," I say to a girl who looks like Nefertiti, "how long has this been going on?"

"Four thousand years, baby," she says coolly. "Go check a history book."

I cannot imagine why I even bothered to ask. The world is ending. So why not party until the final moment is at hand? It makes as much sense as anything else I have seen lately. Slowly, I make my way down the crowded hallway. Two girls and a guy wearing a white raincoat disappear into the bathroom. The door slams shut. I hear the sound of the lock being turned.

"Hey, y'all," someone shouts. "That ain' no community center in there, y'know?"

A crowd forms in front of the door. The big guy with the bush for an Afro rattles the doorknob with his hand. Then he slams both of his palms against the door so enthusiastically that I know for certain that the entire wall is about to tumble down. Not that it will stop the party. People will just keep right on dancing in the rubble.

"That door comes down," a deep voice calls out from inside the john, "some somebody gonna have to deal with me. . . ."

"Doan shoot, baby," one of the girls cries from inside the bathroom, laughing so hard she can barely speak. "We comin' out with our hands up and our noses open!"

"Some brother got hisself a piece?" Nefertiti asks me. I note that she is holding her very own beaker of the tea in one hand.

"May I?" I ask, reaching for it.

"Suit yourself," she says, letting me drink off half of it without changing the expression on her face.

Taking the beaker back from me, she empties it down her throat. "Lawd," she sighs. "I hate to see it come to this. . . ."

I move away. My path is blocked by three guys who are as wide across as barn doors. Two of them squat in the three-point stance. The third gets ready to take the snap from center. "You fine," the quarterback shouts when he sees me. "Yeah. You good right where you are. Now, make like you the Redskin middle backer. Be comin' in on my man Sonny here like you on a dog, wavin' your arms around and shoutin' all kinds of dee-rogatory shit relatin' to his parents and his home town of Bogalusa, Louisiana. Then I can show these sorry suckahs how come it was we got ducked so bad las' Sunday. . . ."

"You guys *Giants?*" I ask in wonder. The center snaps what looks to me like either a frozen squab or a Rock Cornish game hen. Sonny rears up from his three-point stance, growling down low in his throat like a bulldog. I step aside to let him past me in the narrow hallway. Carefully the quarterback checks his blocking. Then he lets fly. The bird turns in a perfect, frozen spiral as it whizzes past my head.

Sonny catches it on his fingertips going the other way. He tucks it lovingly into his chest. Then he reaches out with his other hand and pulls the girl who looks like Nefertiti towards him. She smiles. The two of them disappear into the kitchen.

"Ree-group!" the guy in front of me bellows, thrusting both of his arms into the air so the huddle can form around him. He wears a pair of cut-off jeans and a T-shirt that has to be at least four sizes too small. Party clothes.

"Ain' that jes' like Sonny?" the quarterback demands sorrowfully as I edge past him down the hall. "Hit him right in the hands and now he'll be gone for days tellin' folks how it was him who made the play in the first place. Now, nex' time you rush the passer, boy, keep them hands up. Otherwise, y'all gonna end your playin' days in Hartford. . . ."

"Right," I say. From now on, I will *always* keep my hands up whenever I dog.

In the back bedroom, an entirely different party is going on. The smell of sweet cologne is overpowering. A bored looking guy in a three-piece suit gazes down at the thick gold watch on his wrist again and again, as though he is dying for someone to ask him where he got it. "All right, Chaz," someone says. "Now that you finally learned to tell the big hand from the little one, what time is it?"

"Time you bought yourself a watch, Nee-gro," Chaz replies, with dignity.

"Quiet down in back there," a guy standing by the bed orders. Then he dumps the entire contents of a plain brown suitcase onto the mattress. "I got a train to catch and no time at all to waste playin' around." Reaching into the pile of clothing heaped before him, he pulls out a striped tie. "Ain' gonna need this no more," he notes. "How much you give me for it?"

"Half a buck," Chaz calls out.

"Half a buck? This a *good* tie, Chaz. Raw silk."

Chaz sneers. "Raw rayon," he says.

"Ray on my ass sometime soon, Chaz," the guy who is selling says pleasantly. "You'll like it fine. Forget the tie. We come back to it later. How much for this shirt? This a *good* shirt. . . ."

There are no bidders. "Fellas," the guy who is selling says, surveying the room at large, "I can't be hangin' out all night long playin' Bloomingdale's basement wit' yous. How 'bout these pants? Come from a *good* suit . . ."

"How about the box?" Chaz asks.

"What box, ugly and ignorant?"

"That box of a suitcase they oughta ship you back to Georgia in, home boy. That suitcase."

"Oh, ten bucks."

"Make it five and you'll get out alive," Chaz counters.

"Make it ten," the seller shoots back. "And we'll do business again."

"Say four or I'm out the door."

"Five and cut the jive. Chaz, this a *good* suitcase. Mark Cross. Let me see some cash, now."

Chaz takes the suitcase off the bed. He inspects it all over for nicks, bumps, and bruises. Then he reaches into his pocket. Grudgingly, he hands over a five dollar bill. The guy who is selling snaps it loudly in the air. "It *is* legal, gentlemen," he announces. "And oh so tender. Now, how about these socks? These *good* socks. . . ."

Chaz comes towards me carrying his prize. "How 'bout you, little brother?" he asks. "Need yourself some luggage? Twelve bucks and we got a deal. . . ."

"Don't I know you?" I ask.

"I don't believe you do, my man."

"Come on, you're *somebody*, right? Where do I know you from? TV? Movies? Stereo radio?"

"Since you insist," he says, looking down at me, "I, my man, am one of the Famous Flames."

Chaz has just stepped over the line. "You, my man," I say, "are full of shit."

Chaz sighs. "Hold my coat," he says to no one in particular. "I'm gonna have to teach this boy some respect. Whip him everywhere but on the soles of his feet."

"With what?" I demand, ready to go. "Your tongue?" Before he can recover, I say, "You Bobby Byrd?"

"No, I ain't."

The advantage is now mine. "You Bobby Bennett.

"Not him either."

"Then are you . . . ?"

I stand there with my mouth open trying to remember the name of the third Famous Flame. No one knows it. Not even James himself. Of one thing I am certain. It is surely not good old Chaz.

"Lloyd Stallworth," someone says softly behind me.

"That's it. Lloyd Stallworth. And you ain't him either, are you?"

I am actually in the same room with someone who knows the name of the third Famous Flame. "Quit playin', Chaz," she says. "And tell the truth. For a change." I turn my head. I am standing next to the finest looking girl I have ever seen in my life. Her golden skin glows as though she has just returned from a long stay on the quiet island. Her big eyes are soft and sweet. Her mouth is kind. A cluster of honey colored freckles dances across the bridge of her perfect nose. If all this were not enough, she also knows the name of the third Famous Flame.

"Have mercy," I moan, looking right at her. She giggles. I mean, the girl actually laughs. As though she already knows everything about me yet does not mind.

"You funny," she says.

"Funny *strange*, you mean?"

"Funny *funny*," she says. "I saw you in the kitchin chokin' on that rib and I started gigglin' right away."

"What is it about me that you like best? My dynamic personality? The way I dress?"

She just keeps right on laughing. Everything I say is an absolute scream. I am looking at a stone angel all right, dressed all in white no less. A tender sender. The perfect one and only. High school, here we come. I cannot believe that it is finally happening to me.

"Like something to drink?" I ask. "A chicken leg? Tuna-fish sandwich with the crusts cut off? Name it and it's yours."

"Whoo," she says, letting her breath out all at once. "Someone sure got themselves a head start tonight, didn't they?"

"Yeah, well. It's been a tough year. . . ."

"I bet," she says, her eyes crinkling up merrily at the corners.

"Come on, sugar," Chaz says, stepping between us. "Time to go."

"Oh, Chaz," she says. "I don't think I want to just yet."

"Told your mama I would get you home by sunrise, sugar. Don't make a liar out of me now. . . ."

"If my mama even knew I was out with you, Chaz, she'd make me stay home every night for a year."

Chaz looks me right in the face. The least he can do now is

tear my head off my neck with his bare hands and then eat it. Poor Chaz. He cannot believe that he is being aced out. Still, it is definitely happening all the same. I am making a murderous stretch run in the last eighth of a mile, closing the gap between myself and the leaders as I pound towards the finish line with my skinny neck stretched out just as far as it will go. As I cross the wire, it is not even close. No photo, nothing. I am a winner, out in front at last when it really counts.

Chaz shakes his head. He picks up his suitcase and goes out through the door, muttering softly to himself. I will never, ever see his face again. It really kills me to think about it. It surely does. But then he only brought it on himself.

"Listen, sugar," I say eagerly, "what's your name?"

"That's it," she says.

"What is?"

"My name. Sugar . . ."

"Don't pinch me. I know I'm dreaming but I don't want to wake up. Not yet."

"Oooh," she says, sticking out her perfect cinnamon tongue.

"What kind of name is Sugar? For a person, I mean . . ."

"My daddy gave it to me. He was a joker, just like you. Not that it stopped my mama none. Want to know my last name?"

"Sugar," I say, never meaning anything more in my entire life, "I want to know everything about you. I want to see your smallpox vaccination mark. I want to run my fingers over the little scar on your knee where you fell on broken glass when you were six. . . ."

"How do you know about my scar, magic man?"

"Comes with your ghetto background. . . ."

"Fifth Avenue and Eighty-second Street, you mean. Cohen," she says.

"What about it?"

"That's my last name," she giggles. "Cohen."

"You're Jewish?"

"Only from the neck up."

"Sugar Cohen?" I say repeating it out loud. "As in 'sugar cone'? Don't tell me. You've got a nickname too, right?"

"Bet I do, honey."

"Tell me slow. My heart can't stand this all at once."

" 'Sprinkles'," she says, pointing to the freckles on her nose. "Chocolate and vanilla, with sprinkles on top."

"Sugar baby," I moan, "let me be your sugar daddy. . . ."

419

"Oooh . . ."

"You can melt in my mouth *or* my hands . . ."

"Oooh-*whee*," she laughs. It is a high sweet burbling sound that echoes like water rushing over rocks in a cold, clear mountain stream. "Will you listen to the man! Good thing my mama can't hear you. You wicked . . ."

"I might be bad, Sugar, but I ain't evil."

"Do tell."

"I mean, I could be sweet for you. And you wouldn't have to ask me twice neither. I'd get it right the first time."

Taking my hand, Sugar leads me back into the living room. No river deep, no mountain high can keep us apart. We are on the very same wavelength, the one right at the very end of the dial, the station that only comes in late at night when your room is dark and the moon shines through the window as you lie there with your head on the pillow, jumping, twitching, and shaking in time to the music. Together we are going to bring the new year in right. Even if it does take us all night long.

When we get out in the middle of the floor to dance, people actually fall back to give us room. I know it is Sugar that they are looking at but it does not matter. "Let's dance, honey," she whispers.

"I don't dance, Sugar. Not ever. It's not what I'm good at."

"*Everybody* dances, baby."

"Sugar, you are so fine. I never met anyone like you. I feel like someone just opened a window in my heart. I can feel a cool breeze blowing right through me. And I can't believe I actually just told you that, either. . . ."

"Anybody who can rap like that can dance, honey."

"Not me . . ."

Reaching out with her soft, cool hands, Sugar puts one on either side of my face. She cradles my injured brain like a battlefield nurse administering emergency first aid. "Just wait on it, silly," she says. "It'll come . . . in time."

Sugar starts moving up and back to the music, not doing anything really fancy like I know she can, but just floating along inside the beat. I lean towards her wonderful face. I breathe in the deep, woodsy smell that comes off her neck. Pine needles and holly berries. Spidery ferns that sprout right up through the snow in the very heart of the darkest winter known to man. It is Christmas at last, on New Year's Eve. Sugar is the only present beneath my tree, wrapped in white with a big red bow that I alone can undo.

As it all goes spinning madly around, I spin with it. I whirl like a top to the music. The planet itself is turning in circles. So how can anyone stand in one place and still pretend that they are alive? I start to dance.

A little James, a little Wilson. Can't forget that wicked Mr. Pickett now. A little Temptations. Don't be shy. I cannot help but fly. I waggle from side to side. Nothing falls off and hits the ground. Sugar laughs and nods her head. Suddenly, I want to show her every last step I have ever seen anyone do. Splits, turns, scissor kicks, behind-the-back doo-wop drops, and all-out, running front somersaults. But there is no need. We are just dancing together.

Someone finally takes "ABC" off the turntable, replacing it with Smokey and the Miracles doing "More Love." Thank you, God. The great DJ In The Sky is looking out for me alone tonight. I slip my hand around Sugar's back. Under her white lace dress, I can feel her skin grow warm where I touch her. A steamy tropical current runs up her spine. We move together. We glide, touching heart to heart.

I bury my nose in her neck. Smokey starts stretching it out behind me. His haunting falsetto fills the room. The room itself starts to expand from the inside out. The dance floor is suddenly as big across as the football field in Harvard Stadium. We have all the time in the world. This song will never end. Instead, we will just go right on dancing, two pools of liquid mercury flowing into one another again and again. A drop of sweat falls from my forehead on to my cheek. It might just as well be a tear.

When the music ends, we stand together holding one another. Slowly, I open my eyes. "Guess what?" I whisper. "What?" she asks. "We just won the spotlight dance," I say. "Did we?" she sighs. She moves her head so that she can look right at me without stepping away. "What's the prize?"

"Should I tell you now, or show you later?"

Sugar starts to laugh. Then she casts her eyes to the floor. "Don't look now, honey," she whispers. "But I think you got some business of your own to take care of first. . . ."

I turn my head. Lesley stands behind me with her coat on and my jacket in her hand. I have almost forgotten that we came here together. Why should I bother to remember? Soon, smiling Rob will come to take her away. At the moment, Lesley looks awful.

Her eyes are red. She keeps wiping her nose, as though she has suddenly caught a vicious cold.

"I'm going home, Paulie," she announces.

"Fine," I say. "I'll get you a cab."

"I'm gonna let the two of you work this one out," Sugar says, moving away from me.

"Don't . . ." I plead, grabbing for her hand. But Sugar is already out of reach. The dance is over. Lesley has seen to that.

"Soon as you're through," Sugar says with a smile on her face, "I'll be here. If you want me. . . ."

I look at Sugar and know that this is true. I can put Lesley into a taxi and come back and she will still be here waiting for me. It is just the way she is. Lesley grabs for my sleeve. "I want to go home, Paulie," she says, *"Now."*

"That's *my* line, isn't it?" I ask. Holding up my hand with the fingers spread out towards Sugar, I say, "Five minutes. No more, no less."

Sugar nods. Then she heads towards the kitchen. Lesley watches her go. Turning towards me, she says, "I saw you dancing with her. You never danced with me like that."

It is perfectly true. There are a lot of things I should have done with Lesley that I never got around to doing. Now, it is too late for both of us. Not that it matters. Lesley has Rob heating up in the bullpen, eager and ready to go. In many ways, she is just like me. Lesley has to have a move on the side so that when her current thing falls apart, she will not drop off the bottom of the world. Then again, maybe we are not alike at all.

In the elevator, we stand next to one another with nothing to say. The shadows under her eyes have deepened into angry red bruises that will never heal. Her skin is chafed and raw. I have never seen her look less attractive. Yet for some reason, she is standing right on top of me, slowly rubbing her hand along my arm.

"You liked it with me, Paulie, didn't you?" she asks. "No complaints in that department, were there?"

"No complaints," I say bitterly. "Not from Rob either, I bet. . . ."

Pounding her fist against my arm to underline each word, she says, *"You . . . left . . . me.* What was I supposed to do up there all by myself? Join a convent?"

As far as Lesley is concerned, I am guilty. Guilty as charged and guilty as hell. In her eyes, I will be forever more the boy who cannot dance. I am the one who left her up there on her own with winter coming on and the icy wind blowing through all the cracks in the walls of her lousy apartment. I am the one to blame.

When finally we get into the street, Lesley just completely lets go. She sags into me so that I have to half carry, half drag her to the curb. Big tears roll slowly down her face. She chokes and gags, crying like a child who has only just discovered that tears themselves do not always make a difference.

It hurts me just to look at her. Her sobbing is painful to hear. And I am the one to blame. "Don't make me ride up there alone," she pleads. "Please? Drop me off, then take the taxi back here by yourself."

It is the least I can do. Now that I want Sugar, Lesley needs me. It is a game of hearts that no one can win for losing. Lying on the sloping couch in the old man's living room with the steam hissing in my ears, I would sometimes imagine how good it would feel to have Lesley beg me to do something for her. The moment is finally at hand. Only I feel emptier than ever before, empty and guilty and old, and confused, as always.

That this is our last night together, I know for certain. Sugar and I have many yet to come. I can just ride uptown with Lesley, drop her off, and then return. Sugar will be waiting. Until hell freezes over. There is no mistaking the look I saw in her eyes as she disappeared into the kitchen. That look was no lie. That look was the single truest thing I have ever seen in my entire life.

So I have to test it, the way I test everything, by increasing the pressure until I find the single weak spot in the system that will always spring a leak when the water is turned on full. I owe it to everyone concerned. Because when I leave Lesley this time, it has to be for good. There can be nothing left between us. Nothing but empty space.

I hail a cab. I help Lesley into the back seat. Then I climb in beside her. I take her hand to let her know that even though everything between us is about to end, I am going to do my best to be kind. When the cab pulls to a stop again uptown, I pay the cabbie without even turning around to watch him pull away again. The city is filled with taxis tonight. I can always find another one when I come back down.

On first dates, the rule is that you have to walk the girl right to her door. That is definitely the rule all right. Only as Lesley and I go up the curving stairs together, we both know that we are not going to stop by the door. What we both deserve, and what both

423

of us need, is going to happen. Once we get inside the apartment, we can hardly wait.

We are on top of one another like a pair of maddened animals. With our coats still on, we paw at one another, growling and groaning. We are not making love. This is something else again. Our bodies grind against one another in a mad contest to see who will give in first. My hand burrows under her coat. It is my hand all right. I can see it plain as day before me in the cold, stinking darkness.

I tear at the front of her blouse so violently that little buttons go flying everywhere. I hear them roll to the far corners of the room. My other hand goes under her skirt, and then her panties. I pull off her bra so that her breasts come spilling out. It is my hand and my mouth, only it all belongs to someone else. The angel of death who hovers above us as we roll and grind and moan.

I have to prove what I already know. Death is stronger than life, every time. It is the only form of dishonor always worth courting, just for the hell of it. No matter who you are, no matter what you have done, no matter how hard you have worked to make a life, when you die it all just becomes nothing again. Nothing is what I want now, the very same nothing that is claiming my grandfather. I have to journey by myself through that desert of endless perfection where everything equals zero and it is always cold. Not even the *Shema* will help me now. I am plunging down, lower than I have ever gone before, towards black and awful emptiness. I have chosen death over life without thinking twice about it. Now, I am rushing towards it with every stroke. Lesley's mouth comes open. Her powerful dancer's legs pin me to the mattress. The springs beneath us creak and groan in protest. She draws me close and holds on tight. I feel myself disappearing inside her. This is the most awful thing I have ever done in my entire life. No matter how long I live, I will never be able to forget it or explain it to anyone, myself most of all.

Just as savagely as it began, it starts to end. My soul is being wrenched from my body once again. I can see it being flung from the very edge of the planet into darkness. Slowly it floats out into the void where life has no meaning, silence is the only sound, and death rules over all.

I hear myself screaming even as Lesley screams into my ear. From the next apartment, someone begins pounding on the wall. Then they too begin to scream, in Spanish. All the animals are howling in their miserable little caves tonight, baring their teeth and baying at the moon as they lie in the filthy mess they have made of their lives.

The two of us come together as we have never done before, joined as one in the center ring of a circus without a ringmaster, a pair of performing animals doing the only trick we have ever learned. Kids holding paper cones of popcorn and pastel-colored clouds of cotton candy lean forward, watching in silent horror. Shattered bits of what once was human between us are now piled high around the bed, like sawdust.

For a moment, it is quiet. Then the noise from the street begins. Automobile horns blare. Garbage cans roll sideways along the sidewalk into the gutter, clanging loudly. Cherry bombs explode inside all the sewers with a deep, percussive boom. The entire city is under attack.

Lesley and I have brought the New Year in right. Now everyone is celebrating along with us, ghouls, goblins, witches, warlocks, zombies, pimps, and grinning junkies linking hands in a great circle that stretches around this tortured island of concrete and steel.

Slowly, I get up off the bed. I turn my back on Lesley and start to dress myself in the middle of the room. I have to get away. If I hurry, maybe I can still get back to downtown in time to throw myself at Sugar's feet and beg for her forgiveness. She will understand. It just was something I could not help.

When I turn around again, Lesley is lying on her side talking on the phone. Slowly, she pulls the tattered remains of her torn panties over the very end of her foot, holding her leg straight out from the hip in a perfect point. Realizing that I am staring at her, she smiles. Then she hangs up the phone and slides the receiver back into its cradle.

"Calling out for pizza?" I ask, the sound of my voice strange and foreign in my ears.

"Just speaking to Rob. . . ."

"What about?"

"He's coming up."

"Coming up? Here?"

"Not for another half hour, Paulie. We can do it again if you want. You know, now that I'm *really* in the mood . . ."

I will never be half as good at this as Lesley. It is the only game she knows how to play. If anyone is still bothering to keep score, she is the winner at last. So I guess that congratulations are in order. Turning my back on her in disgust, I go to the door. I open it and walk down the hallway. Suddenly, it is completely silent in the building. The new year has come and gone, just like that.

Out in the street, I start walking slowly downtown for no good reason, ignoring the taxis that cruise right by me. I am in no great hurry. I have all the time in the world. Finally, I have discovered exactly who I am. A refugee, in flight from myself and all those who are just like me. So long as my pursuers do not take from me what little I can call my own, I am willing to strike any bargain and meet any price.

Like my father and his father before him, I am a survivor. For the first time in my life, I comprehend the real meaning of the word. The awful horror that comes along with it I cannot even begin to describe. Only those who have already lived through it on their own would understand, and they are precisely the ones who do not wish to hear.

Epilogue:
ANOTHER
YEAR

I AM SITTING in the very last row of the great church on Fifth Avenue where they never lock the doors and you do not have to show proof of age or your driver's license to get inside. Even on New Year's Eve, there is no cover charge. Advance reservations are not required. I am not alone either. In every pew, lost souls who drifted in during the night are sitting with their heads bowed and their hands clasped, meditating in silence or sleeping it off. Some are already on their knees on the cold stone floor, praying.

Above my head, the great stained glass windows are just beginning to take on color. They gleam softly in the first light of day. Against all odds, the sun is rising once again. On the white altar cloth beneath the giant cross that leans against a wall made of tiny angels carved from stone, it says in pure gold letters, "O God, My Heart Is Ready."

It is all so very clean. So subtle, silent, understated and clean. In here, I can sit for as long as I like without being bothered, knowing that no one wants anything from me. Although I am certain that my grandfather has never once set foot in a church in his entire life, I think he would understand why I am in here now. There is nowhere else left for me to go.

In Jerusalem, the *kohanim* no longer pronounce the priestly blessing twice a day from a raised platform by the Temple. Only a single wall of that great structure still stands. Yet I am still alive. As for him, I cannot say, one way or the other. I know that the love I feel for him is not dead. That love is a single seed, waiting to be planted so something new can grow that I can truly call my own. From that seed, the line will continue.

Above my head, the blue and purple rose window catches fire with the promise of another year. At the moment, I am sure of one thing, and one thing only. Come what may, my heart is ready.

TIMOTHY FINDLEY

"writes like a magician."*

You will be entranced by the depth
and force of his novels.

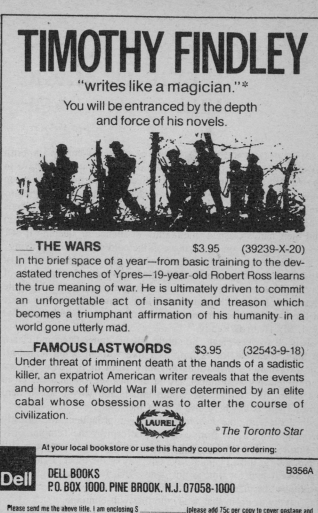

___ **THE WARS**　　　　　　　$3.95　　(39239-X-20)
In the brief space of a year—from basic training to the dev-
astated trenches of Ypres—19-year-old Robert Ross learns
the true meaning of war. He is ultimately driven to commit
an unforgettable act of insanity and treason which
becomes a triumphant affirmation of his humanity in a
world gone utterly mad.

___ **FAMOUS LAST WORDS**　　$3.95　　(32543-9-18)
Under threat of imminent death at the hands of a sadistic
killer, an expatriot American writer reveals that the events
and horrors of World War II were determined by an elite
cabal whose obsession was to alter the course of
civilization.

LAUREL

The Toronto Star

Laurel Goldman's moving first novel is about 26-year-old Jay Davidson, a troubled young man now on his sixth visit to the psychiatric ward. The poignant, disarming story, in the tradition of *Catcher in the Rye* and *One Flew Over the Cuckoo's Nest*, is "full of fine things. Miss Goldman manages to be funny and sad, something only good writers can do."

—Anatole Broyard,
The New York Times

When you're totally at sea, trying to navigate an ocean of private confusions…when you're trying to find a way to cope in a baffling world of paralyzing fears and overwhelming complexities…when, like Jay (a.k.a. Jesse James) Davidson, you walk the thin line between madness and sanity, searching for a solid place from which to launch yourself into life, you are forever SOUNDING THE TERRITORY.

 **$3.50**